The GALACTIC Mage

John Daulton

This is a work of fiction. All characters and events portrayed in this book are fictitious. Any resemblance to real people or events is purely coincidental.

THE GALACTIC MAGE

The phrase "The Galactic Mage" is the trademark of John Daulton.

Copyright © 2011 John Daulton

All rights reserved.

ISBN: 1466276843
ISBN-13: 978-1466276840

Cover art by Cris Ortega
Interior layout by Fernando Soria

DEDICATION

For Lori. My Orli.

ACKNOWLEDGMENTS

I'd like to thank the people who helped make this possible. My wife for her patience and unending support; my mother with her lofty visions and tireless cheerleading; Dr. Doug Rice for his wisdom and honesty; my editor, Joyce, whose keen eye put the polish on this (fortunately for you all!); and to the core group of people who have read my blogs and satire over the years, laughing at my jokes and keeping me from thinking I was only writing to myself.

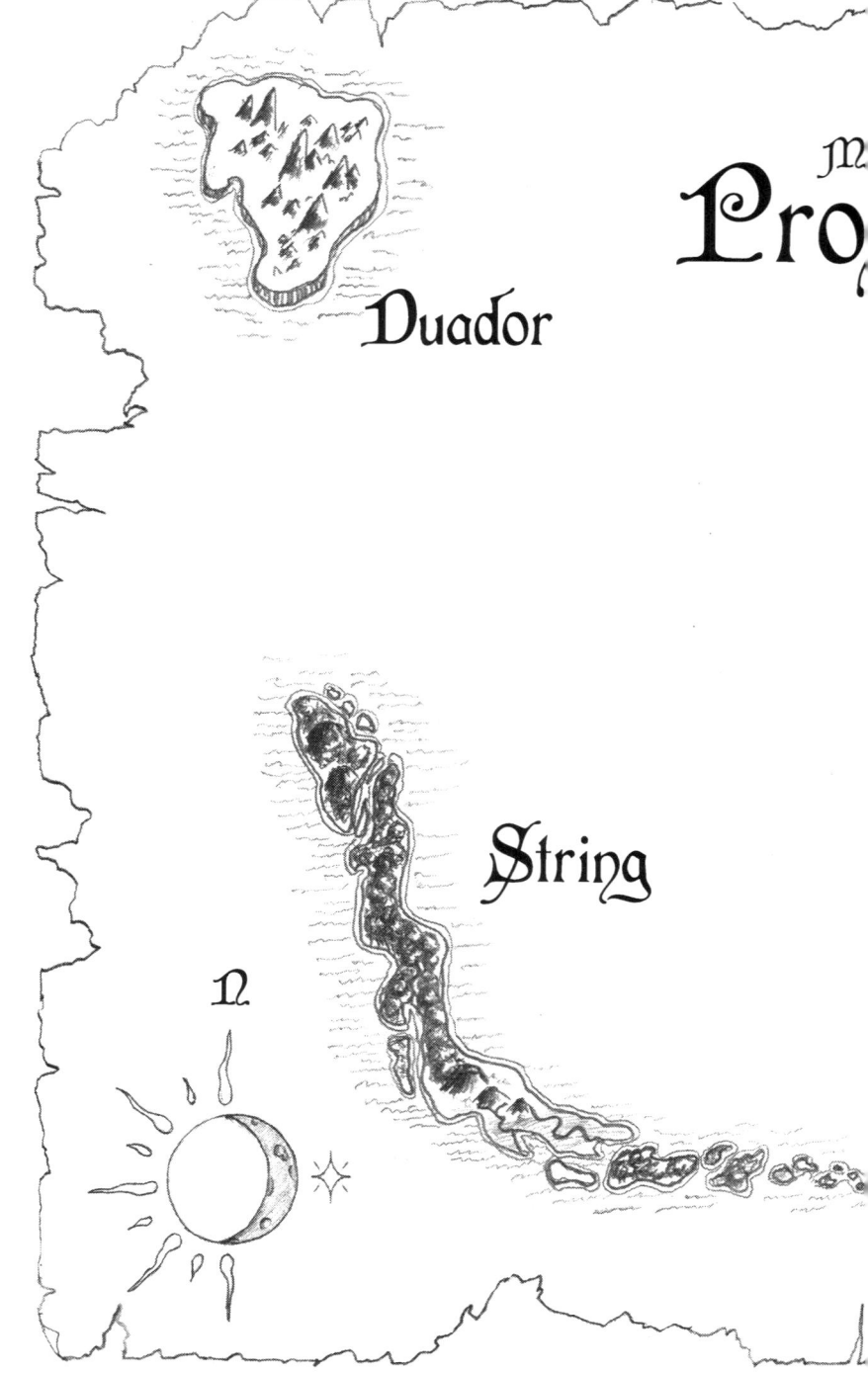

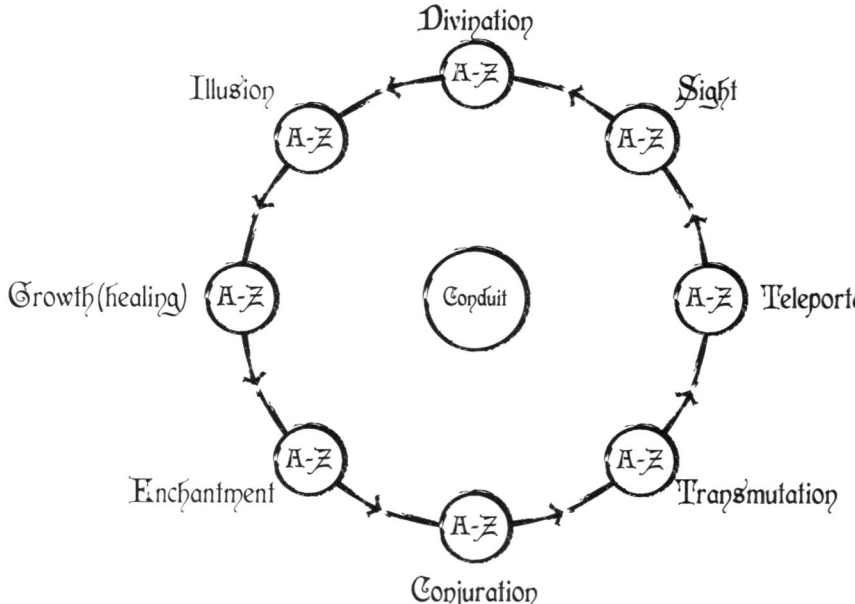

Chapter 1

Altin Meade stood staring at the face of Prosperion's bright pink moon shaking his head. Another night spent casting spells at that elusive luminous disc and still nothing. His temples throbbed. For two years running, he'd spent almost every night up here atop his tower, casting his strongest magic in an attempt to reach her, but every night, like tonight, he got nowhere. Failure was infuriating. Especially since she was right there. A huge round light right above him. Huge. Pink Luria, bright as could be, and yet impossible to find.

He groaned, half sigh and half snarl, and placed his palms upon the parapet, looking away from Luria and out into the expanse of moonlit meadow beyond the castle walls. Failure was exhausting too.

A gentle breeze blew down from the mountain behind him, tumbling over the cliffs and whispering through the courtyard at his back. It stirred leaves that rustled and danced unseen in the courtyard below before wafting up to him with the scent of dew damp stone. He shivered as the gust ruffled the tangle of his dark hair and crept inside his robes. An ivy leaf brushed against his ankle, but he was too tired to scratch.

The breeze moved off, over the parapet wall and down through the ivy leaves, out into the meadow where it rippled the knee-high grass in shimmering waves, dimly green but bloodied some by the light of the reddish moon. Altin watched it move off into the distance until it was lost in the silhouette of Great Forest and the glow of the coming dawn. He groaned again. Morning already.

Closing his eyes hoping, he tried to calm the tempest in his head, but failure seemed to be the morning's theme. Casting against the principles of magic did not come without a price.

He turned to go downstairs, seeking his bed beneath the battlements, and discovered that in the concentration of casting over the last few hours, he hadn't noticed the ivy growing around his foot. He pulled on it reflexively. The vine responded by coiling tighter around his leg. "Gods be damned," he spat, and yanked more vigorously trying to extricate himself. That made it worse. "Lady Synthia's ghost," he snarled. "Let go!"

Curses, however vehement, were not going to be enough to tame the residue of the great Lady Synthia's magic. No ghost, this was raw, lingering power, still active despite Lady Synthia being dead these last hundred years. Altin could swear all he chose, but it would not be enough to disengage the reaching ropes of these old, enchanted vines.

Lady Synthia had been an incredible sorceress in her day, possessing more growth magic from the Healing sphere than anyone living for a century before or since her death. And so it was that, in an incredible feat of herbal-magic, she'd brought forth this enormous growth of animate ivy upon which the enchantment still lingered to present day. It was a truly awesome spell she'd cast. Unfortunately, she'd lost control of the spell almost immediately upon completing the incantation, and the twisting mass strangled her on the spot.

After rending her limb from limb, the clutching tentacles of groping green then snaked about Calico Castle for the better part of a month until the keep's resident master, Tytamon, had managed, with the help of several Growth wizards from the Healers Guild, to unravel enough of Synthia's enchantments to make it safe to live at Calico Castle again—so long as they gave the entangled tower a measure of respect. For a decade and a half, no one could get within twenty paces of the tower, but eventually the ivy's magic began to decline.

Now, a good century since, the vines barely had enough magic left to crawl about at all. Most of the time they slept and groped very little unless compelled to move, and they were even more "normal" the farther from the roots they grew. While still relatively strong near the ground, the magic at the tips was hardly a problem anymore. Except occasionally, like now. And unfortunately, when Altin was in a mood.

He yanked again, furiously trying to wrench his ankle free, but the vine was in rare form this morning and willing to give Altin a tussle for all his worth. Altin, however, had no such inclination. His night of futile casting had made his temper short, and so without thinking, he muttered the words for a fist-sized fireball and conjured it at the vine.

The downside of this idea was that, given the relative weakness of Lady Synthia's magic this far from the roots, the ends were no longer magically resistant to attack, not from axe and not from fire, and especially fire the likes of which Altin Meade could cast. And so they ignited easily and began to burn furiously.

The upside of the fireball idea, however, was that Altin's foot was freed by the vine's reaction to being set alight. He almost had time to sigh in relief before he realized the consequence of his act. Almost.

"Son of a harpy," he swore as the flames began to spread

across the web of ivy on the floor. He panicked briefly then collected himself and ran for the scrying basin filled with water not far from where he stood. He tried to hoist it up, intent on running it to the fire for a dump, but the large container was too heavy for him to lift—too much book time did not come without some negative physical effects.

Grunting and heaving and with thighs that trembled as he hove, he gripped the basin's bottom edge and tipped it up to pour some water out. The initial wave sloshed over the edge, crashing against the bottom of the parapet and running back towards him where it soaked his bare feet and the hemline of his robes. If he'd thought about it, he might have at least sloshed in the direction of the fire. Nonetheless, when at last it was empty enough to lift, he stood with his watery weapon in hand only to realize that the flames were now much too big to be dealt with so easily as that. In fact, the flames were spreading across the feebly enchanted vines more quickly than he ever would have thought, and apparently with no concern for the puddle he'd made upon the floor. Ironically, he actually wished that a bit more of Lady Synthia's magic remained. But no such luck. The vines flamed up as if responding to his thoughts, roaring like they'd just found a patch of kindling doused in oil. The heat forced Altin backwards a step.

The crisscross of vines carpeting the flagstones began to writhe more furiously, apparently aware of their impending doom. The little puddle began to steam. Altin, wanting to avoid a pending doom of his own, threw the remaining water at the flame and cast the basin aside. Sparing a moment to lament his lackadaisical attitude about pruning back these vines last month, he turned and made a tactical retreat. Ducking through the low doorway that led down into his rooms, he descended the short stairwell and hurried away from the growing heat. He paused near his bed, his tired mind awhirl. A book. He needed a book to find a spell.

He darted over to the single shelf above his wood-frame bed and began leafing through volumes trying to find a water spell that would put the fire out. He needed to act fast before Tytamon discovered what he had done. The ancient mage would misinterpret this for sure. And Altin's project was already on defensive ground.

Meanwhile the fire upon the battlements began to rage. By the time Altin found a rain spell that would work, his tower was nothing less than a massive torch, the flames fully engulfing the tower top and now working down the ivy along the outer wall. Fortunately, the lingering herbal magic grew stronger with each foot the fire tried to descend, and so its progress was being slowed, but up top, it was far too late. Altin's neglectful attitude towards those vines had the battlements fully engulfed in flame. Altin could no longer go up there to fight the fire without serious risk to himself, and so he had to run all the way down three floors of spiraling stairs, across the courtyard, through the castle's front gates and out into the meadow where he could finally cast his extinguishing Rainstorm spell from the safety of the grass.

He commenced the incantation, and soon small clouds began to gather above the tower, blotting out the moon and the few stars still bold enough to face the rising sun. A few moments later the tiny storm clouds produced a gentle, localized rain that snuffed the conflagration in a sizzling hiss of steam. The clouds dissipated almost as quickly as they had come, and Altin grimaced as he looked upon the scene.

The fire had burnt halfway down the tower all right, and it left the upper half scorched entirely black. Tendrils of steam rose into the sky, dimly visible in the pale light of the approaching dawn and chasing gray smoke into the air in a crooked line smudged by an indecisive breeze. Water ran noisily down the blackened brambles in little rivulets that traced the curves of charred ivy until gravity or the terminal end of a charred thorn sent drops thump-thumping down upon the broad leaves of the uncooked ivy below. What remained of the ivy wound a green scrawl around the tower's lower half, marking perfectly where Lady Synthia's lingering magic had resisted and kept the flames at bay.

Altin shook his head. There was little chance Tytamon wouldn't notice this; it looked like someone had plucked the tower up, tipped it, dipped it halfway into an inkpot and then set it down again. A brain-dead bat couldn't help but notice such a thing. And Tytamon was neither brain-dead nor bat.

Altin let go a long weary breath as he gazed upon what he had done. It was just such things that had given this weathered old keep its name. The workings of young magicians just like Altin, magicians with access to six of the eight magic schools, had beaten the poor old keep into its present architectural malaise. At least in this instance, however, Altin's little mishap hadn't gotten him killed. And the mess up there could be cleaned. That wasn't historically the case.

No, the truth was that Calico Castle got its name because Sixes always kill themselves. Altin could hear that old saying echoing in his head like a children's sing-song as he stared at the muddle he had made. Those were the first words his ancient mentor had spoken to him when they'd brought him to the keep eleven years ago. "Calico Castle got its name," the old man had said, leaning down so close that his wiry old whiskers had brushed against Altin's nose, "because Sixes always kill themselves. You hear me, boy? You're a Six. And Calico Castle is *my* house." At the time Altin had been properly terrified despite having no idea what any of it meant, but now he understood it far more than he liked.

However, on this day, he had not destroyed a tower, not

like so many Sixes before him had, and he let his gaze run from his own tower—easternmost amongst Calico's five—to the south, nodding as if trying to convince himself. At least he had not done that.

The south tower, as an example of the nature of a Six, was a story involving a pair of Sixes and a pair of centuries not too long past that ended in vastly more destruction than Altin's little morning fire had wrought.

Calico Castle was originally built a thousand years earlier and entirely from stone taken from the mountains against which the keep was built. The whole compound abutted a sheer cliff face, tucked beneath the massive and looming peak of Mt. Pernolde, with its residents dwelling perpetually in the shadow of that gray granite monolith looming some two thousand paces into the sky above. The whole of Calico Castle started out completely gray, nearly camouflaged against the charcoal hues of Mt. Pernolde, and the whole of the keep was built from stone quarried from the same mountain range. Originally, there was nothing about the old keep that could be considered calico at all. However, the introduction of Tytamon after the Orc Wars were won, and, more to the point, Tytamon's willingness to take on the mentoring of the nation's Sixes, is what lead to the castle's inevitable aesthetic decay. Which returns focus to the south tower specifically.

Visually, the south tower still had a large element of Pernolde granite gray making up its bulk, but near the uppermost floor was a large patch of black stone, just a spot really, that marked where Victor the Volatile had blown apart his chamber with a bit too much enthusiasm for conjuring fireballs. In addition, the south tower had at the top, and worn rather like a crown, crenellated ramparts that were made of huge blocks of white marble, a pristine halo of imported elegance brought from the far south as a gift of the Church and meant to appease the gods for what the clergy deemed a "perverse sacrilege of ambitious arrogance" perpetrated by a Six named Finnius Addenpore. Finnius, up until the lightning storm that killed him and subsequently beat upon the south tower for three straight weeks, had promised to be the greatest diviner in all of history. Obviously, that destiny did not work out.

Calico Castle's other towered corners were hardly better off. The north tower was a total loss, a heap of gravel and broken stone that was cursed and could never be rebuilt. Ponpon Fountainglass, a Six and a master enchanter of historic proportions, had somehow managed to enchant himself out of existence and, in the doing, doomed the northern tower in the process too. Whatever he'd done, and no one knew, he'd made the tower absolutely unapproachable. Not even the Enchanters Guild had been able to figure out what poor Ponpon had done, and after a time, even those devoted fellows had given up.

The western tower was only granite gray at its base, the rest of it having been redone in red clay and capped with a shiny brass dome seven centuries back out of respect for its deceased resident Six, Melane Montclaire, who is secretly credited (or discredited) with the discovery of demon conjuring. Unfortunately, an especially large beast she summoned ate her one evening and then spent the better part of an hour bashing its way out of the tower before Tytamon managed to capture it and eventually send it back. A promising career ended, and another tower down.

Frankly, were it not for Tytamon, there would be no Calico Castle at all. Partly because it was he who found himself in the unenviable position of being the only Eight of Eight in the land and therefore the obvious mentor for any Sixes that might come along, but mostly because he was the only one that stood a chance of undoing whatever mayhem they might, and inevitably did, cause—much like the situation leading to the near-roasting of Altin's tower could have become.

However, the fire was not a complete disaster, and unlike all those Sixes before him, Altin was not dead. At least not yet. The fire hadn't killed him, and if he could hide this present mess from Tytamon, he might survive his mentor's wrath as well. But as Altin gazed up and saw that the traitorous breeze had turned the smoke towards Calico Castle's lofty central tower, Tytamon's abode, he realized that he probably wasn't going to pull that off.

And it was just as he thought it that Tytamon came striding out of the castle gates. His gray robes were open at the chest, drawstrings whipping about and wiry white hairs bristling chaotically from within. This uncharacteristically disheveled appearance suggested that not only was the great mage aware of Altin's latest magical mishap, he had been awakened by it too. This circumstance was further evidenced by the waggling strands of wispy white hair that stuck out in every direction from beneath his wrinkled sleeping cap, bobbing feather-like with each angry step of his approach like butterflies bound above his ears. If any doubt lingered in Altin's mind, the expression of molten rage disfiguring Tytamon's gray-eyed face made the situation clear. He definitely knew.

"What in the name of Dunnagan's dragon are you doing this time, boy?" The ancient magician practically erupted as he approached. "The sun isn't even up yet and you're trying to burn my castle down?"

"I. Um," Altin managed. It really was rather complicated to explain.

Calico Castle's other residents were now straggling to the gates as well, but none of them dared say a word or venture into view. They just peeped around the gate like a stack of heads spitted on an invisible pole. Despite the keep's size, there were only six people living there outside of Altin and Tytamon, but to the last of them, none dared to cross either magician—the elder out of respect and the younger out of fear, not fear of Altin's temper or anything untowards in his character of course, but fear of, well, random fires, for example. They all gawked at Altin's misfortune from the safety of just inside the gates, except for a tiny blonde child who couldn't see around all the rest and so stepped boldly out to afford herself a better view. She tilted her head slightly sideways and frowned a little as she watched, ignoring the hissing sounds coming at her from the adults ensconced behind the gate.

"Well?" Tytamon was waiting.

"Well," explained Altin, "technically, it's not my fault. You see, I'm not the one who conjured the vines, so, in a way, I can't be blamed for what happens when they attack." He followed this up with an expectant half grin, knowing full well it wasn't going to work.

"You're going to burn my house down and blame it on Lady Synthia?" Tytamon's beard quivered as he glared at Altin with ice-lance eyes.

Altin sighed. He'd been down this road before, back when he blew up the gardener's ox. And when he teleported a basilisk into the kitchen by mistake. Oh, and there was the time he enchanted a Breeze spell on a cold stone that ended up destroying a barn, a shed and two chicken coops. He winced inwardly at that. The list got longer the more he thought about it. He decided it might be best not to argue any more.

"Gods be damned, Altin. It's not just my castle. It's you. For the love of life, you have to have discipline. You're a Six. Look around you!" Tytamon's arm swept through the air in a gesture meant to take in the mismatched colors of the keep. "You of all people have to think before you cast. You don't have Circularity. You have all that power, but you don't see it all; you can't with only six. How many times do I have to tell you—do I have to beg you—to think before you cast?"

"It's not like that," Altin said, having some ground to stand on here. "I wasn't working when the fire caught. It was just the vine. I shot a fireball. A reflex, that's all. I wasn't overreaching. I swear. It was just an accident."

"You only fool yourself, boy. Ignoring the gorgon doesn't make her go away."

Altin glowered back at his mentor, frustrated and prepared to protest further, but there was such intensity in the old man's eyes that it took the energy from Altin's hastily forming defense. Even if the old wizard was wrong in assuming Altin had overreached, he was right about the rest. But Altin had learned so much more since he'd been working on his own, and that exploding ox incident was over a year ago. A groan rattled at the back of Altin's throat, but he grit his teeth and let defiance go. He wasn't going to win this one and he knew it. Tytamon just didn't understand. Tytamon had no faith.

"Yes, sir," Altin said, the words like vinegar in his mouth.

"Well, at least you had the presence of mind to get it out," Tytamon said, taking in, accepting, and moving past Altin's contrition in less than a breath. "I'm assuming the fire was only in the vines and not inside to burn your books?"

"Yes, just the vines."

"Well, good. That way, when you get the ashes cleaned up, you'll be able to go through them and find a spell to remove the smell of smoke from my curtains."

Altin looked up and saw that the treacherous breeze was still blowing the last remnants of smoke and steam into the windows of Calico Castle's massive central spire, the only one of Calico Castle's five as yet unmolested by magic gone awry. He rolled his eyes.

Tytamon watched as Altin looked up. "Yes, that smoke," the old mage confirmed.

"Of course. I'll get that too." Altin let go a long breath in anticipation of an awful day.

"Indeed," said Tytamon and turned back towards the keep.

Altin watched as Tytamon waded through the grass and reentered the gates, sweeping the muttering house staff and grounds crew back inside with his arms out wide. Their eyes lingered on Altin a moment before they reluctantly allowed themselves to be brushed back into the castle—all except the little girl, who ducked under the dangling sleeve of Tytamon's robes like a tiny towheaded bull bursting through the cape of a matador. She would not be so easily shooed away. She smiled a wide smile at Altin and waved enthusiastically. She started to call something to him, but a woman's flour-covered hand darted out from behind the gate and snatched her from view before the words got past her eager lips. This left Altin finally alone. He harrumphed and spat into the dirt. What did they know? Any of them.

He returned his attention to the tower, now half black and half green, neatly divided in two distinctly "painted" halves. He groaned. Calico Castle at its best. At least those infernal vines wouldn't be a bother for the next few months. But he wasn't looking forward to cleaning up the mess. He wished he had anything else to do.

A familiar screech reached his ears just as he started back into the castle. He turned and surveyed the skyline above the forest to the not-so-distant west. It took him a second to spot it, but he soon made out the form of a dragon winging its way towards him above the trees of nearby Great Forest. Taot. The dragon must have spied the smoke and been concerned. For a big fire-breathing brute, Taot was quite motherly sometimes. The forest-green reptile flew steadily closer, and Altin could hear the rush of air under his mighty wings as he neared, circled, and prepared to land upon the grass.

If recklessness could gain nothing, how would Tytamon

explain Taot? Nobody else had a dragon to call their own. Nobody. Only Altin. He was even willing to admit that trying to tame it had been reckless initially, but it had worked out in the end, which had to count for something. Oh sure, Tytamon would probably argue something like, "And the point of a pet dragon is...?" To which Altin would say, "Prestige." At which point Tytamon would likely add, "Which is useless and completely not worth the risk. You could have been killed just as all the other would-be dragon tamers have." At which time Altin could say, "But I wasn't." But then Tytamon would likely just return to his original point, that there was no point in having a dragon to begin with, which was why Altin so assiduously avoided having that conversation with Tytamon at all—that, and because the old man simply bristled every time the dragon was around.

To be honest, Altin actually thought that the great magician was afraid of Taot, but he wasn't exactly sure why. He was sure Tytamon could destroy the dragon easily enough if push came to shove, but he figured there was something superstitious involved. Tytamon was of the old, old school, and dragons held a place of reverence a millennium ago that they no longer did today; their mystique was gone and they were slowly being hunted out. Their time of awe was before the Magical Revolution, before the power of Language had harnessed the power of mana. The people of Prosperion no longer needed symbols like dragons; they no longer needed the stories of old. They had themselves to view with awe. Only the last remnants, like Tytamon—*the* last remnant—held on to the old stories at all.

Which worked in Altin's favor. It was nice to have something on the old man. A dragon to keep Tytamon from thinking he had Altin all figured out. Because he didn't. Altin was not reckless. Altin was not going to kill himself. And Altin refused to believe that he was just a Six.

As Taot settled to the ground, Altin looked up at the mess of his tower and groaned. Six or not, dragon or not, his head still throbbed from last night's effort, and he was completely not in the mood to go clean up. What he needed was something to clear his head. Something like a cool wind blowing in his face. He turned and sent a simple telepathic greeting to Taot who was getting a drink from the little creek that ran out from beneath the trees.

The dragon returned what roughly translated to a telepathic grin, clearly satisfied that his little human friend had not been burnt to a crisp. Fire was something it was abundantly familiar with. Taot followed this with the sense that he was feeling in the mood to fly too, having just dined on a fat grizzly bear and in need of either some exercise or a nap.

Altin glanced back at his tower as he put his fingers to his temples and rubbed his aching head. "A nap would be good too," he sent back to the dragon. But he knew he'd never get away with that for long. At least a dragon flight would take him out of sight for a while and give his head some time to rest. With a sigh, and grunt when the dragon leapt mightily from the ground, Altin found some solace in the presence of the wind.

Chapter 2

After a refreshing flight on Taot's back, Altin returned to the tower and went about the labor of cleaning up the mess the fire had made. The breeze had blown soot and ash down the stairs into his chambers, and there was spotty black dust on absolutely everything. Better soot than flames, he supposed, as he had been admittedly lazy about casting fire-resisting enchantments on his books. He made a mental note to get on that very soon.

Nonetheless, his books were fine, and he went through them looking for something to expedite the cleaning of his room. He found a Minor Tornado spell which he cast and set to the task of vacuuming up the mess. Once cast, the miniature tornado looked like a twenty foot serpent of whirling wind that had had way too much wine to drink. It seemed to stagger about the room on the tip of its tail, stumbling into every nook and cranny as its funnel head searched for somewhere to disgorge what it had imbibed. It finally waggled and arced its wide-mouthed way to the window where it snaked a length of itself through and began vomiting ash into the meadow below. Window found, the tail end continued to move about the room sucking up whatever tidbits it could get. Altin's expression contorted speculatively as he watched. It wasn't exactly methodical, but he supposed that, while a bit awkward, it would suffice.

Satisfied that his room would eventually be soot free, he went back up to the battlements to have another look. This was going to be a bit more difficult to clean. Near the parapets, the mess was more than ankle deep, and large chunks of half burnt ivy stems jutted from the mounds of gray, promising to be both annoying and filthy to pick up. He contemplated another Minor Tornado spell, but realized that in order for it to do anything with the larger chunks of charred vine, he'd have to cast the tornado a bit bigger than was safe. Not to mention, given the direction of the wind, if the thing decided to spout on the wrong side of the tower, the ash might be carried up to Tytamon's window above. He already had Tytamon's curtains to attend to as it was. With a grunt, he went back down stairs and thumbed through his books, realizing with each turning page that he was probably going to have to clean this up the old fashioned way: with shovel, broom and pail. He groaned. How demeaning for a wizard of his skill.

For a time, he simply refused to do it, and he lay himself down on his bed and stared at the ceiling while the Minor Tornado did its work. Eventually, he drifted off to sleep, getting some well-needed rest. However, he woke a few hours later to the not-so-gentle sensation of the tornado sucking on his face.

"Good gods!" he sputtered, gasping for air as the spell snatched the breath right out of his lungs. "Attack!" He bolted upright and looked furtively about, then quickly regained his wits. He must have been more tired than he thought.

Blinking sleep away, he saw that his room was now free of ash, and so, in the absence of anything better to do, the little twisting tube of wind had begun to meander aimlessly. But for the near suffocation, Altin was quite pleased with the outcome, and he dismissed the tornado spell with a satisfied nod. Now for the mess upstairs. With a sigh, he set himself to the chore.

Later that night, after several hours carrying buckets of soot and charred lengths of ivy out to the gardener's refuse heap, and after a hasty lunch and two more hours trying to find a deodorizing spell for Tytamon's curtains, Altin was finally able to return to the much more important task of magically seeing towards the moon.

He climbed atop his tower, a little tired, but feeling better for the completion of the work. The sky was clear and black, strewn with the millions of lights that had been calling him outward for what felt like his entire life. They seemed both an invitation and an insult, a promise and a threat, daring him to come out to them and yet forbidding him to try. And then there was Luria, loudest of them all. The moon. Sweet, pink Luria, lady of the night, dark mistress of moods whose aspects were true to her gender: beautiful, powerful, unpredictable and sublime. Some nights she was as red as blood, angry crimson and almost too dark to be seen. Other nights, like tonight, she was pale pink, almost white, appearing soft as if just powdered or made from the petal of a rose.

She was still low on the horizon, and Altin waited patiently for her to draw near, rising higher and nearly straight above. He knew the distance to her was far, and he wanted her as close as she possibly could be. He was willing to be patient. He'd been at this task for two years already; what was another hour now?

He moved over to a crate pushed up against the crenellated wall, filled with enchanted seeing stones. The crate was blackened from the flames, and two sides of it looked as if they might crumble if he tried to pick it up. He sighed. At least the stones inside remained unharmed. The seeing stones were fist-sized river rocks he'd enchanted with a location spell so that he could find them wherever they might go. His project of the last two years had been to teleport them as far as he could into the night, and then use sight to find them and have a look around.

Sight, like teleportation, required that magicians be familiar with the locations to which they wanted their spells to go. Sorcerers simply could not travel to places where they had never been—not in body, not in mind. And since Altin had absolutely no idea where Luria actually was, at least not precisely, he couldn't directly target any magic there at all. He had to know a place intimately to cast magic to it. Period. Knowing that something was "way up there, right there, where I'm pointing" just didn't get it done. Not directly, anyway, and so Altin was having to, in essence, crawl towards it, step by step, breaking the fundamental rules of transportation magic and casting with a guess, exhausting himself each night and having to start again the following day. But the seeing stones helped him find his way, sparing him from starting over every night from scratch. At least with them he could start from where he left off the night before and not "all over again." But even with the stones, it was proving to be an interminably long road. Apparently Luria was a lot farther off than anyone had ever guessed.

Resigned that his task was to be one of many years, he set himself to the work of yet another night of blind casting. He plucked a seeing stone from the crate and cradled it in his hands, savoring the smooth, cool feel of it as he gazed back up at Luria tempting him across an unknowable expanse of sky. And he waited.

Eventually she was high enough for him to begin. Deeply familiar with the teleporting spell, having used it nearly every night, he needed no notes or spellbook to prepare. He took a deep breath, closed his eyes and began the chant that would send the seeing stone from his hands out into the sky, hopefully far beyond his best attempt from the night before.

Soon after he began the incantation, he felt his mind open itself to the mana. He probed the curling wisps of deep purple mystery, touched it gently and let it flow into his brain. He gathered the dark vapor in, using his mythothalamus, the gland of magic, to collect and then roll the mana into a thin thread, one end of which he fed into the center of the seeing stone. Tracing the line of mana back out into the night, he pushed his mind up into the coursing sea of nebulous blackness and began seeking the furthest seeing stone cast the night before. The enchantment on the stone throbbed faintly across the distance, its magic beacon pulsing through the darkness and drawing Altin's sight straight to it after only a moment's look around. There, he thought as he centered his mental balance out upon that stone. It was the only target he could see.

Within the mana, as his mind currently was, Luria herself was only an idea. Unlike the enchantment that illuminated the seeing stone drifting out there since last night, he could not see the moon within the mana stream at all. The moon, like any form of normal matter, existed outside of the mana stream. The only way to find things through mana was to know them magically, to memorize the signature they left as they moved through the sea of teeming blackness from which all magic grew. His enchanted stones had a vibrant signature, almost like a magic scent; he could find them easily. But unknown Luria did not. Size didn't matter; seeing magically was about familiarity. He could not see the moon, because in this place, in the stormy mana sea, he did not know where it really was. He had no way to find it. He had no familiarity. And so, as he had every night before, he was going to have to guess.

With last night's stone as guidepost, he pushed the mana thread past it, thickening the stream as he drew more power into his mind, shoving outward with every ounce of his might, up to where he felt Luria just had to be. He pushed against the conflict of his ignorance—the bane of all magic but the divining kind—and very quickly he found that he could push the thread no further. This was as far as he could go. He anchored the thread to the nothingness and returned his focus back to the seeing stone he held. With a flick of his mind to make certain that his mana thread was still securely bound, he drew the thread back into the recesses of his intent, imbuing it with the elasticity of his will. He stretched it taut and then let it go with a silent mental snap.

He opened his eyes as the stone vanished from his hands. There came the familiar sense of release as the mana left his mind and a faint sucking sound as air filled the space once occupied by the stone. He had to wait a few moments after the cast for his head to clear—blind casting was a brutal thing to do—and then he could see how far his stone had gone. He hoped that this time, unlike all the other times, it would be floating at least somewhere near the moon.

He used a basin of water, a new one as the old one had been burnt beyond repair, to serve as an enchanted scrying well in which to locate the seeing stone. Scrying was a far easier form of seeing than direct sight was, and using the basin helped conserve his energy during the long nights of casting blind. The down side of the scrying spell was that he couldn't move the view around within the basin's frame; and there was no sense of smell or sound to be gotten from the watery spell at all. But it did what it needed to do. The view the scrying basin afforded him was simple: either Luria would be huge and his seeing stone was getting close, or it would not. It would either look noticeably changed, larger and filling the scrying basin with its pinkish light, or it would still be hanging as it always was, distant, the same size, and still excruciatingly far away.

And it turned out to be the latter case. Luria still loomed far beyond the tiny seeing stone, looking no different from the seeing stone's location than it did from Altin's tower on Prosperion. It was as if he'd traveled no distance at all. Again. But he was not discouraged. This was the pattern he'd fallen into over the many long months since he'd begun. It had become an old familiar dance. And so he pressed on.

He used the information he got from the new seeing stone as the founding location for the next—once he saw the stone in his basin, looked through it from its location high above, he then knew the place, even if it was just a patch of empty darkness somewhere in the night. Technically, he'd been there, and it became a patch of empty darkness that he was now familiar with. It was also helpful that teleported objects left a mana trail that lingered sometimes as long as several hours. And it was with this added aspect of the magic that Altin could cast an improvised Hop spell, making quick jumps possible, which helped distance and energy efficiency. Hopping was a form of teleportation that allowed for double, triple, and even quadruple teleports, like skipping stones on a pond if a teleporter was sufficiently powerful and skilled. Altin was both. Teleportation was Altin's primary school, and one in which he was ranked a Z.

With his bearings settled on the newest seeing stone, Altin took another enchanted river rock and began once more to chant. He followed the same procedure as before, but this time aimed the string of mana precisely at the newest stone, guided by and linking to its trail. He summoned the mana necessary to send this seeing stone up to where the last one was, and then let it go, intent on hopping this one off the first and doubling the distance with almost no more effort than he'd used for the last attempt. He felt the stone leave his hands and the reverberation in his mythothalamus as the new stone streaked up the mana trail and skipped off the other one, whipping right on by and taking Altin's quest another step further into the night. Then came a second mental jolt, solid like that sense transferred up a croquet mallet when one's ball has been precisely struck. The stone had reached its final resting point. Altin tried not to allow himself any undue optimism as he opened his eyes and moved over to the scrying basin for a look.

Still nothing.

He had to make an effort not to become angry, just as he'd had to curb his hope. This was the dance of his every night. He took another stone and began again.

And again.

And again.

For six hours he hurled stones into the night, and for six hours he still made no progress. Each spell, always targeting an unknown place, took a hundred times the mana that it ordinarily should. Perhaps a thousand times more. The ambiguity by its very nature made such things impossible to know. But each attempt sapped a portion of his strength, the cumulative effect like rubbing one's soul against coarse carpet, over and over for far too long, allowing friction to build and heat to grow until the outer parts begin to chafe and burn, and finally it begins to tear through to the tender places beneath the surface where discomfort gives way to frustration, and frustration to anger, and sometimes, when the pain is great, to fits of rage.

Just the thing to kill a Six.

With all of his anger teeming, boiling like a cauldron in a fire, Altin prepped the last stone in the box. He was going to be goddamned sure this infernal stone got to Luria if it was the last blasted thing he ever did. He closed his eyes and reached out into the night, seeking the mana. His rage was further frustrated by the lack of mana; he'd tapped most of it from the region with so many attempts tonight. His patience was gone, and he was not about to wait for mana to flow back into the sky. He found himself absently cursing Tytamon for likely having used some mana too. A thought flickered across his mind then; somewhere deep inside, he heard the alarm go off. He'd lost his focus. But he caught himself in time.

He cursed silently and let the wisps of mana slip past him without drawing any more in. He shook his head. Definitely just in time. One does not draw mana in without having a use for it. That was a great way to blind one's mythothalamus forever and never cast again. He let out a long breath, chasing the mana back into the night, then opened his eyes and slumped to the floor against the parapet wall. Discipline. At least he had that. But by the gods it was so damnably frustrating.

He took several moments just to catch his breath. He was exhausted. He hadn't slept long enough today. Rather doggedly, he raised his head and stared back up at Luria with defiance in his eyes. "You'll see," he rasped. "One day you'll see."

But it wouldn't be tonight.

Chapter 3

The meadow was vast and verdant, as level as any surface back on the ship, and the enormity of it allowed Ensign Orli Pewter to run more freely than she'd ever run before. She was jubilant, even ecstatic, as she ran. The sunshine was warm upon her face, caressing her pale skin, ghostly white after ten years trapped beneath the fluorescent lights of an interstellar ship, and it touched her with golden rays of honest radiance. A breeze blew through the meadow, bending the shiny stalks of grass in shimmering waves as she ran against it, adding her own speed to the velocity of the floral scented air. Touched with hyacinth, sage and wondrous varieties she'd not yet catalogued, the fragrant wind drove tears of joy from the corners of her eyes as she sped along, salty rivulets blown over her temples to mix with the sheen of perspiration that cooled her alabaster flesh. There was so much space down here, on this planet, on Andalia, so much room to run. Andalia was a real world, a world of soil and trees and grass. A world of bugs and birds and temperatures above and below sixty-eight degrees. Andalia was freedom. It was paradise.

Except, it hadn't always been. The truth of the matter was, Andalia was the scene of a great and mysterious tragedy. Andalia was a world that had been populated only a few scant decades in the past, and not just sort of populated by animals and bugs, but completely populated, with people. Humans. Just like back on Earth. Andalia had been filled with people and dotted with cities that glowed brightly on its surface like a phosphorescent skin, thousands of cities, their electric lights shining into space. Orli had seen the images a hundred times before. But they were images taken by satellites that no longer orbited this world. Images of lights that no longer shone. The Andalian people were gone, and their cities were as well. In fact, this very meadow where she ran was supposedly the site of a large Andalian city called Persepiece. But there was no city here, and no trace that there ever had been one; there was only this vast, suspiciously level meadow where Persepiece should have been. At least if the maps were right.

And the maps were the most vexing thing of all, and what became so troubling to the fleet. There were no ruins here either. There were no ruins anywhere. There were no bodies. There were no wasted towns or lines of decimated vehicles marking the last desperate attempt of a fleeing populace. There were no burnt-out villages, no mangled skeletons of downed skyscrapers, not even any scattered human bones. There was nothing. Only wilderness. It was as if there had never been any humans on Andalia at all.

The fact that there had been humans on this planet, a discovery made some thirty years in the past, was odd enough. The first radio signals, and subsequent video feeds, had been startling to the people of both worlds, even unfathomable to some. Who would have thought the same species could have evolved on two completely separate worlds? Even more confounding was to think that such parallel evolution took place at roughly the same time. But none of that mattered now, at least not exactly. As strange as simultaneous evolution might seem, the Earth ships were here now, here based on belief, and, after traveling ten years, come to see and come to save. And now there was no trace of any humanity at all. The strange coincidence had become a tragic mystery.

When the fleet left Earth, they'd known they might find decimation when they arrived, even allowed for the possibility of annihilation; the last message from Andalia after all—a flickering video image of an Andalian astronaut, his frantic message garbled and unintelligible except for one word, "hostile"—had been warning enough that something was amiss. No other communication ever came after that. But they certainly hadn't expected this, hadn't expected nothing.

And so it was that Orli found herself here now, part of the fleet sent from Earth to discover the nature of the threat that had brought twenty years of interplanetary correspondence abruptly to an end. The fleet was assembled quickly, the technology barely tested; its mission was not only to bring aid if there was anyone left to help, but also to intercept anything "hostile" that might be coming for Earth next —an "anything" that had been formally deemed Hostile in memory of that astronaut's presumably dying words.

However, while Orli was here on Andalia and officially part of the fleet, she hadn't come out of any great curiosity or need to avenge some lost Andalian space-chat friend as many others had. No, she'd been far too young to be concerned with Andalia when she was brought aboard the ship. At twelve years old, she'd been more interested in playing soccer and having sleepovers with her friends. The death of her mother and the knee-jerk reaction to that loss by her father, Colonel Pewter, in volunteering for the fleet had taken her entirely by surprise. And frankly, she resented being here. One personal tragedy had led to another, longer one. She felt trapped by fate and unable to escape, which is why she liked to run. Running made her feel like she could get herself somewhere, even if it was only on a treadmill or on the little track around her gardens aboard ship.

And then there was running down here. It was amazing to run down here. Here she had this meadow to run across, and there was even a stream to leap if she ran down at the meadow's southern edge. So what if there were no Andalians to be found? No Persepiece. It wasn't like she'd known any of them anyway. She knew that thinking like that was heartless, but, for now she was just happy that she had somewhere real to be. Somewhere besides the ship.

She ran through the meadow for the bulk of an hour. Just running, straight as a laser for mile after mile, the only obstacles an occasional tree, young elms mostly, some fledgling oaks and two varieties she'd never seen. Her sinuous legs stretched to their fullest as she ran, happily unfettered as it seemed she'd never been before. She sprinted in hundred yard spurts, and for the first time in her adult life, she got to feel how fast she could really go. It was exhilarating, and nothing could slow her down.

Nothing, except for Captain Asad.

"Pewter, what are you doing out there? All quadrants have already been checked."

She stopped abruptly, panting, and reached up to tap the com badge pinned to the collar of her uniform. "I'm...," she paused, still panting and needing a moment to think. "I'm getting one last specimen," she said, "something I saw when we made the last sweep." She scanned the ground furtively and picked the first small weed she spotted near her feet—in case he was watching her through the sensor feed from their ship, the *Aspect*, orbiting above.

"You have enough of that shit already. Get back here, we're about to leave."

Ugh. What a horrible thought. She didn't ever want to go back to the ship. Not now. She wanted to stay here forever.

This place was a botanist's delight, filled with new species to discover, things only Captain Asad could think of as "shit." And there were animals and sunshine and weather of every kind. Imagine: rain and sleet and snow! She could see the snow on the mountain peaks far off to the east, and she wanted to go see it, to touch it with her hands, to taste it and feel how cold and wet it was. But she hadn't been allowed. Check the city sites, and that's it. The admiral's orders. In, out, back to the ships. That was the mission. But there was so much more to see.

"Pewter, you have your sample. Now get back here immediately."

So he *was* watching her. She growled. He was right that she had enough samples already, but, given that she was under surveillance, she rotated her belt pack around from behind her back and opened up the pouch. She tucked the scrawny weed—it was an odd looking little thing—into a sample bag and zipped it safely back inside the pouch. No sense giving Captain Asad reason to call her bluff. He may have hated the fact that fleet protocol had forced him to, as he'd put it, "waste a spot in the landing team on a botanist," but his disregard for her particular discipline also made him ignorant of it as well. He wouldn't know a good specimen from a bad one if she fed it to him on a fork. She slid the pouch around behind her back again, and, satisfied that she'd sold the lie, she straightened and turned back towards base camp. At least she'd get to run.

And run she did. She was quite breathless by the time she returned, renewed inside despite her body's fatigue. She trotted into camp, planning to get a bite to eat before crews took the mess tent down, but Captain Asad intercepted her before she made it there.

"Pewter, you had orders not to leave the camp. Give me one reason why I shouldn't have charges drawn up."

"I had to get a sample," she said. "I already told you that.

It's a very rare specimen; one I've never seen." She reached behind her, intending to retrieve the scraggly little weed to make her point.

"Spare me," he said. "You're the first botanist ever to be field trained in the vacuum of space. Everything is a species you've never seen."

She groaned, rolling her eyes. Why was he such an asshole all the time? She turned and headed for the mess tent. He'd already ruined everything the run had done for her.

He grabbed her by the arm and spun her back around. "You're not dismissed, Pewter. You disregarded a standing order. And now you're adding insubordination to the list."

"Take your hands off of me or I will tell my father you've crossed the line." Her voice was even, and she enunciated every word.

His dark eyes met her icy blue ones, returning her defiance with venom of his own. But he did release her arm. He hated when she pulled the daddy-stunt on him, and she knew it. He knew she knew it too, and it really pissed him off. She was glad. She loved pissing him off. He was the outlet for everything she despised about her life in space. He spun and walked away.

She snorted and resumed her course for the mess tent. Inside, she immediately spotted her long time friend and surrogate brother, Ensign Roberto Levi. He saw her as she came in and made room for her to sit once she'd gotten a tray of food.

"Eww, you're all sweaty," he remarked, pinching up his face and feigning disgust as she settled in next to him.

"Hey," was all she said, a mutter. She was too annoyed to acknowledge his artificially effeminate display.

Noting her demeanor, he relented immediately. "What's up?" He could tease her about something else later anyway.

"Nothing," she said as she stabbed at her plate, oblivious

to the food. "And everything." She let the fork fall into the tray. "Asad is such an ass."

"It's true," Roberto agreed, not bothering to finish what he was chewing before he spoke. "But he's supposed to be a great military mind. Maybe assness comes with the package." He pressed a tawny fingertip to a few of the larger crumbs that had tumbled from his mouth, then reclaimed them with a slurp.

"Asininity," she said.

"What?"

"The word is 'asininity' not 'assness.'"

He grunted. "Whatever. You knew what I meant."

She retrieved her fork and resumed prodding at her food. It was a rare moment when she didn't take an opportunity to follow up on one of her little literacy jabs, and Roberto had known her long enough to recognize it as a warning sign when she did not. So they sat in silence for a while.

Finally she spoke again. "I don't want to leave."

Roberto nodded, but remained silent. They'd covered this topic every day since landing a week ago, ever since Orli had had her first run through real air and endless meadow grass.

"Maybe the Hostiles, or whoever it was, were just passing through," she went on. "Maybe this whole thing was just like some horrible galactic drive-by, and now they're gone."

"Sure," he said. "All gone. They were probably just passing through." He took another bite. "But I wouldn't hold my breath."

"I would." She looked completely earnest. "I mean, come on. We haven't seen anything to suggest the Hostiles are still around, right? So why leave? It seems so stupid to waste a perfectly good planet like this, to just pack up and go."

"You're thinking with your heart again."

"So what if I am? Changes nothing. Look at the facts.

There's nothing here. Nothing. Andalian or Hostile. It's stupid to leave."

Roberto, more inclined to the majority trend towards caution, silently acquiesced. She was intractable when she got like this. Diversion was the only way. "I know. How about we leave you down here first? Just, you know, for a few years to test your theory out."

"Fine with me," she said, but she sighed anyway, resigned. He was right even though he hadn't said what he really meant. Whining wasn't going to change the facts.

"You can say 'hey' for me if the Hostiles show back up though," Roberto pressed, intent on cheering her up. "Tell them I got caught in traffic but really wanted to be here for them. You know, because I care."

She allowed herself the vestige of a smile. "You mean you'd really leave me? You wouldn't stay and be my brave protector in case they did come back?"

He feigned horror. "With *you*? Look at you, all sweaty and hair blown everywhere. You look like crap! Besides, what am I supposed to do against aliens that take out whole planets? I mean, I'm badass like that, but still, even I have my limits." He drew his sidearm and gave it a gunslinger's spin.

Orli groaned and her eyes darted about, fearing the captain would catch him messing around with his gun. "Stop it!" she hissed.

Roberto holstered the weapon, grinning. "Besides," he said, "we already figured out a long time ago you and I ain't compatible romantically, remember? And since that's out, what am I supposed to do while we wait? I mean, a man of my particular attractiveness will better serve humanity up there with the fleet. The women need me."

She wrinkled up her face. "The blind ones, maybe."

At least she was smiling. "You see, it's that attitude right there that's going to get you stuck on a planet alone some day."

She laughed. They both did. But Orli knew his larger point was right: it was foolish to stay, or at least it was until they figured out what was going on. Deep down inside she knew that it was true. It was logical. But oh how she hated logic sometimes. Logic was cold and sterile, like the ship; it was white and clean and smelled of disinfectant and filtered air. It was not like a grubby world filled with dirt and mud and bugs that bit and stung. That's how life was supposed to be. Who wanted to be sterile all the time? She sighed and slowly began to eat.

When they were done with lunch, they both had work to do before the landing party was ready to lift off, but they promised to have dinner together later on that night. She didn't want to be alone her first evening back aboard the ship.

Roberto went to finish prepping the landing craft for takeoff, and Orli went to the small tent she'd been using to store plant and soil samples. Half-heartedly, she began to pack up her equipment, stuffing it into shipping crates with far less care than she normally would. It was depressing work, but mindless, and after a time her thoughts wandered to the mystery of the Andalian circumstance.

It was very hard to believe after all. The whole disappearance thing. The examination teams truly hadn't found a clue. It was frightening really. Of all the scientists that had come down here to have a look around, teams from over twenty crews, she was nearly the only one with anything to bring back aboard ship. And none of her samples had anything to do with the vanished populace. All she had were plants and dirt. The forensics teams had found nothing. The architects and engineers found nothing. The metallurgists found nothing. It was the same for everyone. Not a thing. Not one molecule of anything anywhere to suggest that there had ever been human beings living on

Andalia at all. Not one single thing.

And it was this total lack of evidence that had started people talking amongst the fleet, talking about a trap, an alien trick meant to bring them here like this. Much chatter was being bandied about the fleet regarding suspicions of varying kinds. Some were beginning to suspect that there had never been any Andalians at all. For many, given the planet's absence of humanity, the perfect likeness to the people of Earth began to seem clear proof of the existence of some elaborate trap instead, as if their own images had been conscripted as part of some galactic ruse. How unlikely had it seemed when the Andalians were first discovered? Just their existence was statistically farfetched. How absurd was it that they could be so like humans in almost every way?

The answer was: very absurd. And now, with no evidence of such a populace on Andalia, the suspicion that there existed some form of trickery had begun to take root throughout the fleet. Five short days after landing, the entire focus of a decade's journey had begun to fall apart. Such was the anxiety amongst the crews and, frankly, the anxiety of an officer corps that found itself with no direction anymore, that the admiral had called for a council of the fleet. The ships' captains and all the administrative brass were to assemble in person aboard the admiral's ship: the fleet's mission had to be redefined.

Contemplating all of it, frustrated by it all, and not wanting to go back to the ship anyway, Orli stuffed the last of her equipment into a large plastic crate and clamped it shut. She turned and plopped down on its lid, putting her face into her hands. She did not move until they came and nearly dragged her to the small spacecraft that would carry her away.

Once on board the *Aspect,* she morosely went about cleaning up and stowing the equipment she'd taken down to

Andalia. When she finally had everything back in its proper place, it was time for dinner and her agreed-upon meeting with Roberto in the ship's mess hall two decks up.

As she moved through the chow line, all she could hear were people talking about the "Hostile trick." She was trying to focus on how much she hated being back onboard, but by the time she'd gone all the way through the line, the endless chatter on the topic got her worrying about it too—not so much about the "trick" itself, but about what the fleet would do. When she found Roberto, she sat down next to him and asked what he thought about it.

"So you think it was really just a great big lie?" she asked, nibbling at a carrot she'd probably grown herself. "You think we got set up?"

"By who, the Hostiles?" He loaded his mouth with semi-synthetic potatoes and spoke around the food. "Nah, I don't think so. I mean, why would they? They haven't attacked Earth yet as far as we know. And if the point was to lure us out here, well, it's thirty years to pay off if you track it from first contact to now. Seems like an awful lot of time to set up an ambush to waylay—what—a thousand people? I mean, what's the point?"

"I don't know, maybe they needed some slaves or something. Or maybe our genetic material."

"Hmm," he said, his eyes lighting up. "You mean like breeding stock?" He contemplated that for a moment, his enthusiasm for the idea growing with such speed that he interrupted her reply. "Oh my God. That's it! That's the answer. Breeding stock is exactly what this is all about. I can't believe I didn't think of it sooner."

Orli looked at him dubiously. "What?" She almost hated to ask.

"Seriously. They did all of this for me."

"Who did? The Hostiles?"

"Yeah. The Hostiles are actually hot space chicks. They

needed some of my sweet Latin love, baby! This whole thing was just a plot to get me here. I should have seen it sooner. It's so obvious. Of course they would wait for that. Totally worth a thirty-year scheme in my opinion."

"It would be." She laughed. "God! You're such a pig. And you do realize they would have started their plan to get you like, what, six years before you were born, right?"

"Maybe they can see into the future."

She feigned total exasperation. "You're like a child. Can't you stay focused for two seconds?"

"No. But you love me anyway." He gave her his most charming look before shoveling in another bite.

She tilted her head and let out a slightly disgusted sound. "Yes. I do," she admitted, causing him to grin triumphantly before she added, "But you might want to wipe the gravy off your face before the alien women arrive."

His smile turned meek for a moment as he grabbed a napkin and dabbed his chin, but the lasciviousness came quickly back. "Hey, what about the men?" he asked. "This could work out for you too. They could have alien guys, you know, like drones or something. Rough, manly types, with grizzled beards and dimpled chins, all pecks and abs and stuff."

"Wouldn't that sort of negate their need to bring you out here? I mean, why would they want to downgrade?"

"Ouch," he said. "That was wrong."

"Just pointing out the flaw in your reasoning."

"Don't mess with a good story, damn it. Try to play along."

"Fine," she said, eyes twinkling. "As long as these drones are romantic and intelligent... I'm in!" She laughed.

"Leave it to you to screw up a perfectly good fantasy with crap like that," he said. But he was laughing as he spoke. "You and your damned old fashioned ideas."

She beamed proudly back at him. "Yep."

"Well, either way," he said, "here's to breeding stock." He held up his cup in a toast to rampant intergalactic sex.

She giggled. "To breeding stock." She clinked her cup against his and they shared a few moments playing off the depravity. But after a while, the conversation inevitably drifted back to the matters at hand. "So, seriously," she said, finishing off her standard issue chocolate chip cookie, "what do you think is going to happen next? Think we'll head home since there aren't any Hostiles for us to fight? Because if we don't go home...," she hesitated, hating to even say the words. "I overheard people actually suggesting we go out to find them, that it's our duty to the Earth to search them out. That could take—that could take the rest of our lives. I don't want to stay on this ship forever. I can't. Can you?"

"Hell no," he said, leaning over to a neighboring diner and asking if he was going to eat his cookie too. Apparently he was, so Roberto returned his full attention to Orli. "I don't even want to be on this damn thing as long as I have been. Man, if I'd had any idea what my mom was signing us up for, I'd have kicked her ass."

"You were fourteen. How could you know?"

"Yeah, well, I'm twenty-four now, ain't I?" He made no attempt to disguise the bitterness that came suddenly to his voice.

Orli remained silent. Roberto's mother had died two years ago of a brain tumor; he couldn't even be mad at her anymore, though at times he still was. Orli was his family now.

"Well," Roberto went on after taking a moment to let his emotions subside, "I hope the captain doesn't talk them into going out to find the Hostiles, even though I know he's going try. He's been itching for a fight since the day we left—Hell, probably since the day he was born. I bet he'd stay out here forever if he thought it guaranteed he gets his war. I almost feel sorry for him, poor bastard. If the council votes to go home, he might not get his wish."

"Well, there's no mystery in how he's going to vote."

"Nope. None."

They sat in silence for a while, suddenly melancholy, but apparently the young woman sitting next to Orli, Ensign Paulson, wasn't getting to her cookie fast enough, so Roberto reached over and offered to help her out. She frowned and raised an eyebrow at him, pulling her chin back against her throat as she moved her hand protectively over her dessert. "I don't think so," she said. She turned to Orli and gave her a look that seemed to say, "How can you eat with this guy?"

Orli shrugged and smiled back. "It's part of his charm. He grows on you after a while."

"So do hemorrhoids."

Both women laughed, and, after a moment, Roberto did too.

The announcement came over the ship's intercom a few minutes later: "All docking personnel, return to your stations. Last resource teams are inbound. Drive teams and engineering, report to stations, ignition at oh-four hundred."

"Damn," said Orli. "There goes any chance of one last trip planet side. God. I almost wish I'd never gone down there. Now I have to think about it for another ten years. I'm not sure I can take it."

"It's only seven if we go straight back," said Roberto. "The detour cost us three years, remember?"

She groaned. "Seven or ten, what's the difference? I'll be an old hag by the time we get home. Twenty-nine or thirty-one. Who gives a shit? I hate this ship." She got up and stormed out of the mess hall, leaving her tray behind.

Roberto watched her go and sadly shook his head. He understood her pain; he knew it well, hated to see her miserable. And despite all his best efforts too. He sighed and stacked her tray onto his.

"You better hope we ain't headed out to find them," said

the woman whose cookie he'd tried to commandeer. "She 's going to be even more pissed off if that's the case. She needs to get on her old man to make sure that doesn't happen. That's what she needs to do."

He nodded as he got up. "It'll take more than her old man to stop it, though. Colonel Pewter is only one council vote. The rest, well, fear, bravado and ten years of boredom can make for some crazy shit when you mix it all together. And Asad ain't the only buckaroo in the fleet."

"Oh, you aren't lying about that," she agreed. "Not at all."

Chapter 4

Altin awoke the next morning much as he had the one before, aching and in pain. He knew blindly teleporting his seeing stones at the moon was extremely inefficient, and he began to fear that even with his vast power it was not going to be enough. To make any more progress he'd have to enlist a whole horde of magicians. He'd need fifteen or twenty more teleporters, at least two or three seers and a conduit. What was worse, he'd need teleporters that were N-class or higher, which meant it wasn't going to happen. The only teleporter he knew above an N was Jacob the Stick, a two hundred-year-old mage credited with the establishment of the Transportation Guild Service and who would be the first to tell Altin that his quest was pointless. But Altin didn't need the TGS's founder to tell him what he already knew. At best he could scrounge up a couple of G's and an H or two, maybe get lucky and find an L, but if Altin's progress was any gauge, and it was, he being a Z and all, that combination still couldn't get it done. They might help him double his distance, even triple it, but he'd been doubling and tripling distances himself over the last two years and that hadn't gotten him noticeably closer either. No, he needed something else. But what?

He groaned and gripped his head between his hands. He could feel his pulse throbbing at his temples and a wave of nausea washed over him as he sat upright in his bed. Dealing with the massive distance to Luria was really beginning to take its toll, and he still didn't know how far away it was. All he knew was that the effort of trying made his head feel as if it would burst every morning now. He felt as if he'd stayed up all night drinking heavily from kegs of ale and rum, draining them entirely by himself.

Thinking of ale and rum made him think of old Nipper, which in turn made him think of breakfast, as Nipper would certainly be in the kitchen right about now. Maybe that would help. The keep's weathered steward would have something for his head, and Kettle, the castle's matronly cook, would have something for his stomach as well. Inspired, he climbed out of bed and went to clean himself up a bit before heading downstairs.

The flagstones were cold on his bare feet, chilling his soft skin as he made his way across his room intent on the basin of water sitting on an ancient dresser near the wall. A gothic window near the dresser let in the bright sunlight of a clear spring morning, and the scent of pine came from the forest on the chill breath of a westerly breeze. Altin dabbed a towel into the clean water in the basin, changed sometime early this morning by silent servants who trod on mouselike feet and who had been changing water and bringing bread every morning since he'd come here eleven years ago. Reflexively he looked to the shabby plank table at the room's center and sure enough there was his loaf, as it always was, as it likely always would be. He still wasn't quite sure which servant brought it every day. There was probably more than one, but he figured most likely it was Kettle, or maybe that little squeaker, Pernie, though he doubted the six-year-old could contain her hyper nature long enough to be stealthy for such a task. Whoever it was, it was a convenient fact, and allowed him the freedom to go days without having to leave his rooms.

He lifted up his robe and sponged out the more generally offensive areas beneath and was about to head down the spiral stairs for a real breakfast when he heard the low rumble of a dragon's call. Since there was only one dragon that ever came anywhere near Calico Castle, he went to the window to send a telepathic "good morning" to his friend.

Taot soared over the treetops to the west and glided low towards the tower. He spotted Altin's little man-head sticking out of the window and flew towards it eagerly, swooping up at the last minute and breathing a cloud of sulfuric fumes through the window by way of a draconic joke. Altin coughed, stumbling back into the room gagging and waving his hands in front of his face as his eyes watered and he choked on the noxious gas. The dragon sent a telepathic version of reptilian laughter, followed by a stone-shaking roar of merriment. Apparently Taot was in a playful mood. Unfortunately, dragon humor did not come without considerable consequence.

Altin staggered back to the window and thrust his head out into the cool morning air again, gasping for breath. Fortunately, the breeze brought some relief, and soon he was recovered enough to watch the mighty creature soar across the plains in pursuit of a herd of elk now sprinting for their lives. Altin watched as the dragon rose high above the ground then swooped low and gracefully plucked a fat buck from the rest of the herd as easily as Altin might pluck an apple from a barrel he walked by. Taot landed in the grass and immediately set to devouring the still thrashing beast, tearing strands of dripping red from it ravenously until it moved no more. Altin grimaced and turned away.

Taot's grisly feast wasn't quite how Altin would have chosen to be reminded that he too was in need of food, but he was reminded just the same. Having already forgiven the dragon's sulfuric sense of humor, he sent Taot a message of warmth and affection and then headed downstairs ready for a breakfast of his own.

As always, the morning kitchen bustled with activity. Nipper was preparing a huge boar for tonight's dinner while Pernie watched the carnage with awe and reverence. Occasionally she emitted an "eww" or "yuck" as the old man worked and yet still found herself compelled to reach for the knife and ask if she could have a turn. She'd clearly forgotten the broom she was supposed to be using, and it now hung limply in her hands, dipping dangerously close to the fire. Altin decided to keep an eye on that, having had enough of fires for a while. But at least she hadn't noticed him.

Stout Kettle, culinary queen, mistress of the kitchens and temperamental master of both frying pan and rolling pin, was busy rolling out the dough for yet another loaf of her wondrous bread—six-time winner of first prize at the county fair and more than partly responsible for the extra layer of belly flesh that had begun to form around Altin's otherwise slender frame. He walked into the kitchen and she immediately came to him and pinched his cheek hard enough to redden it for several minutes to come. "Mornin', sweetie," she said. "There's a good boy. Can't be out castin' yer spells all night without havin' a good meal fer it after, can ya? Sit ya down and I'll fetch ya some vittles fit fer a king."

Altin groaned and rubbed his face. This was why he avoided the kitchen most of the time. However, she wasn't exaggerating as to the quality of the meal, and a few moments later found a heaping tray of fried pheasant's eggs, ham and homemade goat's cheese sitting before him, along with the warm, homey smell of a loaf of Kettle's bread not two minutes out of the oven, just waiting on some butter and a knife.

"Ya look like a pig's arse what sat in a sty," commented Nipper from across the kitchen as Altin dug into his meal. Apparently he'd given in to Pernie's unyielding persistence and stood rubbing his tired old back as the little girl stabbed gleefully, an act both ghastly and unappetizing, into the body of the boar with Nipper's knife.

Altin, grimacing as he watched the child enthusiastically massacre the carcass, nodded at Nipper's remark. The way his head hurt and his body ached, the old man's assessment likely wasn't far from the truth.

"Now, Nipper," Kettle scolded, "what kinda way is that fer ya to talk to the young master? And him tryin' to eat an' all. Have some consideration, won't ya?"

"I'm considerin'," Nipper retorted. "An' I'm considerin' he looks like a pig's arse what rolled in shite. Boy too dim to sleep. Up all night castin' his magic, no carin' fer his body. Like as if he made of stone. Gonna get him killed, just like the othern."

"Oh, now you stop," Kettle said. "Altin's too smart fer that, ain't ya lad?"

Again Altin nodded, stuffing his mouth with a newly presented slice of steaming bread, the butter still melting into its sumptuous fluff. Not only was he half-starved, the bread gave him a chance to not respond.

"I seen the last two," Nipper pressed on. "I watched 'em. Always come down here lookin' just the same. Don't know why they keep sendin' 'em here like that. Weren't nothing Tytamon can do. They just kill theirself ever' time. And this one getting' close. I can see it in his face; his wore out pig's arse face. Just like the rest. Same face. Tired of watchin' 'em die."

"Nipper! You stop this instant or I'll have at ya with this here pin." She raised her rolling pin menacingly. Nipper seemed to take the threat seriously despite his out-ranking the woman in both position and years.

A thumb-sized chunk of pork suddenly flew into his face, startling him and sticking wetly to his cheek. "Gods above, child!" he said as he quickly retrieved the knife from Pernie's hands. Much longer and the carcass would have been fit for only sausages and stew. He shot a look Altin's way, something between anger and concern, and then returned to his work carving the boar, absently batting the girl's hands away as she continued groping for the knife.

Altin knew the old steward saw something that should not be ignored. Nipper wasn't so much different than Tytamon in that way. But, he also knew that he was still casting with discipline. Neither Nipper nor Tytamon ever gave him credit for having discipline. He'd stopped himself last night, just as he should, just as he always did. Altin was in control. He wished they would understand.

"Ya want something fer yer head," Kettle offered. "I keep some willow powder in the cupboard over here fer just such a thing." She shot a glance towards Nipper, then tipped an imaginary bottle to her lips.

"Yes, please," Altin answered. "It's really bad this morning. And while I don't think Nipper needs to worry about me killing myself, I have to admit, I think I'm pressing the edges of my skill. It's pretty hard on me come mornings. I'm starting to think I won't be able to do it after all."

"What?" Kettle looked shocked. "Not gettin' to yer moon? Don't be silly, child. Ya was born to do it. Ya just haven't found the right way about it yet is all. Don't ya start with that givin' up talk or there be no more bread waiting mornings down here to warm ya up. You'll make do with that old, hard yesterday loaf ya always get if'n ya start with that down here. Ya hear me? I won't have no quitters. Not in my kitchen."

He smiled politely and sighed. "Yes, Kettle." She was kind—if nosey and ultimately annoying. He ate silently while she began talking about Miss Madeline, the farmer's daughter down the way a league or so, and for whom Altin had nothing approaching interest or desire. Madeline was a nice girl, but about as sharp as the corners on a melon; and frankly, Altin had no time for vapid fawning farm girls anyway. He had work to do, and the last thing he needed was some illiterate furrow-raker doting all over him in awe of his magic—not to mention his proximity to the legendary wealth of Tytamon the Ancient. No, that was exactly what he didn't need. He had no time for girls.

Somewhere between Miss Madeline and an argument with Nipper regarding the number of cloves required for properly preparing a boar of that size, to which Altin paid no attention at all, Tytamon came into the room. Suddenly everyone was quiet and fell into a most professional demeanor, Nipper sending Pernie to the chicken coop with a basket and a "shush, just do it" when she started to protest.

The staff wasn't generally intimidated by the great mage, and Altin heard their silence as if someone had rung a gong. Absorbed in his thoughts and food as he had been, he feared there might be something he had missed.

Tytamon clapped a hand on Altin's shoulder as he neared, offering a "good morning" as he sat down next to Altin on the bench. No evidence of anything untowards there. Altin harrumphed silently in his head.

"Good morning," he said, eyeing the older mage for clues.

The truth was, Tytamon came down here often, but this morning it didn't take any great feat of perspicacity to suspect that, given Altin's beleaguered appearance and generally battered condition, this morning was not going to follow a normal course. The servants were savvy enough to understand, even if Altin was not, which was why a moment later found the room evacuated but for the two mages sitting there.

"You emptied the sky last night," Tytamon said without

precursor. "Two nights in a row."

"Yes, I did," Altin agreed.

"*I* don't even empty the sky, Altin. Not unless I have to. And I can count the times I've had to on my fingers and toes. At your current pace, you will surpass me in such instances by a good seven hundred years. Don't you think that's pushing it a bit?"

"Yes," said Altin. "I am."

"Care to explain why?"

"No, but I'm sure you'll milk it out of me eventually, so I might as well, right?"

"Might as well." Tytamon reached over and sliced himself a thick piece of Kettle's bread. He buttered it and took a bite. "By Hestra and her seven-headed son this is good."

"It's always best right out of the oven."

"Indeed," agreed Tytamon chewing slowly and contemplating the succulent nature of the treat. "You know, this bread is like the death dance of the male novafly. An exquisite moment in time, almost impossible to catch for most, but those who have seen one erupt talk of it for years. One of life's subtle gems. Generally, those are the best."

Altin nodded and took another bite. Kettle's bread could only buy him so much time. How was he going to explain it to Tytamon? It wasn't like he'd done anything wrong. He just pushed a bit, found a limit, and stopped. That was good magic. Solid application of the principles of experimentation. Nothing less than could be found in every reputable magician's notebook from every century for essentially all of the Magical Revolution. So why was he having such a hard time making himself explain it to the one person who knew this better than anyone else alive?

"So," said Tytamon after cutting another piece of bread. "What does one do with that much mana? Hmm? I can only assume you haven't landed one of your fancy rocks on Luria yet, or I would have heard the rapturous shouts last night.

So what's going on? Tell me, and maybe I can help."

Altin moaned. The old man was always so calm and patient. Why did Altin seem to forget that all the time? He locked up a little inside whenever he had to go to Tytamon for help. The defensive reflex was worse when Tytamon came to him, normally because his errors were so easily observed. He drew in a deep breath and let it all spill out.

"I can't do it. I can't get there. It's too damned far away. I've hit the limit of my power and I'm no closer now than I was two years ago when I figured out how to enchant the seeing stones. I can suck the night dry of mana and still not even make a dent in finding it. It's damnably far away, Tytamon. You have no idea how far away it has to be from here."

"Well, you're right about that; I don't. But I can guess that if a Z-class teleporter with your gifts hasn't figured it out after all this time, it must be pretty far."

"I can port myself to Duador in one shot, no hop, damn it. How is it that I can't even three-hop far enough to change my perspective on the moon to something I can see? Something at least noticeable to the eye?"

Tytamon leaned away from him, a bushy eyebrow raised. "Duador?" He remained calm, but a genuine storm brewed behind that cocked gray cloud upon his brow.

"Only once," Altin hastily amended. "Just once, a year ago, to see if I could do it. Just there and back, not even a full minute in between. Just time to breathe and recast."

"There and back? That's it?" He was looking straight through Altin and the young mage felt certain that Tytamon was using some subtle O-class mindreading on him. He hadn't the courage to try a lie.

"Well, ok, there and then to String, and then back here." As soon as the words left his mouth he knew that Tytamon was going to blast him on the spot, or cast a six-month silence spell on his tongue, or worse, throw him out of

Calico for good.

"You three-hopped around the whole planet?"

The reply caught Altin off guard.

"Well, yes," he answered reluctantly. "It was three full ports, actually, but I could have done the whole thing in one shot knowing what I know now about the distance. It wouldn't even be hard."

Tytamon looked amazed. He appeared to be about to say so, and then checked himself, saying instead, "Why in the name of Lord Morton's moustache would you do something so ridiculously dangerous as going to Duador? I mean, the elves on String could have done any number of things to you for trespassing, much less breaking a five-hundred-year-old treaty... but Duador? Good gods, man, that's insanity. Is there any place worse that you could go? Next thing you'll be telling me you...." He cut himself off. "Foolish boy."

"Look," said Altin, his ire up a bit. "I'm not a foolish boy. I'm twenty-two. And I knew exactly what I was doing. I spent the entirety of eight months prior to that jump reading up on Duador and on String. I knew exactly where the demons arrived, and I knew exactly where the hordes should be in their ravaging rounds. I scried out my landing twenty-seven seconds before the cast, landed exactly on target, and was gone before a puff-adder has time to strike. Same goes for String, adding fifty-eight seconds from the time I scried it out as well. What I did may have involved some risk, but the way I did it was neither foolish nor reckless. It was calculated risk, necessary to my work, and I put in the book time just like you always insist I do. You are right to be mad at me for doing it, but you are wrong to think I did it foolishly. I did not." He stared back at Tytamon defiantly, his lips and hands trembling.

Tytamon studied him for awhile, a long silence before beginning to nod. Altin was at least a year older than the rest had been, more disciplined too. The look in the aged sorcerer's eyes suggested an internal debate. "But why did you do it?"

Tytamon was stalling. Altin knew. He just didn't know why. "I needed to get an idea how far I can jump. I needed something as a measure. And now I have it. That was all. I'm trying to do like you taught me. One tiny detail at a time. Each chip from the stone moves closer to the statue; the finer the detail, the finer the work. I get that. I swear I do. I'm not just another reckless Six."

"They're not always reckless, Altin. They lack circularity. We've had this conversation before. That much power without access to the whole circle of magic limits your ability to work that power safely. You can't know what you don't see because you've never seen it, can't see it. For ninety-nine-point-nine percent of humanity, lack of circularity doesn't matter. But when you are a Six, it does. The law of circularity is proven, Altin."

"Well, I'm not a Six, so it doesn't matter."

"Your guild card says you are."

"They're wrong. I skipped divination on one side and growth on the other, and yet still hold K-class in illusion? How does that fit into the law of circularity?"

Tytamon really didn't want to have this argument again.

"It doesn't, that's how," Altin pressed. "I'm either a K or better in healing, or I'm a K or better in divination; it's just latent or something."

"You're twenty-two. Nobody is that latent. It's never happened."

"Eight of eight never happened either. Not until you."

The problem with bright young apprentices was that sometimes they made argumentation tedious. And on this particular topic, Altin was unyieldingly adamant, and, unfortunately, at least possessed of a logical case, if not a reasonable one. He drove Tytamon to fits, and quite despite the great magician's considerable experience with powerful young mages. However, Tytamon would not allow himself to be drawn into this fight again today. Besides, he had something else in mind. "Look, do you want my help or not? We can argue about your Seven-ness some other time."

Altin stopped abruptly, ignoring the sarcastic undertones. "What kind of help?"

"I realize that it will likely be the death of you, but I know how you Sixe... Sevens can be if you don't get your way. I didn't stop Finnius from defying the gods and getting himself fried by divine wrath; I let Synthia play with her mermaid soil; and, my coupe de grace, I allowed Miss Montclaire to destroy herself and, in the process, facilitate the genocide of an entire race. Why should I not help you out as well?

"Sadly, Kurr has no better mentor for you kids, and, well, I have no better method of mentoring than to advise caution and give what advice I may. You're going to chase your dreams with or without me, but perhaps, with some luck and a few friendly suggestions, you might live to realize your potential. Just try not to level the castle this time. You people are so hard on these old walls."

There was something of resignation in his bearing, a weariness, as if he, like Nipper, did not want to endure another dead apprentice, another round of grief and chaos and the rebuilding of broken towers and sundered hearts. But he was willing to do it because it needed to be done. He seemed reconciled to it now. And apparently the time was right to try.

"Come with me, boy." He got up from the bench and strode purposefully from the room.

His aged legs carried him swiftly, belying his feeble frame as he passed through the central courtyard and unlocked the massive steel door that guarded the entry to the underground sections of his tower. Altin had never been down here before. He followed Tytamon down flights of stairs that carried them a couple of stories down. Finally they emerged into a low, dark basement, the ceiling only a hand's width above Altin's head. Altin followed Tytamon, guided entirely by the rustling of his robes, until Calico's master reached for a lamp hanging on the wall, finding it by memory in the Stygian blackness, and a moment later it sprung to light, illuminating the space around.

The entire room was clutter. Pure clutter. Crates were stacked everywhere, against every wall, piled in every corner and heaped about the middle of the room. Where there weren't any crates, there were barrels and casks. Atop the barrels and casks there were small boxes and sacks and elegant chests and little piles of assorted things like books and cloth and vials of mysterious liquids, powders and gels, all of which combined to give off the most curious of smells, metallic yet with a hint of flowers and perhaps a bit of burning hair. The room was filled literally to the rafters with various objects and containers too numerous to count, and all were covered with layers of dust as thick as a slice of bread. The dust was soft and powdery, of such fine consistency that it began to waft into the air, stirred up by their footsteps and the breezes created through the fanning motions of their pendulous robes and vacuous dangling sleeves. The rising dust coated Altin's mouth and the inside of his nose, its dryness and the musty taste causing him to sneeze and cough, which only made the situation worse.

"Juice of a werebat," Altin spat, coughing harder and pressing a fold of his sleeve against his face in an attempt to filter the particles in the air. "This is awful."

Tytamon, seemingly unaffected by the dust, wasted no time with any of the boxes or barrels and headed straight for a low, iron-bound door made of thick oaken planks mounted on the room's furthest wall. Altin scurried through the jumble and stood near the ancient mage, waiting expectantly and blinking at the dust that was drying out his eyes.

Tytamon placed his hands on the rough wood and spoke a few words of magic. The door's cast-iron handle flamed for a moment as a magical trap disarmed. Altin had to blink a few more times, waiting for the stain of the magic's brightness to leave his retinas. Tytamon pulled a ring of keys from a pocket in his robes and unlocked the conventional lock that was in the handle too. He turned to Altin for the first time since leaving the kitchen and said in a voice so low and foreboding that it startled the younger man to chills, "Don't utter one word of magic in here. Not one. Not even a thought. Do you hear me?"

Altin, wide-eyed and with goosebumps rising on his back and arms, nodded affirmatively. Not a word.

Tytamon opened the door revealing a tiny chamber, barely three paces across in either direction, and stepped inside. Altin followed. The ceiling was too low for his six-foot frame by about two inches, and so he had to stand awkwardly, alternating between ducking his head and spreading his legs. Neither worked very well, but he made do and looked around.

Shelves. Three sets of shelves, that's all there was to see. And the sets against the left and right walls were almost empty. On the right side, the lowest shelf held a skull of some sort, a twisted, toothy looking thing the species of which Altin couldn't even hazard a guess. To the left, on the upper shelf there sat a little jewelry box, tiny, hardly bigger than a bar of soap, and upholstered in lace, once white but now brown with age and dust. A miniature silk bow on its curved top was the little box's only decoration, and the bow was so old that it had lost all but the faintest tinge of pink. But neither of these were what had brought them here, for Tytamon went directly to the shelves mounted on the room's farthest wall.

These shelves had several things on them, most of which meant nothing to Altin. There was an old oil lamp and something resembling a lute. There were two tattered books that looked as if Tytamon had dug them out of a thousand-year-old grave, and there was a small leather pouch, no bigger than a dehydrated pear. And it was to this last that Tytamon went. He took it off the shelf gingerly, and looked back once more at Altin. "Not one word of magic. Or we're both dead."

Altin watched breathlessly as Tytamon pulled open the drawstrings and poured out the pouch's contents into the palm of his weathered hand. Three small stones, ugly, yellowish and roughly the size of a peach pit each. That was it.

Altin frowned.

"Liquefying Stone," Tytamon breathed, raising his hand towards Altin and lifting the lamp so Altin could get a better look. The lamp's golden light augmented the stone's strangely crystalline luminosity, as if the outer surface were transparent, like crystal, but the inside something else. Altin tried to look deeper into it, unconsciously taking the lamp from Tytamon and leaning down close. Experience suggested that the light could go deeper into the rock, should go deeper, but it just didn't; it just seemed to disappear. It was like looking into a mirror that only reflected you but not the rest of the room behind. You knew the room was there, that you should be able to see it, but it just wasn't there. He commented on this oddity aloud.

"It's not that the light doesn't go in," said Tytamon. "It does. It just doesn't come out. It can't. Which is why you must always keep it covered when you aren't using it. Mana isn't the only thing this stuff can amplify."

"So what is it?" Altin reached for one of the stones as he asked the question, half expecting Tytamon to snatch them away.

"It's an amplification stone. A huge amplification stone. Freakish. Not like those meager potions the Conduits try to make."

Altin nodded, he liked where this idea seemed to be going, but he didn't say anything as Tytamon went on.

"You know how much mana you drew last night? Well, you can pull twice that much if you're touching one of these and you don't know what you're doing—sometimes even if you do. You can pull that much, even in a single cast."

Altin scrunched up his face in disbelief. "How? Once I get what I can reach, it's gone. Cleared space is cleared space. Or does the stone extend my range?"

"Boy, you have no idea." He dropped the other two stones back into the pouch and drew the strings tight. "I've kept this stuff secret for years. I don't even keep the things I know about demon summoning as hushed as I do Liquefying Stone." He waggled the pouch in the air as he spoke to emphasize his point, sending a little cloud of dust billowing around their heads. Altin coughed as the centuries-old sorcerer put the pouch with the two remaining stones back on the shelf and motioned for Altin to leave the claustrophobic little room. Altin happily obliged, gripping the single stone tightly in his hand.

"No magic," Tytamon reminded him as they exited.

"I know," Altin answered, impatiently. He wasn't a child anymore.

"Can't be too careful," came the reply as the ancient mage locked the door with the iron key. He pushed Altin towards the exit, remaining behind and making no move to renew the magic lock on the door until Altin was all the way across the room. When he had recast the lock, he rejoined Altin and they started up the stairs. "You need to keep it covered. And not just in your pocket. A hole in the lining and you're a dead man."

Altin promised that he would, but couldn't help glimpsing

at the stone. The cautions were really starting to pile up, almost enough to curb his enthusiasm for running up to his tower and testing out the stone. Almost. And it was just as he was having the thought that Tytamon reached out, viper-like, and snatched the stone from his hand. "You can have it when your headache is gone and you've had proper rest. You can have it tomorrow. Now run along. I have things to do to prepare."

Altin frowned. "Prepare for what?"

"To prepare for what you're probably going to do to my castle. Now go. I'm old and need a nap myself. Belly full of Kettle's bread and I hibernate like a bear."

With nothing to do but wait, and no possibility of rest between now and then, Altin hustled to his room to search his library for any reference he might have missed to the Liquefying Stone. Tomorrow would be the day.

Chapter 5

Altin woke the next morning early and excited. Darkness still lay upon the land, and he had to pace about the top of his tower for over an hour before the sun rose high enough for propriety to allow him to go and pester Tytamon—to go and gather the Liquefying Stone and begin the task of learning how it worked.

He ducked through the narrow door leading down from the battlements, half doorway, half hole in the floor, and came into his chamber. As he moved towards the dresser intending to quickly run a comb through his hair lest he look too desperate to begin, he noticed that in the hour of his pacing someone had brought the loaf of bread to his room as they always did and placed it on the table. He chuckled. All these years and only now had he finally narrowed down the hour. As he looked at the bread in the shadowy, early morning light, he caught a glimpse of movement, a tiny scurrying spot of gray barely darker than the shadows around the bread. He squinted at it and with a word summoned a tiny flame to the candle sitting at the table's center.

The light appeared so abruptly that the little mouse froze for a moment, the candle flame glinting in its tiny, black spot eyes. It sniffled in Altin's direction for a moment and the young wizard could see that it held a portion of his daily bread in its pointy rodent teeth.

"Why you hairy little thief," Altin cursed. "That's mine!" He considered shooting a miniature fireball at it, but recent events stayed his spell. The mouse gave him no time to consider a second option, however, for it was off like a dart, off the table, across the flagstones and into the safety of a dark crack in the wall, not too far from the stairs leading back up to the battlements.

Altin made a face at it as it vanished into the hole. "That's all I need. Mice." He resolved himself to let Nipper know, as such things fell under the old man's jurisdiction, and allowed the promise of the Liquefying Stone to rinse away any further consideration of the furry pest.

Near the recently nibbled bread was a stack of books, a thousand pages of fruitless research done yesterday that had garnered him not one word about the Liquefying Stone. He picked them up and headed downstairs. He stopped on the second floor of his tower, his personal library—an extensive collection by any standards for someone of his relative youth—and meticulously re-deposited the works before heading to the kitchen.

Tytamon was already there when he arrived, and Altin cursed himself for having wasted so much time pacing the battlements in the name of timidity. Nipper was nowhere to be seen, and Kettle was busy looking busy in the presence of her ancient master. Little Pernie was sweeping ineffectually around the hearth, but she looked up and, with no pig butchering to distract her this time, saw that Altin had come in. She grinned excitedly. "Hullo, Master Altin," she said, beaming at him like a tiny towheaded sun. "I saw a lizard already today, out on the well, but he was still stiff with cold because when I tried to wake him he wouldn't move at all, no matter how many times I poked him, and I did a lot because he fell into the well and still never moved all the way down. I hope he will be okay, but I don't know if lizards can swim or not, but he was green, just like sir's dragon. You should have seen him."

Altin rolled his eyes. "That's nice," he said and quickly turned towards Tytamon.

"Pernie, hush," Kettle admonished the child. "Them's got business to talk. No time for silliness."

"Oh, I don't know," said Tytamon, furrowing his brow at Altin briefly before leaning to peek round him towards the girl. "Lizards can be serious business too." He stood and stepped around Altin, fixing Pernie with a grin. With a few words and the wriggling of his thumbs, he created a bright, illusionary lizard on the ground between his feet. "Did it look like this?" he asked. He sent the illusion scurrying across the floor towards Pernie, who screeched with glee and leapt for it, pouncing like a cat. Her hands clutched right through it, at which point it disappeared, causing her to spin round and round like a kitten chasing its tail, searching everywhere, giggling and even lifting Kettle's skirts to have a look between the woman's feet. Kettle gasped and pushed the child away, though she couldn't help but laugh. Giving up, Pernie looked back at the old mage, wonder in her eyes and still giggling for all her worth. His grin grew. Extending his hand, he reproduced the illusion there on his palm, allowing it to rise and float slowly through the air towards her again, dangling as if invisible fingers held it by the tail. Seeing this, she became nearly hysterical with laughter again, and peels of high-pitched merriment echoed through Calico Castle's labyrinthine halls as she jumped for the wriggling fiction while Tytamon teased her, bobbing it up and down and keeping it just beyond her reach. After a few moments of this, Tytamon relented. But right as the magical lizard was finally within her grasp, it burst into a pink cloud of rose petals, real ones, that rained down upon her for nearly half a minute. Somehow she managed to squeal even louder than before, and she danced about in the shower of flowers trying to catch all the petals as they fell.

Altin winced at her jubilant screams, closing one eye and marveling that none of the crystal goblets on the shelf behind him shattered with the piercing shrill of Pernie's noise. By the gods that child was obnoxious, and Tytamon was bringing it on, making it even worse; you'd think he'd know better by now.

"Pernie!" scolded Kettle finally, clutching at her ears. "You'll bring the orcs down out of the hills with all that racket." She turned to Tytamon and added, "An' yer encouragin' her with all that fancy stuff." Kettle's smiling eyes did not reflect the nature of her words, however, and Tytamon only continued to grin. When the petals finally stopped falling, Kettle handed Pernie the egg basket and pushed her out the door in the direction of the chicken coop. The child began to protest, but a look from Kettle choked the words before they could get out. "That's enough lizards an' flowers for one mornin', thank ya. Get ya busy now."

Kettle turned, curtseyed to them both, and followed the girl outside.

Altin shifted his weight impatiently until they were out of sight. "All right, I'm ready to try the stone. I slept well last night and cast nothing. I'm fresh as April dew."

Tytamon, still grinning as he watched the departure of Kettle and the girl, turned back to his apprentice, the merry glimmer in his eyes becoming something that touched on sorrow and perhaps a bit of sympathy. He shook his head and let out a long breath. Altin ignored it all, figuring the old man was having second thoughts about the Liquefying Stone. He kept his mouth shut. This was not the time to give Tytamon any reason to change his mind.

After a moment, Tytamon reached into his pocket and

pulled out a small towel, bundled up tight, and set it on the tabletop between them. They both stared at it for a while.

Finally the great wizard spoke. "I can feel your impatience."

Altin swallowed. So much for hiding it. Tytamon didn't miss much. "I can't help it," he said. "What did you expect?"

"You can't be impatient with the Liquefying Stone."

He knew Tytamon was going to say that. "I know."

"Look, just understand this: this stone is going to dump mana on you. You think you understand what I am saying, but you don't. It will be like striking flint to steel looking for a spark and then having your dragon breathe on you instead. When you go to make your cast, you need to try to draw almost no mana at all. Even then, you're going to be shocked at what you find yourself pulling in. So, make sure you pick a spell that allows you to channel extra mana, something that gives you an outlet to improvise and unload, okay? You will need it for the first few tries; I promise."

Altin listened carefully to every word. It made perfect sense. If the stone did what Tytamon suggested, he might find himself overwhelmed with mana, overcome; even with a mythothalamus the size of his, he could only channel so much. He could be fried—either literally fried, as in dead, or magically fried, burnt out, his mythothalamus cooked and his magical sight lost as surely as a destroyed retina costs a person's sight. "I understand," he said, looking Tytamon square in the eyes. "I honestly think I do. Is there anything else I need to know?"

"No. Just that. Start slow. Keep it simple, and keep it small. Oh, and remember to keep the stone covered when you're not using it. That's the most important thing. Keep it covered, and keep it away from you. Accidental contact is fatal with this stuff. Understand?"

"I understand."

They stood staring silently across the intervening space

at one another, waiting. Altin wanted to just out and ask if he could go but didn't want to seem any more impatient than he was.

"Go," said the weathered mage, looking very tired. "Just go."

Altin gripped the wadded cloth firmly in his fist, raising it to chest level and invoking a triumphant "yes!" With that he turned and ran back to his tower, victory finally at hand.

When he'd mounted the tower he stood briefly surveying the land around him. The gray wall cliffs beneath Mt. Pernolde climbed high behind him, looming protectively at his back as the Great Forest spread itself far into the west, a deep green that faded to gray as the horizon blurred it into the distant sky. Everywhere else, to the south and east, lay the vast plains of Merimak, rippling in the gentle wind as far as the eye could see. It was beautiful, and the day was beautiful, and it was the perfect day to finally find the moon.

A small, weather-beaten and largely burnt table, with a matching and equally decimated stool, stood near the passage leading down into his room. Gingerly, he placed the bundled Liquefying Stone upon the table and patted it softly, as if it needed to be soothed. He needed to find the right spell for trying out the Liquefying Stone. But what?

He thought about it for several long moments, coming up with many options—and none. He ran back down into his room and took one of his old notebooks from the single shelf above his narrow bed where he kept his most valued and his most frequently used books. It was a notebook from his second year of tutelage under Tytamon, filled with simple, easy-to-cast spells that any D or E-class mage could work with a bit of instruction and some practice. He decided this was probably the safest place to start. Simple and small, just what Tytamon had ordered.

He leafed through the book for a time and came across

the perfect spell. A growth spell—not natural growth, for Altin had no skills in healing magic, but a basic expansion spell from the conjuration sphere instead: take something and make it bigger through the addition of material, more like packing a snowball than nurturing a tree. "Easy as tossing a toad," he said aloud.

He read through the spell notes several times, it having been many years since he'd used this particular spell, until he was satisfied that he knew it completely and by heart. The words were simple and the inflections elementary to produce. As he looked them over, they came back to him with an old familiarity. At length he was confident he could start.

He snapped the book closed and, bringing it with him just in case, headed back to the battlements. Now that he knew what he wanted to do, he just needed something to do it to, something small, small enough that if he drew too much mana, he could simply make it a little bigger than he planned when the spell began. He looked for a chip of stone or some gravel, casting his eyes about the ground, searching along the rounded edge at the base of the parapet. At last he spotted one, a tiny rock, roughly round and about the size of a pea. It would do perfectly.

He placed the little rock on the floor, dead center of the tower which was roughly twenty paces across and encircled by the parapet, broken only by the open doorway down to Altin's room. He took the wadded towel from atop the burnt table and moved to the crenellated wall. He flipped open the notebook and reviewed the spell once more, just to be extra sure.

The plan was to grow the stone to the size of a cantaloupe, but if he drew too much mana, he could make it as big as he needed too, big as a watermelon or big as a cow. Size didn't matter. The spell allowed for channeling power directly into the object, which was why it was the ideal spell to use for this initial try. Drawing a deep breath, he put the book down on the wall behind him and opened up the towel.

He studied the stone for a moment, holding it in his hand and examining it for the first time by the light of day. It still seemed dark inside. And it was an ugly stone. Vomit yellow. He marveled at how it could be so sickening, even giving him a sense of vertigo the longer he looked inside, nausea. But if it unlocked the mystery of the distance to the moon, it would be the most beautiful thing he had ever seen. And so he began to chant.

The words to the spell were simple, "Ma'h alta megan. Sen horra pen." That was it. Basic elven words, used more for their ability to focus the mind than for any power inherent to the sounds themselves. All of magic language worked like that, at least for humans. Learned by rote, spoken words served to hone the thoughts to the task at hand. And there was something to the musicality of them too, a harmony that worked to bring the mana into one with the magician's desire, binding timing, focus and will.

With great care Altin began to utter the magic words, using a master's diligence to speak each syllable, to layer each note and beat in its exact place and plane despite the remedial level of the spell. He chanted them meticulously, repeating them as he closed his eyes and opened his mind to the mana all around. The sky was full of mana again, the thick, syrupy ether having flowed slowly back into place since his last Lurian attempt. There was as much or as little as Altin wanted waiting for him to use.

Fully cognizant of Tytamon's warning, he reached out for a tiny filament of mana, no more than a whisker waggling in the currents at the tip of a curling wave, a flicker in the ocean of thick purplish ooze. He plucked at it gingerly with his mind, carefully, like picking something out of someone else's eye, and pulled it into his mythothalamus with a gentle tug.

It came easily enough, and Altin gathered the mana cautiously, stretching it out and directing it across the tower into the pea-sized rock lying in the middle of the floor. He pulled a bit more mana from the coalescing mass and broke the new portions into more threads, sending them snaking out like tendrils into the stone of the mountain that loomed at Calico Castle's expansive back. The tendrils spread like a thousand filament fingers and streaked as arrow shots into the cliffs. Some branched down into the earth, while others turned up, seeking in the sky. Each strand played out as if of its own accord, each in search of any substance that could be used, locking on to any molecule of matter and prepared to bring its essence back, to funnel it into the single mana thread Altin had attached to the tiny piece of gravel lying on the ground.

Altin carefully directed the mana out and felt each tendril find a source to tap, subtle vibrations that murmured to him through a net of mana that was all around him now. When it was done, when the tendrils were all locked taut and humming like harp strings tuned and ready to be plucked, he could at last complete the spell. He spoke the last word carefully, meticulously, changing the tempo just enough to let the growth begin. He opened the gate in his mythothalamus and allowed the outbound mana to flow back in, allowing it to run into his head as one lets light in by opening an eye. And oh how it did run.

What started at first as a tiny influx, as soft pulses along a web of wires, turned suddenly into a raging current broken loose as if from a sundered dam. Altin gasped and tried to cut it off, but the torrent began to rage. His tiny threads began to bloat and swell like overburdened veins throbbing the pulse of some infernal monstrous heart. He felt the threads stretch and bend and twist with such fervor it was as if the mana had begun to boil; he fought against it as one might battle the end of a strip miner's hose shaken free of its restraining mount. Terror began to skulk about the back of consciousness, and he tasted bile rising in his throat. What had he unleashed?

He felt the heat growing in his head, the friction of the energy coming much too fast, and he knew that he risked over-channeling if he didn't cut the mana off. Fear made him want to open his eyes and see the gravel on the floor, but he knew doing that would be a disaster, if not an instant death. He could sense the gravel's reflection in the mana, could feel that it was growing quickly, swelling, even looming at him, charging him like a bull.

He ground his teeth and battled against the current washing in, squeezing down the valve in his brain with every ounce of his magical strength. He heard himself cry out with the effort and hovered at the brink of failure as the gate in his mind tried to close but trembled under the enormity of the press of twice a normal sky's-worth of mana. He sent a silent prayer to several of the gods, gods he almost never thought about, as he fought and fought to shut the mana down.

And finally he did. At last he slammed the mental gate, painfully, but down, cutting off the mana just as something hit him like a blow from Taot's tail, striking him in the chest with an audible crack of ribs and bashing him against the wall. His knees went weak as he cut off the spell and fortunately he'd begun to fall just before the impact came, the limpness likely saving him from being pinned, or worse, from being crushed against the battlements. He gasped in agony as his back scraped over the edge of an archer's gap and again as his head bounced off it, then thumped against the floor with a thud. He was dimly aware of a shadow growing over him and then everything went dark.

When he finally came to, he lay silently, breathing and afraid to open his eyes, afraid to discover what he had done. When he did open them, he was still in total darkness. At first he thought he'd fried his vision, and probably his magic too, and panic welled as he lay there dreading that he'd just fulfilled another prophecy of the Six. But after a time, he calmed himself and began to look more carefully around. There was a faint glow coming from around a bend ahead of him. The light outlined a curving surface, revealing that he was tucked into what was little more than a crawl space formed around the edge of the tower by the massive expanse of what was clearly an enormous boulder now—the pebble swollen to something larger than a house.

The glow had to be coming from his room below—in through the window and up the stairs—and he was suddenly grateful for the design of that stairway he'd cursed so many times before, having always had to duck whenever he went down. He twisted, intent on crawling towards the light, but the pain in his ribs nearly blacked him out again. Good gods.

He lay back, panting, and took the time to consider what had taken place, half terrified and half in awe of what the Liquefying Stone could do. He could have been crushed. He could have died. But on the other hand, the pebble was now an enormous boulder, made so with a child's spell and a tiny mana thread. Such power was incredible. But how had it so nearly come undone? How could the mana flow so fast?

As he reenacted the casting slowly in his mind, he began to realize why Tytamon called the stone Liquefying Stone. Normally mana oozed, it ran like maple sap on a cool November night. But not this time. The stone made the mana run like water, liquefied. Fast and dangerous, a torrent, a river raging with melting snow, stronger, even more powerful than a river could ever be, and flowing from everywhere at once. It was amazing and Altin felt himself rejoice. This really was it. He knew at once that this was what he needed to make it to the moon.

But first he needed to clean up his new mess, and

hopefully before Tytamon found out what he'd done. He had a feeling Tytamon already knew, but the old man was a mystery. And in the face of that, Altin would operate on hope.

He groped around in the darkness, wincing at every move, and found the Liquefying Stone lying near his knee. He brought it up near his face and regarded it in the faint glow coming from around the parapet's curve. "Tricky little bastard, I'll give you that," he said to it. "But you're the ticket for the trip." He laughed, then winced and nearly puked, and then slowly, painfully, made his way around and down into his room.

He wrapped his chest as best he could with some rags lying in a corner—he'd deal with his ribs later—and bundled the Liquefying Stone in an unused strip. He placed it on the table near the mouse-nibbled bread and headed downstairs, out into the meadow. The best way to deal with his pebble problem was from the outside, not from underneath its bulk.

Once outside he looked upon his creation for the first time and almost had to laugh. The pebble was indeed enormous now, and, cradled in the battlements like it was, it looked like a giant snowball on a cone, just like the vendors sold at fairs and festivals, icy treats sprinkled with colorful fruit juices and perfect on a hot summer day. Only this one was not colorful, it was slate gray, the gray of Mt. Pernolde. Altin couldn't help think there was something to be said for the fact that at least when he screwed up one of Tytamon's towers, he kept to the color scheme. He chuckled at his own silent joke, but laughter made his ribs hurt, and it was mostly nervous laughter anyway. He had to get rid of that gigantic thing.

He made a few practice gestures with his arms to see how much the movements of casting would hurt and consequently subject his spell to failure, or even further disaster, but he found that he could manage. Casting wouldn't be pleasant, but discipline would get it done. Discipline was the cornerstone of good magic.

He chanted a familiar teleporting spell that brought him atop the large boulder and looked dubiously around. No, this wouldn't work. If he tried to shrink it back to normal while standing up here, he would have a twenty-foot fall if the boulder shrank too fast, and given his condition, he wasn't willing to take the risk. However, the circumference of the enormous rock exceeded that of the tower itself and thus eliminated the option of a stance on the parapet. That was a problem. This particular spell required that the caster be within at least twenty paces of the target and holding it in full view. The tower was forty-feet high, and even were it a bit shorter, the angle required for something constituting a full view took him well beyond range. He studied the curtain wall beneath him with a grunt. Close enough, but posing the same angular problem as did standing on the ground.

It was then that Altin heard Taot coming in for his morning meal. He turned and watched the dragon glide in as he normally did around this time of day. There was the answer. He saw that the dragon had already spotted him and he hurriedly sent the obstreperous beast a message conveying the sense of injury and a need for delicacy—just in case Taot was in the mood for some rough and rib-exploding joke. The dragon replied with feelings of concern, best described as a brown sense, and something like worry for the pack. Altin had often struggled to explain dragon emotion to people since the day he'd tamed the creature, but no one ever understood. One simply couldn't ascribe color to emotion and expect anyone to understand.

He reassured Taot that he was fine, just bruised, and sent a sense of urgency along with a request for a short ride. The dragon responded with mild annoyance, but was willing to comply. Dragons were such moody things.

Altin quickly teleported back to the meadow and called the dragon to him with a thought. He clambered aboard as soon as Taot offered him his neck, and nearly fainted with the effort halfway up. He received another thought of concern from the dragon, this one tinged with a questioning element regarding strength, darker, a probe on the dragon's part, checking to be sure Altin had not gone weak or been wounded past the point of worth.

Altin sent back raw power, channeling a swell of mana with the telepathic note, a large bubble like a mountain pregnant with lava but not yet ready to burst. The feeling Altin conveyed was not a threat; it was just a statement that the dragon could understand. Animal magic was raw, reflexive and made by instinct, not by thought. Dragons in particular understood how magic worked, at least in their own way, and they understood power very well. Taot knew what Altin meant, and his concern was abated by the show of strength. He was just making sure Altin was still worthy of respect. There was no room in nature for the weak. It was not a matter of love; it was a matter of life and death.

Altin patted him on the neck to assure him there were no hard feelings and then directed him to fly up close to the tower top. Taot responded silently and leapt into the air, the pure power of the leap, launched by muscles thick as pine trunks, jarring Altin once again to the point of nearly passing out. He gasped and fought against the spots that swam in his vision as the dragon cleared the distance between them and the tower with two sweeps of his enormous wings. Once there, Taot hovered, his wings beating against the air with long, measured strokes that had Altin bobbing in the air. Altin sent Taot an image of exactly how he wanted the dragon faced and, once achieved, shifted from the straddling position to his knees. He made a few more practicing gestures, getting used to the rhythm of Taot's wings, and, once comfortable, began the reverse version of the stone-expanding spell.

It was much easier than it had been only a quarter of an hour before. The spell became simple again without the Liquefying Stone, like he remembered it from his youth, and in a matter of moments the boulder was just a pebble once again. Altin breathed a sigh of relief. He looked around to see if Tytamon was anywhere in view, checking the windows of the great central tower, still high above despite his being on Taot's back. He saw no gray whiskers visible in any of its windows, loops or holes. He could finally relax.

When it was done, Taot deposited Altin as gently as possible atop the tower and flew off with a screech of delayed hunger towards the herds that roamed the vast expanse of Tytamon's meadows. He'd had enough of his human, now it was time to eat.

Altin watched him go, thanking him with a thought, and then turned to the little piece of gravel, picking it up between two fingers and regarding it with a smile. It worked. The Liquefying Stone worked. It posed a few problems, sure, but that was just about figuring it out. At least now he had something to go on; now he had the start. Experimenting with magic was like swimming in an icy mountain lake; jumping in was the hard part, but from there it was just a matter of getting settled in. And that was exactly what he had in mind to do with the Liquefying Stone: get settled in.

Chapter 6

Orli had to wait almost two weeks before the council came to a decision regarding what the fleet would do. Apparently the debates upon the admiral's ship were as heated as they were long. The hawks among the officers wanted to press on to the next two star systems in search of the Hostiles, while the doves had argued for turning around and heading straight for Earth. And then there was the large contingent of officers who, like Orli, felt that after ten years in space, it was time to take the sure thing and just settle on the vacant Andalia which was essentially sitting in their laps.

Neither the doves nor the settler factions fancied the notion of another fifteen years in space, which is how long it would take them if the fleet decided to go on to both of the nearest solar systems and have a look around—a year and a half to the closest, and another five to the one beyond that. For the doves and settler factions, doing so amounted to a "gross period of time dedicated to the blind search of vast emptiness and a colossal waste of our lives." For many, to carry on was nothing short of a death sentence, a slow but certain demise from age aboard the ship.

The arguments had been heated and more than one near

riot had occurred, but in the end, the three sides managed a compromise of sorts: the hawks gained a mission to the nearest of the two star systems by arguing that the safety of Earth was entirely in their hands and that at least *some* effort should be made to procure it before they "turned tail and fled;" the settlers agreed to stay aboard their ships for the duration of that mission before being deposited back on Andalia prior to the fleet's returning home, which would appease the doves at mission's end. Everyone agreed that the nearest solar system was the most likely source of the Hostile activity anyway, given its proximity, and so, that was that. A three-year compromise robbing Orli of another huge chunk of her life, unless she went back to Earth, which would make it ten. She had no intention of doing that. Andalia was fine. Anywhere was fine. Just not here on this ship.

When she heard the announcement, that she'd just been volunteered for three more years, she collapsed amongst a patch of tomato vines she'd been tending in the ship's large nursery and cried. It was the third time in as many days that found her weeping amongst the leaves.

When the sobbing subsided a bit, she pulled her hands out of her dirty garden gloves, wiped her eyes and lay back onto the damp soil to stare up into the bright lights above. Rows of unnaturally straight fixtures manufactured for precise balance of all spectrums of light, adjustable to the finest degrees a gardener might desire and as pleasing to the eye as a kick was to the throat. She used to be grateful for them, for their ability to sustain her little seven acres of nature, but now she hated them. Now she could not help but compare them to the Andalian sun, feeling the incompleteness of the manmade light.

The Andalian sun was hot and genuine and shining golden all around; it touched her directly, its rays reached down and warmed her with a real caress; there was no arbiter, no mediating events, it was just her and the sun, connected. But not these lights. They had no heat. They were sterile. White. Their heat was a lie, snuck in from vents near the ceiling, spaced around the room at fifty-yard intervals. Spaced and paced by man and machine. It wasn't real. It was fake heat, piped in to make the misty air heavy, and tropically hot. But it was all a lie.

Orli wanted to go home. And so she cried. Often.

The months following the announcement that the fleet was moving on to the next star system were tough on her, and for a time she became terribly depressed. Slowly, however, with help from Roberto and mandatory weekly visits to the ship psychologist as ordered by her section chief, she began to come out of it for the most part and could focus on her work. In fact, she buried herself in it and used it to hide from thoughts of life beneath an open sky, thoughts of birds and bugs and clouds and gentle scented breezes. Most of the time she pulled it off.

Most of the time, she found herself in her lab going through the various specimens that she had brought back from Andalia with greater diligence than was her research habit prior to having gone planet-side. Truth be told, prior to her specimens being released from quarantine, prior to Andalia itself, there hadn't been much for her to research anyway; most of her lab work had merely been in discovering things already discovered. She'd made several of these during the last ten years, shocking revelations that excited her and reminded her why she'd gotten into botany from the start, only to find out that whatever epiphany she'd had had been discovered centuries earlier by someone else. It was annoying, and a little embarrassing too. But now she was doing real botany, cataloguing things that had never been catalogued before, discovering things that were actually new.

"They're going to teach college classes about you

someday," Roberto pointed out, meandering into her lab and interrupting her work as he usually did when his shifts on the bridge were done. "I was thinking of you down here with all your Andalia plants everywhere. You realize that you're the first person to be messing with any of this stuff? You're going to be famous. You know that?"

She smiled secretly before turning around with a serious face. "I'm happy to know that our weapons specialist spends his time thinking about flowers rather than paying attention to his job. It makes me feel so secure."

He gave her a look of boredom. "As if there's anything to shoot. At least you have something to do down here now. I still have the same boring shit every day for the next...." He stopped himself from making any reference to the long journey ahead. It bothered him, but not like it did Orli, not after Andalia, and he knew it.

She turned away from him and prodded the azalea she'd been looking at when he came in. It was just that. An azalea. Nothing special about it at all. Nothing. Except that it came from Andalia and not from Earth. She'd really begun to marvel at that over the last week or so. While she was really enjoying trying to classify some of the new species she'd found, it was the old species, the Earthlike species, that had the most significant ramifications in her mind. It seemed so entirely impossible that species could evolve exactly the same on two completely different planets in two entirely different solar systems. The miracle of life itself seemed impossible enough, but for life to happen and evolve on identical pathways seemed entirely beyond belief, and, frankly, gave evidence in her mind that the Andalians had in fact been real, not some Hostile trick. She had always been aware of the debate over the likelihood of such parallel evolution, but, perhaps more than anyone, she was in a position to really begin to understand the reality of such an amazing circumstance.

"Don't you think it's odd," she said, taking the potted plant and turning to face Roberto again, "that an azalea on Earth could be an azalea on Andalia too? Doesn't that seem to defy the principles of evolution?"

He scrunched up one side of his face, pushing his tawny cheek upwards in a contemplative way. "I don't know," he said. "Maybe there's just something inevitable about that particular survival technique—whatever it is plants do. You're the botanist; I don't know the terms. But, you know, maybe there's something that goes on along the way that just has to be dealt with in whatever way azaleas deal with stuff, you know? I mean, pretty much everything on Earth breathes air, right? So, we all came to the same strategy there. What's the difference?"

She nodded, considering. "True."

"I mean, they kinda already argued this out about the Andalians themselves anyway, didn't they? You know, them being human and all. It's pretty much the same deal I imagine."

"Yes, I'm sure it is. But still. It's so... odd. I mean, if you look at the diversity of life on Earth, it seems that there would be similar differences on other planets too, exponential differences at that."

"Well, I know you're not a big fan of God, so I won't spend too much time on this, but, well, that's where faith comes in. Falls under 'God's plan' in my book. You agnostics got to find your own answers."

She gave an ironic half laugh. Sometimes she wished she had faith too. It would help to think her life wasn't just being wasted out here, that there was a reason rather than just blind and piss-poor luck. She stared down into the azalea's blooms, stroking its petals gently with a slender-fingered hand. It was a long while before she answered. "Well, whatever it is, it's very interesting. And this one is the healthiest specimen I've ever seen. It's so much more robust than mine ever are. I'm going to bring a few of mine into the quarantine and see if they'll cross pollinate."

"Hell yes," Roberto cheered. "Now we're talking. Earth plants getting it on with alien azaleas. Oh yeah." He whooped and gently slapped the azalea on one leaf. "My brother," he said to it. "Get it on."

"My God, Roberto, is that all you ever think about?"

"For the most part," he conceded, grinning.

She shook her head, but the smile on her face belied her irritation with his endless prurience. She appreciated his humor more than anything else on the ship.

"Well, you need to get out of here," she said. "I'm still on duty for another two hours." She darted her eyes at the lens in the upper corner of the room indicating that a superior might at any moment notice that she was goofing off.

"Roger that," he said. "See you at dinner."

She waved him off and went back to work. Returning the Andalian azalea to its place on a shelf at the back of the lab, she brought out the small leafy weed she'd picked on her last day on Andalia, the one she'd picked because the captain called. It was perhaps the least attractive of the samples she'd taken; it was small and flat-leafed, with no bloom and nothing particularly intriguing in its coloration. Its primary appeal lay in the fact that it did not appear to be anything that grew on Earth. It had similarity to many varieties, but seemed to match none. She'd already spent the bulk of two days looking through the computer archives for a genetic match and hadn't found one, although there were several that were close. Her little weed was almost a dandelion, just a few genes off, and it was almost any one of seven varieties of thistle too, again just a few genes away. What was really fun, at least for her, was that the little plant might even have become some sort of fern had it not taken a side road somewhere in its recent evolutionary past. But it was none of the above. It was simply its own thing. As different from anything found on Earth as the azalea was exactly the same. It was a question and an answer all at once, but she wasn't quite sure what the question was and therefore had no way to take meaning from the reply. She sighed. Maybe there was something in the soil that could tip her off.

She scraped a bit of dirt from the little plant's roots onto a glass plate and set it under her microscope. She punched up the view on her monitor and shifted to the lens she wanted. She heard the whine of the tiny motor as the nosepiece turned and a moment later the dark micro-world of Andalian soil came into view.

For the most part it contained exactly what she expected it would, assorted core minerals found throughout the universe and an array of organic material consisting of decomposed plants and some entirely generic bacterium. However, there was one thing that stood out as delightfully new: a fungus, a tiny spore nestled in with all the rest, and just one, apparently dormant, waiting for whatever it was that would bring it back to life. Orli felt the thrill of discovery for about the twentieth time since beginning her work on the Andalian samples. Here was something new again. Another thing to look into and another place to hide from her misery. Maybe she could get a few more weeks out of this one. A few weeks of intrigue that would help her pass the time and avoid thinking about how hopelessly far off having a real life was going to be. And so it was with a thin veil of enthusiasm masking the specter of depression that flitted about the dark places in her mind that Orli set herself upon the spore. Maybe this time the question and the answer would finally line up.

Chapter 7

Three days passed before Altin was ready to use the Liquefying Stone again. He took the time to fly into Leekant and see Doctor Leopold about his ribs—the Y-class healer fixed him up splendidly—and he spent a great deal of time over the following two days gathering river rocks and filling two wooden crates with them, making them into seeing stones, each meticulously enchanted with Altin's combination of light and homing spells. Once he had enough for a few weeks of casting, he was ready to try once more for Luria, this time with the Liquefying Stone.

On the fourth day after his first use of the Liquefying Stone, he felt that he was sufficiently healthy to have another crack. He spent the bulk of the morning and a portion of the afternoon expanding gourds along the banks of the small creek that meandered out of the woods not too far from Calico Castle to get more comfortable with the amplification offered by Tytamon's ugly yellow stone. He didn't want to waste too much strength on such activity, however, and as the sun drooped in the western sky he decided he was ready to get to work. The real work of getting to the moon.

An hour and a half later found Altin atop his tower, once

more gazing upon the bright face of Luria. She was full tonight and cast a pale pink light across the land, her gentle kiss softening stern Mt. Pernolde and setting Calico Castle in a celestial glow. Altin could not have asked for a more propitious night.

He had the Liquefying Stone in a small wooden bowl now, placed upon the parapet before him and still covered with the cloth. His scrying basin was near the two crates of seeing stones at his feet by the wall, and he'd reviewed all his spells for the last hour of daylight and even a few minutes more by candlelight to be extra sure. Tonight was not a night to make mistakes.

He offered a quick prayer to the goddess of luck, hoping that she didn't hold it against him that he never prayed, and stooped to take a seeing stone from the nearest crate. He plucked the Liquefying Stone from its bowl, and, glancing once more into Luria's lovely face, began to cast his spell.

His mind opened to the mana currents, and he could see the dense cloudy vapor seethe and pulse as he reached into its depths with the Liquefying Stone pressed against his flesh. The dangerous mineral made the mana thin, angry seeming, and Altin knew that he was still going to have to take it slow. Watery mana meant he could run much more of it through his mind, but he still had to control the pace—and a few bloated gourds hardly made him master of it yet. He clutched a tendril of mana and pulled it down into the seeing stone, tying it firmly to the heart of the river rock in his hand, then cast his mind outward towards the moon. He looked about for one of his previous seeing stones off of which he might try a hop, but he realized as he did that doing so meant he would in essence be missing the point of the Liquefying Stone.

Eschewing the previous stones, he aimed his mind at the heart of where Luria ought to be, like an archer targeting an invisible buck, then fixed a line of mana into the vague ambiguity of the intervening night.

He braced himself for the strain of a blind teleport and, pulling back on the strand of mana in his mental grip, he let the seeing stone go with a snap of emptied space. He opened his eyes as he let it go, and was surprised at how little pain the teleport had caused. It stung, but only a fraction of how much this ambiguous casting normally did. The softened mana seemed to have the unexpected benefit of mitigating the pain that came with casting incongruent spells. This was a pleasant surprise. Perhaps the Liquefying Stone forgave the breaking of some rules, or at least bent them around a bit.

He set the Liquefying Stone back in the bowl and covered it with the little towel, then went to his basin and cast the simple scrying spell that would find the seeing stone that he'd just cast away. Sure enough, there it was. But, just like all the other times, Luria looked no different from the vantage afforded by the stone than it did for Altin standing in his tower now.

But he was not deterred. He was used to this, and he hadn't tried very hard. He hadn't pushed the Liquefying Stone's effects at all. He nodded at the image of the seeing stone floating in the darkness reflected in the basin and set his jaw. The Liquefying Stone was going to help, but he was still going to have to do the work.

He took another river rock from the crate and, reclaiming the Liquefying Stone, he prepared for a second try. He decided to go for distance rather than skipping off the last, and this time he allowed a bit more mana to run into his head. He thickened the strand of mana streaking into space, making a rope of it rather than a thread, and when he drew it back, he actually released it with a grunt, practically shouting the last word of the chant that let it go.

The release was awesome and, while uncomfortable due to ambiguity, it still did not cause the normal degree of discomfort that blind casting always had. Altin was growing increasingly optimistic as the resonance of the stone's arrival out in space echoed back along the mana stream.

He dropped the Liquefying Stone back into the bowl and flipped the towel over it again. Returning to the water basin he quickly conjured up the vision of the little orbiting stone. Not much different than last time. But this time, Altin was almost convinced, there was something new. Luria seemed to be, maybe, just maybe, filling the water in the basin a little bit more than it had before. Just a little. He couldn't even be sure. But his heart began to pound. He reached down and measured the distance between the edge of the bright pink disk shimmering in the water and the wooden sides of the basin. Four fingers of water in between. He would pay closer attention to that detail after the next cast.

With a growing sense of hope, he forced himself to calm, resuming his place before the wooden bowl. He took another seeing stone and the yellow amplifying rock and began to cast again. This time he allowed himself to gather more mana at the start, not just planting a cord of mana into the center of the seeing stone, but completely encasing it in a beam of mana, thick as his thigh, before sending that beam up into the night, once more seeking the place where Luria ought to be. When he drew it back, he put every ounce of his mental strength into the pull, and then he let it go.

It vanished with a crisp pop and Altin actually staggered back from the energy of the release. The seeing stone hit the other end of Altin's mana line hard, and he could feel it as it echoed in his head, different this time, a new feeling, a sense of progress.

He stuffed and buried the Liquefying Stone back in its bowl and scrambled to find his latest seeing stone in the basin's watery eye. When he finally called it up, he did not need his fingers to tell him that he was close. The little stone hung dead center in the image like a freckle on Luria's face, which was now a bright disc of light that entirely filled the basin's view.

Altin let out a whoop. Finally! He'd finally made a dent. He couldn't believe it. He'd hoped he would. He'd dreamed he would. He'd calculated theoretically that he would. But always there was the doubt. And now it actually seemed as if it might come true, all the dreams, all the years of work, and just when hope was wearing thin. He leapt about the tower in bounds of glee for a few moments, waving his arms in the air and defying Luria to stop him now. But he didn't let elation carry him away.

Progress. He'd made progress. But he was still not there. He did know, however, or at least began to know, just what it was that the Liquefying Stone could do for him and his quest. So with a deep breath to calm himself and to center his mind back to the discipline required for the task, he set himself to landing a seeing stone on the moon.

It took him the bulk of the evening to do it too, but finally, as Luria was threatening to leave him behind, to duck behind the woods for yet another night, Altin got it done. His use of the Liquefying Stone had gotten better and stronger with each successive cast. By the end of the evening he was launching stones at Luria with strands of mana that were more akin to ancient oak trunks than anything that might be called a thread. And so it was that two hours before dawn, he finally let a seeing stone go with such force that the recoil down the mana stream told him without looking that he had in fact finally landed on the moon. There was no distant echo this time. The reverberation he got was that of a solid hit, a dull thud like a sack of grain dropped into the dirt. There could be no mistake.

He tossed the Liquefying Stone back into the bowl and covered it quickly, hustling to the basin to confirm what he was sure he already knew. And there it was. Lying on the ground. Lying on red ground, reddish soil that looked dusty and dry, like rust. There were a couple of pebbles, also red, but no blades of grass or even different colored rocks. Just red. But it was wonderful, and he was ecstatic.

But it was not enough. Altin wanted to see more. The scrying basin limited him to just a forward view, point to point, which happened to be looking directly into the dirt, so he could see nothing more. The whole point of casting these seeing stones out there with their enchanted homing spells was so that he could use them to become "familiar" with an area, thus allowing him to cast a real seeing spell, one with sight, sound and mobility. Once he'd done that, once he checked it out a bit, then he could finally go himself. But first he had to see, and despite his being exhausted from casting all night long, he knew he had enough strength to do this much more. Raw emotion would give him the strength his body lacked.

He had to go downstairs to the shelf above his bed to get his notes on the seeing spell that he intended to use. The candle on the table had burned out hours before, and it was annoying that he had to take the time to replace it with another one. He was amazed at how much strength conjuring that small flame took, and he realized that without the Liquefying Stone in his grip, he was already past his limits. That last cast had taken everything he had. He closed his eyes and drew in several deep breaths. He had to have the strength for one last cast. He couldn't leave that stone up there for another entire day. He simply could not bear the wait. He had to have some strength left, some. Just enough, the Liquefying Stone could do the rest.

He forced the little flame to appear on the candle with a snarl of effort, and once its flickering light filled the darkness, he took it to his bed and retrieved the book for which he'd come. He nearly staggered returning to the table and flopped down into a chair, absently noticing that the little mouse had apparently been hard at work on yesterday's bread during the course of the long night.

He flipped through the pages and found the spell he was looking for. It was a fairly complicated spell and it took him nearly an hour to read it through to the point where he was sure he had its every measure down. At length he was convinced he did, and pushed himself doggedly up, teetering as he rose, and took two stumbling steps towards the stairs before collapsing to the floor. The last thing he saw was the little mouse's face sniffing out at him from the hole near the stairs as it prepared for another foray up to Altin's bread.

"Master Altin. Master Altin." Pernie's soft and frightened voice came creeping slowly into Altin's dreamless sleep. "Wake up, Master Altin. Please, wake up." Her tiny hand gripped his shoulder and shook him repeatedly, a tinge in her squeaky voice suggesting that if Altin didn't wake up soon, didn't get off the floor, she was going to send another wave of shrieks echoing around the keep. She was terribly distraught.

Altin slowly came to, his ears ringing and eyes feeling as if they might burst like pumpkins beneath a giant's boot. His head pounded and for a moment he thought he might throw up. He closed his eyes again, rolling over onto his back and trying to breathe through the waves of nausea. Pernie's hand still trembled upon his shoulder as she continued to shake him. "Master Altin, get up. You're scaring me, Master Altin. And you're bleeding from your nose. Please get up."

Altin opened his eyes and struggled to sit up, bracing himself with his arms stretched out behind him on the floor. Pernie was staring into his face, little blue eyes wide with curiosity and fear. She'd never seen a great magician lying on the floor before. Her expression told him that such a thing posed a threat to her notion of stability in the universe.

Dimly, his mind cleared enough for him to realize what

had taken place. Yes, he'd definitely pushed too hard. He blinked a few times and tried to clear his thoughts. It occurred to him that he couldn't let Pernie tell anyone what she had seen. That could be disaster for his work.

He forced a smile upon his face, even though the motion of his cheeks made his eyeballs scream silently inside as fireballs exploded in his brain.

"I'm fine," he said in a rasp. "Just a little tired. It's ok, Pernie. Even wizards get tired sometimes. We're no different than little girls when it comes to that."

The unsettled expression on her face left immediately. Apparently the universe was fine again, perhaps even better at this rare kind word from him. "Usually you're sleeping in your bed, sir," she informed him, nodding in the direction of his rickety old bed with its tattered, straw-filled mattress. "Never seen ya sleepin' on the floor before." She shrugged as if it were something she'd simply overlooked. "I brought your bread for ya, though." She started to smile again, but then a look of horror came upon her face. "Oh, but I'm never supposed to wake ya up. Oh, oh...." Her eyes widened as a new kind of fear suddenly took hold. She turned and darted out the door.

"Pernie, wait!" Altin called, but was too late. "Damn it."

He couldn't have her tattling all over the castle about having found him on the floor. It was likely enough Tytamon knew about the giant pebble. An unconscious Altin, bleeding from the face and with his next spell still in hand was enough to cost Altin access to the Liquefying Stone for sure.

He tried to rise and rush after her, but he knew immediately that he'd never catch a child as swift as that. Not in his current condition anyway. With a wince of resignation, he closed his eyes and teleported himself to the bottom of the stairs.

He appeared on the flagstones a step outside the door and swayed, woozy with the effort, just as Pernie came sprinting down. He shook his head to clear it, which had almost the opposite effect, and grabbed her by the shoulders as she prepared to bolt past him and across the yard. She screamed at his unexpected appearance, and he shushed her with a hiss.

"Pernie," he said, leaning down and looming in her face, which was barely a blur in the thunder of his throbbing head. "Pernie, listen, you woke me up. You did. But, I'm not going to tell, okay. You're not in trouble. All right? You don't have to be afraid. Nobody has to know."

"Ow," she whimpered, glancing at his hands gripping too tightly into her flesh and looking up at him again with eyes that were frightened and with tears streaking the dust upon her cheeks. He couldn't tell if she was in disbelief at this stroke of luck or if she thought she was in a scary monster's grasp. Frankly, he wasn't too sure either. He relaxed his grip a bit.

"Listen. I'll make you a deal, okay?"

She nodded, barely discernible.

"All right. Here it is. You don't tell anyone that I fell asleep on the floor, okay? And for me, I won't say a thing about you coming in and waking me up. How's that? Is that fair?"

She sniffled and nodded slowly back at him.

"You promise?"

"Yes," she said. "I promise."

"Okay. I promise too." He released her shoulders and stood up, swaying. "Here, shake on it," he said, extending a trembling hand down to her. She hugged him instead, catching him entirely off guard as she wrapped her little arms around him and nestled her cheek against his hip. He had no idea what to do with that, and she made him entirely uncomfortable standing there. He patted her awkwardly atop the head until at last she went away. Hopefully she would keep her word.

Once Pernie was headed quietly to the kitchens, Altin dragged himself back up into his room. The teleport down the stairs had cost him what little strength the slumber of collapse had brought. Light was beginning to fill the chamber from the window and Altin knew he needed rest. He took one last glance at the spell book lying on the floor and resigned himself to scrying up to the moon later on tonight. He hated to put it off, but he didn't even have the energy to wag a finger at the mouse, which now sat imperiously atop the new loaf of bread, nonchalantly nibbling on Altin's food. Instinct told him that he should shoo the creature off, but instead, the powerful magician collapsed upon his bed.

Chapter 8

When he finally awoke early the next afternoon, Altin was excited enough by the prospects of the day to be un-phased at having to share his breakfast with a mouse. Granted, had the thieving little pest been in sight, it would likely have suffered some horrible, magically wrought fate, but it wasn't, and so Altin tore off a large chunk from an unmolested portion of the loaf and scampered up to the battlements to survey the skies above.

The sun wouldn't set for another two hours, and Luria wouldn't peek up for a bit longer than that, which gave Altin the time he needed to clean up a little and to review the complicated seeing spell in his notes. He wanted to make sure he had it down perfectly; he didn't want any mistakes—there were more than a few ex-seers in asylums around Kurr staring blankly at the walls, drooling, mumbling and forever lost to magic gone awry. The gods only knew what they were looking at, and Altin had no intention of finding out. He certainly had no intention of leaving his mind somewhere on the moon.

And finally it was time. Luria rose triumphantly into the night about half an hour after dark, and Altin wasted not one second in delay. He planned to try this spell without the

Liquefying Stone at first. Seeing magic was more technique than power, and he thought that this spell might still be within his natural range now that he knew where Luria "was." He wanted to find out. And so he began.

Leaning upon the parapet, he closed his eyes and muttered the spell beneath his breath. There were no gestures for this spell, only a gentle rhythmic sway. He did as much, allowing the motion of his body to rock him back and forth, a wave washing from shoulder to shoulder while his palms remained planted on the coarse stone.

Seeking the seeing stone that lay on Luria's red soil, Altin found it almost immediately, sensing its enchanted beacon clearly from across the mana stream. He let his thoughts fall into the currents then, let the mana sweep him away, his consciousness buffeted forwards towards the seeing stone as his body stayed at home. After only a few moments Altin's sight opened upon the moon, emerging as the mana curtain was, in essence, drawn aside.

Everything was dark, or mostly so. Almost night, like failing twilight or just before dawn. He had to struggle with a wave of dizziness as his vision swam, his bearings all askew, for there was no sense of gravity or ground when using sight like this. He had to center visually, the horizon giving him the only clue, but once oriented, he was able to have a look around.

He was on a barren plain, a desert perhaps, though devoid of any desert plants. Devoid of any desert anything, frankly. Just soil. Reddish gray in the wan light of the enchanted seeing stone, pebbly and without the faintest ripple caused by a gust of wind. And it was silent. There was not a sound at all. Not a bird's chirp, a bee's buzz or the slightest breath of air. It was eerie. At first Altin assumed he must have cast the spell wrong, but confirmed with a quick mental review that he had not. He thought it might be the distance, perhaps something unanticipated by the spell. But for now, he let it go. It was just quiet. But at least he was seeing on the moon.

He was exultant with this success, and he had to struggle to maintain his calm so that he would not lose contact with the spell. He glanced down at the seeing stone that would have been lying at his feet, were his feet actually there with him, and briefly noted how different it looked from everything else around. It was so very round and large compared to all the other rocks. He had an urge to reach down and stroke it, to comfort it and thank it for its work. The thought occurred to him that this particular seeing stone would be there for the rest of time, unknown leagues from its home and with no chance of ever getting back, making him nostalgic on its behalf. Such thoughts reminded him that he could turn around and have a look up into the sky, realizing that he could have a glimpse at his own world, a view of Prosperion and of Kurr. Almost tentatively he turned his vision round and looked up into the night.

Back in the tower his body gasped as his vision filled with the radiant wonder of his home world high above. The view was spectacular. Prosperion was a giant blue ball, massive and bright, draped in places by a veil of lacey white clouds swirling and stretching across vast leagues of beautiful azure sea. His planet seemed to have a thin layer of mist around it too, a glow like a translucent shell of shimmering energy, wafer thin and from this distance looking no thicker than a folded handkerchief.

On the right half, just now fully around the horizon, he could see what had to be the continent of Kurr. It was shaped just like the maps back home said it was: the Gulf of Dae cutting in exactly where it should, the Daggerspines crisscrossing darkly in the north, and the Great Forest large enough to be an ocean of green at the center like an arboreal bull's-eye at which he might throw pebbles from up here. He grinned and just stared for the longest time appreciating the magnitude of what he saw. It was odd to think that he was looking down on himself, knowing that the smile he had looking down on Kurr was really a smile looking up at the moon instead. It was just a delightful paradox, and he allowed himself to take it in.

After a time, he realized that he should get busy and look around. He couldn't channel mana forever, after all. Besides, there had to be more to Luria than just this rocky desert plain. One advantage of the seeing spell he was using now was the spell's ability to "run." However, he had no landmarks or promising features to draw him to any particular place, so he decided it made the most sense to just run towards what appeared to be the coming dawn. And so he did.

He pushed his vision along, slowly at first, no faster than a horse could lope, but after what seemed almost twenty minutes with no discoveries of note, he decided to speed it up a bit. Soon his vision was racing across the surface at speeds the fastest of the Queen's clipper ships could never hope to match. He zipped across the landscape, rotating his view as he went, searching for anything that might hold his interest and give him a reason to stop for a better look.

A short time later, he intercepted the sunrise and that gave him a moment's pause. The sun came up all right, but by all nine gods and several of their pets, Altin had never seen it shine so bright. The sun seemed more radiant, more intense up here than it did back on Prosperion. Much brighter. Too bright. Altin made a mental note of that, a reminder to prepare for that reality when he finally came up here himself. And come up here he would, of that he was completely sure. But when he did, he'd make sure to be prepared for the incredible heat.

The sun's brightness explained the vacant desert upon which he now stood. The more he contemplated it, the more it made perfect sense. Luria was much closer to the sun being way up here like this. It stood to reason that it would be subject to greater heat than Prosperion ever was. And as he glanced about, back towards the darker regions he'd just come from, it occurred to him that when it was daytime down on Kurr, Luria was actually farther away from the sun as well. He began to think that it might get very cold up here at times too. In fact, he suspected he might find snow somewhere if he just kept up the search. That could explain the difference in Luria's appearance on the horizon back at home, so red sometimes, yet pink when highest up above, made so by the dusting of snow. It all became so obvious to him now, and he nodded down in his tower, certain that he was finally figuring it out. Perhaps if he moved quickly enough, he could catch the snowfall somewhere before the vicious sun had time to melt it all away. He was certainly ready for something new to see. Even if only a river of melted snow.

As he pushed his vision across the barren waste, he finally spotted something on the horizon that indicated a change of scenery. He approached it rapidly and soon found himself, in essence, standing at the edge of a very large and very deep crater. By his estimate it was perhaps a half a league across and roughly a hundred paces down. There was an odd little mound at the bottom, centered precisely, that looked about twenty paces high by fifteen or so across. He was happy to go down and have a look.

The edges of the crater were craggy, but lacked the evidence of erosion that running water usually made. When he found no cracks down in the crater's bed, it was clear that this particular depression did not get the runoff of his anticipated snows, that it was not a dried-out lake bed or anything similar. There certainly were no fish bones to be found. He speculated that if the heat was as intense as it had to be to burn off the waters in the cycle of a day, there likely were no fish anywhere on the moon. He began to wonder if there was anything up here at all.

The small mound was exactly that, a small mound jutting up abruptly from the center of the enormous hole, featureless beyond a depression at its very top, rather like a miniature volcano that had yet to blow. Altin spent the better part of twenty minutes zooming his vision around it in hopes of something more. But there was nothing else to see. And the silence began to annoy him now.

Life was full of sound. Even the quietest places on Kurr were alive with sound. The most remote meadow in the deepest wood still had the whisper of the wind or the rustle of squirrels and birds amongst the trees to prove that life was taking place. Bugs flew by on noisy wings and animals called out in anger or in glee. Even the rain makes sound when it falls upon the ground, be it on stone, grass or even sand that's nearly soft as down. There's always noise. But there was none of it here. Nothing to hear at all. And it vexed him more and more as time went by.

He ran his vision up and out of the crater and began to scour the moon some more. Faster and faster he pushed his sight, as fast as it could go. But there was still nothing. Finally, frustrated at his lack of adequate speed, he pulled out of the spell and brought his vision back to his real eyes in the tower, back to Prosperion and Kurr. He needed the Liquefying Stone if he wanted to go faster.

He moved over a crenel to the wooden bowl and took the stone from beneath its cloth. This will make me swift, he thought as he clutched it in his fist. I want to find the snows tonight.

He carefully recast the seeing spell, cautious not to overdraw the mana with the ugly yellow stone. Even with caution, he found himself practically slapped back onto the surface of the moon. His vision filled so suddenly with the red expanse that he nearly stumbled from surprise. He steadied himself and prepared to resume his search from where he'd left off, intent on moving quickly now with the help of the yellow stone.

The Liquefying Stone softened the mana immensely though, making the nebulous matter almost too soft to be properly malleable for this. He had to practice pushing it around for a bit, kneading it and trying to mold it into the shape he needed for the movement portion of the Seeing spell. Mastery took him a while, but eventually he became used to shaping the squishy mana and was able to put it to the task. He smoothed out a sheet of it, flattening it with long sweeping strokes of his mind, then began to roll it up, bending it around, fashioning something of a funnel in his mythothalamus. He channeled more mana through it then, holding the funnel's shape taut, like lips pursed to whistle or blow, and then he let the mana through. Soon the coursing currents pushed his sight along, jetting him across the moon's red surface faster than a ballista bolt.

He traveled around the moon in an unthinkable display of speed, the featureless terrain a blur beneath him as he zipped about. He spent the better part of five hours traveling at such a pace, discovering several more craters, much like the first, although varying in size from some no larger than the Queen's arena to some so vast that he could barely make out the opposite edge. But in the end, they too became featureless in their own way, and eventually he found himself heading back round into darkness, the sun setting at his back.

Here, he thought with some renewed optimism, here is where I finally find the snows. Of course here. He moved gradually further from the dwindling light, realizing as he did how silly he'd been to expect snow while he'd been moving through the Lurian day. Giddiness must have made him dumb. He laughed silently at himself as he pushed on with fresh energy, traveling onward until the landscape was completely lost in darkness once again, and this time there was no seeing stone to cast even the faintest glow. He had no idea that anything could be so black. Even the stars were no help, and there were so many more of them than he'd ever seen before.

He took the time to look up, to stare out into all those tiny points of light, so many of them, the same constellations he had always known and a few new ones too. There were new stars now, stars he'd never noticed before. Some filled in the old constellations in places that were empty when viewed from Kurr, remaking them, unwinding figures and characters that millenniums of myths had made and creating new ones in their place, nameless images, frightening and foreign and making Altin feel as if he were suddenly all alone.

And oh how dark it was. There was no darkness on Prosperion like this, not unless one was locked in a dungeon deep beneath a castle's walls. Only the absence of stars marked where the night sky ended and Luria's surface curved away, a pitch black crescent marking a horizon that seemed ready to swallow him if he ventured any farther than he had. He paused. What was the point of exploration if he couldn't see a thing? Such darkness would have him running circles until he tapped his magic strength. And there was no way to cast light to accommodate a seeing spell. He made a mental note to maybe work on that one day. But he would not venture further into the dark.

Instead, he took the time to study the sky again, marveling once more at the stars so spectacular and bright. They too were brighter than at home, like the sun had been. He became increasingly aware of how much closer he must be now, how much nearer to the heavens—if there really were such things.

All those little windows, pinpricks leading into the realm of gods, divine light winking through the holes in the universal dome. It seemed somehow bigger from up here on Luria's distant sands. Almost possible. He laughed. Maybe.

But more impressive for sure. More dangerous and amplified. And yet despite the ominous darkness and the odd sense of infinite proximity, the stars still screamed for him to come to them. He could hear them call his name. The breathy whisper of a lover, a distant siren song. Something. Some inexplicable draw. And he knew as he looked into the sky that there was death out there. Death in all that dark and unknown space. Death for him.

How many men had died upon Prosperion's vast and open seas, died seeking for the sake of curiosity? And what were oceans compared to this? What was this for a Six?

But he knew as he looked up into the star-spotted heavens that he would dare to seek them anyway. He was not a Six, he told himself. And he would not die like one. But he would dare to face the gods if there really were any of them to see. Finnius Addenpore had defied them and never left his tower. Perhaps that was the reason why; perhaps he should have gone to them instead. Either way, Altin was not afraid. If the gods were out there, that was fine by him. He would fly up and greet them, fly through one of those little lighted vents, right up into their world and say "hello" in his most robust and daring voice. "Hello," he would say. "I am Altin Meade, and I am not afraid. I have found you, and there are some things I want to say."

He felt himself fill with hope and yearning and, unexpectedly, with anger and despair. What things? He felt tears come into his eyes, tears burning far away from here. Tears of a man on Kurr right now alone, apart even from himself.

The strange wave of emotion passed, replaced by a more humble sense of awe, the sense of which was still incredible and that kept him lingering, dreamlike, for quite some time. Finally, after he had no idea how long, a rumble in his belly reminded him of passing time. An image of himself shifted in his mind, changed from a triumphant Altin to a less god-defying one, an Altin sitting in a puddle of his own drool and staring out an asylum window filled with bars. He decided that perhaps it was time to call it a night.

With one last glimpse up into the stars, Altin let the mana go.

Chapter 9

The elevator was halfway to the bridge when the first impact shook the ship to its rivets. Orli was nearly knocked off her feet as the elevator lights dimmed and the memory stick in her hands clattered to the floor. The jolt was over as fast as it had come, and Orli scrambled to retrieve the evidence of her latest discovery. She wondered what had just happened to the ship.

She was immediately dismayed when the battle stations alarm was called and red lights in the elevator began to flash. The door slid open onto the bridge where Captain Asad was barking orders and trying to calm his flabbergasted crew. "Strap in, everyone. Do it now, and keep your heads. This is what you're trained for."

Orli heard the clicking of buckles and the slide of rough restraints being pulled taut around several nervous sets of bowels. But there was something in the captain's cold, ever-present sternness, normally so damnably annoying, that had an immediate mellowing effect. She could see it working on the bridge crew as they prepared themselves to fight. It seemed the Hostiles were finally at hand.

"Carrey, hard to starboard. Face it. Give it a smaller target if nothing else. Hartford, eighty percent to forward shields.

Let's get a lock on that thing. Levi, lasers at full and arm the nukes."

"Yes, sir," came in unison from the three as they immediately set themselves to task. Orli watched with mouth agape, barely remembering to step through the elevator door before it closed.

The image on the huge forward monitor showed a large object, an orb of indeterminate size, hovering somewhere outside the ship. She glanced out the two long narrow windows that ran round the forward corners of the bridge but couldn't see it through either one.

"What the hell is that thing?" Roberto asked, his eyes darting briefly to the screen above as his fingers tapped at his controls.

"Hartford?" said the captain, redirecting the question to the young lieutenant to Roberto's left.

"Still scanning, sir," she answered, her fingers matching Roberto's for speed as they both played upon the lights beneath the console glass. Captain Asad scowled at the monitor, his impatience checked only by the sheer force of his disciplined inner core. Finally Hartford gave a reply. "It scans like a planet, Captain. Metals, silicates and trace organics." She paused a moment, rechecking to be sure, "Yeah, it's all there."

"How big is it?" the captain demanded, squinting out through the window to the left of the main monitor trying to find it in the night.

"Eighty meters in diameter, sir, perfectly round. Very dense. Three-point-two grams per cubic centimeter."

"Which means?"

"Thick, sir. Very dense."

"Like a moon, then?"

"Possibly, sir."

"Well, then what the hell hit us? It couldn't have been that thing. We'd already be dead."

"I have it here, sir," piped in Roberto. "Look."

"Put it up," Captain Asad ordered. An instant later a lower quarter of the main screen held an image of a long shaft of a dark substance, stone-like, hurtling away from both the ship and the strange orb. "What the hell is that?"

"Granite, sir," came Hartford's quick reply. "Granite, traces of obsidian, gold and lead."

"What? Are you telling me that thing threw a goddamn rock at us?"

"Yes, sir. That appears to be the case. The... missile," Lieutenant Hartford seemed to hesitate for want of a better term, "is moving away from us at five hundred and eighty knots."

It was then that the coarse looking sphere began moving at them again. It did not start slowly and accelerate as a ship would have had to do, from dead stop and gradually increasing velocity, but instead it was instantly in motion, careening directly at them at an astonishing speed.

"Impact in eleven seconds, sir," Lieutenant Hartford informed them.

"Evasive action," ordered the captain.

"On it, sir," said Ensign Carrey. Orli gripped the doorframe of the elevator as she watched in utter shock. She knew enough about the ship's maneuverability to know that there was nothing Carrey could do. Those paltry little aspect rockets were useless in a situation like this. She wondered if she were watching her death blow on its way. From the way the tendons showed in the captain's neck and the way Roberto kept glancing up at the monitor on the wall as he frantically keyed the controls, she could tell she was not the only one.

"Shoot it, Levi. Shoot it now, goddamn it."

"Already on it," Roberto said, tapping a light that was finally blinking beneath his sweating fingertips. "Lasers hot, in two, one, firing."

Streaks of red light darted into the sky, splashing upon the surface of the onrushing orb and creating a dull orange glow. The orb shifted its trajectory immediately, not a diversion or the angular movement of changing course, but an impossible switch of its location to a path that was slightly left of where it just had been. Not a great distance, but enough to leave the lasers firing out into the stars, swinging hopelessly after the orb, but no longer on the track. The glowing hot spot on its surface immediately cooled and went away.

"Get it back, Levi. What the hell was that?"

"... I don't know," stammered Roberto. "The computer had it locked. It shouldn't have lost it. Maybe a glitch." Orli could hear the dull sound of Roberto's fingertips tapping the console, his flesh thumping against the glass as he desperately tried to get the lasers back onto the surface of the orb.

Finally he did, but this time, the orb didn't glow beneath the attack of focused light. Nor did it make any effort to change its course. It sped away a short distance and once more came to a complete stop, allowing the lasers to beam on it steadily now, apparently unconcerned.

"Something's different, sir," reported Lieutenant Hartford.

"I can see that," he said. "What happened to the lasers? They were working a second ago."

"That's what I'm telling you, Captain," Hartford pressed. "It's different. Its surface shifted—is shifting. Look." She punched up a zoom on the monitor and suddenly the view closed in on the surface of the orb.

At first the orb's surface had appeared to be rough and mottled brown, but now it was fading to solid black, its surface transforming before their eyes. The area upon which the lasers beamed was already completely black and had become smooth, glassy and highly polished like a mirror. In seconds, the lasers were doing nothing to the orb at all, and the crew watched bewildered as the ship's lasers were split into a million smaller beams of light, divided into fragments as thin as wire and reflected harmlessly into space. The rest of the orb was changing color and texture too, the rough brown vanishing as if being devoured by an onslaught of glazed black.

"What in the good goddamn is that?" the captain demanded. He was getting tired of asking questions and irritation began to creep into his voice.

"Obsidian," Hartford replied a moment later. "Volcanic glass."

"Shouldn't the lasers melt that?"

"Yes, sir, they should. Apparently it's not exactly the same obsidian that we have back on Earth."

"Apparently."

"Nuke it," ordered the captain. "Send two."

"Yes, sir," said Roberto.

The orb was suddenly on the move again, once more coming straight at them.

"Nuke it now, Ensign."

"Firing, sir."

The missiles streaked out from beneath the ship, their passage marked by the blue flames of their rocket trails. Everyone on the deck, including the still unnoticed Orli, watched breathlessly as they hurtled towards the orb.

The orb came on in the face of the missiles, seemingly unconcerned. It shifted its position again, just at the point of impact, too quick to see, and didn't lose a moment charging onward towards the ship. The two missiles shot harmlessly by and began to dim with distance against the backdrop of the stars, target lost.

"Oh my God," shouted Roberto at the screen. "Did you see that shit? Goddamn it, there is no way I missed that shot, sir. They can't do that. It's impossible. Nothing moves like that."

"Calm yourself, Ensign. Bring them back," ordered the captain. "Hit it when it passes by. Make sure they're far enough away."

"Yes, sir," said Roberto, tapping in commands to swing both missiles around and muttering anxiously under his breath.

Orli was in complete agreement with her friend. She'd watched it happen too. The orb had just, well, not been where it was anymore. The first time she'd seen it, it seemed like a really eye-defying move, but not this time. There could be no mistake. That orb had shifted its place in space. There was no other way to describe it. Quick as a blink, one second it was there, the next it was beside itself, as if the space itself had moved. The maneuver was, as Roberto had pointed out, impossible. Physics did not allow for such a thing.

"Brace yourselves," the captain ordered, clutching the rail at which he stood. He alone was not strapped in. He and Orli, who, unnoticed, did not yet count.

"Impact in seven, six, five...," counted down Lieutenant Hartford.

At roughly a hundred yards away, the orb once again made one of its impossible spatial shifts, and in the breadth of a breath, it shot harmlessly by, just missing the ship by a few meters to the port side. But in its place, and still quite on target, came another of the long granite shafts, thick as the I-beams comprising the framework of the ship and plunging at them with horrifying velocity.

Fingers beating upon the console, Roberto forsook the vanishing nukes and managed to fire a laser instead, just at the last moment, and not with enough energy to destroy it, but with enough to push the orb's projectile slightly to the side, just off course. Still, it struck the ship a glancing blow that was hard enough to throw Orli to the ground. The captain nearly fell as well, but managed to keep his footing with help from the sturdy rail.

The ship's targeting cameras followed the granite shaft out into the stars. The captain noticed on the main view that the orb had actually gone off to retrieve the first of its mineral missiles still hurtling into space.

"Is that thing actually chasing down its first shot?" he queried his sensors officer.

Hartford tapped up the zoom on the aft camera. Sure enough it was. They watched in amazement as the orb pursued its missile and, passing it by slightly, moved directly into the projectile's path. The orb slowed then, allowing the granite weapon to strike dead center in the middle of its bulk. Rather than dealing damage, however, the shaft vanished inside the orb, slipping back into the surface as if the orb were made of nothing more than mud.

"What in the hell?" the question came from everyone on the deck, whether spoken aloud or not. Including Orli, who did speak it aloud, and suddenly all eyes were on her.

"Pewter! What the hell are you doing up here? There's a battle stations alert." The captain's face was instantly red, and Orli knew that every comment he'd ever made about her unfitness for military service had just been confirmed for him. "Get back to your station, goddamn it."

The look on Roberto's face seemed to suggest that he too was incredulous as to why she was here standing on the bridge. She met his eyes with a grimace and shrugged, holding up her video stick in attempt at some defense. Apparently now was not the time.

"I, I...," she stammered. "I found something I thought you'd like to see." The heat coming off of the captain silenced her. "It can wait." She turned and jabbed at the elevator control, willing the doors to open with all her mental strength.

"It's coming back, sir," said Lieutenant Hartford, inadvertently coming to Orli's aid. "Impact in fifteen, fourteen...."

"Roberto, pull off another shot like that last one and you're a lieutenant come breakfast, you hear me?" Orli was no longer on the captain's mind.

"Yes, sir," came Roberto's reply.

The ship shuddered again just as the elevator door slid open and Orli prepared to step inside.

"Got it," cried Roberto triumphantly just as the missile bounced off the ship's beleaguered shields. "Little sooner than the last time."

"Figure out a way to keep them off of us completely, and I'll recommend you for promotion to admiral before the day is done."

"Yes, sir," Roberto said with growing confidence. "You got yourself a deal."

"Your chance is on its way," announced Hartford immediately after Roberto spoke. The orb had retrieved the second projectile already and was now rushing at them for yet another shot.

Roberto was quick enough on this pass to time the lasers just as the mineral shaft began to emerge. He managed to hit the tip of it and knock it entirely off course.

"Good work, Ensign," complimented Captain Asad again. "Is that you, or the computers?"

"Me, sir. If you watch real close, it turns sort of yellowish, like sand or something, right before it shoots. You got to time it off of that, I think."

"Keep it up."

"Yes, sir."

The orb retrieved its first shaft again and swung round to make another attempt. Orli found herself too mesmerized to leave and dawdled at the elevator, holding the door open and reluctant to press the button that would take her down.

"Why do you think it keeps doing that?" Carrey wondered aloud. "It's like it only has two bullets or something."

"That's probably exactly why," agreed the captain. "It has to conserve resources just like we do."

It came in for another pass, and again Roberto was able to misdirect its shot, although only by a matter of inches this time, causing the captain to growl and Hartford to shoot him a sideways glance.

"It's not a perfect science," Roberto said with a negligible shrug.

"I saw the yellow spot this time, though," confirmed Hartford.

"So did I," said the captain. "And I bet it's soft as a baby's belly. Roberto...."

"On it, sir," said Roberto, anticipating the captain's command. "I'll have a missile on its way too. Going to be tough, though. Missiles are slow."

Again the orb came round and made its pass. Everyone on the bridge, including Orli, was staring at the screen looking for the telltale yellow spot. By the time Orli spotted the sandy colored dot, Roberto already had both lasers playing on the emerging shaft, and the blue dot of a nuclear missile was streaking towards it too.

The orb darted easily away from Roberto's nuke, but it was never in any danger from the shot anyway. Roberto had over-compensated too in anticipation of the orb's physics-defying speed. However, the orb's projectile did not fare as well, and thanks to a bit of luck, as Roberto would admit a few days later, it was blown to dust by the sluggish nuke, which struck it full as the lasers pushed it directly into the missile's path.

The bridge crew burst into cheers, Hartford pounding Roberto on the back, and even Orli could not contain a shout of glee. Once more several pairs of eyes swung round to take her in. She smiled meekly and pressed the button numbered "five." The last thing she saw as the door slid shut was the scowl raging upon the captain's face.

Chapter 10

Altin awoke the next day, once again, late in the afternoon. He hadn't even been aware that he'd gone to bed, but at least he found himself *in* bed and not on the floor. That he'd managed to control his exuberance over his accomplishment enough to sleep was a bit of a surprise as well. It was nice to see that his discipline was working even when his conscious mind was not. Apparently running one's sight around the moon took more energy than he had surmised. The added benefit of the Liquefying Stone's bending of magical rules was a danger he'd do well to keep in mind.

He climbed out of bed, his head a bit sore from last night's effort, and ran back up to the battlements to make sure he'd properly stored the Liquefying Stone. He had. That was a relief. He was taking great pains to make sure his habits with the dangerous little rock were safe ones and becoming reflexively so.

Satisfied that all was right on the tower top, it was time to address the gnawing in his stomach. He hadn't eaten properly in a while and he was famished. Judging from the position of the sun, moving steadily down towards the horizon, he might be just in time for supper. He ran down the stairs, taking them three at a time, and soon emerged in the large dining hall where dinner was always served and quite despite his being absent from it at least half the time.

The chamber was huge and high-ceilinged, fit for a banquet with at least five hundred guests, but spider webs in the rafters high above spoke to the frequency of such events, and one could smell the musty scent of age clinging to the ancient tapestries hanging along the walls if the cobwebs were not evidence enough. Tytamon no longer felt compelled to entertain.

The weathered old sorcerer was already seated at the end of a table that was far too long for one man alone. Altin headed towards him eagerly, bare feet slapping audibly on the flagstones as he jogged, the sound echoing up into the cavernous shadows above and sending spiders scuttling for crevices amongst the oaken beams.

"Good evening, young Altin," greeted Tytamon as his apprentice took a chair to the aged magician's right, sitting before a plate, silverware, goblet and napkin that were all in place, set, as always, in expectation of his irregular appearance. Places for both magicians were set every night, waiting, always the same, and the servants had no end of complaining about how often neither of them arrived. Many a great meal had gone to waste in waiting for these two to come downstairs to eat.

"Good evening," Altin replied, sparing no time in spearing a slice of mutton from a wooden tray with his fork. He stabbed a second slice, and with equal disregard for formalities, he added, "I finally did it. I put a seeing stone on the moon."

"Really?" said Tytamon, sounding genuinely impressed around a mouthful of boiled carrots and pouring wine from a bronze decanter into Altin's cup. "So you pulled it off at last. The Liquefying Stone has made the difference we hoped it would?"

"Entirely so."

"That's splendid news. Splendid news, indeed. A first for Kurr. A first for the world. You should be very proud."

Altin nodded and stuffed an enormous chunk of mutton into his mouth, chewing ravenously.

"So what did you see? Are the stories true? Did you see the satyrs and the Never Ending Dance?"

Altin snorted, his mouth too full to laugh. He gulped his food, masticating just enough to choke it down. "Hardly," he said. "There's nothing up there. It's desert. All desert, I'm almost sure. I need to spend more time exploring it, but I'm fairly certain there's actually nothing going on up there at all."

"Really? Nothing? Wouldn't that be a terrible shame."

"I'm sure the Church will be annoyed."

"No doubt about that. You'll want to be careful how you let that information out. No sense causing a ruckus just on the heels of such a momentous accomplishment."

Altin almost spat. "I'm not one for politics, Master. Perhaps I'll leave the announcements up to you."

"Well, I'm happy to deal with the Queen and her court, but the press is up to you."

"Well, we just won't tell them, will we?"

Tytamon laughed. "The greatest diviners in all the land don't find things out as fast as some of those journalists do."

"That's what happens when you have no magic, I suppose. Blanks. I imagine it beats digging ditches though. Getting paid to snoop on others must be easier than having real work to do."

Tytamon grew momentarily stern. "You know little enough of real work, young man, and much less of the lives of blanks. You'll do well to not harbor such contempt for the decent, common folk of this land. It's those people upon whose hard work and success this nation is built and dating back long before the Magical Revolution came along."

Altin lowered his face to his plate so that Tytamon could not see him roll his eyes. "Yes, sir," he said as he took another bite. The man was such a mood killer.

Tytamon resumed the previous line of conversation and prodded Altin's enthusiasm quickly back to life. "So what are you going to do after exploring Luria some more? What next?"

"Well, I think to begin I'm going to go up there myself. The Liquefying Stone seems to have a really nasty effect of exhausting me, even though I don't quite feel it coming on. I think I'd rather teleport up and then do the rest of the exploration from there. I can teleport around without the stone, use my normal magic, and maybe get a lot more done. I'd rather not sleep entire days away if I don't have to. The Liquefying Stone does not come without a cost."

"This is very true," agreed Tytamon. "However, you do get more and more used to it as you go along. It's rather like the warriors who exercise at lifting rocks. The more rocks they lift and the heavier ones they choose, the stronger they become. Working your mythothalamus with the Liquefying Stone can have a similar effect. To a point." He punctuated this last with a flourish of his fork, sending a bit of meat soaring half the distance to Altin's plate.

"Why don't we use them all the time, then?" Altin asked. "It seems silly to leave such an important tool buried in a dusty old room."

"It's because of the dwarves. Because of Duador."

"You mean Melane Montclaire used the Liquefying Stone to summon the demons on Duador? Is that why there were so many?"

"No. But that is why the stone cannot be used at all. If man or, admittedly, man and elf, could do such a monstrous thing as what was done to the dwarves without the use of the stone, think what could be done *with* it? Think of it, Altin. You are young, but you understand the many hearts of men. You've read the histories of the ancient empires. Can you imagine Korgon the Beast or, worse, the terrible Cerrina Coldfist having access to one of those little yellow gems?"

Altin nodded as he accreted a stack of carrots on his fork in a series of successive stabs. "Another ice age. I can see it now."

"Exactly."

They ate in silence for a time, both matching the names of various villains through the ages with the atrocities they might better have been able to commit with help from the Liquefying Stone. It was a sobering thing to contemplate.

"So why did you give one of them to me?" Altin asked after a time. "That seems rather risky, really, now that I think about it."

"Because I know you well enough to know...." He let the sentence trail off.

"To know what?"

"I just know you."

"Did you divine it? Have you already seen? So you know I won't go mad?

Tytamon was silent. Altin watched the man eat. Almost eight hundred years and yet some things remained impossible to hide.

"You did divine it, didn't you? So what did you see? What happens? Was it clear enough to tell?"

"It was like they always are, Altin. Vague. Suggestions. Images that, as usual, tend only to mean something after the event has passed."

"That's a deflection if I ever heard one. Look, if I'm going to die because of the stone, I'm fine with it. I've resigned myself to it. You know what they say about Sixes."

"I thought you weren't a Six."

Altin laughed. "I'm not. I'm just trying to get you to tell me what you saw."

Tytamon laughed too, but his expression mellowed just as quickly as the mirth had come. "Mostly blackness, Altin. That was all."

"Well, of course you saw blackness," Altin replied, taking another bite, as if relieved. "I'm traveling into a vast and awesome night. What else would you see? You're divination simply gave you a glimpse into the sky."

"Perhaps," said Tytamon. "But I didn't see any stars."

"Divination is always short on details," Altin countered quickly.

"Spoken like a mage who's never cast the school."

"I'm blank there, why would I?"

"You said yourself that your being blank in that school defies the laws of circularity."

Altin groaned, fearing another debate about his Six-ness coming in the wake of Tytamon's dark divination. "Well, I'm not going to kill myself, so your spell probably meant something else. Maybe I'll get the plague and die, and the Liquefying Stone can just go back downstairs." He stuffed another huge chunk of mutton into his mouth, chewed it quickly and then added, "It's not like I don't have the rodents in my room to catch plague from anyway."

"You have rats in your tower?"

"Just a mouse." He swallowed and took a drink of wine. "Just one. I'll get him. I was trying to make a joke."

Tytamon recognized a subject change when he saw one and took the cue. He was not in the mood for an argument with the boy either. Altin could be easily brought to ire some nights. Once more he returned the conversation to the moon.

"So, you're planning on going up there yourself soon, eh? What is that going to entail?"

Altin finished off another bite of meat before replying, washing it down with wine. "I have a few things to do first. I reckon it's as hot as Taot's breath up there; the sun looms huge in the sky, so I need something for that. And, perhaps paradoxically, I believe it can get very cold too. So, I'll have to get a new fur coat, maybe mammoth skin. I don't think I've worn mine in several years and I'm certain it no longer fits. Other than that, I think I'm mostly ready to go. I may make a fast-cast amulet to get me home, just in case something unexpected happens. Just as a precaution. Rather waste a night on one of those than be plagued by something that fulfills your nasty divination dream."

"I didn't say it was nasty, just ambiguous. And I think a fast-cast amulet should be a requirement at the very least, if not perhaps even considering sending a surrogate explorer first."

"Surrogate explorer?"

"A rabbit or a lamb. Just something before you go yourself. Something... expendable."

Altin chewed slowly as Tytamon finished making his point. It was a good one. Caution over speed. "You're right," he said at last. "You're entirely right. I should have thought of that myself."

"We can't all be geniuses," Tytamon chided over the edge of his wine cup.

Altin gasped and made a show of being completely taken aback. They laughed and eventually the conversation moved on to other things.

After dinner Altin returned to his library to search within his shelves of scrolls and tomes and books. He had a lot of work to do. First, he had to find a teleport spell that would work on an unwilling target, for he assumed that whatever he sent was not likely to be too excited about going to the moon, even if it didn't understand. Second, if he was going to protect this surrogate traveler from Luria's raging sun and life-defying cold, he would need to find some spells that would account for that as well. A mountain of research. He definitely had a lot of work to do.

Chapter 11

Altin woke late the next morning after a good meal, several hours of sleep and a night's reprieve from using the Liquefying Stone. Sometimes the body just needed time to recover, even a young body like his. He got up and after a quick wash and change of robes, prepared to go down to the goat pens to procure himself a surrogate traveler to the moon, when a motion on the table stayed his hand upon the door. The mouse was back and once again having its fill of Altin's morning bread.

"All right, mouse, that was your last free meal," he said as he began the words for a minor fire spell. He conjured a tiny fireball, a miniature meteor no larger than a grape, and held it hovering above his hand. He was just about to throw it when he got another idea instead: the moon did not require a goat. Nor did it require a rabbit or a lamb. In fact, the spell that Altin had discovered in his research last night, called Teleport Other, only required a "willing subject," an "enclosed or encapsulated subject" or, as now, "one too simple to fight against the magician's will." This last had come with a caveat regarding emotional states and elevated will, but this was a mouse after all; how emotional could it possibly be? And a mouse would do just as well as a goat for simplicity. Altin growled at the little beast and moved towards it with a malicious grin.

Crouching, he circled round to a position where he would be hidden from the mouse's view by the curve of the bread. On tiptoe, he approached as silently as he could, cursing the rustle of his robes with every step. He snuck up quietly to the bread and, hands cupped ready to pin the mouse securely to the table planks, he lunged over the top of the loaf. The mouse darted from beneath his grasp and leapt to the floor. Altin knew this game and dove to intercept. He actually caught the creature as it was about to enter into the safety of the crack, but the defiant little beast twisted in Altin's grip and bit him on the knuckle, sinking its tiny teeth nearly to the bone.

Altin released it with a yelp. "You little monster!" he cried as the mouse vanished safely into the hole beneath the stairs.

"It won't be that easy," Altin vowed rising from the floor. "I'll have you yet, you'll see." Jaw clenched, he scanned about his room for something into which he could teleport the mouse. He spotted the wine cup he'd brought up from dinner last night sitting across the room on the nightstand near his bed. That would have to do. He began chanting his familiar seeing spell. Once within the magic, he let his vision sink down onto the floor and then moved it into the dark recesses of the mouse's hideaway.

He snaked his vision through the passage, up and down, left and right, until at last he found the mouse resting contentedly in a tiny little chamber illuminated by a crack in the tower's outer wall. Several bits of bread crust were strewn about the tiny lair, one of which the mouse was lazily nibbling on as Altin's vision brought it into view. A small patch of straw in a corner revealed that the mouse had also made itself a bed, apparently intent on setting up permanent residence. Altin suddenly understood why his mattress had recently sprung a leak. He grunted at this revelation as he let the mana go; such vandalism would soon be coming to an end. Having what he needed from the seeing spell, familiarity with the place, he could now cast his newly learned teleporting spell to catch the little whiskered thief.

Certain he was within the requisite twenty paces needed to start a teleporting loop, he began the chant that would send the mouse directly into the wine cup by his bed. He smiled grimly, efficiency in action; he would capture the rodent and get a practice run with the spell prior to a Lurian attempt—forked lightning splits two trolls, as they say.

Having spent the night studying the spell, it was fresh enough in his mind to come off without a hitch, and after a few gestures and a brief dip into the mana stream, Altin teleported the mouse from its nest directly to the cup of wine. And it was to wine that it went, for apparently Altin had not finished his libation last night. The mouse suddenly found itself nearly drowning in several inches of the alcoholic beverage and, quite baffled, began to flounder about, squeaking dreadfully in the panic of its plight.

Altin released the mana as he uttered the last word of the spell and quickly ran to the cup, intending to cover it with a book from the shelf above before the mouse could scramble out. But upon arriving at his nightstand, he discovered the mouse in desperate circumstances indeed. He actually felt a moment's pity for the rodent as he watched it struggle in the wine, its little paws scrabbling desperately at the slick brass sides of the goblet, grasping for a hold while its hind legs kicked furiously to keep its head above the surface of the wine. Picking up the cup, Altin went to the window and, covering the cup with his hand, poured off the liquid so that the mouse was no longer forced to paddle for its life. It was not his intention to torture the pesky thing, merely to send it to the moon.

Once the cup was empty, Altin righted it and moved back towards his bed planning once more to place a book atop the goblet, but the mouse, wet and squishy now, and with dry "land" from which to launch itself, began bouncing off his palm in an attempt to leap out and escape. Over and over it leapt, determined at all costs to break through Altin's palm and run for the freedom of its hole and becoming more and more agitated as moments passed, squeaking hysterically, and beating itself into a frenzy against the cup and Altin's hand. Altin began to worry if this was the "emotional state" that the spell description in his book suggested could give a target an "elevated" and spell-denying "will."

The soggy mouse was remarkably strong for its size, and as it continued to leap for freedom, the thought came to Altin that had the wine cup been empty, he might not have caught his prey at all. The mouse would easily have jumped out and run off before Altin could have gotten to the nightstand and grabbed a book. Imagine having been twice outwitted by a mouse, and in a single day. How humiliating to even contemplate. He also realized that now, in the time it was going to take him to replace his hand with a book, the mouse might still leap out and get away. The little crumb raider continued to keep him at something of an impasse.

But then the mouse began to slow, its leaps becoming less and less frequent, its squeaks less piteous, until at length the mouse no longer moved inside the cup at all. Altin chanced a glimpse between his fingers to see if the little biter had finally given up. It had.

The mouse was just sitting there in the bottom of the cup, a small puddle of wine still sloshing beneath its red-stained feet as its little sides heaved in the effort to catch its breath. Its gray coat was stained purple now, and it gazed up at Altin through eyes that were cloudy and glazed, the once alert black dots now dull, apparently by the fact that the mouse had had far too much to drink.

"You're drunk," Altin laughed. "How perfect. This solves my 'elevated will' problem after all, assuming that's what you were going to try to do." He raised the goblet into the air. "Here's to you, my plague-ridden little friend. You and your trip up to the moon." He looked once more into the cup, but the mouse no longer seemed concerned. Altin was glad of that. He really hadn't wanted it to suffer, physically or emotionally, and intoxication was a splendid piece of luck.

For security's sake, he placed a book over the cup anyway then retrieved the tome that held the spells for protecting the mouse from the extremes of heat and cold. Despite the mouse having a fur coat of its own, Altin decided that spells for both ends of the thermometer were the safest bet. He would have to tone them down some—he'd practiced last night with a sheep or goat in mind—but it didn't take him long to make the adjustments, and after a little less than an hour he was ready to make the casts.

He uncovered the anesthetized rodent and poured it out onto the table, prepared to catch it with the cup again if it tried to run away. It did not. It stared blankly into nothingness, and Altin felt that it was safe to begin. He put the cup down and began the chants that would lay the protective spells upon the mouse. First he cast the Sunscreen spell, which was, at its core, the same simple spell that every mother with B-class enchanting skills or better had cast on every child at every beach during every summer since the Magical Revolution began, and probably even before that. Only this particular version had been beefed up for workers at hard labor in the desert quarries and for some polar expeditions as well. On top of these augmentations, Altin had made a few adjustments of his own, based on his suppositions about Luria's proximity to the sun.

When he was done casting that one, he cast the Winter Warding spell he'd found—a lucky reference to it listed in the same book that had discussed the Sunscreen spell's application as protection even in icy climes. It took him a bit longer to cast that, it being slightly more complex, but after just a few minutes of preparation, the mouse was ready to go.

Altin took the time to dry the mouse's fur a little on his robes before he started the cast that would send it on its way. Its body was limp and warm beneath his fingers, and Altin could not help thinking how delicate it seemed as he felt its little shoulders and tiny hips shifting beneath its skin as his thumbs worked the cloth of his robes against the grain of sodden fur. He dried it a bit more thoroughly, just in case. No sense putting the Winter Warding spell to unnecessary stress.

When the mouse was satisfactorily dried, Altin took it and the book containing the Teleport Other spell up to the battlements to make the cast. He went up there not because he needed to, but because it seemed the right place to be. Casting had an emotional center too. Once up in the fresh air, he placed the mouse on the parapet, away from the wooden bowl and the Liquefying Stone. He was certain he did not need the Liquefying Stone for this since he knew exactly where he intended the mouse to go. The mouse began to stir, and Altin knew the wine would not keep it "willing" for very long, not after so much preparation time. The moment to send it on its way had come.

He glanced once more through the Teleport Other spell in the book, making sure he had it correctly in his mind and, turning slightly to get the sun out of his eyes, he began the chant. The spell was not difficult for a Z-class teleporter, and it wasn't long before the mouse vanished with a minuscule hiss of air. Altin could tell by the feel of it that the mouse had landed where he'd planned, just near the first seeing stone, and he practically leapt to the scrying basin to get an instant view of how the mouse's trip had gone.

It was only a few seconds before the image in the water came into view. And Altin nearly staggered back in shock. The mouse lay broken in the red Lurian dirt, turning grey in the wan light of the seeing stone with its skin split open and little crystals of red, like garnets, floating away from it in the oddest sort of way, slowly, almost drifting as would something in a dream. Its tiny black eyes were broken, ruptured like fine caviar poked with the tine of a fork and then forgotten by some distracted party guest. The insides of its body, protruding through rents in its fur, seemed as if they'd been frozen hard as stone, a monument in miniature to an eviscerated mouse.

But how could that be? What had happened to the winter ward? Could it really be that cold up there? The warding spell was supposed to make one "impervious to cold," and it had been tested in the worst conditions Prosperion was capable of dishing out.

Something had gone terribly wrong. Altin stared into the scrying basin and found himself suddenly going numb. He'd almost sent himself up here. He'd been planning to do it only a night ago, to go alone. Had Tytamon not suggested a surrogate, that would be him lying up there, broken open like a stomped gourd and spewing frozen agates of blood into a dreamlike night. And why did they float like that? What in a gorgon's mirror was going on up there?

Altin suddenly cursed himself for his lack of divination. He found himself wishing that he could do it, wishing that he had made himself try to learn that school of magic more often in the past, wishing he'd pushed beyond what he knew inside was just a block. He'd always written off his unwillingness to attempt the school to laziness, procrastination and perhaps to a bit of disbelief despite what the Sorcerers Council had concluded back when he was a boy of just eleven years. What did those old bureaucrats know? Half of them were has-beens anyway, washouts whose limited intellects denied them the ability to do anything with the gifts they'd been given, regardless of their class. Besides, divination was a bore. The answers were always so ambiguous, meaningless mostly, if they even came at all. It was such a waste of time.

Except for now. He would really like the insight that a good divination might have brought him at this particular place in time. No one else knew the sequence of events like he did. No one had done and seen what he just had. No one ever could. But now he was going to have to get a Divination done, and done by someone else. And there was no room for error; he had to know precisely what had happened to the mouse, which meant that even Tytamon's O-class Divination was not going to be good enough. And now was certainly not the time for Altin to try to learn, not when his life had a stake in the answers being right.

There were only two diviners that he trusted with this task: Ocelot, a crazy witch living deep in the Great Forest was one, but she was too odd, and her eccentricity made Doctor Leopold, the other choice, the more desirable of the two. Though a couple of classes less than Ocelot's Z, the doctor was an expert at medical things which gave him perhaps an edge on Ocelot for this particular cast. And, well, gazing into the water at the shattered remnants of the mouse, Altin concluded that this was a decidedly medical thing.

He felt a pang of guilt as he looked into the basin, his fingers remembering how the tiny creature had felt not so long ago, gently stirring in his grasp as he'd dried it on his robes, its diminutive body soft and warm, still filled with life. He glanced down at the purple stain on his gray robes and his eyes misted for a moment as he realized what he had done. He'd wanted the mouse dead before, true, but that was different. This was an accident. An accidental death was not the same. An incredible sense of guilt began building in his guts, his mind started to whirl and fill with the strangest thoughts, images of fire and of a falling oak tree, of... was that Pernie in a pale blue dress? A voice in his mind cried, "Murderer! Incompetent!" and a wave of dizziness threatened to rise behind his eyes.

He cleared his head with a violent shake, stomping his foot and willing the thoughts away with a grunt that rattled in his throat. What the hell was he thinking? It was just a mouse. A mouse! Vermin. And he'd made progress with it too. That was the point of sending a surrogate after all. Wasn't it? To discover and to learn. So the lesson was there. Now it was time for the next step.

He cursed the weakness from his mind, forced reason slowly, thankfully, back to bear as he drove the absurd imagery away. He mumbled inside his head for stability. What did he know? What did he know? He knew now that he could teleport things to the moon without the Liquefying Stone. That was one. And he knew he needed work on the Winter Warding spell too. That was another thing. See? Some good had come from the cast in that. He just needed to focus back to calm. That, and he needed answers for the rest of what went wrong.

After a few moments, he was himself again, free from unproductive emotions like guilt and insecurity. He took a deep breath and began the cast that would bring the mouse's body back. Once it had returned, Altin wrapped it in a cloth and called to Taot for a ride. It was time to go to town.

Chapter 12

No crew members were seriously injured by the impacts of the Hostile projectiles, and the ensuing hours that Orli spent at her battle stations post, in sick bay assisting the triage nurses in the infirmary, were primarily filled with sitting alongside the other medical staff watching the events outside the ship on the sick bay monitors. As events go, there wasn't much to see, for the mysterious interstellar orb had made no more passes at the ship after Orli left the bridge. Apparently Roberto's destruction of what appeared to be one of its only two projectiles had been enough to run it off, at least for now. But a few hours had to pass before anyone really believed that the orb had actually called off the attack.

Called off, but not in retreat, the orb now hovered a few hundred kilometers off the starboard bow. Distress signals had gone out to alert the other ships, and orders were given to tighten the formation—the fleet having spread itself as they traveled to increase the chance of detecting Hostiles along the way. Obviously that strategy had worked, albeit a bit better than they had hoped, and the fleet was rushing to close ranks and come to the *Aspect's* aid. It was clear that one-on-one was not the way to face the enemy... ships?

Which was the latest debate taking place throughout the fleet, and particularly amongst the *Aspect's* crew: what exactly was that thing?

Orli sat amongst chattering nurses and her duty officer, Doctor Singh, as the lot of them argued possibilities back and forth excitedly. "It's a spaceship, all right," asserted one of the nurses as Orli stared at the image of the orb on a monitor mounted on the wall. "There's probably some wicked little bastards inside of that thing right now, looking back out at us wondering the same thing. 'What the hell is that chunk of metal out there?' they're saying."

"I'm not so sure," said Doctor Singh running long sinuous fingers down the sides of his mouth as if stroking a moustache that was not there. Bright cuticles stood out beneath his nails as he traced the lines of his dark face absently, pulling his lips into a scowl for a moment before thumb and forefinger parted and followed the lines of his smooth shaven jaw. "It might be a ship," he said, "but I'm thinking it might be something else instead. An organism. An animal of some kind. Like a space mollusk or something similar to a tortoise or a snail."

"In space? Are you serious? It's too cold. And there's nothing to eat," argued the nurse.

"Maybe it replenishes its energy from nearby suns. We do. Why not it?"

"That doesn't mean it's alive."

"True," Doctor Singh agreed. But Orli could tell that he was not convinced. The idea of a creature living independently out in space did seem rather absurd. But nothing was impossible she supposed.

A downgrade in alert status was ordered shortly after the fourth hour of the orb's withdrawal. Level Orange was announced and, despite being endlessly on edge and prepared to return to her station in sick bay at any moment, Orli was compelled to go back to her normal post in her lab and nursery.

Once there she was far too anxious to work, and she spent more time simply staring at the lab monitor watching the orb hover out in space, waiting. But waiting for what? She wondered if maybe it was hurt, too tired to move and suffering from the loss of its long mineral shaft. Maybe it was like a bee, she thought. Maybe having lost its stinger, it was doomed to die. She began to think Doctor Singh might have a point. She made a mental note to mention her bee theory to him the next time she was in sick bay, which she hoped would not be for a long, long time.

In the meantime, she needed a distraction. Staring into the monitor at an unmoving object with no defining features beyond roundness and drab brownish gray coloring was enough to drive a person insane. Sometimes she felt she was close enough to losing her mind already, so, to distract herself, she decided to have another look at her little fungal spore—the one with three types of DNA, the discovery of which had brought her to the bridge at the same inconvenient moment that the orb had decided to attack.

She'd been puzzling over the complicated DNA sequence for a day or two prior to her incident on the bridge. At first it just seemed odd, an expectedly unexpected alien kind of thing. But as she studied it closely and scoured every record she could find for something that would shed some light on the oddity that she'd found, she realized that her fungal DNA had three consecutive strands rather than one long and confounding alien one. That had been the epiphany. The fungus wasn't defined by one freakishly long strand, but three separate ones, three that were totally shuffled up and assembled seemingly at random in a single strand. That's what, in the end, she'd finally figured out. Which led her to discover further that her fungus was essentially three species and not just one as well: it was fungus, bacteria, and virus.

None of the three distinct species, when the strands were reassembled in her computer models anyway, came out exactly like anything found on Earth, but they were similar, much as many other Andalian samples had been. Many of the plants Orli had taken from Andalia had been some exact matches to species from Earth, like the Azaleas had been, but there were many completely new species on Andalia as well. But even amongst the new species, none were so alien and dissimilar that they might not have evolved on Earth at some point given a few different random mutations along the way. The DNA strands in the spore were in keeping with this idea, similar, but not exact. However, the fact that the spore had all three sequences mixed up in one long strand was entirely alien, and there had been nothing else in her samples from Andalia to establish such a precedent. This spore was, in itself, unique from all other species she had seen, whether from Andalia or from Earth.

Granted her Andalian samples were limited in scope, but the concrete evidence from Earth supported the bulk of the Andalian genetic trends as well: things either were what they were, or they were something else, but they were never both, and certainly not a combination of three. Gender switching amphibians and cocoon-morphing insects were about as shifty as anything ever got, and it had been with considerable delight that Orli had chanced upon this discovery and felt it significant enough to bring to the captain's eye as well. She'd even been foolish enough to think that he would praise her work and maybe, just maybe, even offer a promotion or at least some token of respect. Given that scowl she got as the elevator closed, however, she was fairly certain her news would not impress him in the least. Particularly not now. Not while they were under attack. Not while they were maybe even currently at war with the Hostile race—assuming the orb even turned out to be a Hostile at all.

She shuddered to think of that. What if they were at war? What if she was? And what if that thing wasn't a Hostile ship, or even a Hostile mollusk like Doctor Singh had said? They were certainly in a war with it now; that was sure. Hell, they could be in two wars now if that thing turned out not to be a Hostile in the end. What a horrible thought. Her whole short adult life had been an unwillingly military one, stuck on this ship and with little choice in the matter. She couldn't even be on the same ship with her dad because of the stupid fleet protocols. Everything was just military now. Military, military, military. There was no such thing as a civilian anymore. Even those who'd originally signed up as civilians had eventually succumbed and joined the corps. Like Doctor Singh. He was just a doctor when he signed on to go, but in time they told him he was a captain too. He still laughed at that. But eventually he went along. All of them did. Ten years was a long time to buck a trend. And now they were at war in keeping with that trend, going along, almost as if they'd brought it on themselves.

With little else to do, and no longer willing to be mesmerized by the monitor and fear, she shook herself and decided to continue working on the mystery of her single fungal spore. Maybe there was more to find now that she knew that there were three separate things to see. And besides, the captain had much larger concerns for now.

Cursing herself for having thought to seek his praise, she brought her tiny sample out and put it under the microscope again. It still looked like just about every other fungus she'd ever seen. Unique in its own way but, still, a fungus just the same. So where was the evidence of the other parts of its DNA? Where were the other traits? How could two-thirds of this spore's genetic programming be so entirely masked from microscopic view. She was tempted to hit the damn thing with fungicide just to see what it would do. But she had no second sample and was reluctant to destroy her only source. She realized she had no other choice but to try to grow some in the lab.

Fungi could be tricky things, so she would have to be extra careful with this particular experiment. First of all, such a thing required that her immediate supervisor, Doctor Singh, and Captain Asad both sign off on the project before an alien species replication could begin. Those were fleet regulations. Which were boring and which she abhorred.

However, she had not elected to become a fleet officer on her own, and therefore, in this particular instance, and given the particular nastiness of Captain Asad's most recent scowl, Orli felt that it was entirely acceptable for her to bypass those protocols, especially because she knew how to grow a fungus properly and how to keep it safe, and because she already knew what the captain was going to say.

Orli was good at what she did, and she knew exactly what to do. She began by clearing out a large cabinet near the far wall, removing all but the middle and lower shelves. She hung a heat lamp inside and put it on a timer set for low light and medium heat. Next she would install a mister in an upper corner, set to spritz twice daily a small dose of water and air, and then she would seal the cabinet doors, airtight and leak-proof. After that, she would build a double-chambered tent by securing successive plastic sheets to the wall, ceiling and around the cabinet on the floor, completely surrounding the cabinet in its own space, sealed tight in the inner tent and enveloped by a perpetual fungicidal cloud in the outer one. She even activated the quarantine misters to spray disinfectant whenever the lab door opened for added security. The little spore had no hope of escape should it try some nasty fungal trick.

But, she was going to let it grow. And at last she had something significant to do.

It took her most of two days to procure the parts and assemble the outer two chambers for her little quarantine to the point she was confident that it was both functional and safe. But at last she was done with it and could place the single Andalian spore into a petri dish and prepare to make it grow. She set it in the confines of the cabinet next to a microscope that she had committed to this task; not even that would escape her airtight tent. The petri dish looked so small sitting there on the wide, waist-high shelf: a single, round plastic container, transparent and filled with a red bed of organic compounds that any fungus should absolutely adore. She hoped she'd done it right, set it up so that the alien spore would grow, but what did she really know about this variety anyway? She really wanted this to work, felt she needed it to. For her own sanity.

Roberto had promised her that cataloguing Andalian plants would get her name into the botanical history books, but she knew that while this was probably true, it would only be as a footnote. Nothing of dignity. She was just the schmuck who happened to be standing in the right place when the landing teams went planet-side. Nothing more. She would get no credit for brains, just for the labor of putting it down for everyone else to read. Anyone could pick a plant, and anyone could put information into a data file. That was not enough for her. Not enough to keep her going for very long. No, this fungus, this was the real work. This was the discovery. Three species in one. She actually had something to be enthusiastic about. And she could hardly wait for it to grow.

But she would have to wait, for shortly after she got the petri dish settled in place, and after a suitable period of time standing in the fungicidal fog and then carefully zipping the outer plastic chamber closed, the alarms went off, recalling the crew to full alert again. She glimpsed over at her monitor, having gotten used to the image of the orb floating out there over the span of a pair of days, and felt her heart begin to pound inside her chest.

Now there were two.

The second one was larger than the first, perhaps by nearly half as much again. And the two were linked together, joined like cells about to split. They must have come together very fast—or else the bridge crew had been very slow to raise an alarm—but they neither split nor merged together all the way after that. They simply joined as they had, and now seemed content to just float out there in space.

Orli felt panic tighten in her stomach as she considered the chance of winning in a fight against them both. Roberto was good, and his instincts had probably saved their lives, but even he could not react fast enough to deal with two. And if they did merge all the way, how huge would a stinger be on a bee as big as that?

She switched the screen to the starboard view, and then to port and stern. Damn. Still no other ships. They were only supposed to be two days apart. Those were the admiral's orders when the fleet had left from Andalia so many months ago. What was taking them so long? There should be at least one other ship by now, if not two. Meanwhile, the clarion rang and she had to get back to the infirmary before they could accuse her of having dallied twice in as many days. Doctor Singh was a kind man and had acknowledged her tardiness last time with only a frown. But she didn't want to push him. He was a superior officer after all. She wasn't sure she could handle any more stress beyond what she already bore.

With one backward glance at her monitor, at the empty space where another ship should be, Orli went out into the corridor, having to pause and wipe the sting out of her eyes as the sterilizing mist she'd set to spray caught her unprepared. "Shit," she cursed, wiping at her face. She'd forgotten how much that stuff could burn. But she was determined to leave it set that way until she was finished experimenting with the spore.

Blinking the disinfectant from her eyes, she began to run. Triage duty called. She only hoped that this round would be as uneventful as the last, although she really had her doubts.

Chapter 13

Leekant was a modern city, not as large as the capital, Crown City, certainly, but close enough to the royal home to enjoy the luxury of being near the Queen. The city's greatest wealth came from its booming lumber trade. Located at the edge of the Great Forest, and right at the convergence of the north and south forks of the Sansun River, Leekant was ideally located to cut trees and to ship lumber, and the many products that Leekant craftsmen could make from it, to Crown. The city also boasted an agricultural base to rival any of the plains towns across Kurr, and once more had the Sansun River to thank for getting its produce to Crown City faster, cheaper and in greater quantity than most other towns could ever hope to do.

Leekant was divided into four quarters, as most post-Unification cities were, and it was to the Guilds Quarter that Altin intended to go. Doctor Leopold kept his offices in a large medical complex near many of Leekant's other physicians, and so it was that Altin guided Taot to a grassy knoll about a half-measure outside of the city walls, close enough to make it a short walk. Normally he'd land a bit further away even than this, but he was in a hurry and so risked landing within sight of wandering eyes. The whole way over he'd been watching the mouse's body slowly thaw within the cloth, and he'd been briefly tempted to have the dragon land upon the doctor's roof. But, of course, he did not. No sense throwing the city into panic, much less bringing arrows and lightning bolts down on both his and Taot's heads. The city guard would not tolerate such a thing.

So instead he landed on the grass and dismounted, sending Taot off with a grateful thought. He could teleport home, there were no restrictions going the other way, but it was expressly illegal to teleport into town. Cities were busy places, and even if one used a scrying spell to find a safe place to port, the time it took to leave the scry and cast the teleport was often enough for someone or something to move into that spot. Teleporting one's self into the same location as another object or person was a recipe for instant death; two bodies so combined could make an awful mess. And besides, transportation via teleport was the domain of the Teleporters Guild, of which Altin was required to be a member by the laws that guided such things. It would not do to step on the guild's toes. They were a very powerful guild and had the ear of the Queen. Which is why Altin found himself walking into town.

He came in through the city's north gate and strode down the cobbled streets, bare feet forming with each step to the surface of every stone he trod along the way, some more comfortably than others, and some not comfortable at all. He suddenly wished he'd thought to strap his sandals on, but he hadn't, so he had to grin and bear it as best he could.

The buildings in the Guilds Quarter were generally uniform: three or four stories above a ground level that was open to the air and held aloft by thick trunks of local wood columns, aligned in orderly rows and serving as stilts to accommodate the occasional Sansun flood. The roofs were all thatch excepting for the Patient Peacock Inn, which sat on the corner across from the medical center and had upgraded to tile roofing made of clay. Most guilds and merchants didn't bother with such things as the Enchanters Guild had sealed up every roof in the quarter long ago, making the thatch impervious to water, fire and rot. But Old Bucky Falfox, the inn's proprietor and perpetual candidate for mayor, had decided that it was important to modernize, wanting to "keep up with the times." Perhaps not the smartest move politically, considering his proximity to the Enchanters Guild headquarters only a block away, but it was a lovely sight and a testament to modernity.

Seeking it as landmark, Altin weaved between ox carts, foot traffic and the occasional nobleman on a horse until he spotted the reddish tile of the Patient Peacock's roof. Finally he'd arrived. He darted between a foursome of city guards in burnished plate armor, one of whom snarled at his impudence with a curse that made a woman passerby cover her young daughter's ears. Altin ignored the verbal exchange that followed as the mother scolded the blushing soldier vehemently and hopped up onto the wood-plank sidewalk that would lead him to Doctor Leopold's office. A half-minute later found him stepping through the familiar iron-bound door.

The doctor's reception room was large and well lit, lined round with chairs along the walls and with plants in two of the four corners, potted and growing as lushly as anything a forest could produce, their health a testimony to the growth magic of the doctor who worked within. A painting of the Queen hung regal and smiling to the left of the receptionist's desk, facing him as he walked in.

Lena, the buxom, green-eyed brunette who worked the receptionist's desk, looked up as he entered and, seeing who it was, smiled widely, her crimson lips parting to reveal perfectly straight, snow-white teeth, also as flawless as modern magic would allow.

"Hello, Altin," she cooed. "Back so soon? I hope it's nothing serious this time? How are your ribs?" Her face became the definition of concern as she leaned forward to scrutinize him for signs of harm, the motion incidentally causing her shoulders to squeeze inward and forcing her cleavage to bulge spectacularly from her bodice in her most alluring way.

Altin rolled his eyes and exhaled audibly in an attempt to stay the onslaught of her inevitable advance. She was always like this when he came to see the doctor, and she had no concept of decency or guile. But she was beautiful. He could not deny her that.

"No, I'm fine. Ribs are fine. I just need to see Doctor Leopold if he is in. Is he?"

"Well I don't know, exactly," she replied, turning her face slightly and giving him the slender curve of a long, delicate neck while batting her eyelashes as coquettishly as she could. "I suppose I could go check for you if you promise to be a little nicer this time."

"Nicer? I'm perfectly nice. And isn't that what they pay you for? Please, I'm in a hurry." He raised the bundle of cloth containing the mouse before him as evidence of the urgency of his quest. Faint red stains bleeding through the cloth indicated that the body was beginning to thaw in earnest.

Even he was normally not *that* abrupt with her, despite his implacable disregard for her advances, and she took it as a sign that perhaps there was something serious after all. She looked a little hurt though, and Altin could see that she seemed rather to deflate. "Fine," she said. "I'll go get him. Have a seat."

Altin sat as Lena disappeared through a door behind her desk. He sighed impatiently as he waited, glaring about the room not really seeing anything in particular. There were several newspapers and some guild pamphlets on the table at the room's center. He picked up the *Teleporter's News* restlessly, laying the mouse down in his lap so he could have a look inside. He flipped through the pages rapidly. Nothing, as usual: something stupid about a new kind of lizard, something else about a hike in guild member dues… he tossed it back on the table, too edgy to read such triviality. What was taking Lena so long? He spent a few grueling minutes watching two fish swim lazy circles in a bowl on Lena's desk and was just about to stand and pace the room when the familiar figure of Doctor Leopold stepped out from the door behind Lena's post.

"Altin, my boy, back so soon? Don't tell me I botched the job on your ribs. I hate to give money back. You know I'm a miser when it comes to gold." He laughed a fat, jocular laugh that rippled through his thick jowls, down the stairwell of his layered chins and all across the great globe of his belly. "I'd rather take it out in trade." He laughed again as Altin assured him that his ribs were better than they had ever been.

"Good, good, lad. What now then? You look healthy enough to me." He looked Altin up and down as he spoke, his eyes fixing on the towel that was slowly turning pink. "You haven't got a finger wrapped up in there, have you? Or maybe a toe? I didn't notice you favoring a leg when you stood up."

Altin glanced over at Lena, who had returned to her desk but was still standing, close enough to him that he could smell the lilac scent of her perfume. She swayed rhythmically as she smiled at him, her body gently sinuous although she barely seemed to move. He thought for a moment she might be trying to cast a spell. But that was silly. Lena was a blank.

"I'd rather discuss it in private, if that's okay with you," he said to the doctor.

Lena snorted, barely audible, just a breath, and returned

to her desk. Thwarted again.

"Of course, my boy, of course. You know the way."

The ponderous physician motioned grandly through the door and Altin, clutching his swaddled mouse, went inside. They quickly traversed the short maze of halls leading to Doctor Leopold's office, and Altin threw himself into a familiar chair. The doctor waddled in after him and plumped down into a squeaky leather chair that screamed and creaked in protest to the load it suddenly had to bear. The doctor was wheezing noticeably from the trip back to his office and took the time while he regained his breath to study Altin with keen, intelligent eyes. After a time he glanced at Altin's bundle. "So what's in the towel?"

"A mouse," said Altin. "And I need you to tell me what went wrong."

Doctor Leopold was familiar enough with Altin's work to know what this visit was all about. He rose up and reached across his cluttered desk, Altin meeting him halfway and handing the bundle into his stubby-fingered hands.

The doctor laid the bundle down and unwrapped the mouse. He took a few moments to regard the dilapidated little corpse before letting out a low whistle. "Pretty mangled. What did you do to it?"

"Well, that's mostly what I'm hoping you can tell me. All I know is that I sent it to the moon."

"The moon? Luria? You mean you've actually done it?" The doctor looked up, his face radiant with pride. "Congratulations, young man. That was a long time coming. But I knew you'd manage it one day."

"Yes, thanks," Altin said, dismissively. "But look at the mouse. That's how it came back. I anticipated that it would be very cold, and maybe very hot. So I cast Sunscreen and Winter Warding spells on it. But, well, they didn't seem to work. I believe I was right about the cold. But I'm not sure what went wrong."

Doctor Leopold studied the mouse again as Altin leaned over his desk expectantly. The body was still largely frozen, only the edges of the wounds were beginning to soften up. The doctor muttered under his breath as he prodded the mouse with a letter opener taken from a drawer. "So it is. So it is."

After what seemed an interminable length of time, Altin asked, "Well? What do you think? Can you divine it or something? I absolutely have to know. I can't do anything else until I do."

"Yes, I can certainly see that," the doctor agreed. "Give me a moment to find the spell." Doctor Leopold hoisted himself up from the chair and moved to a bookshelf where he kept some ancient-looking tomes. He pulled one down and leafed through it until he found the spell he wanted. He turned through page after page of the spell for an unbearable length of time, reading over the magic meticulously, well past sixteen pages by the time Altin grew too impatient to continue counting anymore. Finally, the doctor spoke. "All right, this is the one. It's a place to start." He waved Altin away, batting at the air with the back of a pudgy hand, "Give me some room, will you?"

Altin retook his seat and watched as Leekant's legendary healer closed his eyes and began to cast his divining spell. The casting seemed so much simpler than the spells that Altin had to use. The doctor didn't move his hands at all, pressing them together palm to palm, fingers steeple-like and held beneath his chin. But the cast went on for quite a while. The doctor sat there in his chair, chanting, for what turned out to be a little over an hour. It was no wonder Altin couldn't force himself to try the damnable divining school himself.

Once the doctor had finally finished invoking the magic, he spent a great deal more time immersed within the spell. Altin figured that Doctor Leopold was likely traveling around through the tiny spaces within the mouse and posing the question "why?" to the harmonies of truth that supposedly vibrated across the mana stream when one divined. At least that's what Altin had read; that's what the books said divination magic did. Altin honestly had no clue. And he didn't really care. At least not now. That's why he was here. He didn't have time to mess with prayer.

Finally, after another half an hour examining the mouse's corpse, Doctor Leopold came out of the divining spell. "Wyvern's wings, boy. What have you got yourself into? What killed this mouse is no child's game. Luria is a horribly dangerous place."

"Yes, I gathered that myself. So what, beyond the cold, took place?"

"For starters, I wouldn't say 'beyond the cold' so casually. You have no idea how cold it is up there. There's nothing on Prosperion like it. If water freezes at zero degrees, and we measure our southern pole in wintertime at negative ninety, your moon is at least three times that cold. Maybe more. Divination is not really meant for measurements like that. But I got the sense of three, so take that for whatever it is worth."

"Ok, so it was just the cold. I need to strengthen up the ward. I can do that. Was there anything else? You were looking for an awfully long time."

"Yes, there is." He paused. "This mouse died instantly."

Altin nodded.

"But it wasn't exactly from the cold."

Altin raised his eyebrows expectantly, having nothing else to add.

"Sort of a cold boiling. It suffocated. But didn't have time to gasp. It's as if the air was just sucked out of its lungs, from its everything, replaced by nothing, and then it froze from the inside out. Just like that." The doctor snapped two thick fingers in the air above the shattered mouse to illustrate his point. "I've never seen anything like it. I don't think even your elemental power could summon an ice spell on a mouse and do what Luria did to this one. It's almost beyond comprehension." He raised his squinty eyes and pinned Altin to his chair with a stern glare. "Altin, you're meddling with things that might not ought to be meddled with. Do you understand? This is the kind of thing that gets Sixes killed."

"Gods be burned," Altin spat, bolting up from the chair. "Not you too. I thought you were on my side. I get enough of that at home." He reached over the teetering stacks of parchment records and mashed the towel back around the mouse quickly before snatching it away. He stormed to the door.

"Altin, wait," the doctor called after him. "Come back."

"If I want a lecture, I'll go see Tytamon," Altin said, striding out into the hall.

"I'm not going to lecture. Altin, I'm sorry. It just came out. I know you have as much advice in Tytamon as any one man could probably ever stand. I'm sorry. Come back. There's more that you should know."

Altin hesitated, but was giving the oddball Ocelot a serious second thought.

"Altin, come back and sit down. Don't make me apologize again. I'm too old to be humble to a boy. Sit. And give me back the mouse." There was something accusatory in his tone despite the words themselves, an implicit suggestion that only a child would continue walking out. Altin ground his teeth for a moment and then swallowed back his pride. He needed to know everything there was to know, and he didn't want to waste time chasing the eccentric Ocelot through the woods.

He set the mouse back where it had been on Doctor Leopold's desk and settled himself into the chair again. There followed a long period of silence before the doctor finally began to speak, skipping directly back to the subject at hand. "Another thing you need to know is that there is no moisture in the... air." He hesitated on the word. "No. 'Air' is the wrong term. It's difficult to explain. The sense I got was of gasping, but, because of the instantaneous nature of the event, there isn't time to know. But it was dry cold, although that doesn't really tell you much. The spell seemed to convey an inverted drowning feel. I felt as if I was drowning for lack of water, or such was the sense the divination gave. Air that was not air." The doctor went on for several more moments, prodding at the idea with new, yet still ambiguous terms, trying to pin it down from different angles with different metaphors, until finally concluding by saying, "But such is the nature of divining, which you already know. You get clues but rarely any answers. The gods are tricky in this way. I hope it helps."

"It does," said Altin, his mind churning with possibilities. "It doesn't tell me much, but it tells me something. I'm just not sure what. At least not yet."

A knock on the door was followed by Lena's voice, filtered through the oak. "Doctor Leopold, Lady Falfox is here to see you again. She says the headaches are back."

Doctor Leopold groaned and raised himself up out of his chair with the help of hands pressed upon the desk. "What about the headache I get every time she shows up?" he muttered to Altin as he rose. "What's for that?" He laughed then groaned again. "There's nothing wrong with that woman that a hard day's work wouldn't cure."

He came round the desk to Altin and offered his hand. Altin took it, thanking him for his time, and Doctor Leopold gave Altin a look that could have been the beginnings of another warning, but the glint in Altin's eyes stayed it on his lips. The doctor nodded and smiled, then placed a hand on Altin's back, gently directing him to the door.

Altin swung the door open and found himself face to

face with smiling Lena, obviously familiar enough with Doctor Leopold's habits to know that it would be Altin emerging from the office first. He nearly collided with her as he stepped out into the hall, and for a moment their faces were only a hand's breadth apart. Altin could smell her perfume again and the sweetness of her breath; she must have been eating something made with mint. "Oops," she said innocently, placing her small hands upon his chest in a show of modest self defense—although somehow she couldn't quite manage to push herself away.

"You're going to get blood on you," Altin said, stepping back and opening his gory wad of mouse only inches from her face. Seeing its contents, she screamed and leapt back from him in terror, her pretty face twisted up into a mask of purest horror before she turned and ran back down the hall. Doctor Leopold made no attempt to hide his mirth and chuckled at Altin's back as they followed slowly in Lena's wake.

"That was almost cruel," he said between receding waves of chortles.

"She deserved it," Altin said. "She's always doing things like that. Practically smearing herself all over me every time I come."

"She likes you, boy. Any fool can see."

"I can see. And I'm no fool. She's a tart, and I have no time for her."

"Oh, I think you're being too hard on the girl. She's sweet. And quite something for the eye."

They fell silent for a moment as they came out into the waiting room, Doctor Leopold nodding politely to Lady Falfox as he walked Altin to the door.

"I don't have time for sweet," Altin said as they neared the exit. "I have my work to do."

"I think it's more than that." Doctor Leopold started to press the point, but, once more, Altin stayed the physician's tongue with just a glance. He looked over the doctor's shoulder at Lena, now sitting at her desk again, and couldn't help notice that she was wiping the corners of her eyes with a lacey handkerchief. She glanced up at him briefly, green eyes luminous with tears, then quickly looked away, finding safety in watching her fish swim around the bowl.

Altin beat back a rising tide of guilt. He hadn't meant to make her cry. He hated that feeling. The guilt. It made him even angrier than before, and he returned his attention to the doctor, barely suppressing an urge to snarl. "Thank you for your time, Doctor. You'll put it on Calico Castle's bill?"

"You're welcome. And this one was free of charge. Call it my contribution to history. Maybe you'll mention me in your notes."

"I will," said Altin. They clasped hands once more and Altin strode back through town and out the city gates, his mind a jumble of images, ghosts of broken mice and of women crying behind their fish.

Chapter 14

Altin's teleport brought him back atop the tower just in time to see Taot swooping down on a doe running for her life out in the meadows not far beyond the castle gates. In his present mood he was more than happy to watch the dragon do his work. A dragon's life was simple and to the point. Instinctual. But not Altin's. Everything was so damn complicated all the time.

Taot snatched the fleeing doe out of the grass, clutching it by the head and giving a quick whip to snap its neck. Once the doe stopped struggling, the dragon landed in the meadow not too far from the creek and set himself upon the meal. Altin, leaning on the crenellated wall, morosely watched him eat. Hurting Lena's feelings was really working on his mind. Was he really such a lout? Thinking of it reminded him of the horrified look on Pernie's face the other day. He'd scared her half out of her wits too. Actually, he'd treated her even worse.

He grunted derisively at himself. What was wrong with him? What a vicious thing he had become. Just look what he'd done to the mouse. He'd killed it, horribly, essentially blowing it to bits, and for what? He still didn't know what the problem was. And Doctor Leopold's answers had been vague. Such brutality and he didn't even have an explanation to make it seem as if he'd achieved something for the merciless outcome of his act.

He wondered if perhaps he should try to find Ocelot after all; he needed to know. What he really needed was to be able to divine it for himself. He knew he could if he wanted to. Or at least that's what he'd always told himself. He just couldn't make himself. And why? What in the nine hells was wrong with him? He'd never shown an inclination towards laziness in his life. So why?

Watching the dragon eat seemed to embody all these things, all the complexity and inexplicability of... of just everything old and new. The dragon tearing into that carcass seemed cruel on the surface, but it was for a larger purpose in the end. The carnage had a point. Or so he told himself. But it was an animal point. And why the dragon and not the doe? Maybe the point wasn't a good one. Ugh. It was all so damnably complicated. He hadn't meant to make her cry. He didn't mean to make anyone cry.

He was tempted to teleport back to Leekant, march back in and at least apologize to Lena. But he knew if he did that she'd take it for more than it was worth. His purpose was not to trick her, and he certainly did not want to lead her on. But he hadn't meant to be cruel either. Although, it really wasn't entirely his fault. She came at him like a charging mastodon most of the time, dangerous but visible from half a league away. And she was relentless. Always. And it was just a bloody mouse. She worked in a doctor's office after all; she should be used to the sight of blood.

The more he thought about it, the more he realized he was being a stupid emotional fool. The woman would be fine. And he had work to do.

Taot finished his meal and let out a roar of satiated delight. Altin sent him a greeting, which the dragon returned with a sense of lazy ease. Deciding that some company would be good, Altin went out to the meadow and gave the dragon a scratch behind his massive ears. Taot lay flat to the grass, moaning, a low rumble in his chest like boulders rolling down a hill. The dragon's thick hide made deep massage a chore, like kneading saddle leather, and Altin's hands quickly grew tired, but at least there was one creature on the planet he'd managed to not damage in the last few days. Which was something, because lurking in Altin's mind was the reality of having to make another try at the moon. And he certainly wasn't going to send himself. Not now.

He was going to have to send another surrogate, and he needed to figure out how to keep it from blowing up. He had no intention of doing *that* to something else. But the doctor had spoken of "drowning without water" and "air that was not air." What could that possibly mean? It meant nothing. It's either air or it's not air. And you can't drown if you're not in water. That was absurd.

The cold was easier to contemplate. Altin had been adapting and upgrading spells since he was seventeen; it was one of his gifts, an intuitive magical perspicacity. He was certain he could amplify the Winter Warding spell well enough to abate the cold, no matter how cold Luria actually got. And he would do the same for the Sunscreen spell, just to play it safe. Having no options for the other part, Doctor Leopold's mysterious ramblings, he felt the best use of his time would be to begin modifying the hot and cold wards tonight, a task grounded in certainty, which was what his beleaguered brain needed for a time. And with that decision made, he gave Taot one last pat on the massive, scaly nose and returned to his tower after a quick stop in the kitchen to procure the evening's meal.

He woke the next morning feeling much better. He'd made progress on the protective spells and had come to terms with his percolating sense of guilt. He resolved to be nicer to Pernie from now on and to apologize to Lena while making it clear that his apology meant nothing more than that. And he resolved to do the latter part after lunch. Because first he was going to have another try at Luria.

He needed to test the power of his wards, so he decided to make his next attempt by sending up a potted plant. At least if that went bad he wouldn't have any guilt. He went down to the gardens and dug up a small tomato plant, and dumped it in a terracotta pot. Gimmel, the groundskeeper, caught him in the act, and scolded him for having done such a thing himself.

"That's what I is fer, young sir," Gimmel said as he pushed Altin out of the way and proceeded to dump out Altin's recent work and then replant it in a larger pot. "Ya gots no room fer the roots in yer litt'l pot, sir." He scooped in a sandy looking mixture from a gunnysack as he worked, then braced the plant up, tying it to a V-shaped pair of sticks. "Make it grow healthy an' strong. 'Maters big as yer fist, you'll see." Gimmel held up a grubby, clenched fist to prove his point.

Altin didn't have the heart to tell him that the plant was likely to freeze to death in about an hour, and in his mind he could already see the three small cherry-sized tomatoes ruptured like the mouse. So instead he smiled and thanked the man, and then took the plant back up to his tower. It was time to test the wards.

He recast both protective spells, newly modified to forty times their previous strength. Altin was taking no chances this time. The new spells took about three times longer to cast, but time was not an issue, caution was. When it was done, Altin was ready to send the plant up to where the mouse had lost its life.

Again eschewing the Liquefying Stone for a teleport that was all his own, he cast the spell and shortly after heard the hiss of air that said the pot had disappeared. He went immediately to his scrying basin and called up the image of the plant. He saw it sitting there in its terracotta pot, half illuminated by the dull golden glow of the seeing stone which still lay where it had landed on Altin's first successful cast and half in the dark. Again it was nighttime in that place, which was good. The location would be very cold with the absence of the sun, hopefully as cold as Luria could get.

He watched for quite some time, tense with anticipation, eyes locked on the little red bulbs dangling from the vine, waiting for them to pop. But they did not. The plant looked as comfortable as a plant could be. And so Altin waited. After about an hour he was satisfied that his new Winter Warding spell had worked. Now he wanted to check his heat spell. He couldn't move the plant directly, so first he had to bring it back.

Once he cast the recall spell, he tapped the sides of the pot gingerly with his finger, testing for the effects of extreme cold. The pot felt no cooler than if it had been sitting there on the parapet all along. He felt the cherry tomatoes too, holding each one in his hand, feeling its round red skin, room temperature against his own. Altin was glad of that. He had defeated the unnatural lunar chill.

Now he had to find the sun.

He used the scrying basin to check the edge of the first crater he had found during his exploration of the moon. Having spent time there while seeing, he was familiar enough with that location to call it up easily in the water as he gripped the edges of the wooden tub. Unfortunately, the enormous lunar cavity was also in the dark. He grunted. No help there. He switched the view in the basin to another of the craters that he'd found, the largest of the ones he'd come across, and, sure enough, that one was in the light of day. Without delay he cast the tomato plant back up to the moon.

Once again he stared into his scrying basin and once

again the plant seemed perfectly at ease. Its leaves were not curling up and crisping in the heat, and there was no smoke or steam coming up from the damp soil in the pot. Altin smiled, satisfied that at least his temperature wards were figured out. Or at least seemed to be. He decided he'd give the plant a few hours up there just to be sure, and he used that time to cast the better seeing spell so that he could have a bit more time up there himself.

He didn't spend more than half an hour looking about before determining that Luria, like before, simply had nothing beyond the craters and barren landscape for him to see. The moon was a remarkable disappointment aesthetically and seemed a terrible waste of space. To be honest, the best thing about being up there was the view of Prosperion down below, which he did take a bit more time to appreciate.

Prosperion was beautiful from this vantage. And big. Looking down at it, at its massive blue sphere was humbling; it made him feel so small. She glowed like a jewel too. He traced the luminous layer of light that radiated around the planet with his eyes. Like a protective energy shield, he thought, something cast there by the gods, a divine enchantment meant to keep them safe. It amused him to think it might be humanity's warding spell, and he chuckled. The patterns of the clouds, for the white swirls could be nothing else, were breathtaking, and Altin watched with increasing awe as a vortex storm rotated magnificently above the dark spot of Duador. The more he studied it, the more he calculated the storm's relative size to other features of the globe, the more impressive it became. He figured the demons were getting a violent soaking as nature ran its awesome course, and likely getting blown around furiously as well. But he knew instinctively that the storm would not be enough to wash the island clean. The blight of human arrogance would not so easily rinse away.

Duador depressed him; he'd never had to look at it like

this. The entire race of dwarves, extinct in a matter of eleven days. Talk about magic gone awry, he'd only killed a mouse. One spell, eight men and a conduit, and a continent was lost. Such power, such fragility, was frightening to think about. The cruelty of which men were capable was almost as awesome as that storm. Perhaps more so. Sometimes he thought that the gods should never have entrusted men with magic. The obliteration of the dwarves, as accidental as it may have been, was evidence enough. Humanity had been fighting a righteous war, or so the histories said, and they only sought victory, not genocide. They had no idea the power that they held. Sometimes Altin felt like that.

Which brought his mind back to Lena, and to little Pernie too. Why did hurting them bother him so much? He tried to tell himself that it really wasn't that big a deal, but it was. He decided that now was the time to act on his promises to himself. And besides, the new warding spells had clearly worked.

He returned his vision and the tomato plant back to their rightful place on Kurr. He still didn't know what to do about the "air that was not air" and the "drowning without water" thing, but he had decided to get the other problem off his mind. For the being-nice-to-Pernie part, he had time for that day-to-day. But Lena was another matter. So, for starters, he was going back to Leekant to apologize to her for having been so mean.

Taot was still nearby, so, struggling for the discipline to avoid breaking teleporting laws, Altin flew back to town again. He landed on the familiar knoll and hustled back through the busy streets. When he reentered the office, Lena once more greeted him with a smile; however, this one was not so eager as it had been the day before. She was a resilient girl, but the sting of his cruelty had not yet gone entirely away. "Hello, Altin," she said, studying him as if noticing something new. "Is everything okay?"

"Yes, everything's fine," he said, haltingly at first. "Listen. About yesterday. With the mouse thing. Sticking the guts up in your face was pretty rude. I wanted to, you know, apologize for that. It was a mean thing to do, and I'm sorry. I didn't mean to make you cry."

Her smile warmed, spirits rising as dough becomes bread in an oven's warmth. "Oh, Altin, that's okay," she said, tilting her head slightly to the side. "I know you didn't mean to be mean. And I was... rather clumsy in my way too, so, I'm sorry also."

He smiled back at her, relieved that this had gone so well. "Good," he said. "Then there's no hard feelings. That's great." He hadn't planned on the apology going quite so smoothly, which left him feeling awkward now. "Well. Good. So, then I guess I'll be on my way."

"Wait," she called as he turned to go. "Altin. The Summer Festival is only a few weeks away. You should ask me to go to it with you. I promise I won't say 'no.'"

Altin blushed. He hated dances. And he'd known she was going to make more of his apology than he'd wanted her to. "It's two months away, not a few weeks." He had to quell an urge to tell her to stop hounding him, but it was too soon after apologizing to hurt her feelings again. "I really don't want to think about it just now."

"But you know you're going to go," she persisted. "You always do."

"I don't 'know' that, and I've never brought anyone, have I? I don't even like to dance."

"You have too."

"I have what?"

"Brought someone. You came with Madeline Pender a few years back."

"Oh for the Pearls of String, how do you remember these things? I was fifteen."

"And I was sixteen. Girls pay attention."

"I guess."

"So, will you?"

"Will I what?"

"Ask me to the dance."

"I already told you, it's too far away. I don't want to think about it."

"You're avoiding the issue."

"That's because I don't want to be mean."

"Why would you have to be mean?"

Altin was starting to get angry again. This woman just wouldn't take the hint. He really was trying to be polite.

Lena leaned forward, today's dress even more revealing than yesterday's, and nearly spilled her soft décolletage out onto the desk. "Pretty please," she begged. "Why won't you just ask? Am I that horrible to be seen with that you can't even ask me to a dance?"

Altin averted his eyes, for decency's sake as much as to avoid the question, taking sanctuary in the activities of the fish.

"Just this once, Altin. Why won't you ask?" She was starting to sound annoyed, frustration beginning to mix with some self-created jealousy that had now begun to rise. "Is there someone else? Is it still Madeline Pender?" She paused, as if realizing she had found the thing she'd obviously missed before. She frowned. "No, it can't be. She's got an overbite and freckles on her nose. So who then? Tell me it's not Keiranne Mettlestalk. Please, tell me not her?"

Altin was no longer listening. He was staring at the fishbowl. At the fish swimming there, swimming happily around in their little glass-encapsulated world. Safe in the water, breathing peacefully. Breathing air that was not air. With an almost thunderous clarity, Altin realized that the fish were not drowning, not like a man would, because fish live in water. Men live in air. Air that *was* air, the layer above the sea, the layer that Altin had seen glowing around Prosperion, what he'd absently thought of as Prosperion's energy shield. Suddenly Altin knew what he'd been missing all this time, and the epiphany hit him so hard that he rushed from the room without so much as a backwards glance.

"Wait," Lena called after him, but it was already too late. The door slammed against the wall as Altin yanked it open and bolted out of sight. She stared after him, but stopped on the wood planks of the walkway outside, shaking her head for quite some time. It had to be Keiranne Mettlestalk, she thought. Now she was convinced. But Lena had ways of dealing with women like smarmy Keiranne Mettlestalk, Keiranne with her wiggly hips, doe-brown eyes and ever-pouty lips. There was no way Altin would be taking that woman to the dance. Not a stone's chance for a swim.

Chapter 15

Orli sat with the nurses and Doctor Singh, once more staring at the monitor and watching the orbs hovering out in space. The appearance of the second one had rattled most of the medical staff too, and Orli felt better for having some company to share the anxiety with, particularly when there was nothing proactive she could do.

They watched for a long time, nobody having much to say, when finally the two half-merged orbs split themselves back apart. A computer readout fed from the bridge scan indicated that the larger orb had lost forty tons of mass. Doctor Singh nodded as he saw the numbers at the bottom of the screen. "The new one healed the old one," he said. "Just as I feared it would when it showed up and they joined like that. They are alive. And working together."

His comment reminded Orli of her theory about the bees. "You know," she said as they continued staring intently at the image on the screen, "I was thinking that the orb losing its projectile like it did was something like a bee. You know, if it loses its stinger, it won't survive."

Doctor Singh crinkled up his dark brown brow as he thought about that, bushy black eyebrows knit together almost touching above his nose. Pursing his lips a bit, he began to nod. "You know what, Ensign, I think you may have something there."

Orli beamed. Of course she had something. She wasn't just some stupid girl. It was nice to be recognized for once.

"I think our little hypotheses are worth a call up to the bridge," he said after just a moment more. "Maybe it's something the captain can work with, if they haven't already figured it out."

He tapped a button on the communications console to his left, and soon after Orli could hear Lieutenant Hartford's voice coming through. "Bridge," was all she said.

"Lieutenant Hartford, it's Doctor Singh. Listen, tell the captain we've come up with a hypothesis down here regarding the orbs. Have him call down when he has a chance; it might be of some use in fending them off."

The next voice they heard was that of the captain himself. "What is it, Singh? Make it quick."

"Captain, about the orbs. I have a hunch that they may actually be alive, not space craft, just for what it's worth. And about the missiles that they shoot, I trust you noticed the transfer of mass from the larger orb to the smaller one?"

"I did. Get to the point, Singh. We can chat over tea some other time."

"Right. Well Ensign Pewter here has hypothesized that losing those projectiles might be similar to a bee losing its stinger. We just thought you might be interested to have that...."

"Pewter?" the captain cut Doctor Singh off abruptly with disgust. "Listen, Singh, we appreciate the help. We've already determined the orb was impacted by the loss of mass. But we're good up here without pointless nature analogies to make it nice. We're busy enough as it is. Bridge out."

At least it's not just me, thought Orli as she listened to the exchange. Doctor Singh glanced over at her and shrugged it off. "I thought it was a good idea," he said. "I still do."

"It doesn't really make much of a difference," pointed out a stout young nurse scratching behind his ear nervously as he prepared to take captain Asad's side, "having an analogy like that, I mean. The captain's right. Bee, baboon, or just some damn E.T. Just blow that shit up, right?"

"It looks like we're going to get our chance to try," said Doctor Singh, squinting as his attention was caught and drawn down to motion on the monitor again. "Here they come."

All eyes leapt from the young man back to the screen, growing wide with horror as they watched both orbs streaking in at once. As the two charging Hostiles sped inward towards the ship and in unison released their mineral shafts, the mesmerized infirmary staff grimaced as the ship's two lasers forked towards each one independently and knocked them both aside. They could also see the small dot of a nuclear missile streaking on its way, and a few moments' waiting rewarded them with a bright explosion as the smaller orb's projectile was once again blown into a million scattering bits.

Everyone let out a victorious howl, and Orli reminded herself to give Roberto the hugest hug the next time she saw him. She often teased that he was little more than a barbarian for his consuming love of guns and his constant practicing on the small arms range, but she suddenly found herself unendingly grateful for his sadistic choice of hobbies. He truly was the gunfighter he always claimed to be.

The orbs swung round and appeared to be heading in for another pass. Orli had hoped that having lost its shaft, the smaller one might actually go away, but apparently that was a groundless hope. This time the orbs were further apart, and both swung round to come from behind the ship and at distinctly different angles of approach. Orli knew instinctively that this meant Roberto was going to have to split the screen. If taking the shot meant spotting that tiny sandy place on both orbs at the same instant on two screens, there was little chance he could make both shots. This was likely something beyond even his quick-draw skills.

In came the orbs and once more released their massive mineral shafts. The shaft ejected from the larger of the two was as thick as a railroad car and nearly three times as long. The large orb waited a bit longer to release it than it had before, and Orli watched as Roberto's shot played against the surface of the orb, missing its granite missile by at least a dozen yards. The area of the orb immediately shifted from the dull brown color to the shiny reflective black, and moments later came a thunderous crash as the monstrous projectile smashed against the ship. The lights dimmed and two light fixtures fell from their mountings in the ceiling in a rain of sparks. They swung violently on their wiring as several people shouted in fear and disbelief.

The lights came right back up, however, and a cursory sweep through the ship's various exterior cameras revealed that the ship was still intact, albeit now missing one of its larger communication dishes. A trail of glowing metal debris and bright sparks floated into space from where the dish had been, the sparks blinking out like yellow eyes blinded as the cold of space cooled them to sightlessness and death. The image brought a shudder down Orli's spine. That was close.

"Look," said the stout male nurse pointing at the screen. A pair of nuclear missiles were rocketing after the giant shaft that had just decimated the dish, chasing it and rapidly closing in.

"Go, go," shouted everyone in sick bay screaming at the screen. "Go. Get it!"

Suddenly the larger orb came into the camera's view, and they watched petrified as it streaked across the starry backdrop at incredible speed, apparently intent on capturing the large projectile before the ship's missiles could do it harm. Reclamation was going to be by a narrow margin if the orb managed it at all.

The orb whipped past the missiles and caught up to the giant shaft. It gave the streaking projectile a gentle nudge, knocking it off course just as the missiles came upon the spot. The mineral shaft was diverted, but the ship's missiles were only temporarily put off. They swung round and continued their dogged pursuit.

The orb had to swing itself around as well, but unhampered as it seemed to be by the laws of physics—at least as Orli thought she knew those laws to be—it was fast enough to catch back up. This time it streaked past both the missiles and its own enormous mineral spear and took up a position directly in the projectile's path. Orli could see the coloring and texture at the orb's center begin to change again, shifting to the sandiness associated with the granite beams. Apparently it was willing to risk the hit from the two nukes rather than lose such a humongous portion of its mass. She wondered if the Earth missiles might get inside as well. If they did, it would be by the narrowest margin.

The orb's projectile raced closer and closer and finally made impact with the softening surface of the orb. They all watched in awe as the shaft seemed to sink into the center of the orb. The ship's missiles landed just a moment behind it, and they exploded with a hundred megatons of force.

The orb attempted to shift its surface as the missiles were about to go off, and Orli could see that its texture switched to something that was powdery looking and almost gray. When the flash died down, they could see that the missiles had struck and blown off what was now a large cloud of the dense powdery dust; but for the most part, the orb seemed to have absorbed the blow, caving in on itself, collapsing inward like a deflated basketball on the near side while the far side of the orb shifted to an elastic substance that stretched out before it and helped to absorb the shock. The orb's surface stretched out into space, taking the energy with it, attenuating it slowly until at last the power was entirely dispersed; it reminded Orli of someone thrusting their hand into a rubber glove, several hands all at once. Everyone stared at the monitor, horrified, and after a few breathless moments, the mangled orb began to retract its newly formed pseudopodia until it was once again a perfect sphere. Or at least, nearly perfect. There was a huge scar on its nearer surface now, which Orli attributed to the loss of all the dust, a gray cloud created by the explosions and even now dissipating into space. At least they'd hurt it some. Maybe it would go away. Maybe both of them would.

Apparently not, however, for just then the ship was rattled to its last rivet as another jarring impact struck upon its shields. Orli wasn't an engineer, but she was fairly certain they couldn't hold up to much more of that. She'd momentarily forgotten about the smaller Hostile of the two.

Doctor Singh, first to gather his wits, snapped the monitor back to the bridge feed, and they all watched as lasers played harmlessly off the smaller orb's shifting obsidian skin. They looked on as another nuke shot out in pursuit of the projectile that had just beaten on their ship. The smaller orb was not as fast as the other had been, but still it made an attempt to reclaim its only remaining mineral shaft, trying to outrun the missiles just as the larger orb had done.

It caught up and passed both nuclear and mineral missiles, getting well out in front and then dropping directly in their paths. Orli squinted into the screen as the orb positioned itself to absorb the stony battering ram. She watched it soften up, creating the sandy center, but she also noticed that it shifted its outer portions to the grayish powder that the first orb had used to absorb the nuclear missiles' blows. This one was prepared, as if the other one had told it what to do.

The orb's projectile vanished inside its surface, and Orli grimaced in anticipation as their own missile streaked in not too far behind. The smaller orb was able to transform more of its surface into the powdery gray, and when the missile finally exploded, she saw that there was less of a cloud than there had been with the larger one and more of the stretching glove effect. When the dust finally cleared, the smaller orb seemed to have taken only the slightest of dents. But at least there was a dent.

The larger orb was coming round for yet another pass, and once again they braced themselves for the blow. This time the giant orb let out two shafts, both at once, and Roberto's laser trick was only up to diverting one. Again the ship was struck, and this time when the lights went off they did not come back. The entire ship went dark, even the dim red emergency lights had failed. Orli was more scared than she had been in her entire life. Nothing had ever been so black.

One of the nurses began to scream, and Orli could hear Doctor Singh's white coat rustle as he moved through the darkness and found the woman, comforting her with words of calm resolve. She could see a pinpoint of light as he flicked his penlight on. "Hold it together, people," he announced just as Orli was about to scream herself. It was so dark. Doctor Singh's penlight was almost an insult in darkness such as this. "Backup power will be right up. Keep your heads."

He was right. A moment later the backup power kicked in and all the lights came on. The monitor resumed its images of the stars outside, and the communications console burst noisily back to life—voices screaming as injury reports streamed in.

"Prepare for wounded," Doctor Singh ordered. "We have incoming."

Chapter 16

Altin arrived back in his tower and knew immediately what he had to do. The fish in the bowl had revealed to him what he had needed to understand: the universe was made in layers. It was so obvious now. There were nine layers of hell beneath the sea. There was one layer of sea for the creatures that breathed water, one layer of air for the creatures that breathed air, and, obviously, there were at least two layers of the heavens: the layer that held the sun, the moon and the planets, and the layer from which the light shown through the backdrop of the night. It was so completely clear to him now that he could hardly believe he hadn't seen it all before. He was even more annoyed that none of the great scholars in any of the books had pointed it out. Obviously, it wasn't like they didn't understand the difference between breathing in water and in air, but somehow nothing that he had read, none of those authors, had put the layers together like he just had. It was almost too simple to be believed, but then, that's how the big discoveries usually were.

The air—or whatever served for air on Luria—was not meant for men, just as the air that Altin used was not meant for fish. Each creature could only breathe on its respective layer. Up or down, a device was needed if you wanted to survive outside your own plane—a device like the fish bowl was. You had to bring your own layer with you; that was the simple trick. Altin knew of men who dug for clams and sponges using inverted tubs to bring air beneath the surface of the sea, and clearly Lena's fish were doing fine having, in a manner of speaking, brought their water up into the air. So that was all that Altin had to do. However, he was not quite sure if his bowl needed to be inverted or upright. Did Luria require the fishbowl or the sponge-divers' technique? Of that he had no clue.

He cast a seeing spell back up to the moon and flitted his vision about, but nothing helped him figure it out. At length he decided to cover both bets and just seal himself completely in. It was the safest course. All he needed now was the right spell to pull it off.

He ran down to his bed chamber and got the book from which he learned the two elemental warding spells. He recalled reading something about an igloo spell that might be made to work. He found the passage and read through it eagerly, but it did not contain the details of the spell, only the magician's name: Polar Piton. Altin cursed. He wanted to get started on learning the spell now, not just the act of finding it. He wasn't in the mood to dig through another mountain of books.

He took a few deep breaths, realizing his thoughts were moving in a sloppy direction, towards haste and recklessness, and he forced himself back into a disciplined state of mind. The whole incident with Lena had unhinged him. Incidents like that were why he hated going to town. The more contact he had with the outside world, the more complicated things became, throwing his focus and equilibrium out of whack. He closed his eyes and calmed himself. Agitation was not a good base for doing research. Once he had his impatience in check, he headed downstairs, intent on finding reference to

Polar Piton in Tytamon's massive library as he knew there was no reference to the explorer in his own. He'd read every one and that name did not ring familiar to him at all.

The best way to find a book in Tytamon's library was to ask the ancient mage what he had on a given subject and then ask where it was. Tytamon knew every book he had, and nearly every page of every one as well, for, like Altin in his private library, Tytamon had read each at least once, and, more often, several times. But it was just Altin's luck that Tytamon was gone from Calico Castle at the time, forcing Altin to find what he needed on his own. Which meant it was going to take a lot of time.

Tytamon's vast collection of books was housed on seven floors of his enormous tower, each chamber circular and ringed with shelves stuffed with books, many of which dated back to the earliest days of the Magical Revolution, and some even older than that. Tytamon had been diligent in his early years, cataloguing all his books as he collected them, still enthusiastic in his relative youth and with the joy of creating such a massive resource as this would eventually become. And because of this youthful exuberance and discipline, the top three stories of his library each had several ledgers that listed books by title, general content description and approximate location in the room, which was at least something given that each chamber of Tytamon's huge tower was fifty paces across. The old man could pack a lot of volumes into a space like that, particularly when each room was filled with shelves placed so closely together there was barely room for Altin to walk between them without his shoulders brushing against the books.

Hoping for some luck, Altin went to these upper floors first. He spent a few hours going through the catalogues seeking something that suggested the possibility of finding some obscure reference that might lead him eventually to Polar Piton's work. But he found nothing. There was one reference to "Chills" in a work on the lowest of the three catalogued floors, but it had nothing that Altin could use. So he was forced to the lower four floors and perusing book by book. He tried sending Tytamon a telepathic request, but the old man's mind wasn't open to outside thoughts; he was either blocking or in discussions with someone else. Altin really wished the ancient mage would come home.

He spent the better part of twelve hours working through the shelves before hunger and fatigue got the best of him. He wasn't even a quarter way through the room. One room. He sighed and took himself down to the kitchen to get something to eat. Pernie was there, sitting by the fire.

"Hullo, Master Altin, sir," she greeted him, smiling wide. "I seen yer dragon again today, sir."

"Yes, he was here," Altin said, lifting the lid on a large stone trough that was enchanted with a cold spell for keeping food fresh. He spotted a portion of mutton left over from a few nights back and lifted it out. He realized Pernie was watching him and reminded himself that he was going to try to be nicer to the girl. "He was having his lunch," he added to that end.

Encouraged by this rare attention, Kettle's insistence that Pernie leave the mages alone dissipated like fog before a breeze, and she began to chatter on in earnest. "He's so big. I'm going to have one too one day you'll see, an' then when I'm a powerful wizard like you an' Master Tytamon, I'm going to fly into the mountains and breathe fire on all the orcs an' then there won't be no more an' no one will have to be afraid. I will, don't ya think, Master Altin? Someday, I mean. An' I'll kill them all too. Every last one."

"That's rather extreme, isn't it? Killing them all?" He set the mutton leg on a wooden tray and sliced off a large chunk. "Humans learned a long time ago not to kill every last one of anything. It's bad, Pernie. Even if what you want to kill seems evil at the time."

"Nipper says orcs is what killed my mom an' dad. He says orcs is nastiest of anything. Nipper says the world is better off if they was all dead. That's what he said an' he knows because he fought in the Orc Wars an' has a big scar on his chest. Did he ever show ya his scar because it runs all the way across his whole chest an' belly an' he could of died from orcs?" She was growing excited, and Altin could sense a headache coming on.

He returned the remainder of the mutton to the coldstone box and ate the portion he had cut as Pernie prattled on about the orcs in the hills and about magic and dragons and pretty much everything else that could possibly be discussed in the time it took to eat three slices of mutton and an apple from the basket near the window. When he was done, he smiled at her and tried to find a polite way to leave. Shouldn't Kettle be watching her?

"Well, I have to go back to work," he said at last. "You have a nice night, Pernie."

"You're suppose to have some water with yer food," Pernie said as he tried to leave. "Eight glasses a day for a man yer size. Kettle told me so an' she wouldn't never lie about that. I'm supposed to have six, but I already had mine."

Altin looked at her, bewildered, unsure if even hurricanes had so much wind. And what was he supposed to say to that? He wasn't thirsty. He knew, intellectually, that indulging the child was best, but that would just encourage her for the next time that they met. His purpose in being nice to her was not to endure more of her endless noise.

"I'm not really thirsty. I need to get back to work. So, good night."

"Ok, Master Altin, sir. Have a good night, sir. An' I won't say that ya didn't drink yer water like ya should neither 'cause Kettle gets to scolding if ya miss yer water or won't eat yer greens. So I won't say nothing, I promise." She smiled at him, a genuine full-body smile that was pure as a drop of dew.

He looked down at her and started to smile back. She was cute, he could admit that. He caught himself, however, and kept himself from being sucked in. He always got so uncomfortable around her. He shook it off. All of it. Besides, he had work to do. "Goodnight, Pernie." And with that he left. Several hours passed before he finally went to bed.

He woke early the next morning, just at the break of day, and went immediately back up to Tytamon's library and recommenced where he'd left off. A quick check had proved that Tytamon had not yet returned, and so Altin spent the rest of the day going through each book in turn, sliding them out, opening them, scanning sections for any hint of elemental or shielding spells, seeking the paired appearance of "P"s that would mark mention of Polar Piton's name. Anything at all. But he got nothing.

This really was a horrific way to keep a library, he reminded himself as he went along, much as he did on every occasion that found him on the lower four floors of Tytamon's library over the last eleven years. If Tytamon ever put him in charge of these, the first thing he would do would be to straighten them all out. The city libraries had the new catalogue systems with the enchanted divining mirrors installed. Walk up to the mirror, put your hands on the edge and look into the glass—the next thing you know, the shelf you need is reflected in the image at your back. It wasn't even that complicated of a spell to do if one was a diviner of even marginal skill. Altin was certain Tytamon could do it if he'd just be willing to spend the time. If it was left to Altin, he'd have to pay to have it done. Which, given the number of books, would cost a fortune and take an excruciatingly long time to carry off. He understood why Tytamon procrastinated though; each book had to be read into the spell, making the process a painfully laborious thing to do. Divining was always like that, and this was just another example of why Altin told himself he couldn't be bothered to take it up. Divination simply took too much time.

He stopped briefly for lunch—a hot meal at Kettle's insistence as she declared that he was looking "pinched and thin." She'd wandered into Tytamon's library looking for him, having not seen him in a couple of days, and would not be placated until Altin had something warm to eat. Apparently Pernie had ratted him out concerning the nature of yesterday's meal. After eating, he returned and spent several more hours trying desperately to find any reference to Polar Piton and his accursed protection spells. But still he couldn't find a thing, not even a mention of the elusive wizard's name.

Vexingly, Tytamon's trip was a long one, and the ancient wizard was four more days in returning by the time Altin finally saw him and could ask him for some help. He'd only gotten through a floor and a half of the un-catalogued books by the time Tytamon came home.

"Good afternoon, my boy," the ancient mage said cheerfully upon seeing Altin. His parchment skin looked tanned as if he'd been to some distant beach and there was distinct energy in his step. "What are we looking for?"

Altin glanced up at him and had to suppress his annoyance at the old man's healthy, pleasant tone. The chipper attitude seemed to mock Altin's miserable last few days. "Polar Piton," Altin said. "Anything on him at all. I haven't found a thing. I have more references to him in my small library than you do in this whole damn collection." He was being a bit melodramatic, he knew, but he did still have two-and-a-half floors to go, both of which were more than thrice the size of his collection on their own, and he felt it important to let his frustration through.

"Hmm. Polar Piton, you say." Tytamon stroked his moustache where it ran round his mouth and blended with his beard. He was too well rested to be bothered by his apprentice's surly tone. "Not familiar with the name. What's he famous for?"

"Nothing, really, just some arctic region stuff. Polar exploration mostly, I think. Pretty minor, but useful industrially."

"Ah. Well, perhaps that's why I haven't heard of him. Always a fire man myself. Never had the thing for the cold spells like you do."

"I like fire."

"I know. Not my point though. Anyway, I can save you looking any more. I don't think I have it. In fact I am certain that I don't."

"Damn. Then I'll have to go to Crown."

"If it matters, then indeed you will." He smiled happily, as if a great problem had been solved, annoying Altin to no end. "Say hello to Karroll if you run into her; I haven't seen her in an age."

"Let's hope I don't," Altin said, grimacing and hating how Tytamon spoke so familiarly of the Queen. And as if Altin was just going to trot up to the Queen's entourage and say, "Hey there, Tytamon says, 'hello,'" if he saw her coming down the street.

"Why not? She's a great old gal. How can you possibly not like the Queen?"

"Liking her has nothing to do with it. She makes me uncomfortable."

"Well she shouldn't. She's very easy to talk to you know. A magician of your stature needs to learn to be at home with the royals anyway. You'll be called before them often enough as time goes by. You will see."

"You might be right, but that doesn't mean I have to go out of my way to be with them right now."

Tytamon just laughed. "Fair enough, my boy. So when will you leave?"

"I'll leave now."

"Now? You're not going to teleport are you?"

"Not all the way." He turned his eyes towards the book that was in his hands.

"One day you're going to get caught and the teleporters are going to have you whipped. Or you're going to land inside a pig and that will be the end of it for you."

"I'll be fine. I do it in the air anyway. In flight, on Taot's back."

"You could land inside a bird."

"The bird would land inside us. But it won't. I mean, what are the odds? And I always look before I leap."

Tytamon started to say something, a word that began with a sibilant sound, but cut it off. "You'll do what you want, regardless of what I say. I hope you find your book."

"Me too."

With that the elderly magician turned and headed for the stairs. He looked tired suddenly, as if the rest he'd gotten from his trip had just been washed away.

"I am careful," Altin called to his back.

"Transportation Services has 'clean rooms' for a reason, Altin," the old magician said, standing in the door. "The entire system, of which you became a part when you joined the Teleporters Guild, was devised for a reason. The systems in place today were devised over centuries of slow, painful and meticulously wrought understanding. Much of it bought at horrible cost. TG's policy didn't just happen by mistake."

Altin moaned, annoyed. "I know. You think I didn't pay attention when I was there? I just don't feel like standing in line. And I don't want to pay for something that I can do myself, and with far less effort."

"It's not your money anyway."

Altin looked away, cheeks coloring, but then turned back. "You brought me here. I didn't ask to come."

"No, they brought you here."

"Whatever. You could have turned them down."

Tytamon recognized a pointlessly combative stance when he saw one; he'd seen enough of them in nearly eight hundred years to know. He smiled, a wan, resigned thing, and turned his back to go. "You'll do what you want, Altin. Good night."

Altin watched him until his feet, climbing up the slowly winding stairs, disappeared behind the lintel of the door. He blinked into the emptiness, wondering what had just gone wrong. He couldn't help thinking that he'd just done it again. Whatever "it" was. One thing was sure; he was getting tired of people making him feel like this. Really tired. With a grunt, he turned and stormed out.

Chapter 17

Altin appeared two leagues outside of Crown, Taot never having lost a wing-beat and already quite used to teleporting with Altin across the skies. Altin always prepared him for the jump, and the dragon seemed little phased by it anymore. They were very high up, and from this altitude the massive city was little more than a great blur of grays and browns packed into a box and surrounded by a patchwork of assorted fields whose various crops gave the whole scene the look of a giant earth-toned quilt.

Crown City sat at the junction of the bloated Sansun river and its largest tributary, the Decadent Limb, roughly a hundred leagues from Calico Castle. Spreading for fifty measures in every direction around the city were acres and acres of farmland, worked by a quarter-of-a-million serfs and vassals, and overseen by at least a half-thousand lords and barons, many of whom held titles rooted in dubiously royal blood. Inside the city lay the most modern and disparate assemblage of architecture as had ever been gathered in all the history of Prosperion. Where Leekant boasted unity or at least an overall architectural theme across its four quarters, Crown had nothing resembling a unifying style at all. In fact, the only aesthetic trend in

Crown was that there was no trend at all. Wood buildings stood next to marble, single-story next to nine. Thatched roofs, tile roofs, brass and beaten tin. It was as if the city's founders just threw open the gates and welcomed in anyone who had the ability or willingness to construct. That's not quite how it happened, but it had the same net effect. And yet, despite all this disparity, or perhaps because of it, the city was a uniquely sumptuous whole.

And located at the heart of the city lay the Royal Palace, an opulent undertaking that had required a hundred and sixty years, a thousand magicians and forty-four thousand men to build. Its highest spires reached nearly a half-measure into the sky, and it spanned an area encompassing a full square league. It was, in short, enormous. And there was not one modern amenity that it lacked. No room ever got above or below sixty-eight degrees. Rain never blew through its ever-open windows, and a lightning strike could not catch any of it on fire. In the massive grounds that surrounded it, its trees were the largest anywhere in the land, and it boasted an oak tree that stood over one hundred and eighty paces high and took four full minutes to walk around at the base. In addition, the Royal Gardens swarmed with birds from every corner of the world, including a few species brought from the shores of dangerous Duador and none of which could get past the bird-free wards that were enchanted to keep them on the grounds.

Beyond the palace gates lay the Royal Compound housing King Perfort's University, over nine hundred years old; the Duke of Dorvost Museum; the Magicians' Medical Institute; and, of course, the Royal Library, in which was located, among other things, the only collection of magical works larger than the one found in Tytamon's tower. The Royal Library, however, was not focused on magic alone and comprised a complex of twelve large buildings, each five stories high. It was said that the Queen owned a copy of every book that was ever put into print. And today, Altin really hoped that this was true. He'd wasted over a week trying to find Polar Piton's spell, and his patience was wearing thin.

He sent Taot a down request and the dragon began to slowly spiral towards the ground. Altin directed him to a little copse of trees roughly a measure down stream from the nearest farm and a spot that a quick sweep of a seeing spell had assured him was out of range of any curious eyes. If the locals became alarmed by the sight of a dragon swooping down, the Royal Guard of Crown would be called immediately. Altin knew for a fact that the Queen kept at least four N-class conjurers on duty at all times. He didn't want to dodge fireballs that big, and he was sure Taot felt the same. He just wanted to find a book.

Once they landed, he sent Taot a query as to whether the dragon preferred to be teleported home or to be left to hunt in the surrounding countryside. The dragon's reply was a general sense of aversion to the smell of so many people in a single place. Altin laughed, sending back an agreement with Taot's olfactory assessment of the human race. He cast a quick seeing spell to make sure Taot's lair was empty and then sent the dragon home.

Satisfied that Taot was taken care of, Altin began to walk towards the river, finally coming to the well-paved road that arced in from the fields beyond. The highway ran parallel to the water for a time before veering off once more towards the city gates, and as Altin trod upon it, he could not help but appreciate how good the workmanship in such matters had become. The paving stones were set evenly the entire way, perfectly cut and tightly fit with no rounded cobbles to bruise his feet, unlike back at home—although he had remembered to wear his shoes for this particular trip. The surface was smooth, leveled by magical planes, and the numerous carts and wagons trundling along made a fraction of the noise that they would had they been bumping over Leekant's cobbled streets. The progression of workmanship and magic was moving forward at an amazing rate these days.

A teamster passing by had seen Altin emerge from the copse of trees along the road and made some laughing remark about having to urinate himself but being more willing to wait than Altin was. Altin smiled and waved as the wagon passed him by. There was no point in pointing the error out.

It wasn't long before Altin had made his way into the city and through the busy streets leading into the Royal Compound. He went to the library's main building first and found a vacant catalogue mirror right away. He grasped the beautifully carved rosewood frame and let the words "Polar Piton" play across his mind. He had no need for divination of his own—the enchantment placed upon the mirror did all the work—and in a moment, behind himself in the reflection, he saw the building to which he needed to go. As he looked at the building in the mirror, its reflection shifted from a view of its façade to one of its interior, indicating a stairwell and a landing upon whose wall was a bronze plaque engraved with a large numeral four. As he made out the number on the plaque, the view in the mirror shifted once more to a row of shelves, showing the end of a row, and once more a bronze plaque, this one marked T.1037.a-T.4909.s. That was all Altin needed to see. The image remained for a few moments after he released the mirror frame, playing through the sequence once again, giving him time to take a strip of parchment from a stack beneath the mirror and quickly jot the numbers down. He replaced the quill in its inkwell and headed back outside.

Five minutes later found him standing at the shelves he'd just seen in the mirror, slightly out of breath for having run the entire way. Even with the directions from the enchanted mirror, it still took him almost an hour to find the right book. There were several with references to Polar Piton, but only one of them ended up having a spell that looked like it might work. The source, an autobiography in the man's own hand, included a spell titled, lamely enough, "Polar Piton's Perfect Parabolic Protection." Altin mused that it was the oddball explorer's penchant for such things that prevented his work from having become more mainstream—his writing was entirely absurd in many places and prone to rambling about his dogs and a woman named Euridia, whom he had apparently loved at some point in his distant youth, and who had clearly cost him any degree of fame because of the obsession that she had inspired, further evidence for Altin of the danger of forming that sort of deep personal bond. However, painful as the reading was, Altin did find the spell and, with some modifications of his own, he was convinced that he could make it work for his purposes.

He took the book to a copying room and began the arduous task of transcribing the spell. It was a seven-page spell and several of the sigils were worn with age. Copying it was the labor of nearly four hours, made so by Altin's decision to have the entire chapter that the spell was in rather than just the notes and by the fact that he took some rather copious notes from other chapters too.

When he was done at last, he could see through the window that the sky had grown dark outside. He sighed. He wouldn't have time to use it now. But he knew that that was best. He was tired anyway, had been tired before he came. No sense getting in a rush and making a "fishbowl" that might leak.

As he contemplated the long walk out of the city that would take him far enough away to teleport back home, he realized that he really should pay a visit to his friend Aderbury first. If Aderbury, or more specifically his wife Hether, found out that Altin had been here and not stopped by, the couple would never let him live it down. Aderbury was a gifted young transmuter that Altin had met during his mandatory service in the Queen's army a few years back. Of all the magicians in his regiment, Aderbury was the only one Altin still kept in contact with, and even that, admittedly, was not often enough. Altin was just too busy most of the time. However, it was still relatively early, and Aderbury wasn't too far out of Altin's way, so off he went.

Aderbury worked in the industrial section of Crown in a large building owned by an architectural firm called Castles, Inc. Aderbury was the firm's fortification pro and there were few men on Kurr who could match his skill for melding stone. The man was an artist, and he was a favorite of the Queen. He was a pretty decent conjurer too, and he and Altin had had a great time showing up the rest of their regiment in casting fireballs the size of houses and ice storms that could make a snowman cry.

Like Altin, Aderbury was a workhorse, and it was no surprise that Altin found him still hard at work in his small office at Castles, Inc., when he arrived.

"They still have you stuffed in this little room?" Altin said as he walked in without bothering to knock.

Aderbury looked up from his design, an expression of delight expanding on his tanned face. "Altin! What an unexpected surprise. What brings you to town?"

"A book. What else?"

Aderbury stood and rushed to clutch Altin in a great bear hug, pounding him roughly on the back. "All that reading's why you haven't got yourself a woman yet," Aderbury said, holding Altin at arm's length to look him up and down. "You could definitely use some sun." He laughed and let Altin go, but then his thick eyebrows rose suddenly above his large brown eyes as inspiration struck. "Dorianna! You have to let me set you up with Hether's new friend. You should see this woman, Altin. By all the gods, you've never seen a bosom so spectacular." Aderbury made a rounding gesture way out in front of his own chest to amplify his point. "And she can cook too. She's almost as good as Hether. Probably be as good if she had someone to practice on." He gave Altin a wink and then, turning, grasped a chair from a desk that sat opposite the one he'd been working at. Altin gave the empty desk a withering look.

"You still have to work with Thadius in here?" he asked as Aderbury offered him a seat. "You built the Queen's private bathroom, for heaven's sake. Why don't they give you your own space?"

"Because Thadius is the boss's nephew. You know that. And he's a Four. I'm just a Two."

"You're a Y-class transmuter. Thadius is what, a C?"

"He's a G. And he's still a Four, my friend. You know how it works. It's letters *around* the dial in this town. That and who you know."

"Well, you do know the Queen."

"Yes. I do. I thought she was going to ask me to work at the Palace full time after the bathroom job. That would have been a nightmare."

"Why? You'd be rich."

"Until I died of boredom. I don't want to spend my life walking around fusing cracks and making miniature castles for little princelings to play war in. No thank you. At least here we get real work sometimes. And, you'll love this, I heard that the Illusionists are going to build an amusement park down in Murdoc Bay. The old man is supposed to put in a bid. I don't know who besides us could build it, except maybe Parson's Palace down in Hast. But those guys are terrible corner-cutters."

"An amusement park in Murdoc Bay? Why down there? That's a pirates' den."

"Pirates have kids too." Aderbury let out a hearty laugh and jumped out of the seat he had only just resumed. "Let's go have an ale or five. I'll send a lizard to Hether and let her know I'm going to be late. Maybe I'll tell her to call Dorianna too." He grinned lasciviously. "They can make us something to eat afterwards, to soak up the ale." He stooped and scribbled something on a scrap of parchment and then crossed the room to a small cage sitting atop a cedar filing cabinet.

Altin rose and pointed in the direction of Aderbury's slightly bulbous belly. "I know what you're thinking, and, no. Besides, I don't want a woman. I'd end up looking like you. I think not. Kettle's bread is bad enough."

Aderbury looked as if he'd just been struck a mighty blow. "What? This is pure muscle." He rubbed his belly for a moment then made a show of flexing. He really was a burly man. His arms, shoulders and back were broad and strong from lifting so much rock. Exquisite transmuter as he might be, his work did not allow him to levitate every stone. "Besides, you can't say no because Hether already expects you. Don't be rude."

"No she doesn't. She doesn't even know I'm here."

Aderbury just snorted and reached into the cage, pulling out a small mottled-brown lizard, not much longer than an unclasped woman's bracelet and with a body hardly thicker than one of Altin's middle toes. Aderbury deftly tied the note to the lizard's back with a piece of string taken from a jar sitting near the cage. When the note was secure, Aderbury whispered something to the lizard that was too low for Altin to hear. "She does now," said Aderbury with a triumphant expression as he tossed the lizard to the floor. The instant its tiny suction-cupped feet struck the wooden planks, it was gone from sight, leaving Altin to wonder if it had run out, gone invisible or cast some animal version of a teleporting spell. "Homing lizard," Aderbury said, grinning at Altin's quizzical look. "What will they think of next, eh?"

Altin was staring at the floor where the lizard should have been. "Where on Kurr did you get that thing?"

"Oh, they're quite the rage," said Aderbury. "It's one of the advantages of living in the real world rather than out in the woods like you. Access to new ideas. They've been a big item now for about eight months. They say they're actually Z-class 'porters. Probably better than you." He laughed at this last part.

Altin frowned at the absurdity of the idea. Z-class animals. Nothing innate had that much power.

"Definitely smarter than you," continued Aderbury, still chuckling as he spoke. "You should read your *Teleporter's News* some time. They just ran an article on them. You still have to keep up with things you know, even out there in the sticks. Everyone's got one now. Some people even get three or four. You should get one too."

"Yeah, well, I've fallen a bit behind in my reading, what with my work and all."

"Yeah, about that. How's the quest for Luria going anyway? I didn't have time to ask."

Altin didn't have time to answer either, as it was at that moment that Thadius Thoroughgood walked in the room.

Thadius, a tall and strikingly handsome man in his late twenties, lean and perhaps a bit too well kept, smiled a flawlessly toothy grin at Aderbury and then, allowing the smile to collapse into a sneer, gave the barest of head inclinations to Altin as well. "Aderbury, dear boy, you're still here and working late. You must take a break, I absolutely insist. Let's go have a glass of wine, shall we? You can even bring your friend there if he'd like to come along. We wouldn't want to leave poor Altin all alone." He drug out the last word, emphasizing Altin's lack of success with persons of the opposite sex. "Perhaps if I buy enough wine, we can persuade some scamp to have a go with him just for charity's sake." He gave a great laugh and clapped

Aderbury on the shoulder as if his joke was the best one ever made.

"Actually, I've already got plans, Thad, but thanks," said Aderbury. "I'll see you tomorrow though, maybe we'll have a glass then, all right?"

Thadius rolled his eyes back towards Altin. "I see. An evening spent at home with him, eh? The misses and all that rot? Old time's sake, I suppose. Delightfully boring, I'm sure. Count me out."

"I didn't hear him invite you," Altin said, unable to refrain.

"Of course not, my boy. I have a standing invite. Don't I, old chap?" He fixed Aderbury with an expectant look.

Aderbury nodded. "Of course, Thad. Anytime." Both Aderbury and Altin knew that Thadius would never take him up, so it was but a little thing to say the words.

It was at that moment that the tiny lizard, or *a* tiny lizard, appeared on Aderbury's shoulder and nibbled him on the ear. Feeling the gentle pinch, Aderbury reached up and gingerly plucked the creature from his tunic and placed it on his desk. Altin could see that there was still a note tied to the diminutive creature's back.

Aderbury read it and flashed a wink to Altin. "Well, Thad, it's time for us to go. Tomorrow then?"

"What's for dinner tonight? I'm suddenly feeling starved for Hether's humble cooking charm," came Thadius' unanticipated reply. Aderbury looked momentarily aghast.

"Duck's liver," said Altin, jumping in. "Duck's liver and mongooseberry pie. My special request since I don't get to town that much."

Altin knew from their time in the service that there was nothing Thadius hated more than duck's liver and mongooseberry pie. The only time Altin remembered ever seeing Thadius drop his eternally supercilious air was when their platoon had been stationed in Hast during the town's annual Mongooseberry Festival. There had been nothing else to eat. He, and most of the rest of the squad, had delighted in watching the pompous baron's son wrinkle up his nose as they were served the same thing, duck's liver and mongooseberry pie, every meal, three times daily for three straight days. Altin had never seen someone come so close to willingly starving themselves to death as Thadius had done. And it was clear from the expression on his face that he had no intention of eating it tonight.

"However, starved as I may be," said Thadius, always quick on his feet, "I think I'd prefer the company of Esmarelda Mendinghand to the two of you." He fixed Altin with a nasty look, then turned back to Aderbury with a smile. "Tomorrow indeed, but it will have to be your treat for making me wait another day. Good night." And with that he swept out of the room.

They both watched him go in silence before Altin shook his head and chuckled behind his teeth. "How do you put up with that day after day?"

"He's a one-trick troll. Once you've seen it, it's easy not to be impressed."

Turning back to the note from Hether, he crossed out her lines and added one of his own. "An ale or two, and then we're on our way," he spoke aloud as wrote. He tied the message onto the lizard's back and then carried the little beast over and set it on Altin's shoulder without a word of warning first.

"What are you doing?" Altin asked.

"Getting you imprinted in its amazing little head." Aderbury leaned in near Altin's ear and whispered, "Altin Meade." He stroked the lizard's back a few times as it sat there under Altin's ear and he repeated Altin's name a few times while continuing to stroke the lizard's tiny head. The lizard seemed unimpressed.

"That's weird," Aderbury concluded a moment later.

"What's weird?"

"I thought you'd never seen one of these."

"I haven't."

"Well, apparently you have, because it's not acting like it does when it imprints someone new. Usually they make this chirping sound to let you know they have your scent. Or whatever it is they do."

"No," Altin said. "I've never seen one before. Honestly."

"Well, this one seems to think you're already in the network."

Altin raised a querulous brow. "Network?"

"Yeah. Once one of them knows you, they all do. That's why the system's been expanding so fast. Some sort of group reptilian mind or something."

"Well, I'm not in it, despite what your little friend seems to think."

"Well, let's try," he said. He took the lizard back and moved across the room. Whispering to it briefly, he tossed it down at the floor and a moment before it hit the wood it was already on Altin's shoulder nibbling at his ear.

Altin laughed and reflexively took the lizard away before it could have another bite. It didn't bite hard, but having a lizard chewing on one's earlobe was the kind of thing one had to be prepared for. Aderbury, however, was clearly amused.

"Damn that's fun. I'm so glad we bought this thing. Now give him back. Or even better, say, 'Hether,' and toss him down."

Altin looked askance at his friend who nodded, encouraging him to try. "Just whisper. They have very sensitive ears."

"Hether," Altin whispered and dropped the lizard to the floor. It was gone in a blink, and soon after, back at Aderbury's home, Hether had her kettles on the fire. Having no way to escape his friend's unyielding invitation, as

Aderbury would not allow him to "skulk back to his work without at least one night among the living," Altin found himself having an entirely delightful evening amongst his friends. His only stipulation had been that Dorianna be left out of the mix, for which he paid in jests throughout the night.

Chapter 18

Orli never wanted to be a medic, and she certainly hated the position now. It was only because she was so inept mechanically, and because she was a complete washout with firearms, that she'd been forced into an assignment involving triage in the event that things went bad. And things were bad. Her aversion to blood was never a problem before because nothing had ever happened before that would require her to be around it, but now something had. Something horrible, and with a scant three-week medic's training—completed four years ago and not practiced since—and with a degree in botany, issued aboard a spaceship no less, she found herself elbows deep in gore.

The large Hostile's projectile had struck the ship's upper deck and crushed an entire cargo hold. Several crew members were killed instantly, and even more were being brought to sick bay with broken bodies and mangled or missing limbs. Blunt trauma was everywhere. Orli scrambled back and forth at the beck and call of virtually every nurse on the staff, running for bandages and assorted medicines. Three times she was asked to hold pressure on wounds that squirted hot blood onto the exposed skin of her forearms where her sleeves and gloves didn't quite touch. The whole thing made her dizzy, and when the young man with the missing left foot began to scream and weep and beg, she had to run for a bucket lest she puke right there in the hall.

There was so much screaming. Big men, strong muscular laborers, were reduced to crying and calling for their mothers, wives or both. She held one woman's hand and watched her slowly die. Doctor Singh had whispered, "It's too late for this one," as he'd brushed aside Orli's pleading hand reaching out to him as he'd moved past her in the rush. Orli took the time to weep for the woman and watched in helpless horror as the life faded gradually from the woman's eyes.

The ship was rocked occasionally as they worked, the orbs not letting up in their attacks, but in the three long hours since the cargo bay was crushed, there had not been another blow as telling as that one had proved to be. Slowly, one by one, the medical staff caught up to the glut of wounded, and after a few more hours of arduous, heartbreaking work, those that would make it were all treated and resting as comfortably as could be. Two-thirds of the ship's small hospital beds were taken, and Doctor Singh could be heard complaining that the bridge crew had better do their job and finish those orbs off once and for all. There simply wasn't room for another mistake.

Orli cleaned up as best she could, and flopped doggedly down in a chair at one of the nurses' desks. The computer was patched to the bridge screen, as most on board were, and Orli watched through heavy-lidded eyes as the ship's beleaguered bridge crew continued with the fight.

Poor Roberto, she thought. At least I can take a break. And his work had started well before hers. She sighed and laid her chin upon her hands, folded on the desk, and watched the scene play out.

Apparently they'd managed to destroy one of the larger orb's projectiles as the fight went on and now both orbs were operating on just one shaft apiece. The orbs had gotten smarter about retrieving them apparently, but it seemed both of them were taking something of a beating every time. Orli scanned the skies for signs of another ship, but still no one else had arrived. The delay was aggravating. Where were they? They were several hours past the two-day mark and Orli found herself hoping someone would be reprimanded for having drifted so far away. It also occurred to her that they might be dogging it, hoping to avoid a fight. That made her grit her teeth. She'd better not ever find out that was true or she'd mangle someone with her own hands.

She watched as the two orbs swept in for yet another pass. It seemed as if they might be moving a little slower than before. It gave her hope that they could tire. Red lasers striped the night and diverted both mineral beams from their intended course. More nukes streaked off after them in what was becoming a familiar dance, both sides waiting for the other to make a mistake. And it appeared as she looked on that this might be that moment.

It was with an impending sense of hope that Orli realized, watching the larger orb chase down its diverted projectile shaft, that it was moving far too slowly. It seemed to be struggling just to catch up to its weapon, much less to pass it by. The nukes showed no sign of anything like fatigue, only the hot blue fire of their burners pushing them towards the shaft.

The orb managed to struggle out in front of its projectile finally, but only barely, and the Earth missiles were only moments from blowing it to bits. Orli watched, holding her breath as the orb softened up its trailing face and allowed itself to slow. Its projectile touched it gently and began to slip inside. The nukes were only a dozen meters behind. Orli could tell the orb was trying not to let the reclamation process slow it down, but she also knew that it didn't have much choice. If a bee required its stinger to be alive, this one might just be out of luck. The *Aspect's* missiles closed in on it ruthlessly and exploded with devastating effect.

The orb did not have the time, or perhaps did not have the energy, to shift its skin to its defensive state. The missiles hit it while roughly a quarter of the shaft was still outside its main mass and caught it with the soft spot still totally exposed. Following the blinding flash, the orb burst like a grapefruit dashed angrily upon the ground, splitting wide open and spewing out glowing red strands of its innards, which Orli would have thought were made from lava had she not known better than to think such a silly thing. She let out a whoop of glee. Shortly after, the entire sick bay, patients and providers alike, were howling at their monitors, watching as the orb slowly bled out its glowing guts. Like the sparks from the broken communications dish, the orbs phosphorescent entrails were cooled to darkness by the grip of icy space, and in the course of just an hour, the entire orb was frozen as solid as a block of ice.

The smaller orb, apparently taken aback by its compatriot's unexpected fate, hovered at a distance for the duration of the hour. But, perhaps on seeing the last bit of heat sucked from the shell of its sundered friend, it launched one more missile-hurling attack. Roberto easily swatted the missile aside with the lasers and launched the nuke that would chase the orb's pounding shaft of rock down and turn it into dust.

Orli watched the monitor breathlessly as the missile's blue light streaked off into the night. She heard herself cheering it on again, as she had done before, but this time the orb did not give chase. Orli knew that something was wrong as soon as she realized that the orb had stopped and now hovered midway down the length of the ship rather than reclaiming its weapon as it had always done before. It was just floating there, a few meters above the hull. She watched with gritted teeth and squinting eyes, hoping that maybe it had just resigned itself to its fate. But she knew she was wrong, and she watched with horror as the orb lowered itself slowly closer to the ship. She could see the flicker of the shields as the weakened defenses—powered only by batteries and generators with the ship's engines still offline, and likely close to drained from such a prolonged and brutal fight—attempted to hold the orb at bay.

The orb began to flatten itself out against the shield, spreading like pancake batter in a pan, softening and losing everything about itself that had once resembled a giant flying rock. As it flattened, it lightened in color too, becoming golden, almost tan, and then, once it was no more than a few meters thick, it began to pulse near the center of its mass.

It seemed to still hover above the ship's metal hull now, but Orli knew that the remaining distance was only given to them by the shields. The space between the flattened orb, now looking for all the world like a jellyfish pressed against window glass, was the only thing keeping it from contact with the ship. And there was something pushing slowly through the shield, something right from the center of the orb. Orli squinted at the monitor, pressing her face almost against the screen before she thought to magnify the view.

"Why don't they just shoot it off?" she heard a patient somewhere behind her say.

"We can't target ourselves," came someone else's dismal reply. "Who would have thought that would ever be something to regret?"

Sure enough, the ship's lasers could not target the Hostile clinging to its hull, and ever so slowly, the orb began working a small part of itself gently through the ship's plasma field. Its progress was painfully slow, and Orli could see the flashing lights of the ship's alarm systems change to indicate a new form of attack. The complementary call came across the loudspeaker a moment later, warning the crew to prepare for possible boarding and small arms combat.

Not taking her eyes from the screen, Orli felt at her hip for her required sidearm. Of course she wasn't wearing it. She hated guns. Which was just as well, she was probably the worst shot on the ship, if not in the entire fleet. Guns scared her. Who would have thought a beam of light could make such a horrible hissing noise, and the conventional rounds? Please. Those were awful. They were practically loud enough to make her ears bleed, and they kicked harder than the hydraulic rams that closed the loading dock doors. No thank you. However, right now having one didn't seem like such a bad idea, and she suddenly wished she'd paid a little more attention in firearms class, or at least to Roberto, who was always begging her to accompany him to the range.

"Oh well," she said aloud, rising from the chair. "If it comes down to me having to save the ship with a pistol, we're probably better off dead. The irony alone would be too great for the fleet to survive."

Doctor Singh came up behind her and placed a hand on her shoulder. Apparently he'd heard her talking to herself. "I'm right there with you on that one," he agreed, moving past her and into the tiny room that served as his office. She watched him open a drawer and pull his own standard issue Colt M-7XR sidearm from where it had been since the day the fleet left Earth. "You better go get it, just the same," he said. "You never know. Irony has its own particular appeal."

"True," she said, returning his smile and feeling a little better despite the knot of fear that was churning in her guts. "I'll be right back."

He nodded and with that she ran back down to the nursery and her lab. Her own sidearm, like Doctor Singh's, was kept safely in a drawer, put away for fear that she might accidentally blow someone's arm off, or perhaps just one of her own. She strapped the belt and holster awkwardly around her slender hips and buckled the thigh strap securely about her leg. The whole thing was absurdly heavy for its size, most of the weight being due to the laser's battery pack, which had likely lost its charge long ago; which also meant that if she had to use the damned thing, she would have to shoot its thunderous conventional rounds. God, she thought as she pulled the pistol from the holster and ejected the clip to make sure it was at least still loaded, please not that; I think I'd rather wrestle the aliens down by hand than have to shoot them with this awful thing. The clip was full and she slid it back into place, pressing it until it clicked. Holstering it, she was now as battle ready as she had ever been. With a sigh towards the peaceful, intellectual sanctum of her experimental tent, she ran back up to the infirmary to see what else was going on.

Alarms were ringing all over the ship by the time she finally arrived. The view on the monitor showed that the orb had finally worked completely through the shields and now it had its proboscis-like appendage attached firmly to the hull. The tip of the orb that was physically touching the ship had thickened up at the point of contact and looked something like a plunger or perhaps a bolt standing on its head. Orli stood beside Doctor Singh as they watched it begin to twist slightly from side to side. Smoke could be seen curling away around the edges of the thickened portion, and, after about twenty minutes of that, Lieutenant Hartford's voice came over the ship's speakers once again. "The hull has been breached," she said, and that was it. The ringing of the alarms was all there was to fill the silence. No one in the ship's infirmary spoke.

She found herself clutching Doctor Singh's forearm as she watched, and, catching herself when he gave a little grunt, she released him, apologizing for the four moon-shaped cuts pressed into his flesh. He nodded but did not take his eyes from the screen for quite some time. When he finally did, it was only to look at the communications com, anticipating a new wave of calls for help.

"I suggest you get a bit of rest," he said. "Ten minutes is better than none, and this might be a very, very long night."

Looking into the monitor at the scene outside, at the orb whose flattened mass now pulsed against the ship, she agreed. As she watched it out there, a smear of color against a vast sheet of speckled black, she realized that it was all just one long night—one long, miserable night. And there was something in the pulsing, the rhythmic throbbing of the monster mounted on her ship, that suggested daylight was never going to come. She said as much to Doctor Singh, who failed to answer for leaning down very close to the image on the screen.

At first she thought he was just watching their fates being forever screwed by whatever that orb was doing to their ship, but after a moment Doctor Singh let out a grunt that had the sound of hope. "Look," he said, leaning away from the monitor and zooming in the view on a section of stars beyond the orb. "Look there, that spot of light."

Orli leaned in and saw it too; it looked like a large star, but growing bigger by the moment.

"It's the *Sarajevo*," the doctor announced. "They're here. Finally, someone's here!"

The *Sarajevo* loomed larger and larger until, after what seemed at least a thousand years, Orli could finally make it out by its features rather than its lights. It came closer, seeming sluggish to her after having watched the orbs move so quickly through the same expanse of space, and when it was in range, two bright laser beams shot out and played upon the surface of the orb still pulsing against the *Aspect's* hull.

The orb split in places along its surface, steaming and bubbling, seeming almost to boil wherever the lasers burned its skin. Small blobs of the lava substance ejected from the cuts, forming glowing globes that floated away to be extinguished by the freezing darkness. She watched as the orb jerked and writhed under the onslaught, and she wondered why it insisted on holding on, wondered if perhaps it had got stuck, or worse, hadn't unloaded all its soldiers onto the *Aspect's* decks. It lingered for a few seconds more, but then finally it released its hold, slowly retracting its proboscis and then moving quickly away from the ship where it resumed its familiar spherical form. Once reformed, Orli could see that the orb's surface was riddled with crevices, gouges and grooves, sorely damaged and wasting no time in shifting its surface to the reflective obsidian glass. The *Sarajevo's* lasers winked out, useless now, and Orli once more marveled at how the orbs managed to shift their shapes and textures as they did. Missiles emerged from the *Sarajevo's* underbelly a few seconds later and rocketed towards the orb, as did a pair from the *Aspect's* arsenal as well.

Apparently unwilling, or unable, to bear the brunt of four more nuclear impacts, the orb shot off into the night. Orli watched it go and allowed herself a smile. She wondered how long the orb could run as she found herself once again cheering for a nuke. "Blow it to bits," she muttered as she watched the missiles go. "Blow it to goddamn bits."

Once the blue dots of the rockets were out of sight, she turned and faced the row of patient-laden beds. There were still a few unused. She glanced up at the ship status lights that continued to flash above the door. She wondered if there was a battle taking place somewhere on the ship. She would have heard by now had there been an alien invasion on the upper decks. Wouldn't she? She sighed. Maybe the *Sarajevo* had made it just in time. Maybe those beds would stay empty after all.

Chapter 19

The more times he read it, the more Polar Piton's Perfect Parabolic Protection spell looked to be precisely what Altin needed. If it did exactly what the enigmatic arctic explorer said it did in his notes, creating a "perfect parabolic shield, anchored firmly to the ground and impervious to sun, wind and cold," the spell could serve to make Altin's fishbowl—or manbowl as the case may be—highly functional. The spell description further claimed that "all aspects of the environment within the shield shall remain constant within the dome unless acted upon by countermeasures or other magical means." He wasn't completely sure what that meant, but he assumed that it referred to air temperature and humidity. There was something that followed about how a cooking fire would not warm up the inside of the dome (or else it would—the writing in the original book had been hard to make out during Altin's transcription; the text was blurred, and whatever had come after that campfire line was rendered completely indecipherable by the passage of time). Piton should have cast the spell on the book, Altin thought when he'd been copying it at the time. But nonetheless, he had what he needed now.

Altin had been studying the spell all morning, or what

was left of the morning after having a long night in Crown enjoying the hospitality of Aderbury and his wife—after which he found himself, as usual, wondering why it was he didn't go see them more. Regardless, the work of a few hours studying, despite a mild, ale-induced headache, made him familiar enough with Polar Piton's spell and its components to try casting it.

The spell called for two small beads of glass, components which Altin had in abundance in a jar in the lowest room of his tower. He ran down, retrieved the jar and was back in his room panting moments later ready for a go at Polar Piton's shield. Holding a glass bead in each hand as the spell required, he carefully re-read the main incantation from the book laying open on the table near the ever present loaf of bread. Confident that he had it right, he focused on a large flagstone near his bed and cast the spell. The cast was complicated, and it took him several minutes to chant it all despite his intention of making his first version very small. But finally it was done, and Altin opened his eyes to see what he had made.

Apparently he'd made nothing.

"What the...?" he muttered, running through the incantation in his mind. He carefully went over each part in his head, checking it against his notes. He hadn't done anything wrong; he'd spoken it precisely as he'd written it down. He wondered if maybe he'd made some kind of transcription error. He really didn't want to go back to Crown.

He went over to the flagstone and gingerly reached out his hand. Maybe it was there, just invisible to the eye. His hand touched something solid where he'd thought the shield should be, something that flickered at his touch. He let out a sigh of relief. All that worry for nothing.

He tapped the invisible surface more soundly and the shield flickered once again, revealing in shimmering outline that the flagstone was now capped by a dome of energy. The shield was longish and roughly cylindrical, like an upturned drinking glass, but with a rounded top and encasing an area about a pace across and not much higher than Altin's knees. He laughed triumphantly. "Wonderful!" he said.

He laid his hand flat against the surface; it felt solid, although there was no temperature at all. He rapped on it with his knuckles and found that the contact made no sound of its own. Interesting, he thought, I wonder how strong it is. He looked around for something to strike it with but, finding nothing suitable, had to run upstairs and retrieve a seeing stone from one of his crates.

Back in his room he struck the shield firmly with the stone. It resisted the blow entirely, shimmering briefly with the contact but showing no signs of stress. Altin gave it another whack. Still nothing. He began to beat upon it resoundingly, even stepping back and hurling the stone at the dome with all his might. The shield held firm.

"Well, it's strong," he said to himself. "I wonder how something like this stayed hidden for so long." But recalling the generally inane nature of Polar Piton's notes, and by implication probably the man himself, Altin suspected he already knew the reason why.

It was then that he noticed a length of straw, tumbled to the floor from his battered old mattress, lying on the flagstone, half in and half out of the shield. He wondered if he could pull it out.

He went round to where the golden strand protruded from the base of the shield and gave the end of the straw a gentle tug. It did not budge. He pulled a bit harder, but he knew instinctively that the straw would break before it could pull through. It would, however, slide up and down easily enough. Altin spent a few moments experimenting with that incidental discovery and found that he could move the straw around the dome in any direction that he liked—up, down and around, as fast or as slow as he wanted—but he could not pull it out. Nor could he push it back through. He wasn't sure what it meant, but he made a note of it on his copy of the spell, along with remarking on the dome's apparent strength. It amused him to think that others might one day read his work, just as he now read Polar Piton's work, and it was nice to be part of the chain. He wondered if Polar Piton would be happy that his spell was once again in service for exploration's cause. He decided that the adventurous man most assuredly would.

Satisfied that the spell would serve as he had hoped, he dismissed the magic, prepared to move the experiment to the next phase. But first he needed a new surrogate to send up to the moon. Lacking another mouse, he ran down to the stables and out to the goat pens just beyond. He searched out a small black and white kid and chased it around the pen for a while. It was as if the little creature knew what Altin had in mind as it darted to and fro, avoiding his clutches whenever he came near. "Knavish beast," Altin spat as the kid scampered beyond his grasp for a fifth straight time. Why were the simple things always more complicated than they were supposed to be?

He approached it slowly this time, knees bent, balanced as he moved with arms out to either side. "Come on now," he said soothingly. "This is a rare opportunity for you." He got within a step of the goat, his feet making sucking sounds in the muck. The goat watched him closely, its brown eyes large and curious, white lashes blinking studiously. "Come on," Altin said again, leaning in and then, snakelike, shot his hand forward to catch it by the scruff. The kid scampered away, escaping along the fence.

"Infernal beast! You're supposed to be domesticated, don't you know?"

He lunged after the animal again with similar results, and it was a matter of some ten minutes before he finally caught it, eventually pinning it against the gate with his leg in a rather awkward piece of luck. But at least he had it in his grasp.

The goat kicked and squirmed and twisted in his grip, bleating loudly, making noise as if Altin were torturing it with thumbscrews and a hot iron. Altin was embarrassed by how much effort and commotion it took to get the goat up into his room, and he did so with utmost speed lest anyone see him so belabored by a goat.

Eventually, however, he succeeded in getting to his chamber, and he decided it best to bind the wiry beast up before he set it down and risked having it run away again. He had no intention of chasing the little rascal around the tower all day long. He carried it to his bed and plunked it onto a blanket in which he quickly and tightly rolled the bleating goat up, swaddling it like a newborn babe. With its legs buckled and pinned against its body, the goat was finally forced to settle down. It lay there, resigned, panting heavily and allowing Altin to at last resume his work with Polar Piton's spell.

Altin took the bundled goat and set it down on the flagstone he'd used before, and once again he cast Polar's shield upon the spot. When it was done, he peered in at the goat to see if it was suffering any undue stress. It appeared just as it had before; its mouth opening occasionally to let out another irritated bleat—although silent, as the sound did not come out through the shield—but beyond that, nothing out of sorts. Altin decided it was time to send the encapsulated creature up to Luria.

Since it had been awhile since he'd last cast the Send Other spell, he went and got the book so that he might have another look. He spent some time reviewing it to make sure he had it right, and when he was done, he sent the goat on its way. Altin heard the pop of air as the shield, the goat and the flagstone all vanished at the completion of his chant.

Now for a look! He raced upstairs to the scrying basin and conjured the view of the goat sitting next to the original seeing stone.

The image came into the water, and Altin winced as he watched the goat writhing about and struggling against the blanket in which it was bound. It flopped about like a fish on land, and Altin felt the cold grip of dread as he witnessed it floundering beneath the dome, kicking and fighting within the blanket, apparently in great distress. Now what had he missed?

After several agonized moments of thrashing, the kid broke free of the blankets and scrambled to its feet. It stood staring out into the barren expanse of Luria's dark landscape, its mouth opening and closing repeatedly as Altin watched. It's gasping, Altin thought with growing horror. It's suffocating, drowning in the air that is not air.

Chills running through him, and waves of guilt, he stood up from the basin, prepared to bring the creature back. But just as he did, the goat stopped gasping and turned and looked around. It walked over to the other side of its enclosure, stopping to nudge the blanket with its nose along the way. It opened its mouth again, once, then nibbled at its hip, scratching an itch. Altin leaned back down, watching.

The goat began moving its mouth again, and Altin realized after a moment more that it was not gasping for air at all: it was complaining, bleating noiselessly into the night, likely calling for its dam. It went on like that for quite some time, but eventually it stopped. Apparently resigned to its fate, it turned and paced around its tiny little space beneath the dome for a while. There was only so much room within the magical confines, and a complete circuit took only a few steps to bring the goat all the way around. Despite the pointlessness of its exercise, the goat paced round and round anyway, until it finally grew weary of that as well. Then it turned back towards the middle and lowered its nose to the blanket lying on the stone again. It nudged the rumpled cover with its snout and then decided to take a bite.

Altin let out a cry of glee. The goat was fine. The spell had worked and the goat had just been frightened for a bit. Polar's shield worked and had proven that perhaps it was a "perfect" protection after all. Altin was ecstatic and began immediately to make plans to send himself up as soon as he possibly could, but, in the name of caution, he decided to leave the goat up there until after dinner to be safe. He would check on it then, and, if all was well, he would be taking its place up there tonight. In the meantime he still had work to do.

The first thing he had to do was to cast a version of the dome large enough to accommodate himself. He spent some time debating on just where it was that he should stand, but it occurred to him that he really didn't want to be up there like the goat, standing in a space hardly big enough to move.

He went back down to the notebook where he had meticulously transcribed Polar's shield spell and looked it over carefully. There was nothing in there that indicated any maximum capacity for the spell, and Altin found himself calculating what it would take to cast one large enough to envelope his entire tower. It was a simple matter of exponential mana draw, and once he'd figured it out, he decided to give his larger version a try.

He went back up to the battlements and began once more to cast a Polar's dome, this time over the tower as a whole. His larger version took quite a bit longer to cast, but, with patience and a few moments of nearly losing the delicate strands of mana required to craft the protective spell, he finally got it done. He opened his eyes and looked out to see what he had made.

But there was nothing. He had a moment's panic, but then realized how absurd his distress was. Of course he couldn't see it. He'd already been through this once. He looked about for something to throw and found the pebble he'd used when he'd first started experiments with the Liquefying Stone. He threw it over the wall and watched it as it flew. It traveled several paces out from the parapet before striking the inner surface of the shield and dropping straight to the ground below. Altin saw the faintest flicker just before the pebble fell. He gave another whoop. It did work. He'd cast it perfectly.

He heard a tinny echoing sound just as he gave his little rejoicing cry, and he turned to watch a bird fluttering wounded to the ground. Apparently it had struck the dome from without and knocked itself nearly out.

Altin grimaced in its direction and shrugged an apology to its tumbling form. Another victim in the name of progress, he tried to tell himself. It was, however, interesting to note that he had heard the sound of the impact from here inside. He told himself to add that to his notes when next he went downstairs: sound came into the dome but did not go out. That made him wonder; perhaps he should check to see if he could teleport objects in and out of the parabolic shield. He decided to use his familiar piece of gravel, so he teleported himself down to where he'd seen it land.

He appeared in the knee-deep grope of Lady Synthia's impudent vines just outside his tower. The vines writhed about, trying to coil around him, but too weakened by the fading magic of their aged enchantment to do him any serious harm. He fumbled about for a moment, arms plunged into the twisting mass, and finally found the little stone. Looking through the shield, which he had to locate by reaching blindly forward until he touched it with his hand, he spotted a large mushroom growing just a step or two outside the dome. Perfect, he thought.

Holding the little stone in his palm, he began the chant that would send it through the barrier. An instant later the gravel could be seen sitting upon the mottled brown cap of the mushroom, as if Altin had set it there by hand. Altin gave it a satisfied grin. A moment after, Altin brought the pebble back, proving that teleporting inside the dome was not going to be a problem either. For good measure, he moved around the dome to where the bird had hit, and, searching it out in the tall grass outside, he cast a spell to teleport it inside as well—a living test, just to be safe before trying it himself.

However, the "living" portion of that idea was pressing the limits of the term. The sparrow came through the shield without any trouble, but it lay writhing at Altin's feet. He grimaced as he watched it and could not help but pick it up. "I'm sorry," he said to the bird. "I guess you weren't expecting my shield to pop into your path." He could feel the warmth of the bird's body in his hands and was reminded of how the mouse had felt when he'd dried it that day he'd sent it to the moon. He found himself once more fighting off an ominous sense of guilt. And with that guilt came annoyance. It vexed him that his euphoria could be so easily threatened by such a simple thing. It was just a stupid bird. He couldn't believe he was actually considering taking the broken bird to Leekant to see if he could get it fixed. What in the nine hells was wrong with him?

He stared down at the bird lying in his hands. It was barely moving, and it was making a wet spot against his palm where blood leaked from a fractured bone that had poked through the skin. Its shiny black eyes, little onyx dots that were beginning to fade, stared up at him blinking. Its tiny beak opened and closed slowly as it uttered faint rasps of anguished breath that seemed an accusation, a proclamation of Altin's capacity for doing magic and dealing incidental death.

He wished he could heal. Why couldn't he heal? What was the point of all his power if he couldn't heal a stupid bird? All this magic. The largest mythothalamus in a thousand years. And he couldn't heal a lick. It seemed ridiculously unfair. And this wasn't like his zero score in divination either. Deep inside he felt that his divining issue was just a block. But healing. He knew he couldn't heal. He was incapable. He didn't know how he knew, but he knew. He would never heal. Never. He grew so angry watching the bird's torment that he dashed it to the ground and crushed its head beneath his heel. Out of its misery, he told himself, it's what needed to be done. He hated it. And he hated that he could not heal. And he hated being helpless; he hated being weak.

He also hated when these sudden moods came on him, and he tried to banish the emotion from his mind. He blamed it on too much to drink last night and found himself cursing Aderbury and his endlessly friendly ways. Everything seemed to try to keep him from his work.

He was just disciplined enough to know that this sudden mood left him in an improper frame of mind to cast. He was tired. He needed to get more rest. Reluctantly, he resigned himself to a nap. He'd sleep this mood off and be ready to cast when Luria was bright against the sky. Tonight would be the night. Tonight he was going to the moon.

Chapter 20

By the time he woke up, Altin had completely forgotten about the bird. He felt much better and much more capable of maintaining a disciplined mind. He even allowed himself the time to eat a chunk torn off the loaf of bread before he went immediately back to work.

He went up to the battlements and had a look around. Luria was darkly red in her waning phase and gave very little light, barely more than a crimson crescent painted upon the face of a black and distant night. Still, the air was cool and refreshing with a gentle breeze serving up meadow scents from the ground below. The perfect night for a trip up to the moon. But first he had to check and see about the goat. He went to the basin and brought up the image of the kid. The goat was curled up on the blanket and for a moment Altin felt anxiety grip him in the guts again. Fortunately, a close-up view confirmed that the goat had merely gone to sleep, its little ribs moving rhythmically up and down proving it still breathed. Good enough. It was time to get to the business of going up there himself.

Turning from the scrying basin, he closed his eyes and began to chant the portion of Polar's shielding spell that addressed the body of the shield itself. The magic dome was still up from when he'd cast it earlier in the day, and he pushed his mind into the energy it contained and had a look around, probing it and checking its every inch to make sure that it was safe. He could feel its energies pulsing, teeming with power, solid and strong. But there were other things he wanted to check on beyond just its strength. Thinking of the fishbowl, he wanted to make sure that his container was not going to have any deadly leaks. He could imagine air hissing out of it through some crack in the stone or through some undetected creature's burrow.

While still immersed in the mana and in Polar Piton's shield, he traced with his mind the segments of the shield where they passed down and around the castle's curtain wall. There were segments of wall in two places where the shield was parted, the shield giving way to the solidity of the stone, straddling it as one's hand might pin a large block of butter to a plate. He spent a great deal of time studying these intersections, concerned for how teleporting the tower out was going to impact those two spots and if there might be places for his air supply to escape. He was glad he did, for, just as he suspected, the shield did not pass through the wall. It attached to its surfaces, tightly, but did not go through. The energy bound itself to the stone blocks as if they were simply part of the "ground" as defined by Polar Piton's spell. Best not to mess with that connection, Altin thought, but he did resolve to include an extra length of curtain wall beyond the shield on each side when he teleported, just to play it safe.

Which left only the ground below. The shield ended abruptly at the ground. It did not penetrate the earth beneath, though it was attached more firmly than the castle was itself. Altin decided that he would have to teleport a cut of ground as well, so as not to break his airtight seal, he could in essence scoop out a solid foundation of earth from below to make sure his shield had a significant "cork" of dirt to stand on when it appeared upon the moon.

Letting go of the mana that had immersed him in the shield, he spent a bit more time exploring with a seeing spell, scurrying around the tower with his magical vision to make sure that nothing was awry. Once he was confident that all was well, he ran down to his room and scribbled a brief note on a sheet of parchment:

Tytamon,
Gone to moon. Will have tower back by morning.
Altin

He teleported the note to a basket that sat on Tytamon's desk for the express purpose of receiving such things and, with that done, ran back up to the battlements prepared to cast.

Unwilling to take any chances, Altin uncovered the Liquefying Stone and held it in his hand. He didn't want to miss leaving something critical behind; the teleportation spell he was going to use was little different than the one he used on himself almost all the time, but it did include a significantly larger mass: his entire tower! He dipped his mind into the mana currents, seething now with the effects of the wondrous Liquefying Stone, and carefully drew off a large quantity of the whirling purple mass. He flattened it with his mind, spreading it thin like a sheet, which he then cast over his tower's Polar shield like a giant net. He pushed the net down through the curtain wall, a pace beyond where the shield was anchored to the stone, and he stuffed its edges down into the very surface of the earth, pulling underneath the tower as well, almost as deep as he was tall, and yanking at it with his mind as if trying to wrap the tower in a sack. He squared it off beneath the tower as best he could, wanting a flat base beneath him when he set the tower down upon the moon, but it was so dark beneath the ground that he had to do much of it by "feel." Snugging the mana net firmly into place, he took a moment to make certain that all the significant parts were tucked inside. They were.

With that portion of the spell complete, he shifted the cadence of the chant for the transition through space and attached a cord of mana from the "netted" tower up to the tiny seeing stone on Luria countless measures above his head. He funneled the mana easily, despite the difference in mass, and found himself on the verge of distraction at how simple the Liquefying Stone made such a monumental task. Once the link was made, Altin drew the tower back, stretching the whole of himself and the entire castle corner backwards in the empty place where mana dwells, and then released it like a shot. The next thing he knew, he was on the surface of the moon.

He opened his eyes and there he was, gazing out into the most enormous night he'd ever seen. Stars were everywhere. Ten times more than he remembered from his seeing spells before. An awesome sight, beyond anything he had even thought to imagine prior to being here. One just doesn't think in terms of this.

And then there was Prosperion. He looked up and saw it, momentarily surprised that it would be "up" where the moon should be. But there it was, shining like an enormous pearl of blue. Real this time, radiant, a far more mesmerizing sky light than Luria could ever be. Altin was suddenly jealous of himself, knowing that most nights would find him back down there with only pink Luria's face to see. How unfair that the denizens of his world had only this small pink disc to gaze upon. After such a sight as this, he wasn't sure he'd ever be so impressed with a face as featureless as was the moon's.

It took him a while to move through his moment of newfound awe. But at length he did, and he paced excitedly around the battlements, looking at everything. As he did, he realized that the tower was tilted just a bit, and it was with some degree of humor that he discovered he'd cut himself out an uneven granite base. His tower leaned like a poorly made chess piece set upon a rocky board of red. Still, not bad for a bit of guesswork he decided, and gave a dismissive laugh. Experimentation was never without its risks. If he'd gotten himself to the moon and all he had to suffer was a five degree incline, he figured he'd done it decently enough. Far more than anyone else had done. At which point he grinned.

He allowed himself to fill with the appreciation for what he had just achieved. Altin was the first man on the moon. Ever. Two magicians had tried before, or so he'd read, but neither had made progress of any note. One had simply vanished several hundred years ago, and the other, a P-class teleporter, was found dead, his mythothalamus burnt to a crisp inside his head. Altin was sure that he now knew why. He glanced at the Liquefying Stone lying safely in its bowl. There was no way anyone could get here without that stone. At least not the first time. The unknown element was just too impossible to outcast. Especially for a P.

But Altin was certain that he could teleport back without it now, at least himself and quite probably the tower. The distance wasn't a problem, at least not for him. The problem had always been the colossal ambiguity that made blind casting such a strain. But now he knew exactly where "here" was. That poor P-class teleporter had never had a chance, as uniquely powerful as he most certainly was—a P rating was no common thing. No, finding the moon was a project for a Z. And here he was.

He hopped giddily about his tilted tower and shouted with glee. It was just so exciting. And there was no one else around to see, so it didn't matter how silly he may have looked. Glancing down from the wall, he happened to spot the little goat sitting out there all alone in the faint glow of the seeing stone below. He gave a start. Poor thing. He'd completely forgotten about the goat. He calmed himself enough to cast and brought the goat and the flagstone back inside, the flagstone returned to its proper place in his bedroom down below. He ran down to make sure that the goat was all right, and, satisfied that it was, came quickly back up top. He was still jubilant, like a child, and it took several more moments to prepare his mind again so that he could make yet another cast, this time one that would take the tower to the edge of the first big crater that he had found while using Sight to explore.

Viewing the yawning hole in person, from his tower, was more impressive than it had been with simple magic sight; the perspective of a flesh-and-blood man, physically present, gave the site a sense of scale that had been missing merely seeing from Prosperion. The scale of the crater, wide and dark, punched into the ruddy landscape as if by the fist of a god, was humbling to behold, spectacular in its magnitude and in its presentation, encapsulated by stars and with bright Prosperion looming high above. Altin could not help but be in awe. He wished that there were someone else here to see it too.

He found himself thinking of Aderbury and his wife. Aderbury would love it up here, and Hether would scream in absolute delight. Then, as one thought tends to lead to another, he realized that this was where Aderbury should build his amusement park, not down in Murdoc Bay. Suddenly Altin's mind filled with images of a giant Polar's dome covering measures of Luria's open space. No place on Prosperion afforded so much land ready to be used. The moon was already cleared and leveled. Imagine the demand. Aderbury could make a fortune up here and leave that tiny office and insipid Thadius far behind. Yes, he was definitely going to pay Aderbury a visit when he got home.

And he also wanted Tytamon to see. He decided at once that he should go down and get him; he should go and teleport Tytamon back up. His mentor had lived for nearly eight hundred years, had seen almost everything there was to see, but he'd never seen this. Altin was suddenly intent on nothing else. And besides, he wanted to see if it was going to be as easy as he thought to send himself back without the Liquefying Stone. In the matter of casting, there was not so much difference between a goat and a man as one might think.

Using the scrying basin to spy out a dark corner of Calico Castle's vacuous dining hall, an area safely behind the mounted armor of a long dead knight, Altin determined that the corner was indeed devoid of any life. So confirmed, he closed his eyes and cast the teleport spell that he felt certain would bring him home.

A moment later found him standing in the dark. His vision took a moment to adjust and, after reaching out a hand to confirm that there was indeed cold metal armor on his left, he knew that he was home. Two tiny spots of light marked where candles still burned on the table far across the giant room, and Altin jogged over to them only to discover that the table had long ago been cleared. He wasted no time and rushed to Tytamon's tower.

He took the stairs three at a time—well, three for a while, then two, and finally one at a time—as he made the arduous trek up to Tytamon's private rooms, but, despite being out of breath by the time he finally arrived, he was still completely energized as he stood upon the landing and beat upon the door.

He was called inside immediately by the sound of Tytamon's gravelly voice. He burst in and without a salutation of any sort breathlessly spilled it out. "I made it," he proclaimed. "I made it to the moon and I'm on the surface right now as we speak, looking up—or down —at Prosperion. It's beautiful and you have to come see. Right now. You truly do. You've never seen anything like it in all your life."

Tytamon raised a bushy eyebrow, just one, cocking his head slightly as the other brow pressed downward over a somewhat doubting eye. "You're where?"

"I'm on the moon. Right now. You really have to see." He was still panting.

"Hmmm," Tytamon uttered, nodding gravely and giving Altin a patronizing look.

"What?" Altin said, seeing the disbelief. "Didn't you get my note? Haven't you seen the tower?" He ran to Tytamon's window and pointed down to the missing section of the keep. He was somewhat taken aback by what he saw. Whoa! He certainly had excavated a large chunk of Calico Castle's wall. But that didn't matter now. He put the vast gap in the fortress out of his mind and gestured eagerly out the window for Tytamon to see. "Look!"

Tytamon moved reluctantly to the window and looked down into the court. "Good heavens," he said. "What have you done?"

"That's what I'm trying to tell you. I told you in the note. I'm on the moon. Right now."

"My boy, you're standing right here. Perhaps you'd better have a seat."

"No, not now. Well, I mean, not *right* now. But... I just was. And I can go back. Please. Just come. I promise it's worth the time to see."

"Ah," said the wizard finally caught up. "So you've really done it, eh? You've actually put a man upon the moon?"

"Yes," said Altin beaming. "And I'm about to put two on the moon if you'd care to come along."

For a moment Altin thought Tytamon was going to decline, to hesitate on the grounds of prudence or some spurious safety fact, but after a brief pause to consider, the great mage put the spell components he was holding back down upon the bench. "You're sure you know what you're doing?" he asked with some slightly nervous collaboration taking place between his eyes, his eyebrows and the corners of his mouth.

"I was just there. And I had a goat up there all day before I went. It's fine. I promise."

Tytamon sighed, resigning himself to curiosity and to fate. His weathered face burst into a grin, the cautious cabal amongst his features put to rest. "Then let's go. Show me to the moon, my boy. By all means, show me to the moon."

Altin, having the Teleport Other spell still fresh in his mind from working with the goat, wove it together with the self-teleport spell, and after a few moments of careful incantation, they both vanished with a sucking of air that left the candles on Tytamon's bench flickering and alone.

They emerged upon the parapet of Altin's tower, and it took Tytamon only a few moments before he let out a low whistle and a gasp of awe. Just as Altin had not so long ago, the great sorcerer stood transfixed before the bright enormity of Prosperion for some long time. When he finally could, he smiled beneath his beard and muttered, "So that's how we look from way up here."

"Indeed," agreed Altin staring up at the great blue wonder above.

There came another long silence as both of them contemplated the nature of what they saw, its magnitude both in beauty and in size. "It's as if we don't even count," Tytamon said at last.

Altin looked puzzled, but Tytamon was too busy ruminating within his ancient mind. After a while, and what looked to Altin as if the old man had wiped away some tears, Tytamon turned round and clasped him by the shoulders. "You've done something great here, lad. Do you realize that? You've done something that's never been done before. A real discovery. I'm not even certain what it means just yet, but it means something significant I'm sure. This is a lifetime's work fulfilled. Your name will be listed as one of the greatest magicians of the age. Queen Karroll is going to have a fit she'll be so pleased."

Altin smiled and basked in the praise. But something in Tytamon's words checked his pride from glowing too blindingly. "It's not a lifetime's work," he said, just to make the record clear. "It's just a spectacular start."

Tytamon frowned at him. "Really? A start to what?"

Altin turned away from Prosperion's bright blue glow and pointed to the stars. "I'm going out there."

Tytamon shook his head in disbelief. "For what, Altin? There's nothing there but stars, pinpricks of heaven's light. And likely not meant for us."

"Well, to begin, there are seven more planets I can find. If there are no satyrs and dancing nymphs up here on Luria as the legends said there were, then perhaps they are on the other planets instead. And how do you know that the stars are not meant for us? The priests say we are the children of the gods. I'm sure the gods will want to see their son if they're actually out there peeping through. They'll be happy when I arrive."

"You don't believe in gods, Altin. Don't invoke them now."

"I don't know what I believe. But I know that there is only one way I'm ever going to find out."

Tytamon continued to shake his head. "There's never enough for a Six."

"Why must you always go to Six? You always do that. I told you I'm not a Six. And you thought I would be dead before I ever got this far, but here we are. Gods. Why ruin a perfectly good moment?"

Tytamon was taken aback by Altin's sudden flare of rage. But the boy was right. Tonight was not the night for the never-ending debate. "You're right. I'm sorry. It's a bad habit, and one I'm trying to break. And this is a spectacular night. We should celebrate."

"We should," agreed Altin, his irritation settling once more beneath his skin. "Tonight. I think I should go get Aderbury and bring him up as well."

"I've got a hundred-year-old bottle of elven wine that is begging to be the first one opened on the moon," Tytamon offered. "I'll go get it while you chase down your friend."

"You mean you're not going to warn me about teleporting into Crown?"

"Altin, I believe you're well beyond listening to me just now. If you don't know the rules by now, you never will. And besides, you've already broken the laws of teleportation as we know them anyway, just by getting yourself up here. Who am I to tell you what to do?"

Altin knew that Tytamon didn't entirely mean that, but it was good enough to suit his mood. "Ok, I'll be back with Aderbury, and you go get the wine." He started towards the scrying basin, but stopped and turned around. "If you think your little U-class teleport can handle it that is. If not, the Liquefying Stone is over there in that bowl upon the wall."

Tytamon conjured the illusion of a fireball and made as if to throw, then cast himself back to Calico Castle with a hiss of emptied air. Altin laughed as he went to the basin to find a vacant room in Aderbury and Hether's house, into which he planned to teleport himself. Twenty minutes later found the four of them sitting round the ragged, half-burnt table toasting Altin and the moon.

"To the moon," they cheered.

"And to the stars," he answered back. "Maybe this time I'll find someone out there besides myself."

Chapter 21

The hours that followed the orb's retreat were a mix of euphoria and angst. Half the *Aspect's* crew were ecstatic about their recent victory while the other half were fighting off a sense of dread and shock. Only the flurry of activity that followed prevented either group from falling fully on either side of the fence.

Orli remained busy in sick bay for several hours after the orb had disappeared into space, but the flow of wounded they'd expected from the orb's apparent attempt to board had never come to pass. They got a few more patients as one of the crews working to seal off the crushed cargo hold had a minor mishap with a ruptured welding tank, but beyond a broken bone and some stitches, there was no longer much to do.

A few hours after the orb vanished, the alert level was once more lowered to Orange, sending Orli back down to the nursery and her lab. When she arrived, exhausted, she went straight through her lab and into the tiny room that was her quarters, barely four by nine, and threw herself atop the bunk that folded out from the wall. Closing her eyes and resting a forearm across her eyelids to block the glare from the light fixture mounted directly above, she tried to breathe

the stress away with carefully measured breaths. God, she was tired. After a while she started to tremble, and eventually to cry.

She'd never seen so much blood in all her life. And the tension was horrible, the fear. And that poor woman. Dead. She couldn't have been more than thirty years old. Orli suddenly wished she'd thought to learn the woman's name. She seemed so young to die, and to not even have Orli know her name was a tragedy. To die alone and anonymous out here, so far away from anything alive and warm that might have cared, to die in the arms of someone who didn't even know your name. The injustice was too enormous for Orli to let go. The whole of this existence was an injustice too enormous to let go.

Everything out here was so sterile and cold. So black and dark and absent of a shining sun. So white and clean and absent of a warming sense of home. It was hell. It had to be hell. Orli thought of the descriptions she had heard and read about hell, descriptions of a hot place burning; a place of endless fire and sulfur's stench; of craggy, undulating ground, filthy and writhing with crawling, hideous misshapen souls in every stage of torture and decay. But that was a joke. Whoever had invented those stories had no idea what hell was really like. Not like Orli did. There was no rot or stench in hell, no filth or heat of fire. There was none of that. Hell was a cold hospital room on a sterile ship. It was a meticulously clean place of recycled air and water that was filtered through a thousand kidneys and six large machines and then kidneys and then machines, over and over and over until it lost all taste—or gained it depending on one's state of mind. Hell was isolation on a ship where people died for stupid things and nobody knows their names. Hell was right here where Orli was.

She shuddered and tried to push the faces of the mangled men and women out of her head, to clear her mind of depressing thoughts about life aboard the ship. A futile task. And the images continued to plague her even as she dropped into a long and sorely needed sleep.

When Roberto finally woke her with a rough shake, she actually felt better despite the nightmares that had plagued her rest. "Wake up. Wake up," he was almost pleading. "Jesus woman, the captain is going to have you freakin' skinned."

"What?" She was groggy.

"Didn't you hear him call? He's been trying to reach you for the last half-hour. I thought he was going to come down here and shoot you he was so pissed. That's why I volunteered to come. They need you up on seven-deck. Now."

"What?"

"Deck seven. Get your botany kit. They need you now. They needed you half an hour ago. Hurry. Jesus. You're so fucking busted."

She resisted the temptation to ask "what?" again and shook herself fully awake. She went to a cabinet and pulled out her field kit as she blinked the sleep out of her eyes. "Why do they need me?" she asked as she headed towards the door.

"Not sure," he said. "Something the Hostile left sticking in the hole. You better run. You can tell me about it at dinner. I'm on a timer too." He patted her on the cheek and then turned and ran away.

She sprinted out after him and went to the elevator at the other end of the hall. A few minutes later found her nearing a large storage room on the ship's uppermost deck. The corridor leading up to the room's entrance was bustling with activity and was cordoned off and guarded at either end. She approached the two marines guarding this end and told them who she was.

"About goddamn time," said one of them, a middle-aged sergeant she recognized but did not know by name. His counterpart, a younger woman, perhaps in her mid thirties, turned her face to the com-link on her shoulder and announced to someone that Ensign Pewter was on her way.

Orli shrugged at the burly sergeant and went through, passing groups of armored marines bristling with weapons of every size. They were clearly ready for a war. As she approached the double doors leading into the storage room they opened and out came a heavy-set man who introduced himself as Lieutenant Commander Gray. "It's this way, Ensign. I assume you've been briefed."

"Nope," she said, a bit nervous with all the guns and the very martial feel that was heavy upon the hall. "I haven't been told a thing."

"The Hostile deposited a substance in the hull breach before it released itself from the ship. Doctors Singh and Salvator have already had a look and neither can make a positive I.D. That's why they sent for you."

Orli could see the familiar faces of both Doctor Singh and Doctor Salvator as she and the lieutenant commander approached. They were standing amongst a group consisting of the captain, a handful of other officers and a few enlisted men situated near a scissor-lift parked beneath a large hole some twenty feet above. The hole was circular and had a very smooth edge, looking as if the orb had been extremely careful in its work before it went away. In place of the steel that would normally have filled the space was a dark greenish brown substance that appeared soft and marginally smooth. She caught herself staring up at it while she approached the group and had to force her attention to the officers as she gave a barely acceptable salute.

Orli exchanged warm smiles with the two doctors and one of the crewmen whom she knew from poker games on the recreation deck. "And this is how we found it when we came in," the Lieutenant Commander was saying as they came upon the gathering of crew. "Sealed tight just like that. We didn't lose a molecule of air."

"You're late, Pewter," snarled the captain. "You screw this up and your court martial begins in the morning, you hear me?"

Captain Asad was always such a joy. She smiled meekly back at him. She really wanted to tell him to die in a fire, but she knew that probably wouldn't do much good.

Lieutenant Commander Gray looked to Doctor Salvator, indicating that his portion of the briefing was at an end. Doctor Salvator picked up where the lieutenant commander left off, pushing her glasses up on her pale and lightly freckled nose. "He's right. Tight as a wine cork and sealed up good. But they're welding new hull plates on as we speak just in case. I'm sure you've seen what happens to champagne when the cork comes out. We're not trusting that thing for a second." She pointed up at the strange substance filling the hole.

Orli cringed as she thought of herself being sucked outside, an unwilling surfer on a wave of escaping air. No thank you. She sent thoughts of gratitude up to the men who were tromping around on the hull outside. A spacewalk was always a dangerous thing, even more so with a Hostile orb lurking somewhere.

"So," went on Doctor Salvator with her slight Texas drawl, "we've been up to have a look, and we have no idea what the hell it is. It's not mineral and it's not organic either. At least not exactly. We tried them both. I've got degrees in geology, chemistry and biology and I can't even make a guess. If you asked me which one it is, I'd have to say 'yes.'" She leaned over to Orli and, gesturing with a shoulder towards the captain, whispered in her ear, "I reckon my psych degree will do me more good than any of the other three; he's going to lose his ever-loving mind if we don't figure out what it is soon."

Orli looked over at Doctor Singh who only shrugged as his reply. This was definitely not his specialty.

"Ensign Pewter," said Lieutenant Commander Gray, "if you could step onto the lift. We'd like to get your examination underway." He touched her lightly on the back of the arm and nudged her towards the scissor-lift.

She moved with him to it and smiled patiently as the pimple-faced petty officer who operated the lift grinned at her with a smirk too smarmy to qualify as professional. She clamored up into the basket of the lift, and the Lieutenant Commander handed her field kit up after her once she was inside. She gave the petty officer a nod to let him know that she was ready to go up. He grinned lasciviously at her again and made no attempt to conceal the play of his gaze up and down her slender frame. She rolled her eyes and looked up at the hole above. How could he be thinking about sex at a time like this? They were all like this, the ones that weren't serious and stern anyway; some things never changed.

The scissor lift jolted as the young man activated the control, and in the space of moments she was lifted to the hole. Snapping latex gloves in place, she reached up tentatively and pressed her fingers against the substance that was plugging up the gap. It gave slightly, like an industrial rubber mat. Only this one was six feet thick. And it was smooth. Not smooth like glass or plastic, but smooth like vinyl generally was.

She spent a few moments just studying it with her fingers and her eyes before deciding to try scratching a sample off its surface for a closer look. She took a scalpel from her pack and a sealable plastic sample bag and reached up to give it a cut. A voice in the back of her head, the one she never listened to, was telling her that this was a horrible idea, and her heart was pounding like a psychotic drummer as she reached up to make the scratch. The instant she did, the strange object went from dark tones to mottled white and gray. There was no sound or motion or jolt of energy, just a color and texture shift across the surface. Just that. But still it scared her half out of her palpitating wits.

"What the hell are you doing, Ensign?" barked the captain, accompanied by a collective gasp from everyone else below.

Her defenses came reflexively to bear as her heart continued to spasm in her chest. "I'm examining the goddamn thing like you told me to. What am I supposed to do, use ESP?" She cringed immediately and wished she could take the comment back, but the unexpected shift of the material had frightened her just as much as it had the rest of them. Adrenaline did the rest. The scissor-lift was already coming down.

She reached up to touch it again before it was out of reach. It was now hard as rock, and rough like rock too. If she didn't know better, she'd say it was rock, likely granite or some other kind of quartz just like the Hostile projectiles were. But how could that possibly be? It hadn't been that when she went up. She looked in her sample bag to see what she'd scratched off. There was a small piece, barely a crumb, but it looked like granite too. She tucked it into her bag and quickly zipped the sample up.

"Ok, that's enough for now, Pewter," said the captain. "Before you kill us all."

Once she'd climbed out of the basket and was once more on the deck, she found herself confronted by several pairs of wide and eager eyes.

"Well?" said the captain for all of them, impatient but apparently recovered and still willing to hear if she'd learned anything despite having given them all a start. "What did you do? What did you find out?"

She'd expected him to berate her for the ESP remark. "It's turned to stone now, if I haven't missed my guess. At least the part that I can see. I tried to scratch it with a scalpel and then it turned to rock. Just like that. I don't know what else to say."

"What do you think it was before?" asked Doctor Salvator. "Before it made the change?"

She had to think about it for a bit. "It looked like an organic compound, but it might just as easily have been petroleum based. Somewhere between sap and plastic. I honestly don't know."

"You're using different words to say the same things we couldn't say," Doctor Salvator joked, though the tension hadn't quite left her doughy frame. She started to add something else but the captain cut her off.

"That's fine, Ensign. You've been remarkably little help. And you are confined to quarters until I have time to figure out what I'm going to do with you. Orange alert and you are half an hour late responding when I call. You're done. Dismissed." He turned to his science team standing near and added, "You may still have access to her if, for some reason, your work requires her—specialty." The last word was accompanied by a sneer.

Chapter 22

After celebrating the discovery of landing on the moon, Altin turned over to Aderbury the project of announcing that progress to the Queen. He figured including Aderbury in the event, and using Aderbury's access to the stoic monarch as an excuse to avoid having to deal with her himself, he could guarantee Aderbury's position as lunar amusement park project-director should that idea pan out. And with that task underway, Altin began the work of moving beyond Luria and out into the night.

If the astronomers were right, the planets should be the closest lights up in the sky and therefore the most obvious places to target next. There were seven planets besides Prosperion, and Naotatica was not the nearest one. But, according to the Church, Naotatica was the planet upon which the elves had originally evolved. As the story went, Melgon Tidalwrath, a second-generation and upstart god, had angered the older Prosperion gods with an act of selfishness and had been banished to Naotatica as punishment for a span of five hundred thousand years. Apparently, again according to myth, when the young god got there, he found the haughty race of elves, for whom he grew an instant hatred, and subsequently banished them to

Prosperion, to the islands known as String, where they have lived ever since.

Altin wasn't sure he believed the story, but at least it gave him a place to start, more hope than the other planets had. Given the inhospitable climate and lack of breathable air here on Luria, it made sense to seek out a world that had a surface usable by an elf. If the elves could breathe on Naotatica, Altin could breathe. So, with that bit of logic behind him, he began the work once more of casting seeing stones blindly into space.

At least this time he had the Liquefying Stone and some small concept of the distances involved. He figured that the other planets had to be much farther from Luria than would be convenient, just as Luria had been from Prosperion. So, with that as a starting point, he cast his first stone out in the direction of Naotatica's tiny green speck of light, casting it twice the distance between his planet and its moon. He knew the planet would be farther than that, but it was a distance he could hold in his head better than just trying to cast it out with nothing shaping his thoughts at all. Going to the scrying basin in his familiar routine, he was a bit disappointed, but not entirely surprised, to see that Naotatica's light was no larger than it had been a moment before. Perhaps skipping a few of the solar system's other planets on the way to Naotatica was not such a good idea, he thought. Still, the hope of the elven origins kept him at the task, and he spent the remainder of the night trying to improve his casts.

He repeated the process for the next several nights: exhausting blind casts, sleep, a nibble from his diminishing loaf and starting over again, casting stones as far as he could make them go. His skill at casting into the unknown, despite the prohibitive nature of such a thing in teleporting spells, grew with each successive cast. He was actually doubling and tripling his range by the end of every working night as his mind began to conceive of distances that never in all his life had he imagined could possibly exist. And by using the skipping stones technique along with the Liquefying Stone, he could really cover a lot of interplanetary ground.

By the end of his sixth day trying, he finally had Naotatica clearly in the scrying basin's view. He stared down into the water, panting from the effort of several hours of casting against the winds of no-known place, and grinned as he saw that Naotatica had grown from a spot like all the rest of the stars into a round light roughly the size of a grape and just about the same shade of green. "Hah, there you are," he said into the water, rippling it with his breath. "I finally found you. I'm coming to get you next."

Energized by his new success, he resumed his casting of the seeing stones. He launched his next stone at the last, intending to skip this one off of that, and have it hop twice again the distance he'd just made. He checked it in the basin and sure enough Naotatica had once more increased noticeably in size.

He repeated the process again, this time skipping off the farther stone. Naotatica was now half the diameter of the basin. He cast another stone. This one had the planet's bright green face filling the basin from edge to edge. Altin was ecstatic. He was going to land on Naotatica tonight.

He cast another stone, this time his excitement giving him strength as if this were his first cast of the night. His seeing stone shot way out past the previous one, and when Altin checked in the water, hoping that he had landed there at last, he found himself staring into a basin filled with glowing green.

"What in the nine hells?" he muttered.

He decided to cast a full seeing spell on the location of the seeing stone and immediately went into the chant that would bring his vision to the little rock. Once there, he looked about and dropped his jaw in awe. Naotatica was enormous.

He could tell that his seeing stone was still very far away from the planet, now that he was here and could move his view about. By tilting his view up or down, or wide to either side, he could see the black of space around Naotatica, but looking straight at it, it completely filled his vision, peripheral and all. But regardless of how large it loomed, the angles required to see the stars behind told him that he was still extremely far away.

He released the seeing spell and decided to cast another stone. He'd try to double the last distance and see where he ended up. He figured he might go right past the monstrous planet, but he was anxious to get there pretty soon. His strength was quickly giving out.

He cast the stone and returned to the basin to see where it had gone. Once again the water was filled with glowing green. This time, however, there was a slightly different look to the color in the water: it had an element of mist, a visual texture of a sort. He quickly chanted the improved seeing spell and once more joined his sight with the actual location of the seeing stone. He immediately felt that he was falling, and, for the first time since seeing anything out here in space, he actually heard some noise.

The stone was apparently falling through a cloudy, windblown mist, and Altin allowed his vision to fall with it, retaining his visual anchor on the stone and feeling as if he were there. The wind was violent up there, and Altin could see the stone, a rather good-sized chunk of rock, being buffeted easily about as it continued to fall through the blinding mist. And everything was green and seemed to glow. Everything. Or nothing. There was not one dash of another color anywhere to be found. Just green. There was enough gradation of texture within the whirling blasts of mist to give him the sense of downward motion, but nothing more. And the volume of the wind was incredible. He had to adjust the auditory portion of the spell after a while as the intensity grew painful in his head. And so he fell.

And he fell.

And he fell.

It seemed he must have fallen for an hour, although he doubted it had been that long, and with every passing moment he kept anticipating, at last, some contact with the planet's surface. But it just would not arrive. His seeing stone continued to plummet for what seemed an impossible length of time, and after pushing himself to the limits of his magical strength, he had to let the vision go. He was exhausted. He simply could not go on. With the last of his energy, he conjured the image of the falling stone back in the scrying basin and locked it there with a simple enchanter's stream. It was all he could do to stagger downstairs and tumble into bed.

He woke the next morning—or what felt like morning given how different the concept became up here on the moon where both the sun and bright Prosperion lit up the sky on schedules of their own—and ate the last of his now quite stale loaf of bread. Losing his access to a fresh daily loaf was an unexpected downside of being out in space. He would have to load up on food the next time he went down.

He took a drink of water from the pitcher on his nightstand and noted that it too tasted rather old. Looking into the pitcher reminded him of his scrying basin on the battlements, and he trotted up to have a look at the stone which was now surely lying on Naotatica's solid ground.

But it was not. It was still falling. Altin could not believe his eyes. Nothing could fall that long. Such a thing was absolutely impossible. It was as if the entire planet was made of air. Green air. He couldn't believe such an absurd idea. How could a planet be made of nothing but howling winds and mist? What kind of planet was that? Surely not one that had spawned the race of elves.

His mind began to wrestle with the new problem that he'd found. It couldn't really be a planet if there was no planet in all that mist, could it? And yet, it certainly looked like a planet when viewed from high above. He thought about it some more. Naotatica had seemed shockingly large as he'd been casting his stones closer and closer during the approach. It was possible, he supposed, that Naotatica could be, well, really, really large. Amazingly large. Perhaps incredibly larger than Prosperion could ever hope to be. Maybe, given the enormity of the distances he was discovering out here in space, perhaps there were sizes of all kinds to be fathomed here as well, not just distances from point to point. He realized that Naotatica might not be subject to all the same size paradigms that Prosperion and Luria had caused him to unknowingly embrace.

Given that idea, he decided that it was at least plausible that the sky on Naotatica was vastly larger, or deeper, than was the sky around Prosperion, much thicker than Prosperion's little translucent shroud of glowing mist. And if this were the case, extrapolated outward by Altin's new respect for possible distance, it stood to reason that a stone falling through a sky that large might take considerably longer to hit the ground than would a stone dropped into the air above Kurr.

But still... all night?

He was willing to believe, however. For now. And so, leaving the basin enchanted with the view of the plummeting seeing stone, he decided that this was a perfect time to take the tower home. He needed to stock up on a few supplies anyway, and he was really hungry for something substantive to eat. He looked up at Prosperion and saw that Kurr was nowhere in his field of view. Judging from the position of the sun, he realized that it was evening back at home and suddenly hoped that perhaps he might be in time for dinner;

a hot meal was exactly what he needed after so much time away.

It turned out he was in time for the evening's repast, and it was over a huge roast turkey, heaps of fresh vegetables and a pudding that rivaled the turkey for size that Altin regaled not only Tytamon but Kettle too with his stories of Naotatica and its seemingly endless sky.

When he got to the part about coming home for want of food, Kettle's face took on a stern and focused look, as if she'd been stewing on this for days. "Well, sir, if ya are goin' ta be flyin' around in space, ya needs a proper bellyfull ta keep yer strength. Any fool knows as much." She shook her finger at him as if he were five years old and had gone out into the snow without putting on his coat, and her momentum began to build. "Gone fer days," she trudged on, "An' not one word ta me about it. And here, me havin' ya—the lad I'm charged with feedin' mind ya—starvin' ta death out between the stars. The hearth goddess herself will have my soul fer failin' ya." With that she got up and stomped out of the room, the two mages smiling at one another across the plentitude of food.

"I can't tell if she's mad or impressed," Altin admitted as he heaped another portion of pudding on his plate.

"Both," Tytamon said around a mouthful of the spectacular dessert. "Mostly impressed, I'd wager. But if she'd boxed your ears on her way out, I wouldn't have been surprised."

Altin nodded and grinned as he took another bite, but when he'd finished his meal and a half hour of discussion with Tytamon about his plans, he found that he had a messenger waiting at the stairwell leading up into his rooms.

"Master Altin, sir," Pernie said, carefully repeating the message word for word, "if ya would oblige, Kettle has need of yer services to fetch yer coldstone box up into yer rooms."

He gave her a quizzical look, but nodded that he would follow as she scampered off into the dark. She led him back to the kitchen where Kettle was still heaping leftovers and loaves of bread and flasks of water and wine into a large wooden crate that she had lined with enchanted cold stones. She speared him with a look as he walked in, and he knew that he was about to receive a lecture from her in no uncertain terms.

"Now yer goin' ta listen ta me, boy. Ya may be the young master in this here castle, but I'm not without some say about what goes on, and there isn't gon' be no flying up in space without no food. Ya hearin' me?" She didn't even give Altin time to nod. "This here crate is gon' be yers. I know enough 'bout yer teleportin' to know ya can send this crate right over there under that table any time ya like." She pointed with her chin at a stout wooden table in a far corner of the room. "So from now on, if'n yer gon't be off fer days and weeks at a time, yer sendin' it back fer me ta fill with food whenever ya need. Do ya hear me, lad? Ya send it right back there. Won't be no starvin' mages on my watch, or it'll be the rollin' pin fer ya I tell ya true. And don't think I won't do it, 'cause I will."

Altin started to protest, to explain about accidents and how Pernie might be playing under the table when the crate came back or something of the sort, but he could tell by the look on Kettle's face that she already knew all about that and would not be hearing his excuses. It was safer to just say, "Yes, ma'am."

She stuffed some carrots into a small basket and loaded them into the crate, then set its lid back on, pounding it down tight with a fleshy, flour-covered fist. "There ya go. Now get this thing out of here, it's takin' up too much space."

Altin smiled and happily obliged. With a few words and a gesture, the crate was sitting near his bed. "Thank you, Kettle," he said when it was done. "You are very kind."

"Don't I know it," she said. "Now get along. Yer taking up too much space too."

He gave her a short bow and a polite smile, the latter of which she warmly returned along with a pinch to his cheek that left a flour print to mask the red mark she'd put there. And just like that, his stale bread and old water days on the moon were at an end.

Once again thinking of water reminded him of his seeing stone, still being seen in the basin up in his tower. He wondered if it had finally hit the ground. He remembered to smile at Pernie who was studying him silently from beside the fire as he left, and then he went upstairs to see.

Chapter 23

The seeing stone, unbelievably, was still falling. Altin might have spent some time on exasperated expletives, but there was something new to see as well. The stone was beginning to glow, as if it were heating up.

He frowned down into the scrying basin and wondered what was going on. He cast the seeing spell that would bring his senses to the stone and once more found himself listening to the sound of violent, howling winds. But he could also hear the seeing stone as it hissed and scorched in the billowing mist. It fell and fell, and as it did, it grew hotter and hotter with each descending yard. And it was only a short time after Altin had rejoined it that the stone actually burst into flames as it tumbled through the endless glowing green.

The flames burned loudly and sounded like a torch held in a raging storm, and all the while the flames grew larger and brighter until at last the stone vanished with a hiss. The falling sensation in Altin's vision stopped.

Anchored to the tumbling stone, his spell had just lost the object to which it was attached, leaving Altin to stare motionlessly into an endless expanse of green. He could still hear the winds howling, but the sense of falling was gone. He wondered what he should do. The stone had been falling for over half a day. Should he press on himself and see how much further he could go? Naotatica certainly seemed an unlikely place to have spawned a race of elves. But he wondered if perhaps he had just not gone deep enough. Perhaps he just had to finish passing through the clouds.

But what, twelve hours of falling through the clouds? Was that even reasonable to assume? If that wasn't completely preposterous, then what did it imply? Maybe Altin had been right before. Maybe it was an entire planet made of air, green, whirling air. But the Elves weren't ethereal things. So they really couldn't be from here. Or else he just hadn't gone far enough down to see. Or else the Church was wrong. He didn't believe half of what they said anyway. Less than half. They seemed to have morality mostly right, but the stories were absurd. Naotatica was clearly not being accurately described. He groaned.

He decided to push his vision further in, and, using his newfound understanding of distance, was able to attain seeing speeds that were beyond him only a few weeks in the past. With some slight modifications to the chant that he was speaking beneath his breath, his vision was hurtling through the apparently depthless mist.

Eventually, even at this seemingly impossible speed, it took another hour and a half until the color of Naotatica finally began to shift. He still hadn't found land, but as he traveled deeper into the planet the scenery began to change from greens to yellows and gradually to the brightest raging white. In fact, it got so bright that Altin once more had to tweak his spell as it became far too bright to see, brighter than staring into the sun. His vision continued on into the brightness for nearly another hour until he was abruptly in the dark.

At last! He'd finally found land. Or so he thought. He

must have gone too far, pushed past and beneath the surface of the soil. He backed his vision out until once more he was in the light. The indescribably bright light. Somehow retracted too far.

Impatiently, he changed his chant back to accommodate a slower speed and tried once more to move downward towards the ground into which his sight had disappeared. It took a bit longer, but once more he plunged his view into total darkness, never having seen the ground's approach.

"What the...?"

He backed out again, slowly. Total, overwhelming whiteness.

Forward, the tiniest movement, into black.

This can't possibly be Naotatica, he told himself. Nobody could live in this much sunlight. And to think, he'd actually thought it was bright on Luria.

But then again, on Luria the brightness obviously came from the sun. Whatever this light was, it couldn't possibly be the sun, not shining through the blanket of clouds Altin's sight had just fallen through. Could it?

Good Mercy and her five favorite dogs. What was going on out here? Did nothing make sense in space? It wasn't like he didn't already think the Church's version of reality was ridiculous, but, after what he'd seen in the last few weeks, even their stories made more sense than this. The whole thing was impossible to comprehend.

However, the one thing he did comprehend was that there were not going to be any elves waiting for him and his tower to arrive. At least not here. And if there were, they were not the kind of elves that he had any desire to meet. Any creature that could live in an atmosphere of fire capable of burning up a stone was not a creature Altin felt he needed to get to know. Taot's acidic humor gave him troubles enough at home.

And besides, he had no evidence that such a race was

even here. Like the satyrs and the Never Ending Song on Luria, the elves of Naotatica were nothing but a myth. It seemed that once again he had spent a tremendous amount of time and energy to discover absolutely nothing at all.

Why was everything out here so entirely empty, anyway? What was the point of all of these places and spaces if there wasn't anyone to fill them up? The waste of time, effort and whatever it was down here serving as land was an outrage, and the possibility that something had created such waste insulted what little grip on anything approaching piety he might tenuously retain. He could not hear the curse words he uttered back in the tower, but he spoke them aloud just the same. This was annoying. Frankly, from his point of view, Naotatica could officially be written off. But, given that he was Kurr's first interplanetary explorer and therefore technically empowered to do so, he thought it only proper that he at least see it in person before he wrote the planet's condemnation forever in his notes.

He retracted his vision back to Kurr and recast the Polar's shield around his tower, preparing himself to go. He immersed his vision in the shield, just to be sure that it was sound before preparing to teleport back out into the stars.

He debated how to approach this new teleport as he was about to go much farther than he'd ever tried before. He could use the Liquefying Stone and try to one-shot all the way to Naotatica, or he could try to hop the tower off of a few seeing stones along the way and get there without its help. Weighing the learning opportunities on either side, he opted for the latter and set himself about the cast.

The teleport worked easily, in fact far more easily than he'd hoped it would. He could have skipped the hop effect entirely had he known how little the distance would actually mean in terms of ease. The simplicity with which he brought himself all that way was due to knowing where he was trying to go. Even though he knew how teleportation worked, it was still surprising that such a distance made so little difference in the end. Compared to how hard it was to cast one small stone blindly out into the night, the relative effortlessness of moving the large tower all the way to Naotatica was incredible to comprehend. But it turned out to be very easy, and he was glad he'd taken the time to try.

He'd aimed himself and his tower at the last seeing stone he'd cast, the one prior to the one that had been falling for all that time. Once more he found himself floating above the surface of the enormous giant green ball, only this time he was there. Despite having seen it before, it was even more breathtaking in person; something was lost when viewing such a vista through a magical device. Naotatica was colossal. It was beyond colossal. Altin simply had no way to express his sense of amazement as he looked on. From there he decided to teleport even closer still, and in a blink, half the night was filled with the titanic green world.

He went downstairs and got his notebook from the table in his room. He brought the inkpot up with it and set them on the table near the wall. He pulled out the rickety stool and, opening his book, began to sketch the planet onto a blank page. There were a few distinguishing lines that ran round the surface of the planet, a marbling effect, which made it more than just a circle on the page.

Beneath the illustration he made a few notes. He described the fate of the seeing stone, and he wrote about his encounter with the point of light and dark. He even made a few comments about elves and the errors of the Church before looking up once more and noticing that his tower had begun to fall. He rose up from the stool and walked over to the parapet. He had to squint into the night to be certain, as the planet's proximal size was such that it made movement hard to gauge, but soon it was confirmed: the tower was definitely falling, and it was falling directly into the giant green world.

At first fear clutched at Altin's chest. What was going on? Was some other magician working against him down below? Perhaps he'd been wrong about the elves. But as he thought about what he'd seen, he shook himself free of such ridiculous thoughts. Of course that was not the case. This was just something new, something else with which he would now have to contend. And he needed to do it before he fell into the planetary mist. He had great faith in Polar Piton's shield against the cold and heat of empty space. But he was not sure he wanted to try it in the whiteness that burned within Naotatica's blazing depths.

Calming himself from the initial grip of fear, he thought for a moment about what spell would serve him best. He could teleport back to that last seeing stone and still have a reasonable view. But somehow that felt like a retreat. And he wasn't yet willing to concede.

He ran back downstairs and went through one of the books he kept on his shelf. There was a chapter on falling that he'd read a few years back while studying flight forms and other airborne spells. He found the pages he was looking for and sure enough he had a spell called Stasis: Falling Stops. It seemed the perfect thing. Only this spell required a feather from a raven's wing and a small bit of lead. Damn, he thought. A bad time for spell components.

He knew he had a brick of lead down in the tower's lowest room, but the raven's wing was something of another trick. He went down and dug out the lead from a box buried beneath a stack of old notebooks and a few sacks of assorted things. He conjured a magical flame and melted off a drop, which he then cooled with a simple spell called "Arctic Breeze."

The feather was still going to be the sticking point. The dead bird from his initial testing of the shield was likely still outside the tower near the wall, but that was a sparrow and would be no help at all. He rummaged around the lower rooms for quite some time, opening boxes he hadn't looked into for several years. He couldn't believe there wasn't a raven feather in a single one.

"What kind of mage has no feathers," he chided himself as he finally gave up and took his bit of lead back up to the battlements. Naotatica expanded before him like a sky-devouring beast, so vast he had to look nearly ninety degrees left or right to see stars on either side. And he was falling faster than he had been prior to going and getting the bit of lead. His memory conjured a vision of the seeing stone bursting into flames and then imagined his tower doing much the same. That simply wouldn't do.

"Fine," he groaned. "I'll take it back for now." Somewhat resignedly, he teleported himself back one seeing stone further than from where he'd first arrived.

From this vantage, Naotatica was still quite large, but apparently whatever was making Altin fall towards its howling winds had no effect upon the tower now. He watched for a while to be sure but eventually decided he was safe. But he still needed a feather. He was not going to let whatever was going on near the planet work against him a second time.

Annoyed by the distraction, he went to the scrying basin and viewed the corner of Calico Castle where his tower normally sat, making sure the area was clear. It was, and a moment later found him once again on Kurr. He sighed and dropped the Polar's shield. It was going to take a while to find a raven if his skill with goat gathering gave any clues.

He sent a telepathic message to Taot to find out where he was. The dragon was several measures away, up in the high mountains courting a female dragon that he'd had a chance to meet. A carnal wave washed into Altin's mind as Taot's thoughts returned, the beast simple and open in its method of communicating what was going on and causing Altin to redden far more deeply than the reddest rose. The uncultured dragon simply had no shame. Regardless of the dragon's lack of propriety, however, Taot clearly was not going to be of any help locating a raven, which meant Altin had to do it by himself.

Annoyed, and impatient to be back at the real work of exploring space, he put on his shoes and headed downstairs and out into the meadow beyond the keep. As he made his way through the knee-deep grass, he scanned about for any trace of a raven. And of course there were none lying handily about.

He walked through the better part of what on any other occasion would have seemed a lovely mid-afternoon, but he saw not the faintest sign of a raven anywhere. He walked along, ignoring the warm sun and the fragrance of wild flowers on the breeze, until at last he came into the woods, where he spent some time in the shadowy darkness growing furious at the fact that there were still no ravens to be found.

"How hard can it be to find one blasted burning bird?" he snarled after another hour of traipsing about beneath the canopy of leaves to no avail. He was sure the forest was hiding its ravens, trying to spite him, showing him every color of bird but black, and he said as much out loud before he finally gave it up.

There had to be a better way.

Impatient, he teleported himself back to his room and went once more into Tytamon's tower. He found the old mage working on one of his favorite never-ending quests, the pursuit of the certainty that he could make diamonds out of coal—not for want of money of course, but out of pure stubbornness after so many unsuccessful years. Altin shook his head as he watched the ancient magician chant out his newest version of the spell and, without surprise, watched the coal vanish in a puff of acrid smoke.

"That's never going to work, Master. I don't know why

you keep trying."

"Well, it should work," Tytamon said, waving away the acrid fumes. "My divination says it can. I just wish the damn clues weren't so unbelievably vague. 'Weight' is the impression I get. 'Lots of weight.' So, I conjure weight. And still, I get...this." He indicated the smoke curling around his head with a gnarled hand. "How much weight can it possibly need?"

"Well, it's your project," said Altin. "I'm sure you'll figure it out. But, before you try again, do you have a few raven feathers that I could have?"

The ancient sorcerer crinkled up his already wrinkled face as he considered where he might have some raven feathers stashed away. After a few long moments he shook his head. "No, I haven't got a one." Then he added, as if an obvious afterthought, "Just go get one."

Altin rolled his eyes and, thanking Tytamon for his time, went back down and out into the courtyard. The afternoon was wearing thin. So was his patience. But he had to make another try. Or else he had to go to town. He really didn't want to take the time for that.

He set his jaw and strode back out into the meadow beyond the gates. He scanned the area for any signs of black but saw only Pernie playing near the creek. He watched the tow-headed child as she raised her slender arm and spun round a tattered, homemade sling. Whoosh, whoosh, two times round, and then she shot a frog that was sunning itself upon a rock. Altin was mildly impressed by her marksmanship but was not inclined to comment lest he be drawn into another rambling conversation with the excitable little girl. He had almost turned away when a glint of sunlight caught his eye.

Pernie had pulled a small knife from her belt and was running towards her prey. Altin watched, recoiling a bit in surprise, as the little girl went to work neatly slicing off the frog's legs where the thigh bones met the hips. Slice, slice and it was done, just as neat as you please. His expression shadowed with disgust. She seemed too young to be fond of such ghastly play. But then he saw her run the two bloody limbs back to where she'd made the shot and drop them into a basket that he hadn't noticed earlier, hidden by the grass. Of course. Kettle sent her out here when it was time for her famous frog leg stew.

He harrumphed and put his mind back to his own hunting task. But as he turned and headed for the woods an idea struck: Pernie. Pernie would be perfect for this type of grisly work. Clearly she had no qualms about blood, and she seemed an excellent shot. Not only that, this was a great way to proceed with his commitment to acting nicer to the girl. Maybe he could kill two birds with just one stone. He chuckled at his cleverness then turned back and called out to the miniature hunter stalking frogs along the creek.

She came immediately, grasping her basket in one hand and her sling in the other as she bounded through the waist high grass, leaping like a little two-legged deer. Her first thought was to proffer the basket to Altin, that he might see the enormity of her catch. "Look what I got," she said proudly.

"Good gods, child," he said peering into it and remembering to sound impressed. She'd certainly gathered enough to feed them all tonight. "Did you save any for the birds and snakes to eat?"

She grinned proudly. "They have to catch their own."

He wanted to be friendly, so he pressed on a sentence more. "You certainly are a good shot with that." He pointed at the sling dangling in her fist. "How'd you get so good?"

She held it up for him to see. It was just two lengths of frayed rope and a pouch made from a piece of burlap. "Made it myself," she beamed. "Practice all the time in case a orc comes out of the hills to get me like Kettle always says they will." She looked genuinely afraid.

"You know Kettle is only trying to scare you into being good with all that orc talk, right?"

"Nuh-uh," said the little girl, glancing furtively up at the peaks behind the castle's granite walls and looking as if she might actually start to cry. "There's orcs up there. Nipper says it too. And Gimmel."

"Well, yes," Altin said, forcing a smile and nodding patiently. "Technically, there are. But they haven't attacked the castle in over four hundred years. Think about it. Would you attack a castle where Tytamon the Ancient lives?"

She had to think about that. "No," she said after a moment, shaking her head. Then she added, "And you."

He let out a breath of relief, satisfied that tears were no longer an issue to be feared. "All right. Good. So, Pernie, being that you use that sling so well, have you ever shot a bird?"

"Oh, all the time, Master Altin, sir. I get quails an' pheasants all the time. Even got a dove right out of the sky. Nipper says I'm Nordark in human form, come up from a fourth level a hell I shoot so good. Says it's unnatural for a girl, but I don't care. Girls can shoot good as boys if they want." She looked tentatively back at Mt. Pernolde and the surrounding peaks. "Never shot an orc though."

"Well, that could work out for both of us then," said Altin leaning down towards her and bracing his hands against his knees. He ignored the part about the orcs. "How about I give you another job for that sling of yours besides shooting frogs? I'll even pay you for it. I'll give you a silver piece if you can find me a raven and bring it down."

"A raven, Master Altin, sir?"

"You know, the black ones that fly around sometimes and make that awful sound."

"The ones with the red spots on their wings?"

"No, not those. It has to be a raven. The bigger ones, no

red spots. I need the feathers from a raven's wings. Do you know the ones I mean?"

She was nodding now. "Is that the only thing you need, Master Altin, sir?" She stared up at him, and he could see she was breathless with anticipation for the task.

"Yes, that's all. Just a raven's wing," he said. "And if you bring it quickly, I'll pay you two silver pieces for your time. He added the second part as an afterthought, but she was already gone before he spoke, sprinting for the woods as if money meant nothing to her at all.

Chapter 24

Only a day after Orli was confined to her quarters, the first signs of illness became apparent among the members of the crew. On that first day, eleven people showed up in sick bay complaining of headaches, fever and violent diarrhea. The ship was put on lockdown immediately, and Orli found herself no longer the only one onboard restricted as to where she went. Nobody was allowed anywhere other than duty stations and quarters. Meals were to be combat rations only and anybody who wanted to go outside of one of these two places had to run the request directly through the captain himself.

But that suited Orli just fine. If there was some disease floating around the ship now, she was perfectly content to stay right where she was. Within hours after the first wave of illnesses were reported, rumors began to circulate around the ship that an alien contagion was on the loose, injected into the ship when the orb thrust its proboscis through the hull.

Through talking to Roberto on the com, and through the regular ship's announcements, Orli gathered that the rumor was being taken seriously and that extreme measures were underway. White clouds of mist began to appear from every air vent on the ship as hundreds of gallons of antiseptic compounds were pumped out into every deck. Orli was glad they were taking decisive action, and she believed there was a chance that the rumors of alien infection were true, but she also had her own private fear as she glanced over at the plastic isolation tent she'd made around the cabinet on her wall. If it was an alien disease, she just hoped it was the orb and not her that had brought it to the ship.

She hadn't checked on her little fungal spore in a few days, and it was with trepidation that she zipped herself into the isolation tent. Before, she'd been excited to look and see if the spore might actually grow, but now she dreaded what she might find. She snapped on a pair of latex gloves and covered her face with a protective mask.

She opened the cabinet and pulled the petri dish out into the light. Looking through the clear plastic of its lid, she could see a grayish spot near the center of the dish. Her whole body tightened in a spasm of guilt and fear. She even felt dizzy for a moment as she realized that the spore had in fact started to grow. Of all the terrible times for success. Suddenly she had to fight back a wave of panic, and her breathing came in gasps as the reality of what she might well have done struck a nearly physical blow. She grappled with her emotions and finally regained some measure of calm, though panic flitted against it like a moth at a window trying to get in.

Replacing the petri dish, she zipped herself out of the tent and climbed onto the workbench beneath the air intake vent mounted in the ceiling. On tip toe, she reached up and opened the vent, pulling out the filter inside. She left the vent door swinging as she hopped back to the floor. Taking a scalpel from a jar against the wall, she cut out a small section of the filter and took it over to a microscope. She was afraid to look.

But she'd lucked out. The filter was clear of any signs of

fungus, and she could at last allow herself to breathe. That was a relief. She took a few more samples from other parts of the filter just to be safe, but in the end the outcomes were all the same. There were no fungi to be found. The epidemic could not be blamed on her.

With that nearly exhausting set of minutes out of her way, she decided she might as well have a look at what it was that she actually had done, since her fungus had finally decided to grow. She zipped herself back into the tent and had another look. There wasn't much to see with just the naked eye, so she scraped a bit of the growth onto a slide and set it in the microscope she'd put inside the tent.

Sure enough, her little spore had taken off and she had quite a colony going on. Her first concern, particularly given her recent scare, was to make sure that the fungicide she was using would actually do the trick in case this fungus decided it did want to get outside.

Using a syringe and the tiniest of needles, she squirted a little drop of fungicide onto the fungus sample on the slide. She looked back into the eyepiece to watch it take effect.

It did not. And the fungal cells were gone. In their place were several bacterial cells, which seemed quite happy to swim about as if they were fish in some microscopic pond.

"You've got to be kidding me," she said aloud, staring down at the scene upon the slide. "That did not just happen." She pulled back from the eyepiece and squinted down at the slide with her own two eyes, as if somehow that might clear things up. There was no way that she had mistaken those cells for fungi when they'd been bacteria all along. No way.

She pulled the slide out of the microscope and scraped another bit of the grayish spot in the petri dish onto a new glass slide. She put it in the microscope and had another look. Sure enough, fungi. Just what she'd expected she would see. Just as she had known she would see.

She retrieved the syringe and dropped a bit of fungicide

on this slide, as she had the first, and quickly looked back into the microscope to see if the fungi were still alive. The cells were alive, but once again there was no fungus to be found. Only bacteria. Same as the first.

She grunted, the corners of her mouth twitching. What could that possibly mean? She suspected the three types of DNA were at work. But could a creature, even a single-celled one as simple as these, remake itself as fast as that? Even with the genetic maps ready to go, an instantaneous shift seemed impossible at best.

But she had no more time to work on it, for it was then that she got Doctor Singh's call. "Ensign Pewter, you are needed back in sick bay. Report immediately." His tone was laden with stress, and Orli knew at once that things were getting bad. "And by immediately, I mean *immediately*." Despite the firm command in Doctor Singh's voice, there was an almost desperate undercurrent in the man's normally unassailable calm. Something was really going wrong.

"Coming," she said.

She tossed the two slides into an empty petri dish then closed it up and set it on the shelf. She capped the fungal sample as well, then, shutting the cabinet, zipped herself out of the tent after spending a moment in the fungicidal mist. Given what she'd just seen, she wondered if there was any point.

Her hands were trembling as she removed all of her protective garb. She'd be donning more in a few moments, up in the hospital section of the ship. As she jogged through the empty white corridors on her way to sick bay, fear of contagion began to grip her in the guts. She couldn't help thinking that she was running to the one place she never wanted to be, the place that had filled her nightmares only a short time ago, a place of screams and blood and fear, and now a place of contagion and possibly a gruesome alien death.

And her fears were not unfounded, for over the course of the next six days, it was in just such a horrible scene that Orli found herself immersed. The alien disease—and it was something alien because it was like nothing any of them had ever seen—had an awful progression. After the headaches, fever and intestinal trouble, came trembles and psychological distress. For many, the psychosis was a simple thing: weeping in corners or curling up in a ball beneath your cot. But for others it was violent and agonized.

The first patient to manifest this aspect of the disease was, no surprise, the first person that had reported his condition at the onset of the epidemic—and by day six, the existence of an epidemic was a certainty as over three hundred people were now infected with the mysterious disease. The first crewman, an older enlisted man normally stationed on deck seven, got his case of trembles near the end of the sixth day. He began sweating and shaking in his sickbed and did so for nearly five hours at which point, as Orli was changing sheets on a bed across the aisle, he suddenly leapt up and charged at her, screaming insane gibberish about aliens and tooth decay as he ground and gnashed his teeth. He slammed into her with his whole body, swinging his fists spasmodically. He was a large man, and Orli was thrown against the wall, crashing into a tray of instruments and falling amongst them to the floor in a metallic din.

The madman dove upon her and started pounding her with his fists, still screaming about the aliens and rotting breath. Orli was screaming too. It took her a few moments to recover from her initial shock, at first panicking and covering her head with her arms defensively, but finally gathering her wits enough to try to fight him off. She kicked and drove at him with her knees, scratching and punching with every ounce of her strength. His dementia was not conducive to effective defense, and she got several punches past his non-existent guard. Two times she palmed him in the nose, the second blow sending a gush of blood across his face and splashing down onto her, onto the front of her pale green scrubs. She realized as she saw the crimson streaks that she was now in a fight that could end with her in this man's shoes next week. The realization caused her to scream even louder as she continued trying to fight him off.

By then, two nurses and Doctor Singh were there, and Orli saw Doctor Singh plunging a needle into the raving man's shoulder as the two nurses fought to pull him back. The bloodied man collapsed onto her a moment later, limp and heavy as death, and Orli scrambled out from beneath him, swearing and trembling with rage and fear.

"Are you okay?" Doctor Singh asked, a dark hand on each of her shoulders and leaning his face down to study hers close up. His expression was one of fright and genuine concern. She nodded that she was, and the doctor ran a cursory inspection over the rest of her body. He saw the blood on her smock. "Did you get any in your mouth or eyes?"

She saw what he was looking at and shook her head, no. "At least I don't think so."

"Are you cut?"

She held out her bloodied hands, still trembling, and they both looked to see if she'd been cut by either the madman's gnashing teeth or clawing nails, or cut by something sharp on the tray when she had fallen, a scalpel or a shard of broken glass. But she was fine. No cuts. Maybe she'd gotten lucky after all.

It wasn't until she was back in her quarters, given a twelve-hour leave by Doctor Singh, that she allowed herself to cry. She sat on her bed and sobbed, shoulders heaving as she let the terror out. All of it. Terror of the patient who had attacked her, and terror for the one that was going to attack her next. Terror of the disease, of the horrible vomiting and diarrhea, of the headaches that made the people scream, of the raging fever and, now, apparently of the dementia that followed the body-wracking shakes. She felt terror of the anarchy that was fast becoming the ship, and terror of the orbs. Terror of death. And perhaps mostly, terror of misery.

"Orli," came Roberto's voice from the speaker on her small desk. "Hey, Orli, you there?"

She wiped her eyes on her blanket and tried to put on her regular face. She blew her nose and, after a moment, clicked on the monitor. "Hey," she said. "What's up?"

"Are you okay?"

"Yeah, I'm fine. What's up?"

"You don't look fine. I just heard what happened. Pennington told me. Are you sure you're okay?"

"Yes, I'm fine. Just scared the crap out of me is all. Really. I'm fine."

"Well good," he said. He looked relieved. "You look like shit though." He smiled.

"Thanks," she said, sniffling. She heard the captain's voice in the background, typically surly despite being too far off for her to make out all the words.

"Gotta run," was all Roberto said before the monitor went blank.

She spent a few expectant moments waiting for the ship-rattling crash of another projectile from an orb, assuming the returning Hostile to be why Roberto had been called away. But after a time she decided Roberto's abrupt departure was due to his having been caught sneaking the time to check on her, and she allowed herself to breathe. She didn't know what she would do if Roberto wasn't on the ship, wasn't there to care. Probably shoot herself or go entirely insane. She sighed. No, it would have to be insanity for sure; she'd never pull the trigger. She didn't have the guts. She sighed again. God, this was such an awful place. And the nightmare had just begun.

Chapter 25

Pernie was as good as her word, and it was with remarkable speed that she returned to Altin with two raven's wings, cut neatly from the bird and sparing Altin from disposing of a corpse. While a bit unnerved by the delight the girl seemed to take in butchery, he had to admit she'd done precisely as he'd asked. She also refused to take the silver coins.

"I never seen Master Tytamon paying you," she informed him. "So I ain't taking money neither since I'm going to be yer apprentice too."

Technically, Altin had an allowance, but still, what was he supposed to say to her? He frowned. This child certainly was difficult. "Well, I won't be taking any apprentices any time soon, so you don't have to worry." It wasn't the perfect evasion, but he figured it would do. He was wrong. The tears that he had so adeptly avoided in the meadow threatened once again to pour, forcing him to quickly add, "But if I do, I promise I'll let you give it a try."

That seemed to hold back the water for now, if barely, and she handed off the severed wings and turned morosely from the room. Altin felt as if he should add something more, something to make her smile, but he couldn't think of the exact right words. There were things he might have said.

He grunted as she disappeared down the stairs, pushing inconvenient emotions aside, then went to the window that faced the courtyard to make sure she had really gone away. He saw her carrying her little basket of frog's legs into the castle proper and knew that he was safe to cast his Polar's shield.

Once the shield was up, he went to the spell book with the stasis spell. He studied it closely and read the description aloud:

Cast upon a falling or levitated object, stasis will grant such properties of location as if the spell's recipient were firmly planted on the ground. The object cannot be moved by force or magic unless there is a more powerful magic at work. Applied physical force can, and will, move or destroy the object if said force is too great, as Stasis does not buttress the target's physical properties in any way. However, the object may be moved about at leisure by the caster through the use of the simple release command embedded in the spell and re-stasised with the same activating word. The effect lasts for approximately two hours unless enchanted otherwise as per standard extension procedures.

The description went on from there about K-rank enchanters and whatnot, but Altin saw what he needed to see. Stasis was exactly what he wanted, or at least seemed to be, and he wasted no time in beginning to memorize the spell; his tower would not be falling into planets again any time soon. He worked a few hours memorizing it, and by the time he had it cast and sent himself back to Naotatica, he yawned and stretched tiredly from all the work.

He spent another hour in static orbit above Naotatica, back at the point where the falling in had begun, to make sure that the stasis spell was indeed working as it should. Once he was convinced of it, he enchanted it permanently in place. He made the appropriate changes in his notes, and then put himself to bed after a meal eaten out of Kettle's crate.

He woke up an indeterminable number of hours later and wrote a note to remind himself to get a water clock the next time he went to town. It was so unendingly dark out here that he felt he might lose his sense of night and day completely at some point. Particularly if he was going to be out here for a while, which was exactly what he intended to do.

Now that he'd mastered the strange pull of Naotatica, he felt it was time to press on with the next planet in the line. He wished there actually had been a line, however, for according to his astronomer's maps the planets at this time of year were nowhere near aligned. The closest one was the sixth planet in the solar system, Venvost. He squinted up into the night sky and tried to spy where he thought it should be based on his astronomer's charts. But there were only stars speckling the night. He couldn't tell one from the other.

He looked back in the direction of Prosperion and realized how very small it had become. He'd been so focused on moving outward, he hadn't spent any time appreciating just how far away from home he'd come. Prosperion was just a pale blue dot. Hardly bigger than any other star, but still discernable by its hue. The sun was getting smaller too. Not uncomfortably small, but Altin could tell that he wouldn't be able to travel a whole lot farther before being well beyond its range, which made him start to think. What if he did pass so far away that it faded out of sight? What if he got so far away that it disappeared and he could not find his way back. The thought made his stomach clench.

But he knew immediately that that was absurd. He had the advantage of always "knowing" where Prosperion was. That idea was at the core of teleportation law. You just had to know where you wanted to go. But still, it was a frightening thought. To be so far away from home. So far that even the sun might go away.

As a security precaution, he decided he needed to construct a fast-cast amulet to take him home. Or perhaps just to Luria so there would be no danger of someone standing in the way. He remembered discussing it with Tytamon. It was still a good idea, something for just-in-case.

And so he did. The prospect of losing sight of Prosperion and perhaps even the sun was such that Altin was willing to spend the two days required to make his fast-cast amulet. He only had a few flawed garnets in his tower to use, but the gem was not important beyond its purpose of storing the energy and the focus of the spell. Any gem would do. He chose a good-sized garnet, about the size of a lima bean, and trickled the mana into its tiny mass slowly over the course of two days; he even used the Liquefying Stone so he could layer in mana for what he figured would be more distance than he would ever need, a ridiculous amount. Why not? Given the distances he'd discovered out here so far, there was no sense taking chances after all. When he was done, he used a bit more lead from the brick downstairs and crafted a crude mount for the garnet using a transmutation spell from one of his books. He ran a leather cord through it and held it aloft to examine his work when he was done. The amulet was hideous.

He had to laugh at how horrible it looked. He was sure no jewel crafter. He should have had Aderbury do it; the man was an artist when it came to things like this. Oh well, he thought, it's functional and that's what matters. It made him feel a bit safer. It also gave him license to push outward harder too.

Satisfied, and annoyed that he'd allowed fear to cost him two days, it was time to press on. He looked back up into the sky in the direction of Venvost, ready to go. But, it was still not there. Or at least not that he could tell. Just an enormous darkness sprinkled with spots of light. He groaned. He wished he could divine. Finding the general direction of Venvost would be the simplest kind of divination anyone could do. Even B-class divination could provide enough of a feel for him to start.

After scanning hopelessly in the vast night sky, and after six tremendously long seeing stone casts with the Liquefying Stone in the direction he hoped was right, he decided to give divination a try. For all he knew he was casting in entirely the wrong direction anyway. He was not the mathematician Aderbury was, but he knew enough of angles to know that, given the distances he was working with out here, guessing could be an extremely time consuming way to get it done. Harder than finding a tadpole in a tar pit, as Tytamon would say. Altin was certain that he could cast himself around forever out here and never find a planet by anything approaching chance. The size of space was simply too great.

He went downstairs and got his *Divining for Beginners* book from his personal library on the tower's second floor. He hadn't opened this book in years, a decade at the least. He sighed as he blew dust off the top of its yellowed bulk.

He opened it up to the first page, the binding creaking as he did, and leafed impatiently through the introduction which explained the value of knowledge and defined the nature of Divination as "images that work with what you know." He knew what he needed to know. He needed to know where in the last layers of hell damnable Venvost was.

He turned to the page that held the starter spell. It was a very simple spell, and it was a directional one. The instructions read:

Think about your mommy or your daddy, or your teacher if your parents aren't nearby. Then, sit on the floor. Close your eyes and try to picture where that person is. As you think of them, chant the following words to the tune of "My Cat's Paw:" Leenox para meh, foor nah for nah moor. Leenox para meh, foor nah for nah loor.

Altin moaned and snapped the volume shut. The book was infantile. And he hated that stupid kiddie's song. And his parents had been dead for years. And he already knew where Tytamon was, so what use was that supposed to be? He threw the book down onto his bed. He didn't have time for stupid childhood spells.

He went back upstairs and cast four more seeing stones to absolutely no avail. His casts were still improving, and his distances were getting extreme. He could easily cast a seeing stone twice the distance it was from Luria to Naotatica now with the help of the Liquefying Stone. It was amazing what just being able to conceive of the distances out here did to help the casts.

He began to wonder if perhaps he'd already passed Venvost completely by. He moved from his latest view in the scrying basin and cast an improved seeing spell out to the tiny seeing stone he'd just sent blindly into space. He spun his vision round in all directions but still there were no other planets in his sight. There was nothing, just stars.

And his theory about the sun was proving right too. It was almost completely gone when viewed from this most recent seeing stone. It really looked like nothing more than a giant star. Which made him wonder if maybe that was all it really was.

What if the sun was just a star?

The thought struck him like a blow. He stared at the bright spot of light far back behind his tiny seeing stone floating in the night and realized that another cast or two like the last and his sun would be no more significant than any other of those other dots of light sparkling in the sky. It would be just like them. Exactly like them.

Which meant that they in turn might be exactly like it.

The thought was chilling in its magnitude. What if the stars really weren't holes in the ceiling of the sky? What if the stars were suns? Suns like the one that shone down upon Prosperion? And if they were, what if every star had a planet or two around it that was filled with life? A Prosperion for every point of light in the whole seemingly endless stretch of space? What an incredible thought. And it seemed to him as he considered it that it must be true.

Every sun had its own life. And maybe there could only be one place with life near any given sun. Maybe there weren't going to be other people on the rest of the planets around his sun after all. Maybe that was just how the universe worked. He'd cursed the moon for being an empty waste of space. He'd cursed Naotatica too. But perhaps, once again, he'd been thinking entirely too small. He snorted in recognition of this fact and nodded to himself. Maybe there were only so many fish allowed to live in any given solar bowl.

He snapped his vision back into his body and then teleported himself and the tower out to his furthest seeing stone. He stood for a long while looking out into the stars. The darkness was as beautiful as it was vast and terrifying, the stars seeming to crowd together in every swatch of space. He marveled that as close together as many of them might seem, they were likely as far away as was his sun. Perhaps farther. Almost definitely farther. Nothing out here was close. It made him shudder just to think. And yet they called to him, daring him to come outside his tiny little space, challenging him to leap out of his tiny solar bowl and swim—swim with people from the stars. There simply had to be someone else.

But first there was Venvost he had to find. He would not begin another quest until his current one was done. That was not Altin's way. As tempting as the stars might be, he had a few more planets to explore. And it was with a resigned sense that there would be no one to greet him on any single one that he set out to find them just the same. If he did not look for them, perhaps no one else ever would. He would not leave anyone out here all alone.

Chapter 26

Altin's theories involving the vacant states of the other planets turned out to be entirely true, and, though it took him almost six weeks to find them all, and some considerable time scouting each of them out, in the end he was convinced that the races of Prosperion were all that his solar system had brought to life. Furthermore, religion was entirely disproved for him. There was both satisfaction and discontent in that. He'd always been happily agnostic before. In an odd way, the possibility that the Church might be at least partly right, despite his skepticism, had always been something of a security net. But now that had been taken away. Altin's sense of loneliness was complete. There was no one else circling round the sun.

But the revelation helped to drive him on. He knew that there were others in the vast space that he found himself drifting in, there had to be, and he was bent on finding them no matter how long it took. And so it was that he set himself to the task of reaching for another sun—reaching for a star.

He had no particular one in mind, and it was on a lark that he forced himself to use the childish divining spell in picking one out. He sat atop the battlements with the infantile book in his lap and chanted the stupid baby song—though rather than picturing someone he already knew, he decided in his typically obtuse fashion that he was going to concentrate on someone he *wanted* to know instead. He knew that this attitude was probably going to prompt failure, particularly in a school for which he'd been told he had no gift, but such was his mood when he gave the spell a try.

He followed all the steps, just as the book said he should, and, just as he expected, when he was done he felt that he had no answers at all. The only new impression that he came away with in his mind was that now he knew he was a fool—that and, after sitting cross-legged on the floor singing that infernal cat song, he was very glad that there had been no one in the tower to see him try. He tossed the book onto the scorched table near the wall and looked back up into the sky. So many stars and no intelligent way to choose.

But he needed to pick one. So he did. He closed his eyes, vowing to fix his attention on the first one he noticed when he opened them back up. And he did just that. He opened his eyes, picked a star at random from the view, and marked it in his mind with a silent seer's mark. "I will go there," he said aloud and then his newest quest was underway.

Given his work over the past several weeks, he was able to teleport completely out of his solar system in just one cast, roughly four times the distance that Naotatica was from the sun. From there, however, it was back to work with the Liquefying Stone.

He took a seeing stone—both his crates freshly refilled with newly enchanted stones made during a recent trip back home and augmented with the new stasis spell, given what he'd learned from Naotatica about things tending to drift out here—and sent it far out into the night, aimed directly at his chosen star.

He didn't even bother to check on it in the scrying basin, and instead he immediately picked up another seeing stone and sent it skipping off the first. He repeated the process eleven times, growing wearier with each successive cast, before finally looking into the scrying basin to see what he had done. Which turned out to be nothing. No change. No closer than before.

He knew it, of course, and there was no surprise, no disappointment. Just the establishment of fact. He was in for a long haul, and the early stages of this new pursuit were going to be about fathoming new extremes of distance. And so to that he set his mind.

Every day, Altin cast and cast his stones. Every day, for seven to ten hours, he would send seeing stones out into the night, aimed each time at his private, distant star. He cast until he was exhausted, throwing stones so far into the depths of space with each successive spell that by the end of the third week the stones were vanishing from his hands with an almost thunderous crack. After a day's labor, for labor it was, he would collapse in his bed—if not onto the flagstones beneath his feet—following a last attempt and sleep for seven to ten hours. He'd eat, sometimes wash up, sometimes not, and begin again. And so it went for nearly a month and a half, a grueling display of discipline, Altin's will only becoming more entrenched the longer that it took, an obdurate thing buried in resolve with roots deeper than a mountain's and even less pliable. And still his star was no closer. After the month and a half, he'd actually spent two hours on his bed contemplating the nature of his own frailty, of his quest's impossibility, but that moment quickly passed, and he was back to casting again. And so it went for yet another month. And then a month after that.

His occasional trips home—he'd taken to teleporting home every so often in person just to get his laundry done and get more seeing stones—yielded him a scolding from

Kettle for his disheveled look. Pernie stared at him from shadowy corners on those occasions when he arrived, looking almost afraid. A glimpse in the mirror showed that he was indeed a frightful sight, but such things were not in his realm of concern. He had a goal and he would get there if it killed him. No matter what. And to hell with the history of the Six.

At times he was delirious after days of casting endlessly in a row. He knew he was walking on the edge, and he caught himself on two occasions mumbling over the scrying basin with nothing conjured in the water at all. He shook himself to sense both times and put himself to bed. He had an endless headache now as well, had had it for at least six weeks in a row. And he noticed that he didn't smell the same. He caught whiffs of his own scent sometimes and realized that something in his body odor had changed, had turned more acrid, more acidic somehow. And his robes hung off of him like rags. But he did not care. He would go on, would continue to press his limits every day, press the Liquefying Stone. And he was having success when it came to that. The distance of his teleports became something too vast to be explained, even to himself, space so incomprehensible he had no way to describe it symbolically. He simply called each cast a "stone's throw" and sufficed himself with that.

Somewhere just past his third month out—time was really something of a blur—was when he first encountered movement in the eternal dark of night. He'd just finished a string of six successive casts and was sitting on his stool catching his breath and having a bit of cheese when he saw it. He had to squint to be sure that he'd seen what he thought he saw, but sure enough, against the star-spotted curtain of sky there was a spot of total black, round and looking as if he'd caught a portion of space in a yawn. The yawn continued to widen, however, and it wasn't long before Altin realized that the dark spot was moving. Very soon it was looming up at him blotting out a good portion of the night, as much as would a fist held out at arm's length against the sky. It seemed to stop then, and just hovered quietly beyond the tower for a while.

Once more Altin felt himself cursing the unknowable distances of space. He couldn't be sure if the dark spot was huge, like Naotatica, and still very far away, or if it was relatively small and right outside the shield. He took a torch from the sconce by the stairs and walked it over to the parapet, holding it out as far as he could reach. Its paltry flickering flames did nothing to illuminate the black ball dangling in the night.

Altin squinted up at it again and shook his head. It began to move again, or to swell, he really couldn't tell which, and he got an uncomfortable sense of vertigo as it grew considerably bigger and drifted to the side. He wondered if his stasis spell had failed and maybe it was him doing the moving all the while. He quickly mumbled the words that would put his mind inside the Polar's shield. No, the stasis spell was working as it should.

"Hmm," he muttered aloud. "Well, at least I'm not alone. Unless it's just an empty rock." He had to admit that movement did not necessarily mean life. Nothing else since leaving Prosperion had. There was no reason to believe that this spot would offer anything new. In fact, it was his experience that most of the round things out here possessed no life at all, Prosperion being the sole exception to the rule. However, this object did not seem to move randomly or by chance.

He didn't have much time to ruminate on it, however, for the black spot suddenly began to grow again, and the next thing he knew his tower shuddered as if an earthquake had struck.

"Nine hells!" he cried, staggering against the wall with

the violence of the attack. The tower stopped shaking almost immediately, allowing him to regain his balance and to curse again. "Manticore's milk, what did I do to deserve that?"

He cast his eyes around him seeking out the dark spot against the sky. He plunged the torch into the scrying basin to aid his vision; the light had made it difficult to see very far into the darkness. There it was, off to his right and slightly above. It was small again, not much bigger than a walnut from Altin's point of view, and still shrinking. But it stopped a moment later, and once more began to grow. Altin, considered by most who knew him to be a quick thinker, stood transfixed. He was out of his element here.

Again the spot became huge and swept past his tower, once more battering the Polar's shield with an incredible, stone-rattling blow that this time knocked Altin to the floor.

"For the love of Mercy," Altin muttered as he scrambled to his feet. He wasn't sure which would fall apart first, the Polar's shield or his tower, but either way, he couldn't just stand there any longer and let that thing beat upon him like it was, or his adventure through space was going to come quickly to an end.

He looked out at the spot again, once more diminishing in size as it passed him by. It stopped, and then headed back. He knew that he didn't have time to cast a full teleport and for a moment considered using the amulet he had made. But that would be akin to him having run away. He wasn't about to do that.

And just what was this gods-be-damned thing anyway? And why was it attacking him? In fact, how dare it attack him! He'd done nothing to deserve this offense. Only orcs attacked without provocation, not civilized beings like men or even elves. This was an affront to his honor, and he would not be put to flight.

However, the words of the stasis spell came back to him

now: *Applied physical force can, and will, destroy the object if said force is too great.* Altin suspected he'd found the kind of force the spell was talking about, if not of any origin that the creator had had in mind.

With a word he released the stasis spell, granting the tower at least the luxury of absorbing the blow in the same manner that a warrior might roll with a punch or fall away from a truncheon blow. That done, he plunged his mind inside the shield to see how it was holding up. The strands of mana with which it was woven were indeed beginning to vibrate as the energy of the two great impacts struck them like strings upon a lute, but for now it seemed as if they were holding remarkably well. He just needed time to go down and run through his book of combat spells to see what he could use. He was going to put this black spot in its place.

He was halfway down the stairs when the next impact sent him tumbling the rest of the way into his room. He rolled into his bedchamber in time to see the bookshelf empty itself onto the floor.

"Damn it," he spat as he scrambled to his feet.

The candle rolled off the table and fell onto the rug upon which the table sat.

Altin ran over and stomped out the small fire that ignited on the rug and put the candle back in its holder, mashing it firmly into place. He then ran to the pile of books lying near his bed, tossing tomes aside and looking for his book of combat spells. Finally he found the one he needed and flipped it right side round so he could have a look.

He leafed through it hastily, not even sure what he was looking for, when he came across an old familiar spell called "Luminous Aura." Perfect he thought; that would help him see the dark ball better against the night. He scoured the spell rapidly, and memorized it with little trouble at all. Such was the beauty of the *Military Book of Spells*, everything in it was designed for combat efficiency, and it did not hurt that Altin, as a mage in service of the Queen, had been forced to read them nearly every day for the duration of his two-year stint. The incantation came easily back to mind.

But he needed more than just a way to see it. He flipped through some more, looking for something else. The tower shuddered as another impact shook it to its ivy-covered base. He ignored the impact and continued paging through until he found a spell called "Combat Hop," a quick reflexive teleport spell meant to, in essence, "blink" combatants out from beneath descending blows. He thought he might be able to add it to the Polar's shield. It would be fantastic if he could make it work, but he still needed something else. The tower shuddered again, and a light rain of dust and grit fell onto the pages of his book.

He blew the grit away and paged past the fire spells; no need to read them, he would never forget those after the drilling he got with them in the service. He stopped briefly in the section on electrical spells. He wasn't sure if he could conjure lightning out here, but there was a simple version that wouldn't hurt to try. It was a short spell with a single word release. It only took him a moment to get it in his head. He realized when he was done, however, that it required that he touch the target to release the spell. Rushing was causing him to make stupid mistakes and to waste valuable time.

The tower shook again, violent but not as bad as the last. More dust came down and settled on the page. It was like having orcish trebuchets launching boulders as big as wagons against his shield; the raw insult of it was really beginning to stir him to a fury, particularly as he'd done nothing to deserve this unwarranted attack. The candle rolled off the table in the middle of the room again.

He rose and replaced it in its holder once more, and then leafed quickly through the rest of his combat book; there wasn't much else in it that he didn't already know by heart. He'd have to make do with what he knew. Besides, the volume of dust falling from the ceiling suggested he didn't have time to continue looking for a better set of spells.

Back on the battlements, back in the total darkness of the night, he spun round until he spotted the black spot way off to the left and somewhat down below, although it was circling the tower in an odd and oblong way. But, despite the new looping-round tactic, it was growing larger again, returning for another pass. He would not have time to cast the Combat Hop, but the Luminous Aura was an easy thing to do. So, as the spot came on at its incredible pace, he muttered the words and cast the glowing aura upon its charging mass. As soon as the spell took effect, Altin could see it much more clearly as it moved.

It turned out to be a large brown ball of rather rough looking material that reminded him of a coconut without the hair, organic looking and perhaps no tougher than a block of wood. As it rushed in, he saw it open up a portion of its surface and emit a long chunk of something that was obviously very hard given the mighty blow that it struck upon the Polar's shield a moment after the release. The tower was rocked to its foundations again, and Altin watched as the coconut chased down its projectile and reclaimed it into itself, presumably to be used for yet another pass.

"So that's how it works," Altin said aloud. "Well, we'll just see about that." He planted his feet firmly beneath him and waited for the next attack, easily tracking the coconut now thanks to the Luminous Aura spell—and despite the very unnerving round and round flight pattern that the spot was using now. In fact, as the spot moved farther away, it became harder and harder to see, and by the time it was small enough to be considered walnut-sized again, the circular movements were taking it completely out of view. It was as if it were orbiting his tower around the vertical axis for some inexplicable reason.

That's when it occurred to Altin that he'd released the stasis spell.

"Of course!" he cried, and quickly muttered the word that would fix the tower back in place. Immediately after, the coconut no longer seemed to whirl about the tower, although it was now out of Altin's view. He felt the next impact as it struck the stone at the base of Altin's tower. He suddenly wondered if he'd cut deep enough into the granite at Mt. Pernolde's base to hold off such a monstrous blow. His foundation was either going to be a strength or weakness here, and he was now in the unfortunate position of having to find out which would be the case. It was not a pleasant thought.

"All right, these harpoon things need to stop," he said as he watched the coconut nearly disappear above him against the stars. He began the chant that would add the Combat Hop to his shield, hoping he had time to get it off. He met with an ambiguity that made his incantation flounder in his mouth. He had to release the spell midway through, which filled his head with a burst of light, and nearly knocked him to the floor. Incomplete magic was a dangerous and painful thing.

The problem was, casting the spell required he specify from what, precisely, the tower was supposed to hop away. Apparently, he did not "precisely" know what the spot was throwing at him. He tried again, this time struggling to define the object in terms that would activate the spell. Meanwhile, the giant coconut got off another shot.

This impact did knock him to the floor and the disruption of the magic once again blasted his mind with an explosive burst of light, blinding him for a moment and leaving him gasping on the floor. The aggressive brown ball hit the tower twice more before Altin was able to raise himself from the flagstones, and when he did, he could smell smoke coming from down below. He guessed that the candle had fallen to the floor again, and he cursed himself for having twice put it back in the same unstable spot.

He glanced up and saw the coconut coming back for another shot. His hand went reflexively to the amulet around his neck. He could just run away; his room was on fire, and this thing was beating his tower to death.

But he couldn't do it. He would rather die.

He stood up, nearly passing out with the effort and stared defiantly as the brown ball came on. He braced his hands against the wall and waited for the impact to shake him to the ground, staring intensely at the spot and intent on watching its missile every instant that he could. It came, he watched, and then he was knocked to his knees despite his grip on the parapet. But then he rose, immediately, and began to cast the Combat Hop again. He knew enough to get it done now; he'd watched it very close. He closed his eyes and drew the mana to him, gathering it round into a ball of his own, then rupturing it into a thousand tiny threads that snaked out like rays emitted from an invisible star, each one a potential path for the tower to take. Some went far, perhaps a half a measure, others only forty paces or so. Most were somewhere in between. And then he locked the spell on the idea of what he'd watched just pound into his tower, on the idea of a long, stony-looking shaft emitted from a large and charging ball flying through the night. Once that was done, he cast the center of the magic's core, the essence of the spell from which all potential hops were born, into the Polar's shield, watching it as the mana permeated the energies encapsulating his tower and mingled with the threads of the stasis spell. He hoped his impression of the spot's weapon was good enough to work.

With the spell in place, he let the mana go just in time to brace as the coconut was letting lose its shaft again. He grabbed the wall and prepared to take another hit. But then the stony harpoon was gone, as if it had vanished in the night. Altin let out a whoop of glee. Combat Hop had worked. And just in the nick of time. He spun and watched as the coconut chased its weapon down. He allowed himself a smile.

The Combat Hop spell was a bit disorienting at first. Every time the coconut came at him and released its brutal battering ram, the tower leapt away, sliding randomly and instantly down one of Altin's enchanted mana threads. After each pass, he had to search out where the coconut had gone again, as it could be literally anywhere in relationship to his new locale. But that was a small price to pay. The coconut could no longer beat upon his shield.

He cursed at it as it came in for yet another pass, and made a rude gesture with his fist. But Combat Hop had bought him time. Time to go put out the fire before it got too big in his bedroom down below.

He ran downstairs and saw that his rug was engulfed in knee-high flames, and the legs of his table were now beginning to burn as well. I'm sure hard on furniture, he thought as he tried to conjure a small cloud of rain. It was a simple version of the spell he'd used several months back when the ivy had caught fire, but, small as he tried to make it, it didn't do the job. It wasn't a total failure; he got a bit of rain puttering from wisps of clouds that were more mist than cumulus and that tried to form near the ceiling of his room. But what came was such an abysmally small amount of water that it hardly reduced the flames at all. He should have known. There wasn't enough moisture in the air beneath his relatively tiny dome to conjure a storm of any size. He recast the spell, channeling directly at his scrying basin and the pitcher on his dresser across the room. This time it worked, and at once the fire was put out, filling his room with steam and whorls of stinking yellow smoke. The rug was wolf pelt and the smell of burnt hair was going to be in everything for a while. He fought back a gag and went upstairs.

The spot was zooming in for yet another shot and Altin chuckled as its projectile went harmlessly past, the Combat Hop moving him a hundred paces to the side. "Nice try," he taunted as the spot went off and reclaimed its missile yet again.

It zoomed in once more, but, unexpectedly, it stopped and hovered some considerable distance away, appearing roughly the size of a peach, or perhaps a croquet ball. And there it stayed, as if watching him, perhaps recognizing that it couldn't hit Altin with its heavy beams of stone.

Given a moment's thought, Altin decided to send a fireball on its way to test out his theory about the spot being no more resilient than a block of wood. He was about to cast one as large as he possibly could when he found that there were insufficient elements near enough to him for him to get it done in the volume his mental image specified. The fire spell was suffering from the same problem he'd had with the rain spell. Apparently, magic had to be worked a bit differently out in space. He would have to modify much of what he thought he knew. But he had an idea.

He restarted the fireball spell, this time running a mana stream all the way back to Naotatica, figuring on borrowing elements from its fiery core as the answer to his need. At least the empty planet would be good for something, he thought. Drawing from so far away took him quite a long time to do, and as he did it, he realized that perhaps next time the Liquefying Stone would be a better choice for this particular type of spell. However, he had the source he needed already fixed in his mythothalamus, so he worked the spell as it was.

The fires deep inside Naotatica were incredibly hot, and Altin could actually feel the essence of the heat within his mind as he had never done before. Even drawing molten stuff from the heart of a volcano was nothing compared to this. It was thrilling to think he had access to such incredible power. He gathered up enough of it to fill a manor house and attached it to the mana string. Then he let it go, using the distance of three months' teleports to speed his fireball on its way.

The transfer from Naotatica into the space a few hundred paces to Altin's left was instantaneous, and the white-hot fireball went streaking towards the aggressive spot. The effect was almost blinding the fireball was so bright, and were it not for the screening effect of the Polar's shield, Altin felt it might actually have cost him his sight. He watched in awe as the giant ball of incredible heat closed on the coconut hovering out amongst the stars; Altin was certain that nothing could take that kind of heat. But the coconut moved easily out of the way. As if it had Combat Hop as well.

Altin gasped. His brows dipped as he concentrated on this new discovery. No. Not a Combat Hop, he thought, for he had actually seen it move. But still, the spot had moved so fast that Altin was convinced that it had used something similar to the spell. "You little mimic-monkey," he said. "So that's how you're going to play?"

His words were tough, but in truth, if a fireball wasn't going to do the job, he, like the coconut, had no other way to attack his opponent and do it any harm. And so the wait began, neither of them able to strike a decisive blow, or any blow at all, and neither of them going to leave. Altin was damn sure not going to be the first to go. There was absolutely no way he was going to retreat. No way. On that he was resolute. As long as Kettle was back home to fill his box of food, he would stay here until the end of time. No coconut was ever going to scare Altin Meade off like some girl running from a snake. Never.

Chapter 27

Orli's twelve hours of rest flew by, and before she knew it she was back in the nightmare taking place in sick bay. Two more patients had gone mad since she'd taken her break, and the first man, the one who had attacked her, was dead. When she walked back into the infirmary, Doctor Singh was sitting at a monitor with Doctor Salvator leaning over his shoulder also staring at the screen. They both saw her come in and nodded a greeting, Doctor Salvator adding, "Ensign Pewter, you might be interested in seeing this." She beckoned Orli over to the join them at the monitor.

"This is the bacteria causing the disease," Doctor Singh informed her as Doctor Salvator made room for her to stand behind his chair. "We took this culture and forty more just like it over the last week from members of the crew. We've been dosing them with everything we have over the last few days and yet, nothing. It's definitely an alien species, and it is apparently immune to everything we've got."

Orli could see that there were several bacterial cells visible on the screen, wriggling about in a blue-gray solution that looked in the monitor as if it were aglow. These microorganisms looked remarkably similar to the specimens she had found while working with her spore, and so she said as much.

"Really," Singh and Salvator said in unison after hearing what she'd found. "So it was the orbs that took out Andalia." They both nodded as if the last bit of doubt had been eliminated for them regarding the fate of the Andalian populace.

"So, what can you tell us about this bacterium then?" Doctor Singh asked, sounding hopeful. "You've had a great deal more time to study it than we have."

"Well, sadly, I really didn't start working on it right away, so I'm not that far ahead of you guys at all. But I will tell you that my bacteria came from the fungus."

They both frowned. "What do you mean?" said Doctor Singh.

"It came from the fungus. Not off the fungus, but *from* it. My original sample was—still is—a fungus. I only saw this bacterium after I tested one of our fungicides on a few of my fungal cells to check its efficacy. That's when I saw the bacteria. My fungus actually *became* bacteria as a reaction to the fungicide. I bet it's some kind of alien defense."

Doctor Singh crunched up his whole face, doubtful. Doctor Salvator didn't look much more convinced, but she at least made an attempt to hide her reticence.

"I'm serious," Orli insisted. "I did it twice. And if you map the genome—which I did have the time to do—you might find that it contains genes for not only bacterial traits, but fungal and viral too. Do it, and you'll see."

"So you're telling me that this bacterium has genetic material for three entirely different types of organism, manifests only one at a time, and... can change at will?" asked Doctor Singh. Doctor Salvator was no longer hiding anything in her expression.

"Yes. Instantly. Faster than I could get back to the microscope. That's exactly what I'm saying."

"And you're sure it's not just a mask, some kind of

camouflage?"

"I'm pretty sure."

Doctor Singh turned and ordered a nurse to draw new blood samples from several patients to whom they'd been administering antibiotics. He looked back at Orli. "As absurd as it sounds, at this point I'm not putting anything past an alien disease."

"It's not really that much of a leap if you consider the source," Orli put in. "I mean, the orbs seemed to make instantaneous shifts of their exterior depending on what we were throwing at them. Maybe their defenses are change-based, be it ship—orb—armament, or in their germ warfare techniques."

Doctor Salvator gave a low, short hum, her eyebrows lowered, and her mouth tight, moving laterally on her face in a doubtful way. "There's a big difference between armor and life forms. I don't think it's quite the same thing. Although there is a convenient coincidence, I'll give you that."

Doctor Singh nodded, but said nothing. Orli thought that he might be at least considering what she said, but just then a huge racket broke out as two patients managed to reach the neurotic state of the disease simultaneously and began attacking the staff and other patients. One, a dark woman with sunken eyes and gaunt cheeks, began to scream. Nothing articulate, just a high, piercing wail of absolute disconnect. She slapped the cup from the nurse's hand and spit at her, baring feral teeth, pausing her howl long enough to hiss. She swung towards the bewildered nurse and leapt with a strength a casual observer would not have reckoned her to have, her hospital gown flying open, her legs twisting round to clutch the nurse and bear her to the ground. The other, an older man, threw his tray aside and began tearing the tubes from his arms, gripping them in pale fists that looked arthritic the knuckles bulged so much with the rage behind his grip. He lunged for the patient in the bed next to him, who'd been asleep and had to defend himself despite surprise and pharmacological haze as the deranged patient began strangling him with the clear plastic tubes.

Orli and both doctors ran to help, she and Doctor Salvator pulling the strangler off of his victim, Doctor Singh untangling the screaming woman from the nurse. Several trying minutes ticked by before they got both patients sedated, but at last they did, though silencing them brought little relief, for the entire ward was beginning to show the signs of strain. It would only get worse as increasing numbers of the crew went crazy and ultimately died.

And it did get worse over the course of the next few days. The disease was spreading throughout the ship, and, as people got word of the futility of sick bay, many of them began to closet themselves away even if they manifested early signs of the disease. What was the point of going to sick bay if there was no cure?

There came more and more incidences of crew members appearing unexpectedly, already mad in the last stages of the infection, and attacking one another. What was worse, many of them were attacking critical ship's systems: one petty officer jettisoned two of the *Aspect's* four landing craft, and another attempted to blow up the ship's forward water tanks. That would have been a real disaster, and security forces, at least those few remaining who were able to perform that rigorous of a detail, had been forced to shoot the man. He was the seventh death by that particular means in as many days. By the end of the outbreak's third week, the ship's crew was down to half, and of the half that remained, a quarter were showing signs of infection too. And there was no help coming from the rest of the fleet. No other ships were willing to risk their crews on the *Aspect*, not with an alien pathogen on the loose. Rumor had it that the *Aspect's* name had been unofficially changed to the

Aspect of Death in mess halls and recreation rooms throughout the fleet—not mockingly, but in a tragic, frightened kind of way.

All but three of the nurses were dead now, and Orli was frequently forced to work in that capacity despite being untrained. The three nurses were doing many of the duties normally saved for the doctor, as Doctor Singh was working tirelessly on developing a cure—standard treatments were completely ineffective, and he felt his time was better spent seeking their salvation than comforting the doomed. This left Orli performing duties far outside her experience and qualification. However, she was doing so with increasing skill and was even becoming something of an expert at sedating mad crew members regardless of their size. Her small frame and runner's fitness made her quick enough to do it well. She was fast and of the right stature to get inside their flailing limbs and deliver a shot with precision. And she was becoming, with practice, very hard to hit. In fact her reputation in that regard grew over the course of a pair of weeks, and gradually she became the official sedater, being called virtually every time crew members lost their minds.

She reported to the infirmary one shift after an entirely unsatisfying five hours sleep and was greeted by a blinking light on the console that promised to be just such a call. She pressed the key that brought up the face of a very distraught petty officer with a large gash over one eye and sweat glistening on his face. "Duvall just lost it," he said. "We've got him cornered. Security is here, but they said as long as he doesn't come out and make them shoot his ass, you guys have time to come down and help him out. Hurry though." She could hear a man's voice screaming in the background, something about corned beef and a white yoyo with no string.

"Coming," was all she said and clicked off the monitor.

She grabbed the kit with all her syringes and sedatives and, poking her head in to say "hello" and "goodbye" to Doctor Singh, she trotted off.

She'd taken to trotting now. Running only brought the nightmare closer with greater speed. And the outcome was all the same. She'd sedate this one, just like the rest, but it wouldn't make much difference. He'd still be dead in a few hours. The only thing she was doing was saving the security guys the guilt of having to shoot another one. That's what this was all about. No need to run. Trotting was just right. Walking made her feel guilty, made her think she'd lost the last remnants of her humanity, but running got her there too fast. As long as she was willing to trot, she could tell herself that she was still concerned, that she was still human and alive, not just waiting for them all to die and end this slow disaster in the emptiness of space.

She arrived at the waste materials processing plant a short while later, her heartbeat quickened not by the distance but by the nature of the task she was here to perform. She may have done a lot of these, but they still made her nervous.

The petty officer with the cut on his face, the one who had made the call, met her as she came into the vacuous chamber and pointed in the direction of a large tank hissing steam from a cracked pipe fitting. The pipe, broken during the initial fight with the madman, was one of many that angled up into the labyrinthine array of plumbing that ran through the ceiling above or plunged down through the grated floor into a series of tanks and filters below. The huge room was humid from all the evaporative processes at work and remained so despite the huge vents meant to draw the moisture back into the plant's hydro-conservation loop. The stench of the waste treatment process was overpowering, and disgust contorted her features as she surveyed the situation with a cursory glance around.

She could see two men, dark silhouettes in the warm fog

misting up the room, and gauged by their rigid posture that they were security. She nodded to the petty officer and moved to the closest of the security men. It was Petty Officer Morgan whom she'd been running into more and more over the last few days. She lifted her chin in recognition as she approached.

"Where is he?" she said.

"Yo, Pewter," he greeted back. "Over there." He pointed with the end of his rifle.

She squinted, having to peer carefully through the shadows to make out the dark form of a man cowering on the deck behind the giant boiler. He sat on the steel-grate rocking back and forth, thumping his head on the wall behind him and mumbling to himself.

"He got any weapons?" she asked.

"None that we can tell. He was just yelling before, and acting all crazy. Had Tortelli in a choke hold, so I had to shoot him. Got him in the left shoulder, though, not a fatal shot. And he did let Tortelli go." He tipped his head sideways towards the other security officer covering the corner from the opposite side of the boiler, but didn't take his eyes off of Duvall. Sensing that he was the object of the conversation, Tortelli nodded back.

"All right, maybe he's weak from loss of blood," Orli hoped aloud. "I'll go get him out." She took a syringe from her kit and tapped the bubble to the top, clearing it with a squirt. "Wish me luck."

"Luck," said Morgan. "I got you covered."

She crept into the shadows, moving through a partial curtain of steam and slowly towards the man still thumping his head against the wall. Despite being slim, she felt claustrophobic, dwarfed between the two large tanks and having to duck under and step over huge pipes every so often, some nearly two feet thick. Quickness wasn't going to help her much in here; there was hardly any room to move.

She looked back at Morgan around the curve of the boiler and through the mesh of pipes. He was kneeling and had his rifle pointed at Duvall in case the madman got out of hand. She nodded and pressed on.

When she was close enough that Duvall could hear her over the hissing of steam and the racket of the pipes, she spoke to him in a soothing voice. "Hey, Duvall. Hi. Listen, I'm Ensign Pewter. Orli Pewter. I came down from sick bay, okay? I want to help you if you'll let me. Is that okay?"

Duvall continued to rock back and forth and thump his head against the wall, the dull sound of flesh and bone on metal joining with the hiss of escaping steam.

Sweat was running down Orli's face and neck as she moved through the reeking, humid air. She could see that Duvall was soaked from head to toe in sweat and blood as well. The right shoulder of his uniform was almost black with blood, light reflecting off of the wetness, and he looked extremely pale. He'd definitely lost a lot of blood.

"Duvall, can you hear me? Are you listening?"

He made no response, and she moved in closer, hypodermic at the ready, held like a knife poised to stab, palm ready to press the plunger down.

There was a pipe running out of the bottom of the boiler near where Duvall was hunkered down. It came straight out of the tank and disappeared into the wall, two feet off the floor and almost eight inches thick. It was the only thing between her and her goal; Duvall was three feet beyond. Sedating him was going to require that she step over the pipe at the same time she came within the wounded man's reach. She would have to be quick. She'd seen enough patients in this condition to know that apparent delirium was no impediment to sudden bursts of energy.

"Okay, Duvall, I'm coming to you now, all right? I'm just going to give you a shot to help you, okay? Don't be afraid. I'm not going to hurt you; I promise."

She knew he wasn't listening as much as she knew that he was not concerned with whether he got hurt. But the calm in her voice helped her pretend that maybe she actually was. She neared the pipe she was going to have to step over. She stared into the shadows at Duval, wondering if he knew that she was there in any vague sense at all or if he was already gone. She raised her foot and stepped over the pipe.

He leapt at her. "No more fucking corned beef," he cried. "It's all gone now. And the yoyo too. There's nothing fucking left." He tackled her, one hand gripping her neck, the other arm wrapped around her waist. With the pipe behind her knees, she tripped over it and went down hard on her back against the metal deck. The fall knocked the wind out of her and banged her head with stunning force. Duvall tripped over the pipe coming after her and he went sprawling too, his fingernails scratching a long cut into her soft throat as he groped to maintain his hold. Orli struggled for consciousness as the sound of a single shot rang out. She saw sparks as a bullet hit the boiler where Duvall's head had been a half a second before he fell.

Duvall stood up as a cloud of foul smelling steam began spraying out from the tank where the bullet had gone through. He began to scream as scalding liquid scorched the side of his face, but he lunged at Orli just the same, still yelling about the yoyo and its missing string. A second shot rang out just as he dove at her, his body suddenly twisting in the air as he flew. She scrambled against the tank, out of the way as he crumpled to the floor. She rose quickly and turned to see him getting to his feet. He lunged at her again. This time, she stepped neatly to the side and thrust the hypodermic needle into his back as he staggered past. He tripped over the knee-high pipe again and went down hard once more, landing back in the corner where the struggle had begun. This time he didn't get back up.

She went to him and saw that Morgan's shot had hit him

in the ribs, passing through his body and out through the chest. His breath came in ragged gasps. He looked up at her, his eyes wide and terrified. Orli wondered if it was the fear of yoyos and corned beef or if it was the fear of standing at the brink of death. She heard boot steps clanking on the deck coming around both sides of the boiler by which she crouched. She wanted to find a way to conceal the ragged wound in Duvall's chest. At least that. Something to spare Morgan's conscience from carrying the guilt of this man's death with him for the rest of time—or however long he had. But it was too late, Morgan had already seen. The look on his face told her that he knew.

Duvall started to choke, and Orli looked back down at him just in time for him to cough a gout of blood into her face. And then he died.

Chapter 28

Altin's standoff with the coconut-colored spot went on for quite some time. It made no further attacks with its large battering ram, and Altin wasted no more energy on fireballs that the coconut was clearly going to dodge. And since there was no point in even thinking about the lightning spell, the two of them just stayed there for what turned out to be nearly three entire days; Altin was far too stubborn to leave. He was not going to be run off by a giant, hairless coconut. That simply would not do. So he stayed right where he was. He sent his crate back for more food and water while he waited, and he made some adjustments to his shield. He was able to modify his stasis spell to keep the tower oriented on a target of his choice; his new version would keep him from having to look around to find it after every pass. He even attached an activation word to the spell to make the two elements of his revised edition match. He was actually rather proud of his new spell and decided to give it its own name, "Combat Stasis." And it was just as he finished penning the new title in his rapidly filling notes that he looked up and saw that two more of the coconuts had arrived.

One of the newcomers was at least twice as large as the

original that was still floating a few hundred paces away, and he'd decided that the first one was roughly the size of a country church, which meant that the new, giant ball had to be at least as large as a good-sized inn, if not as large as the entire block upon which an inn might sit. The third one was roughly the size of the original, if perhaps the slightly larger of the two, and between them all there was a considerable amount of mass. Altin wondered how long it would be before the three of them attacked. He was fairly certain that Combat Hop would be up to the task, but he thumbed his amulet unconsciously as he watched and waited to see what they would do.

It turned out they were only waiting on a fourth one of the giant spots to arrive, slightly smaller than the rest, and then the fight resumed. They encircled his tower, hovering slightly higher than he stood and no more than an eighth of a measure off. Once in place, all four spots came streaking in at an alarming rate. Altin grimaced and wondered if he were about to die as all four of them released their giant battering rams at once.

And then he was somewhere else, roughly eighty paces away. He laughed. Combat Hop was up to the task of four. "Maybe next time," he mocked. "Try again."

They did, but this time with a different tactic. They came in waves of two, and from slightly different altitudes. But still their attack had no effect, and so they tried again, all at once and coming out of a large formation that started out roughly as a square. Altin laughed and bade them bring it on.

This time, the largest orb held back, slightly behind the other three, and it delayed in releasing its shot a half-second after theirs as well. When the first three released, Altin's Combat Hop blinked him off to one side, but just as the fourth orb let its missile go. The large stony beam struck its mark, likely only random chance, but still a blow so brutal that Altin was nearly knocked out of the tower as he tumbled over the crenellated wall.

The force threw him over the parapet, and it was only by some luck of his own that he managed to grasp the wall before he fell the forty feet to the ground below. With strength born of terror, he pulled himself back over the wall. Once more he considered teleporting himself back home. He couldn't afford for these spots to get too many more lucky shots like that. And even as he thought it, the orbs came in for yet another pass. He knew he didn't have time to scry out the corner of Calico Castle to see if it was safe to bring the tower back. He was less familiar with Luria, but he could get there without looking if the coconuts didn't knock him over the wall in the middle of the spell. But he didn't want to run. And that's when inspiration struck. The thought of having to scry out the castle to see that it was safe gave him the most obvious of ideas. He was a teleporter after all. He could try to use his best skill against them in defense. They'd already proved they had no honor and so relieved Altin of playing by the rules. Sing a song for the siren, as the saying went. Granted, they'd started the music already, but Altin was ready with some lyrics of his own. Magic ones.

Though he had no idea of their emotional state, he assumed they were intelligent and so possibly resistant to his intended method of attack. But they were rather large. Perhaps if they were hollow at all, they might be moveable by the nature of the "enclosed or encapsulated" portion of the Teleport Other spell. Unwilling subjects can be teleported if they've been stuffed inside a box; the mage merely has to focus on teleporting the box rather than the person stuffed inside—this technique was especially useful for the movement of prisoners between penal facilities on Kurr. Altin's intent was to discover if the spots were indeed like coconuts, round "boxes" with occupants inside, or like a snail that's pulled inside its shell. There was only one way to discover this for sure.

Altin closed his eyes and began the chant with the inflection he had used to move the shielded goat and his crate of food through space so many times before, focusing on the spots as if they were containers rather than living things. He channeled the mana with a bit of malice too. When he had enough gathered, a monstrous amount, he slung the shimmering darkness around the first spot like an enormous lariat. Then he sent the other end of his mana stream out and wound it round the other coconut that was similar in size. So connected, he focused his mind on the strand between them, willing it to powerful elasticity, and allowed it to retract like a stretched spring, snapping the two coconuts together into one.

The newly formed mass split open as both spots were forced to occupy the same space at once, an impossible thing to do and yet maintain a physical status quo. The sudden combination of their bulk caused the accumulation to burst open and sent a spray of glowing orange ichor jetting out, spewing forth as if a round and lumpy volcano had just erupted into the night. Altin let out a hoot of rapture as he watched the sundered blob go spinning off into darkness. He wasn't sure if his success was due to the "container" idea or the spots not having the intelligence to resist, but whichever it was, his tactic worked.

He began to chant again, the rhythm of the magic evaporating his emotion into the focus of the spell. He took the smaller orb of the remaining two and once again teleported it into the center of the largest one. Despite the size difference, Altin was confident that it would be enough to do the trick, and it was with great expectation that he opened his eyes after the spell's release. His confidence was well placed, and the merge ruptured a huge segment of the larger spot's side, opening a massive hole in it like a blown caldera, and spraying more of the glowing goo out against the backdrop of the stars. The wounded spot immediately moved away. Not a drifting death, Altin gauged, but clearly in retreat. He watched it go with a look of grim satisfaction on his face until the orange light it left in its wake had vanished from view. That would show them, he thought. You don't mess with a teleporter.

Jubilant in his victory, and now released by it as well, he wanted nothing more than to rush home and tell Tytamon that there were other things living out in space—albeit hostile, angry and aggressive things, but still, something besides the races of Prosperion. The discovery was much too exciting to keep to himself, so, with the thrill of combat still pumping in his veins—and the stench of burnt fur and wood stinking up the top of his Polar's dome—he decided it was time to take the tower home.

After a quick glimpse into the scrying basin to make sure the area was clear, Altin returned the tower to its place, filling the gap in Calico Castle's wall. Once the tower was settled, he released the shield, letting the cloud of foul smoke drift into the sky just as Kettle's scream echoed off the gray stone of Mt. Pernolde.

"She's gone, she's gone! Nipper, she's gone!" came the kitchen matron's piercing wail. Altin had never in all his life heard her make such a sound as that, a shrill cry of terror that pierced his body and chilled like a well-cast ice lance spell. His nerves, still tingling from his recent battle, were pulled taut once again. He ran down the stairs, taking them four at a time as he rushed out into the courtyard.

Kettle was still screaming as he cast his gaze about, looking for her while trying to pick her voice out from the echoes of it bouncing off the castle walls and looming cliff. Her cries were coming from outside and seemed to be moving as if the woman were running towards the hills. He ran through the gates and saw her rushing around the corner of the castle at a speed unexpected from a body as stout as hers. He sprinted after her.

He caught up to her a moment later as she was coming past his tower and running along the stone face of Mt. Pernolde's sky-high cliffs towards the north. He caught her by the arm and dragged her to a stop. "What's the matter? What's happened?" he gasped at her.

Kettle's eyes were wide and hysterical. "Pernie," she screeched, "they took mah Pernie away."

"Who? Who took her?"

"Orcs," she said. "It was orcs. An hour, maybe less. Ya have to get her back. Ya have to get her back."

Tytamon emerged around the corner just then, running towards them with his robes pulled up above his boney knees as if he were a maiden who's just seen a mouse. "What's with all the fuss?" he demanded. His face was filled with the contagion of Kettle's screams.

"They took Pernie," Kettle moaned and staggered a few steps forward in pursuit. "Just snuck right in and took my baby away. There were footprints all around the yard." Her body was exhausted, and raw emotion took its toll. She collapsed to her knees. "Get her. Please, get her. Gods. Someone bring her back." She was overcome with grief and could no longer speak through the violence of her sobs.

Tytamon looked askance at Altin, who could only shrug. The ancient mage glanced around briefly noting the tower's return. His expression grew dark, but whatever it was immediately went away. "I'll divine her," Tytamon said, "since a telepath she's not." With that the old sorcerer chanted the words that teleported him up into his tower. There was no time for courtesy in a crisis such as this. Divination took long enough as it was.

Too long, by Altin's way of thought, and Taot *was* a telepath in an animal kind of way. He sent the dragon an urgent call, and the dragon's reply came immediately back.

He was on his way.

It took the dragon a few agonizing minutes to fly to Altin's tower, and in moments they were in the air. "Which way did they go?" he called down to Kettle as they took off.

The sight of him on the dragon's back seemed to give her a ray of hope, and she pointed towards the east.

"I'll find her," he promised.

"You better," was her reply.

There was something feral in her eyes, a ferocity that sent a shiver down his spine as he urged Taot towards the nearest pass. What was that all about?

They soared along Mt. Pernolde's edge until the cliff dwindled into something resembling a passable incline. There were hundreds of narrow crags that the orcs might have used to climb up into the treacherous terrain, and Altin had to hover above every one, squinting into the shadows hoping for a glimpse of anything that moved. Altin queried Taot if he could recognize Pernie by her scent. The great beast acknowledged that he could; her scent was often on a morning meadow breeze.

They flew back and forth in long sweeps, searching every crevice and every crag. Altin marveled that the orcs could have gotten so far away in such a short time, but once they were in the undulating steepness of the mountains, with all its boulders and scrubby brush, they were in their element and out of his. But Taot knew it well enough, and he communicated to Altin's mind what was essentially an image of a maze as he flew off deeper into the range. They flew for several minutes until Taot brought them to a place where he stopped and hovered in the air. He sent Altin an image of a portion of the land far below, a rocky section of trees slightly to the north with a growth of scraggly woods masking the dark expanse of a narrow canyon. Shrouded in shadow, the canyon was too dark for Altin's human eyes to see inside, so he urged the dragon to fly nearer to the edge.

The dragon refused, however, forcing Altin to cast a seeing spell instead.

In the concealment of the canyon lay a small orc village of perhaps thirty huts and two larger buildings made of logs. Altin had had no idea that the orcs had settlements this close to Calico Castle, much less within the realm of Crown. The Queen would not be happy to know that the orcs were once more beginning to encroach.

He scanned through the huts one by one, using his magical sight to look for any sign of Pernie, although he knew that she could not possibly be here yet, not if Kettle's estimate of time was right. There was no way that the orcs would have gotten here so fast, even if this was where they were planning to bring the girl. But still he looked, trusting to his dragon that this was where the orcs would come.

It took him several long minutes to rush his sight through all the buildings, and he was surprised by how many orcs were living there, at least sixty or so of the large brutish males and perhaps half that again of hideous, fang-faced women and scrapping little brats, all of whom were filthy and covered with mud... and worse. The place was slovenly beyond all comprehension, and they'd barely seen fit to scratch a trench through the middle of town, down the slope, and through which their waste and excrement mostly drained. As he saw his way through the village, Altin was glad that seeing spells did not have the gift of smell. It was an awful place, and Altin could not imagine chatty little Pernie being there.

But she was not there now, and he sent a message to Taot encouraging him to sweep the area and work back down the trail, perhaps they could catch the raiding party when it emerged from whichever hidden path the orcs had used. The dragon's reply was a simple sense of predatory patience, and he did not move from where they were.

Altin was not a predator, and sitting there was vexing.

How could he convey to the dragon that there was no way the orcs would be getting there this fast; not to mention the fact that the middle of a town full of orcs was not the ideal place to exact a rescue. He didn't have time, however, for it was at that moment that he saw six orcs emerge from a concealed crevice in the rocks and begin riding up the trail leading into the orc-filled canyon. Riding on horses.

Since when had orcs begun domesticating horses? They were not supposed to have the discipline for that, or at least that's how the stories were always told. Orcs will eat a horse before its old enough to ride. Impulse over intellect. Everyone knew that. But apparently things had changed.

Sunlight glinted off of Pernie's flaxen hair just as the group disappeared into the shadow of the canyon's wall. Taot's thought was roughly the equivalent of a spoken "there." The dragon followed this thought with what could have been a question mark regarding what Altin would like to do. The dragon was ready to swoop in and burn the village to a crisp. Altin had to remind his draconic counterpart that they were on a rescue mission and that Pernie's life must be spared.

He conveyed a sense of bringing Tytamon first, to help them with the orcs, to which the dragon reluctantly agreed, and Altin cast the telepathic spell that would nudge Tytamon into opening his mind, but the ancient magician's mind was closed. Telepathy was like that. One needed another telepath, for starters, and one could only push at that person's awareness from the outside and hope that the recipient let you in. But Tytamon did not. His mind was apparently blocked by the divination spell that he was casting and Altin was put off. If he had some paper, he could teleport a note. Or even one of Aderbury's ridiculous homing lizards, but he had neither, and he was unwilling to turn back now.

"Fine," he said, sending the thoughts to the dragon as well. "Let's go get her. Drop me off down there." He sent an image of a place below the village near some trees. "Wait till I get in. I'll tell you when to burn it. Just watch out for me and Pernie, though."

The dragon seemed to understand, and Altin hoped the beast could control his natural instincts once the fight began. Taot swooped down into a narrow ravine, not too far off the trail leading into the village, and Altin slid down his neck and dropped onto the ground. He ran as fast as he could up through the rocks and stopped when he got near the canyon mouth. There were two large orcs with halberds standing guard, but Altin didn't have time to fight.

He wished he'd memorized an invisibility spell, but, since he hadn't, he cast a seeing spell instead. He found a place inside the entrance into which he could teleport and hide. Once inside, he did the same twice more and soon was well within the village, hidden in a filthy hut behind a stack of rotting grain sacks and trying for all his life not to gag from the overwhelming stench. From here he could hear Pernie begin to scream.

He cast another seeing spell and pushed his vision through the wall of the hut and towards the sound of Pernie's cries. Two female orcs where stripping her down and smearing her with cooking grease, as a third began dumping a yellowish powder over her that Altin assumed was some kind of flour.

Drums were being beaten now too, and many of the orcs began to dance around the village's central fire, whooping and howling with ravenous delight. From the general rapture surrounding Pernie's preparation, it seemed that they had not had human meat in quite a while. They certainly weren't wasting any time.

Altin would have cast the Teleport Other spell from where he sat, plucking Pernie out, but he was a lot farther than twenty paces away, a requirement of the spell—and that assumed that the little girl was not so hysterical as to qualify as an "unwilling target" as well.

There was nowhere else to hide between here and there, at least no place large enough to enable him space to move and cast without being seen, and so he was going to have to make a run for her from here. He decided it was time to call the dragon in.

He sent a message to Taot, still hovering above, indicating that he'd like the lower portion of the village burned. The dragon did not even bother to reply. The roar echoing off the canyon walls was enough to confirm that Taot was swooping in.

The orcs immediately leapt into action, their movements disciplined and unified. Altin peered through the hut's window and watched several of them run off, even including one of the women that had been preparing Pernie for the pot. He noticed two older orcs emerge from a hut across the fetid trench from where he hid, one of them conspicuously draped in feathers and strings of teeth taken from animals of varying ferocity and size. A shaman, Altin thought. Great. He sent a warning to Taot not to fly too low and included an image of the shaman, trying to convey a sense of sorcery as best he could without the use of words.

Taot's reply was an image of a broken egg and something approaching humor. Altin nodded and sent back a sense of "luck" as he ran to get Pernie from the orcs.

He was spotted immediately upon exiting the hut by an orc carrying a longbow. The orc dropped to a knee and knocked an arrow, plucking it deftly from the quarrel strapped to its thigh. The arrow came whistling in and went right through the sleeve of Altin's robe as he dove narrowly to the side.

He rolled to his own knees and began at once to cast. He didn't have time for a huge fireball, but even Altin's small ones were large enough to do the trick. A bright mass of flame, big as an ale keg, crackled through the air and struck the orc full in the chest just as it released another shot. The arrow thunked into the ground between Altin's thighs, narrowly missing his groin. Altin grimaced down at the arrow as the orc's flesh and armor ignited and began to burn with yellow flames, the orc's cries mixing with those of the dragon and poor Pernie for the span of several heartbeats while it burned. Finally, it fell into the muck and was silent again, its body reduced to a charred and steaming heap. Altin ran on to where he'd seen the females preparing Pernie to be cooked.

The orc women saw him as he ran in. They turned on him and growled curses that were animal and foul, rattling in their throats. Pernie saw him too, and she let go a squeaky plea for help as something like optimism glistened in her frightened eyes. Altin was resolved to stop at nothing to get her out of there. The sight of her like that, terrified and ready to be boiled, fueled his rage and filled him with hate.

The two females rushed at him, their teeth bared in savage snarls and their strong hands brandishing knives made for cutting meat. The first one was in flames by the time she'd taken her second step, struck full in the face by a melon-sized ball of fire. Pernie screamed and had to dive out of the way as the burning woman staggered back and nearly fell on top of her. The second woman, however, sprang like a leopard at Altin before he could cast another spell, and soon the two of them were grappling on the ground. Despite having knocked the knife away, mud, cooking grease, flour and bits of rancid food slicked them both to the point of being nearly impossible to grasp, and Altin found wrestling with her frighteningly difficult. And what was worse, Altin was not nearly as strong as the female orc was, not even by half. Only by the fact that both of them were slippery was he able to escape her clutches long enough to scramble to his feet, and even then the snarling woman thrust a muck-encrusted hand out and caught him by the sleeve before he could step away. He needed to get far enough back to cast another spell. He jerked violently against her grip, hoping to tear free either from her gnarled hand or from the robe itself, but neither would give way.

The orc woman used Altin's violent tugging as a means to regain her feet, scooping up her dropped knife as he inadvertently pulled her up. She lunged at him with the grimy blade, a fluid motion as she rose, and caused him to twist awkwardly to avoid being stabbed between the ribs. He cursed. Caught in her iron grip like this, he could not make the gestures necessary for another fireball. His mind began to race, and he was about to count himself gutted when he remembered the simple lightning spell he'd unwittingly memorized during the standoff with the giant spots. Learning it seemed so long ago now, though in truth it had barely been seventy-two hours. With a sudden sense of calm, he straightened, took her by the wrist and spoke the spell's single activating word.

She was mid-swing, the knife plunging for his heart when he said it. "Avort." Suddenly she stopped and staggered back, eyes wide as she began to shake. The pitch of her screams rose two octaves as currents stored in the earth beneath them coursed through her body in violent waves, drawn forth by Altin's call. She howled and writhed and shook, foam running from her mouth as Altin let her go. She collapsed upon the ground then, twisting and jerking with residual energy until finally she stopped moving all together, a faint whine of releasing air and some smoke wafting up with the departure of her last breath. She was dead. Altin looked upon her body and wrinkled up his nose. Her eyes had come out, and both her palms and the soles of her feet were split wide like over-done sausages, dark blood seeping out from the open flesh and running into the fetid mud in which she lay. Grotesque as it was, it served her right. He spat on her and looked up, seeking Pernie once again.

The little girl lay upon the ground, curled up in a ball, terrified and whimpering. Altin went to her. "Let's go," he said as he scooped her up. He turned and looked down the slope to make sure that he had time to cast the spell that would teleport them out. The whole village was ablaze, and the whole of the canyon was filled with the flickering glow of Taot's raging breath. But there were four orcs charging up the hill at him. Males. He knew he could not fight them off and still keep Pernie safe. But he did have enough time to cast the teleportation spell. And with that he got them out.

Chapter 29

When Altin first delivered Pernie into Kettle's arms, the woman became a virtual fountain of tears and joy. She took the greasy, flour-covered child from Altin's arms and rushed her to a back room of the kitchen, placing her on the cot she sometimes used for taking naps. She ran her hands and eyes all over the girl's slender frame looking desperately for any signs of serious injury. There were no broken bones and only a few cuts, one of which required some stitches, but Kettle delivered those with a capable hand and in short order. Beyond that the child was relatively unscathed.

With hot water from the cauldron near the fire, Kettle washed Pernie down and wrapped her in a towel before taking her back to the cot and rocking her, still trembling, in her arms until at length the child was asleep. It wasn't until then that Kettle said a word to Pernie's savior, and her opening salvo was something to behold.

"You," she spat, coming at him with such vehemence he took a backwards step. "Ya just up an' go as ya please, don't ya? Not one damned thought fer what anyone else is about. And ya takes yer tower an' half the wall an' just go cavortin' around fer weeks at a time; not a care fer the likes of us. No, not you." She drug the rarely enunciated pronoun out in a way that made it worse than any curse she could conceive. "An' ya just left us wide open fer anyone what happens by, ya did, let the orcs waltz right in an' take mah Pernie away."

He started to mumble a reply, but she didn't let him speak, rising and striding into him with a growl of rage so ferocious Altin lost focus in his bewilderment. He'd never seen her like this before.

"If'n ya ever go off an' leave us open fer them orcs ta sneak in here an' snatch her away again, don't ya never come back or I'll cut ya' open myself, ya hear? By Mercy's wrath, I swear I will, mage or no."

There was nothing Altin could say to that. What could he say? And worse than the speechlessness was the dawning sense of dread that came upon him as comprehension began to permeate the barrier of his initial perplexity. As her words seeped through there formed within him an awareness that the furious woman might have a point. A terrible, horrifying point.

A part of him wanted to muster some sort of defense against it as her meaning grew like some wild accusatory weed, but how, when everything she said was true? He had been taking the tower out for extremely long periods of time, and he'd never once thought about the security of the castle or the people living there. Nothing had ever gone wrong before.

He tried to shake the blooming realization away. It frightened him to think he could be so selfish as she accused. He wasn't like that. Was he? He fought to fend the feelings off. No, she was wrong. It's not like the gates aren't always open, he tried to tell himself. And Tytamon didn't even keep anything that resembled a guard on staff.

But his attempts to convince himself were futile even as he had the thoughts. *He* was supposed to be the guard. He and Tytamon. But he'd taken a corner of the castle away instead. He'd excavated a section of wall that was large and obvious and then kept it gone for nearly an entire month, had been keeping it gone for months and months. How could the orcs resist such an invitation as that? They couldn't, that's how. And they'd gotten in because of him.

Kettle turned from him and went to a large cutting board where she began to chop carrots with such fervor that the knock-knocking of the cleaver against the wood made it sound as if there were a giant woodpecker in the room.

Altin considered leaving, but he knew that was the worst thing he could do.

"I'm sorry," he said after a bit. "I didn't think that orcs would come. It's been centuries since they came around." She looked up at him, and he immediately wished he hadn't opened his mouth, or had chosen something else to say. But, it just came out. A reflex.

Fighting back tears, she turned on him in full, the cleaver still gripped tightly in her hand. "Don't ya say another word," she said, and he thought she might actually swing the knife at him. "Ya didn't *think* is right. Damned right about that. Ya got the brains of twenty men, and ya can't manage ta make even one of 'em work. So what's the good of havin' 'em then?" This last was mostly muttered as she turned away and brutalized another carrot, chopping deep lines into the cutting board as she pounded savagely against the wood.

"Well, I am sorry. And you can tell Pernie I'm sorry too when she wakes up. I never meant for anything like this to happen." He turned to go, fighting back tears of his own. He felt so small.

"Tell her yerself," Kettle said, her voice turning icy calm. "Don't look fer me ta bail ya out of that one. Yer the one can look her in the eyes and explain ta her why it was she near got ate, tell her who it was what let the orcs inside. Yer the one ta tell her that, not me. I won't be makin' yer excuses fer ya. Hide from the rest of the story if ya like, hide from all of it, that's fine by me. I'll keep yer secrets, but I ain't savin' ya on this. I had enough of it."

Altin cocked his head and studied the woman for a moment. She looked as if she'd said something she didn't want to say, but she was in no mood to take it back.

"What's that supposed to mean?"

"Ya know damn well what it means."

"No. I don't." He didn't.

"All of it. Why yer here. The whole history. Yer parents. And yer sister. It's all the same story with ya, Altin Meade. Only this time it's different 'cause it *is* yer fault. Ya can't say yer just too young no more. An' I'm not gonna baby ya about it neither. Not no more. Time fer ya ta grow up an' face the truth, an' I don't care what Tytamon has ta say. I'm tired of it all. Yer too old for everyone to be prancin' around secret-like, like yer made of thin ice and everyone's a fat man walkin' on the pond. I'm done with it I tell ya. Done." She had run out of carrots and was now whaling on a cabbage. Coleslaw was likely to appear on the menu tonight.

Altin felt his face heat up as Kettle went on, his confusion growing deeper with each new word. What in nine hells was she talking about?

When she was done, the cabbage essentially juiced and now running onto the floor, he demanded to know just what it was she meant.

"What do I mean?" she said, squaring to him and stepping towards him once again. "I'll tell ya what I mean. I'll tell ya what everyone means but is too a'feared to say. Yer a menace Altin Meade. A sweet, hardworking, likeable menace most times, sure; an' don't think I don't love ya with all mah heart, 'cause I do, but yer a gods-be-damned menace. You've always been a menace. Since the day ya was born." He could only stare. This was not the Kettle that he knew. She saw his apoplexy and relented some. "Didn't ya ever want ta know what happened ta yer parents, Altin? Ta yer sister? Haven't ya ever tried ta ask?"

"They died when our house burnt down. Tytamon said I was only a few months old."

"Did ya ever ask how the fire got set, Altin? How the fire got so big?"

"Well, no," he admitted. What was the point in asking that?

"It was yer magic what done it, Altin. Yer magic started that fire."

Altin laughed, a nervous sound. "Impossible. I was an infant."

"An' magic usually comes around seven or nine. I wasn't born yesterday, Altin. I may be a blank, but I didn't just fall out of the peach basket. Of course magic comes later than that fer most. Fer most, Altin. But not yers. Yers started seepin' out like seeds from a busted 'mater when ya was nary but a babe." She took a tomato from a basket near where she stood and pricked it with her knife to illustrate the point. She gave it a little squeeze and a jet of liquid squirted out. "The way I heard it, they figured ya musta got cold layin' in yer crib. Maybe half asleep. But ya used yer magic somehow an' brought the coals ta life, a raging fire that burnt yer house ta ash. Yer parents died getting ya and yer sister out."

"That's ridiculous," was all that he could say.

"An' yer sister... Do ya remember how that happened, Altin? Do ya? 'Cause that was yer magic too. Ya teleported her into a tree. They say ya was only five or so years old. A sibling fight was all, but ya found yer magic again. An' accident, sure, but that's when the town council started ta figure ya out. That's how ya ended up here, Altin. Because nobody but Tytamon had any chance of reining that kind of power in. Yer a menace an' ya need to get yerself under control. Maybe ya can control the magic now, but ya ain't figured out how ta control yerself." She crushed the tomato in her hand and they both watched silently as the red juice ran down her forearm and into her sleeve.

Altin was in shock. How could he possibly respond to what she had said? Kettle's story was ludicrous. She was blaming everything on him. It wasn't even possible for an infant to use magic and conjure flames. There were the chants and gestures they had to know, distances involved. But even as he had the thought, he knew that those were only the superfluous contrivances of man. Raw power, animal magic, required nothing of the sort. But at less than one year old? The mythothalamus wasn't even fully formed at that age. It couldn't function that soon. And even if it had, what about the fire alarm ferns? Surely his parents had a few of those hanging around their house. Everyone with children did. The alarm would have been raised the moment heat fell upon the enchanted leaves, the plants charged with whistles loud enough for anyone to hear. His parents would have woken up, and the fire brigade would have been alerted too. And what about the fire brigade, where had they been? Surely they would have come in time; it was a modern world after all. Unless the fire had just been that big. Gods, how enormous would it have had to be? He was certainly capable of ridiculously large fires now. But he hadn't even been one year old.

But what if it was true? What if he had killed his parents? And his sister? Neechy. Poor Neechy, not so much different than Pernie in appearance and in size. Had he really merged her with a tree? What a horrendous thought. And how? She couldn't have been a willing subject. And even if she was, he wouldn't have had any idea how that kind of magic worked. Teleportation is much more complicated than conjuring fire ever was.

Prompted by the emotion-laden queries, his mind began flashing images of a little girl in a blue dress peeping out of an empty apple barrel and sing-songing him with names as cruel as only an eight-year-old sister could apply. Horror grew in his mind as the memories came rushing back; he watched her childish face mocking him over the barrel's edge, heard her voice taunting him with "Altin Maltin, Big Fat Paltin" over and over. He could remember the helpless rage he'd felt; he felt its echo even now, clutching his chest like an iron band, growing tighter and tighter as anger turned the screw. He hadn't even uttered a word, hadn't cast anything as refined as the spells that he knew now. He had simply willed her into the tree, willed her with every ounce of anger and hate that a five-year-old boy could possibly employ. And then she was gone, barrel and all. Forever.

A storm raged in his brain, the memories playing out like scenes in some macabre illusionist's tale. He had memories of the villagers cutting down the tree a few days later when he'd finally tried to explain what had happened—even though in all honesty he hardly knew himself. He'd been too young to understand. But he understood when the lumberjacks pried strips of blue cloth out from between the trunk's concentric rings. He'd understood that well enough. And then he'd apparently blocked it out. Until now. Until Kettle. Until Pernie had just about been killed.

Kettle was right. He was a menace. Deep down he'd always known it, always felt the danger lurking there. He suddenly understood why it was that he needed so desperately to get away, why he needed to run to outer space: to be free of anyone that he might love, that he might kill. It was no wonder he never feared for himself. He was not the one in danger. It was everyone else. Kettle was right. And he needed to get away.

He ran from the kitchen, back into his tower where he cast a Polar's shield twice the size of the one he'd been using to protect himself. Under that one, he cast a second, the same as he'd been doing all along. The larger dome would prevent the orcs from coming through. Satisfied, he grabbed the Liquefying Stone and threw himself out into the night.

One hop returned him to his furthest point in space and, wanting to drift, he let go the stasis spell that held the tower in place. With the release of the stasis energy, the tower began to rotate, making the stars appear to slowly spin around. He hoped a coconut monster would come and kill him, or at least send him spinning eternally away. But for now at least he felt as if he were free to float endlessly through the night. He blew out the lamp he'd left burning on the table and sprawled out in the middle of the floor, staring up into the spotted sky.

Kettle's voice ran through his mind over and over, her words an accusation. "Menace," she kept repeating, a horrid echo in the caverns of his brain; it was a curse. And the worst part was that it was true. He was a menace. He was a killer. And he was mean. He was a mean, selfish killer. Realizing such things about himself was mortifying, and yet he knew with absolute certainty that it was completely true. All his adult life he'd fancied himself as an explorer, an academic and a sorcerer on his way to greatness. He sneered derisively as he thought about his selfish dreams. He'd never once thought that he'd be anything but a success—if not with his moon project, then with something else, perhaps something closer to home. But he'd always known that there would be something to validate him in the end. And now he saw that he was only a menace, had always been a menace. Nothing more.

How much death would he mete out before he was finally through? How many more lives would he take through pride and ignorance? His parents and his sister were obviously not enough. So now he killed little girls too, or at least tried to get them fed to ravaging bands of orcs. That's what he did when he wasn't killing helpless animals or being mean to young women who only wanted to dance. Good gods. What a bastard he was. And who was next? Who was next on Altin's list to die, the list of those who had to pay for knowing the great magical menace, Altin Meade?

And suddenly he knew. The blood drained from his face, straight to his guts. He knew exactly who was next. He'd left Taot to fight the orcs alone.

Chapter 30

Orli lived in constant dread from the moment Duvall coughed infected blood into her face. The certainty of contraction hung upon her like a weight, an anchor of paranoia that dragged her already flagging spirits down. The morning after the incident with Duvall, she woke to a rumbling in her stomach. A long, lingering growl, the gastric movement woke her and set her heart racing in her chest. "Shit," she said, sitting up and raising the back of her hand to her forehead to check if she was hot. She waited, hesitant to breathe, tensed like someone in the process of defusing a ticking bomb. She waited, listening, wondering if it would come again, that sound. It had to be the disease; the Hostile microbe had finally taken root.

Eventually the sound came again, shorter this time but still clearly rattling through her intestinal track. Her palms were sweating, but part of her thought that perhaps it was just a hunger pang. It was technically morning after all. She waited for a third instance of the sound, but no more rattles would be heard. And she was hungry. She had only eaten once all of yesterday. She sighed.

"God, I'm such an idiot."

She felt stupid for her fleeting panic, but how else could

she feel after having infected blood blown into her eyes and mouth? She couldn't help but stress when her body made a noise. Every time her flesh felt an unfamiliar itch she felt a pang of dread. Every time a forearm hair caught in the fabric of her uniform she knew it could be the twitch of an infected nerve. A spasm in her eyelid promised impending doom. Anything, and her heartbeat quickened until she was sure, sure that this wasn't the sign she was looking for, the sign of death. And frankly, after only a day and a half of it, Orli's nerves were raw.

"How are you?" her father, Colonel Pewter, asked over the ship-to-ship not long after she had put her mind at ease from the most recent paranoid episode.

"Fine," she said.

"You don't look fine," he replied.

"I said I'm fine. Look, I'm going to be late for my shift." And she abruptly cut the connection off.

"Shit," she said after doing it, and debated calling her father back. But she didn't. She laid herself back down on her bunk. "Goddamn it" just kept racing through her head.

Maybe it wouldn't be her though. Maybe she wouldn't get sick, even after that damned Duvall. She had that hope to cling to. She had made it this far after all. She had managed to hold infection off longer than damn near everybody else. But that was before fucking Duvall choked his disease right into her face. Goddamn it. Why her? She knew there was no reason to hold out hope. Not now. It was only a matter of time.

All that day she monitored her every sense. She had to sedate two more crew members over the course of her long shift, and by the time she went to bed she couldn't even recall who they were or even where she'd had to go. She couldn't remember any significant details of the day. She could only remember the tingles in her skin and wondering if that perspiration was from exertion or from the onset of the fever that would start the countdown to her demise. She remembered trying to convince herself that she was being silly and that there was at least an order to the symptoms of the disease, a sequence; she remembered trying to talk herself down from the point of having a complete inward collapse, but that was really all. Her entire shift was like working in a dream, slow and hazy, with lots of missing parts.

She woke the following morning in much the same state of mind. Lying on her back, staring up at the bright square of light that came on with her alarm, she waited to see if some symptoms had snuck up on her in the night. She checked herself mentally, taking silent account, sensing each part of her body separately and with care. That's when she felt the tiny itch inside her chest that spawned a little cough.

Hypochondria, she thought in the instant after the minor convulsion had come to pass. A hiccup and nothing more.

But then she coughed again, harder, and rattling sounds came from deep within her lungs. She took a long breath, intent on expanding the alveoli and driving out the nothing that this had to be. Fear chilled her, raising the fine hairs on her forearms when the itch grew instead. She tried to hold it back, tried to focus on denying it, but in the end, she coughed. A violent spasm of the lungs so brutal it bent her at the waist.

"Fuck," she muttered into the growing dread. The chill that was upon her drove inside and froze her to the core, waves of it then radiating out in pulsing stripes of fear that prickled her skin as they coursed down her limbs squeezing cold sweat from every pore. She coughed again, and there could be no mistaking the nature of the sound, the whole-bodied instance of an alien disease. No question. Orli had it now. Terror consumed her; every nerve tingled and she felt as if she were static-filled. Then the bottom dropped out of the universe for a while.

Sense returned eventually, though. Oddly enough, beyond the initial gut-dropping throb of horror at the realization she was going to die, she did not remain as frightened as she would have expected herself to be. The discovery was, oddly, something of a comfort in a way. A revelation that, while perhaps not the news she wanted, at least it brought the anxiety and anticipation to an end. At least she didn't have to wonder any more.

As she lay in her cot waiting for the next cough to come, she actually began to ponder what she would be like when she finally went mad. She didn't particularly relish that idea, going mad like that. Part of her wanted to just give up, to not even let it get that far. She considered overdosing herself with something stolen from Doctor Singh's dwindling pharmaceutical supplies, something pleasantly numbing and permanent. Why fight it? And why go endure another sixteen-hour shift of insanity in sick bay, a pointless battle against an unbeatable foe? Why, when, honestly, it was a total waste of time; those people weren't remotely cognizant by the time they were about to die. Orli wasn't even a source of consolation to them when they bit the dust. So why bother? It would be so much easier to just lay here and pass the time alone, maybe watch some old movies for a change—the old, old ones, from way back when they made them in black and white. Those were romantic times. Good times. When men actually loved their women and sex was not just some simple sport. Life was large and complicated, a place where passion could run to its extremes. The world was big and primitive and alive. Not like here. Not like this ship.

She sighed as she laid there, her fingers absently stroking the rough synthetic fabric of her mattress where the sheet had pulled away. She stared up into the light fixture above. No, she would not be going to sick bay today. She decided she was done. There was no point in going on. She knew she wouldn't resort to suicide, but she could at least die after having got some rest. Who wanted to die all worn out? The last several weeks had been an endless, grueling grind that left her exhausted every moment of the day. To die rested would be nice. A real relief.

She debated calling her father and telling him, but she didn't want to see the misery on his face. He'd start in again with all that "every scientist on every ship in the entire fleet is working endlessly to find a cure" stuff again. He'd promise her they were close. She'd have to smile and nod and promise back that she'd keep her wits about her until the ordeal was finally at an end. She'd have to promise she'd be strong. What a batch of crap. She didn't think she had the strength to carry out the lie. And besides, the ordeal really was almost at an end. Almost. Not the end she'd wanted, but at least an end.

A few hours after she hadn't shown up in sick bay, Doctor Singh's voice came across the com. "Orli," he said, "You there?" She could hear worry in his voice. Over the last few weeks he'd become rather paternal; they'd gotten very close. Tragic circumstances, she supposed. "Orli, speak up if you're there," he said. She heard him cough right before he cut the transmission off.

Him too? She sighed again. He was so kind. And there was nobody more likely to find a cure than he was; it was a shame that he would have to die. "Yeah, I'm here," she said, swinging her feet to the floor and punching up the com at the head of her bed.

"Okay, just checking on you. I got worried when you didn't show up is all."

"Yeah. Sorry. I just... you know."

"I know. It's getting hard. But we have to keep on. I think I have it now too." He added this last part as if it were an aside.

She nodded. "Yeah. I heard you cough. Me too. I think I

got it from Duvall the other day. Looks like we're on the short list now, eh?"

"Perhaps," he said. "But I'm not giving up hope. I sent some specifications to the *New Guinea* team for a retroviral that might be the third leg that we need. She's got the best science lab in the fleet. If her crew can't handle it, nobody can."

Orli was tempted to say that she figured it would be the latter, but she let it go.

"So, you coming to work today?" he asked, gently, his tone implying that he wasn't ordering her to if she wasn't in the mood. "I could use the company. Ashley and Mark are too far gone to help anymore. Mark was a real trooper though. I have them both on sedatives. Figure I'll just leave them out until they go, you know?"

"Yeah, I know. Do the same for me, will you? I don't want to go out screaming."

"Done," he said. "Same goes for me if I get there first, okay?"

"I promise."

He smiled into the monitor. The lines around his eyes were deeper and longer than they were a month ago. He looked so tired.

"I'll be up in a minute," she said after a long silence. "Thanks for checking on me."

"You bet." His face vanished a moment later.

When she got to sick bay she saw, to her horror, that Captain Asad was now lying in one of the beds. Doctor Singh hadn't mentioned that. Nothing short of her own contraction of the disease could have shaken her as much. Though she detested him with every ounce of her being, the captain was the singular point of strength on their beleaguered ship. He'd held everything together when under another man the crew might have fallen apart, might have lost its collective head. He was supposed to stay healthy; he needed to. But he hadn't. And here he was lying in the bed sweating rivers and murmuring with delirium. Not the delirium of the last stages of the disease, not those, he hadn't begun the trembling yet, just the regular delirium of deep fever and a body wracked with disease. But that settled it for Orli, seeing him lying there like that. They were done.

That's when Doctor Singh let out a whoop of joy.

She turned to where he sat at the monitor talking to an older woman in a white coat whose wrinkled face and thick-rimmed glasses filled the screen. "Really?" Doctor Singh was saying. "That's fantastic. Get it over here as fast as you can."

"We need a few days to manufacture it," the woman said. "So hold on. It's a tricky process, but it's coming, okay. Tell your people to hold on."

"I will," he said. "I will. Just hurry."

Orli walked up as he shut off the com. "That sounded promising. Any chance that's what I hope it was?" She was surprised at how calm she felt, as if she were watching herself from another room, like an outsider with no reason to emotionally attach.

"They found it," he said. "At least they've modeled it on the computer and it works. They're synthesizing now. A few days, she said. So, we just have to keep it together." He was grinning from ear to ear. "We might just make it after all. And here, this morning, I thought we were goners."

Orli nodded, smiling too, or trying. She wanted to believe. But something inside her told her that it wouldn't pan out. Some form of letdown tomorrow, a glitch, something, that was more in keeping with how things really went. But she didn't want to kill the mood, so she said, "Me too. I hope it works." That was the best that she could do.

They both stood silently for a few moments, caught up in private thoughts, before Doctor Singh shook himself and, after a fit of coughing, said, "Well, until the vaccine is here, let's try to make people comfortable, shall we? We still have a few long days ahead."

Orli just hoped it was less than six.

As it turned out, it was four days before the first doses of the experimental cure arrived in the docking bay, delivered in a remotely piloted transport ship and done in secret out of fear that the remaining crew members not yet infected might mob it and use up the limited initial doses in a panicked effort to remain that way. The first mate, one of the healthy few, and not disposed to panic, knew of the delivery and saw to it that it could be carried off in secrecy, his only caveat being that the captain get an early dose— Captain Asad was shaking violently in his bed by the time the shipment finally left the *New Guinea's* loading dock. Another shipment would be coming in sixteen hours, synthesized by the *Sarajevo,* and more would be coming from the other ships in the hours that followed, but Captain Asad could not wait more than a few hours at best.

Orli and Doctor Singh were there to receive it, both feeble and under siege by raging fever and bouts of vomiting and diarrhea, but, out of sheer force of will, they were intent on being there and seeing this epidemic through, devoted to their friendship where nothing else could get them through. The two men who unloaded the refrigerated crate eyed them both with the kind of looks one saves for a grenade tossed onto the floor, but Doctor Singh's rank and the reputation he'd earned over the last few weeks as a man bent on the survival of the crew kept them from drawing their guns and running him and Orli off. They did not want to catch the disease, but they hadn't quite lost all sense of decency. At least not yet.

An animal urgency trembled in Orli's hands as she and the doctor opened up the refrigerated crate and pulled the first doses of the *New Guinea's* new vaccine from the swirl of fog inside. Doctor Singh's hands shook too, and it was all

Orli could do to not snatch one from him and inject herself ravenously. She managed to keep the urge in check, if barely, and after a few moments both of them were dosed.

"Take it to sick bay," Doctor Singh rasped at the two men, who still stood ten feet away. "Quickly."

The younger of the two men stepped forward and, pushing the lid closed again, grasped the handle. He looked back at his unmoving compatriot. "You heard the doctor," he said. "Let's go." He turned to the two withered medical personnel standing near him and whispered, "Will it work?" There was a fear in his voice that belied his discipline.

"If there is a loving God, it will," Doctor Singh answered. "So pray."

Orli and Doctor Singh dosed everyone in their ward as soon as the crate was in sick bay, starting with the captain whose tremors had begun to subside as they came in, a sure sign that the last stages of the disease were near at hand. Doctor Singh administered the shot and shook his head in doubt. This was awfully late. He placed a hand on the captain's sweating brow and whispered, "Good luck, my friend."

Orli watched Doctor Singh as he went off to administer the experimental drug to the rest of the patients on his assigned half of the room. She lingered for a moment above the captain once Doctor Singh had gone. She peered down into his deathly pale face. He wasn't near as intimidating in this condition as he usually was, and it was for the first time that she realized that he was just a man, no different than her or anyone else aboard the ship. Seeing him lying there gave her an unexpected clarity—in part, a sense of her own resilience for having survived long enough to maybe bring him back—but something more as well, a new respect for him, for the man, the flawed man who had somehow held the crew together, forced them together with that cold voice and disciplinarian's grip. He'd saved them all from anarchy, and he'd done it with all the same frailties that he shared with her. All the same weaknesses. She decided that if he lived, she would try to show him more respect. He'd earned it, even if she knew she'd never like his personality.

"Don't give up, Captain," she whispered. "Keep fighting. Like you always do."

With that she went to dose the other half of the room, fighting against the violent stomach cramps that tore at her insides all the while. If she hurried, she might be able to inject them all before she was too weak to press the plunger down.

Chapter 31

When Altin arrived back at the orc village, the entire canyon was filled with smoke. The village was utterly destroyed, and everything but the two log lodges, which still burned high and bright, was reduced to heaps of ash upon which danced the orange flicker of dying flames. Altin choked and gasped and had to run bent low as he scoured the ruins for signs of Taot. But there were none. In fact he found nothing left alive at all. He sent out a telepathic message, seeking his reptilian friend, but got no reply. Darting from ash heap to ash heap, up and down the slope, he searched everywhere, stepping over burnt orc corpses at nearly every turn. Taot was nowhere to be found. He wanted to tell himself that the dragon was fine, but there was no answer from his telepathic prod. There was nothing, as if the dragon had him blocked, which Taot never did.

He widened his search, cursing himself with every step for being unable to divine—it seemed that every moment of the recent past presented him with another reason for that particular regret. He ran out of the canyon and scrambled up the rocky slope that would take him atop the cliffs surrounding the village. It was a vast area, a plateau, heavy with growth both high and low. Startling deer and pigs and birds of every size, he forced his way through the brush and trees, clamoring over rocks and wading through several small streams, all the time calling out for Taot, calling for his friend.

An hour later, his robes hanging from him in tatters, he finally spotted the dragon lying in a heap, a swath of broken trees marking the trajectory of its crash. He could see that one of his huge wings was fanned flat on the ground at an impossible angle, broken and twisted out of joint. Arrows pierced the membrane of both wings like needles sticking through a sheet, and a huge nasty spear jutted out from between the dragon's ribs. Dark patches of blackened flesh all over Taot's body showed where scales had been blown away to expose the flesh beneath, such damage presumably the work of the shaman's ice bolts and fireballs. Apparently the orc magician had not been such an easy egg to crack as Taot had assumed. And Altin had left his dragon to fight the shaman all alone.

He raced to where Taot's battered body lay and put his hands on the dragon's ribs, praying to all nine gods that there was some breath still moving there. There was. Barely. Tears burned his eyes as he blinked back relief he did not deserve. He knelt at the dragon's head, which was lying in the dirt pillowed by the broken bough of a tree that had come down with him in the crash. Taot's breathing rasped, a barely discernable, a bubbling sound telling Altin that blood seeped into the dragon's lungs. That spear had probably been the telling blow. And Altin could not heal.

He cast a seeing spell straight into Doctor Leopold's office and found that the doctor was not sitting at his desk. He cursed and moved his sight through the wall and into the doctor's examining room. The doctor was there. Altin made a quick assessment, determining that the man lying on the examining table was not likely to move in the next few seconds and aimed his teleport spell to the furthest corner of the room. He appeared a moment later, much to everyone's surprise.

The man, wearing nothing but his socks, was furious as he clutched desperately for the tablecloth and pulled it around his nudity with a gasp. "By the gods, man! I will have you arrested for this."

"Tidalwrath's fits, Altin, what *are* you doing?" demanded Doctor Leopold.

Altin could barely speak he was so out of breath from clawing his way up and down the mountain slopes, and he had no time for apologies. "I need you now. An emergency. I beg you come. Please." The words tumbled out between gasps as he seized the doctor's arm. His eyes flicked to the irate man who was still fuming arrest threats while tugging on his pants. Altin gave him a plaintive look, adding, "You can have me executed later; I truly do not care. But Doctor Leopold, I need you now."

Doctor Leopold had never seen Altin so agitated before, and, albeit reluctantly, he looked the question to his patient hoping for a tolerant respite. The man glowered at the doctor for a moment then studied Altin for a pair of breaths. He too could tell by Altin's ragged look and panting fervor that perhaps an emergency was at hand.

"Fine," he said. "Go."

Altin thanked him with a look of pure relief and gripped Doctor Leopold's arm as if intending to drag him bodily away. A moment later found them standing at Taot's head.

Doctor Leopold staggered back reflexively in fear. "Good gods, Altin, have you gone mad?"

"No, he's mine. This is my dragon. I've told you about him before. Please, you have to help him."

Doctor Leopold hesitated briefly before giving in to curiosity. "What happened to him?"

"Just look," Altin replied as if it should be obvious, but he realized Doctor Leopold needed a moment to gather his wits.

"It was orcs," he added, forcing politeness. That was all the courtesy he could manage. "Doctor, there isn't time. Listen to his breath." He dropped to his knees near Taot's snout and lowered his ear to the fist-sized nostril to illustrate his point. "You see. Listen."

"I don't know anything about dragons," Doctor Leopold protested, eyeing the monstrous creature and clearly hesitant to get any closer than he already was. Altin gave him a withering, impatient look, and finally the doctor joined him on the ground. "You're right, that doesn't sound good," the physician said after leaning down and listening for himself.

Doctor Leopold stood and, moving away from Taot's dangerous looking teeth, went to the area where the spear had been thrust between the dragon's ribs. The doctor felt a bit more comfortable having moved away from that enormous, toothy head. He placed a hand on Taot's scaly side and began to chant a spell, the divination taking quite a while to cast. At length the doctor's examination was begun, and Altin watched impatiently with only fear for Taot keeping his nausea in check. He would kill himself if the dragon died. He was not going to take another life. Not like this. Taot would be the last to die at Altin's selfish hand.

Doctor Leopold spent an agonizingly long time studying Taot with the divination spell, but at length he had enough information that he could attempt to stabilize the giant beast. "He's got eight broken ribs, a ruptured spleen and a punctured lung. The lung's the worst, he's bleeding badly, and I have to stop it before he drowns."

"I'll empty Tytamon's treasury; I don't care if I have to steal it all. Anything. Please save him."

Doctor Leopold paused and looked Altin in the eyes, straight on, an expression dripping with merciless reality. "It's really bad, Altin."

"Please."

"I'll do what I can."

What followed was the longest eight hours of Altin's life. He paced back and forth impatiently as the doctor worked well into the night. Each step Altin took renewed his hatred of himself, and somewhere around the sixth or seventh hour of self-excoriation, he swore off magic for good. He spent the last hour devising the plan that would burn out his mythothalamus and make his conviction permanent. Doing so would be simple with the Liquefying Stone.

Somewhere after midnight the doctor staggered back as he released himself from a long and wearisome healing spell. His face, doughy as it normally was, was even whiter than usual and his lips were almost blue. He was exhausted. Nearly collapsing to the ground, he sat with his back against Taot's armored belly struggling to regain some small bit of strength. Even in the cool night air, sweat ran down from his brow and cheeks, over his corrugated chins and into to the collar of his shirt where the dark wetness had spread during the course of his work to join similar patches radiating outward in his tunic from beneath his arms. "By the gods these things have a lot of tissue to repair," he said. "Damn lungs alone are bigger than a man. Bigger than me."

"Did it work?"

"Yes, lad. The bleeding is stopped. Just. But I've got no more strength to give, so it will have to do for now."

"But what about his wing? And the burns. And the arrows everywhere?"

"Altin, you're a magician. You know what it is to be out of strength. And I've used up all the mana now. We have to wait."

Altin sent his mind out into the mana stream and confirmed that what the doctor said was true: the pudgy physician had indeed emptied out the night. An incredible surgery. He sighed and moved to Taot's head, where he knelt down and laid a hand upon the dragon's snout. He caressed it tenderly. "How long until he wakes up?"

"I don't know, Altin. I've done everything I can."

They sat there in silence for a long time, the doctor leaning his head against the now rhythmic rise and fall of Taot's belly, eyes closed as he tried to get some rest. Altin stroked Taot's face and prayed to gods he hoped might actually exist, prayed that they would save the dragon's life. Or else.

Perhaps an hour before dawn, Doctor Leopold stood up. "Altin, you need to send me home now. I have to get some rest. And I have patients to see in the morning."

"But what about his wing... all the other things?"

"I'll come by tomorrow afternoon and see what else I can do."

"All right, I'll come get you. What time should I come by?"

"I'll send a homing lizard to let you know. Have you imprinted any in town?"

"No. Only Aderbury's in Crown."

"Good enough," the doctor said. He paused, studying Altin's haunted eyes and tattered robes. "You need some rest too, boy. You look like you've just watched a harpy eat."

"I have," he said. "In a manner of speaking, anyway. I've seen a monster do its work."

Altin's tone made the doctor stare at him awhile. But, too tired, he let it go. "All right then. Send me back, and then go get some sleep."

"I'm going to take Taot back to my tower."

"You shouldn't move him."

"I'll place him exactly as he is."

"It's your dragon," the doctor said, lacking the strength for argument. "Send me back."

Altin sent the doctor to his office and then went about casting the spell that would place Taot atop his tower back at home. Resting normally, with wings folded in, the dragon would only have taken up roughly a third of the tower's space, but with one wing spread out like it was, Taot was going to take up a lot of room. Altin had to be very careful how he oriented the dragon as he fixed the positions in his mind to cast the spell. But he managed it well enough, and a moment later Taot appeared on the battlements lying just as if it had been there that he had fallen rather than on the ridge above the orc town.

Taot appeared near the curving parapet not too far from the stairs leading down to Altin's room. His shattered wing was spread across the flagstones, its tip curled up against the opposite wall, and his long tail wound halfway round the tower, circling the edge like a great, spike-backed snake. Altin went around the parapet carefully, checking to make sure nothing was out of joint or twisted in an uncomfortable way. The dragon had enough room to stretch his legs if it woke up, and Altin was satisfied that Taot was resting comfortably before he finally allowed himself to go lay down. The truth of the matter was, he was ready to pass out. He'd never been so depleted in all his life.

It is a rough day when one has to destroy four deadly space monsters; wipe out an entire orc village; nearly kill a little girl; and perhaps successfully end the life of a devoted and magnificent dragon who might have lived a thousand years were it not for one's rampant thoughtlessness. Then, toss in the revelation that one is responsible for the death of both of one's parents and one's sister, and, well, one's energy comes quickly to an end. Along with a few other things. But for those, he'd have to wait. He had nothing left for today.

Practically crawling to his bed, he collapsed in a tattered heap. Tomorrow was not that far away.

Chapter 32

Altin woke nine hours later, every muscle in his body screaming as he sat up out of bed. Rising stiffly and with a groan, he made his way back upstairs. Taot was still unconscious. Considering the horribly broken wing and the pincushion state of its arrow-riddled membrane—not to mention the giant spear still jutting from his ribs—Altin thought it was probably for the best that the dragon remained asleep. Letting Taot rest did little to fill the time, however, and empty time gave Altin too much opportunity to focus on his guilt, on the sense of helplessness that had begun to plague him since he'd brought the dragon home. There had to be something more that he could do. It occurred to him that the dragon was going to need something to eat when he finally did wake up. Procuring Taot's food would distract Altin from his thoughts—and from the awful thing that he was going to do to make things right once the dragon was returned to health.

He went downstairs and nosed around the pig pen for a bit, but Nipper grew furious when Altin suggested slaughtering a prize hog to feed, as the aged steward had put it, "that infernal monster," and so Altin decided that getting a deer was probably a better choice. He went to the stables and asked the groom to saddle up a horse, too sore to want to do the work himself. Happy to oblige, the groom set about the task, giving Altin time to go to the armory and select a longbow and a quiver filled with arrows suited for the hunt.

As he was choosing his weapon from amongst the dusty racks of Calico Castle's ancient weapons store, a shadow moved into the arc of light beaming through the opened door at Altin's back. Altin turned and looked up to see Pernie standing in the doorframe peering into the musty gloom. His stomach abruptly tightened; he wasn't prepared for her just yet.

They stood motionless, looking at each other for quite a while, as Altin tried to make out the expression on her face. The light behind her limned her blonde hair in a white glow, like the silver that trims a cloud, and highlighted stray threads poking out from the fabric of her simple, homemade dress, making them shimmer like luminous hairs themselves and giving Pernie's diminutive frame a soft and radiant air. He could not see her face. Backlit, her expression was lost in shadow leaving Altin to guess what was going on inside her mind. Guilt colored him and he had to briefly turn away.

He made an act of studying an old shortbow he lifted from a rack, but quickly set it back. He owed her more than that. He pushed past the awkwardness and forced himself to speak. "So are you feeling okay?"

"I'm fine," she said. "Just a cut. Kettle stitched it up. You want to see?" She shifted her weight forward, prepared to come into the room.

"No, that's all right," he said, stopping her. "I was there when she did it. Kettle's a good woman. She loves you quite a lot."

Pernie shrugged. "I know."

They stood there for another long moment, Altin wishing he knew what else to say. How does one explain to a child that the horror they just endured, the terror and the pain, was brought on by someone they trusted to keep them safe? How does one go about doing such a thing? He couldn't even fathom where to start. Nervous laughter almost made a sound as he recollected Kettle's accusatory words. "The brains of twenty men," she'd said. What a joke. He couldn't even talk to a little girl.

"So what's the bow for?" Pernie asked, giving Altin a momentary reprieve. "You gonna shoot somethin'?"

He was able to get his breathing started once again. He hadn't realized that it had stopped. "A deer," he said. "Taot needs something to eat."

"Why can't he get it his self? I seen him do it a thousand hundred times."

"He's sick."

"Oh?" She looked puzzled, like trying to adjust to some impossibility. "What's wrong with him?"

"He got hurt. Doctor Leopold treated him though, so he'll get better now." His voice lacked conviction, but Pernie seemed not to notice as she pressed.

"Was it the orcs what hurt him? Because I seen him flying down. I heard him roar real loud. I thought he might be coming after me."

"Well, he was coming to help you, so he was coming for you in a way. He was helping me to get you back. And the orcs did hurt him, but Doctor Leopold healed him, so now everything should be okay."

She tilted her head and studied him for a moment. "Where is he then? Are you going to his cave?"

Altin hesitated, wondering if he should tell her that the dragon was here, up in the tower, or if he should tell her something else. But hadn't he hurt her enough? Certainly she deserved the truth. But this truth might get her killed if she tried to sneak up and take a look; what if Taot suddenly woke up? So he probably shouldn't tell her. Which meant he had to lie, another form of injury. Or was it? Why was this little girl so hard to comprehend?

Little bits of blue. That was why. Glimpses of Neechy danced across his mind, spinning around in her bright blue dress, laughing and playing. Alive before Altin dealt the killing blow. And now there was Pernie. Altin realized as he stood there beginning to sweat why it was he had such trouble with this tiny child. Suddenly he knew. But the knowledge didn't change anything. At least not now, not for this.

"Well are you?" she said again. "Because I can help you if you do. I'm a pretty good hunter, you know, if you need help finding him some food." She puffed her chest out proudly.

He exhaled carefully. "No. He's not in his cave. He's in my tower. Up in the battlements. He's very sick. And you must promise to stay away. If he wakes up, hurt like he is, he might be angry and lash out at the first person that he sees. Promise you won't go up."

"But I could go up with you," she said. "He wouldn't be angry at me then."

"I don't know if even I am safe."

"Of course you are. You saved me from the orcs."

He winced. "Yes. Listen, about that Pernie. That should never have happened, and you should know that the whole thing was my fault."

She looked at him as if he'd just told her Kettle was the Queen.

He needed her to believe him, and he stepped forward and knelt before her to look her in the eyes. "Really, Pernie. It is my fault. They came in through the wall, through the hole I made. I never should have taken the tower out without putting something in its place. I opened up the castle and just let the orcs come right in. It's my fault you got hurt. And I'm really sorry." He forced his gaze to stay in hers, his breath held awaiting her rebuke.

"Is that why Kettle was yellin' at you last night?"

Altin nodded.

"She was yellin' pretty loud. She yelled at me like that when I forgot to shut the gate and all the goats got out one time. Nipper paddled my behind too." She hesitated then, her mind drifting for a moment to the memory of which she spoke. "I bet Nipper won't paddle your behind though," she said at length. "Nope, I bet he won't." She seemed satisfied with this assessment, but felt compelled to ask, "Will he?" with tangible concern reflecting in her large blue eyes.

Altin could not stop the smile that came to his lips, although he felt unworthy of it even as it did. He shook his head. "No, Nipper won't paddle my behind. But I think perhaps he should. I certainly deserve it."

She laughed at that. Apparently the thought of an all-powerful magician being spanked by the cantankerous old man was hilarious. "You could fix it so it didn't hurt," she giggled as she began contemplating the possibility. "You could turn his hand into a pillow or grow your butt into a stack of hay." She laughed louder as she thought about it more. "I wish I could make my butt into a stack of hay. Or maybe a big prickly pear tree." She was nearly overcome with hilarity as she began to rattle off every soft or menacing thing that she might turn her bottom into if only she had Altin's magic to command.

The irony was too great for Altin to share in Pernie's fun, for he had no intention of ever using magic again. He realized now that everyone was right. He was just a Six. The circular irregularity to which he'd clung for all these years meant nothing. And not only was he just a Six, he was a deadly Six, a Six that had been taking people's lives all along the way. His only question now was whether he should burn out his mythothalamus and stay here as a blank on Kurr like he'd decided to do last night, or if he should just vanish into space, one last cast and then drift forever in the night. The latter seemed a more fitting end. Particularly as he watched little Pernie laugh. She was so innocent and full of life. She didn't care what people thought. She was just alive. And she was not cursed like him, not a menace like Kettle said. He wished that the worst thing he had ever done was to let some goats get out.

Pernie ran out of items to list as options for the transmogrification of her backside, and so she abruptly changed the subject as children are wont to do. "So can I help you find Taot's deer?"

Her question caught him off-guard and at first he had no reply.

"Well, can I?" she repeated. "Help you find the deer?"

He didn't know precisely what to say, but he was certain that "no" was not an option given the events of yesterday. "Fine," he said, retaking the shortbow from the rack and grabbing a quiver of arrows hanging on a nail. "You can come along." Why not, he thought. Hells, she'd probably find one faster than he could anyway if ravens were any kind of clue.

The groom saddled a pony for Pernie to ride, and soon the two of them were off across the meadow and out onto the plains. As Calico Castle grew smaller in the distance, Altin couldn't help thinking that he was probably the last person Kettle would have chosen to have watching over Pernie now. He tried to shake the thought. The girl roamed these lands almost daily as it was. She probably *was* safer when he was not around, which gave weight to the option for disappearing into space.

Strips of blue cloth wrapped around his thoughts as they rode along, memory's garrote tightening amongst the imagined sounds of Pernie screaming from inside a tree. He could hear the screams clearly echoing off the insides of his mind, much like they had off the face of the orcish cliffs.

The screams he'd caused her—a gap in the wall was an invitation that an open gate was not; one spoke of vulnerability while the other spoke only of people at their ease.

Sure enough, it was Pernie who spotted the doe and her fawn as they topped a modest hill. "Down there," she whispered, breaking Altin from his trance. "See? By that tree. And look, she has a baby too."

Altin would have ridden right on by if Pernie hadn't spoken up. He blinked a few times, clearing his head, and then looked where Pernie was pointing down the slope. The deer grazed beneath the sweep of a weeping willow's boughs, unaware of their approach.

"Yes, I see them," he said. "You have good eyes." He was reluctant to go after them, however, because the doe did have a fawn. He didn't think Pernie would be too happy about killing the little one. They'd either have to kill it, or leave it motherless, and neither option was likely going to sit well with a child.

"Kill the mother first," she said, "then the little one won't go too far away."

Altin turned in his saddle and gaped at her.

"It's true," she said, misinterpreting his incredulity. "Gimmel told me so, and he hunts all the time."

Altin shook his head and had to suppress a grin. He didn't deserve it anyway.

They dismounted and, after hobbling the horses, they slunk down into the grass, trying to keep the willow tree between them and the pair of deer. The wind was blowing across their path, preventing the deer from scenting them in the air, and they finally made it close enough for Altin to take a shot. His tired muscles protested as he drew the bowstring back, and when he shot, his missile flew harmlessly past, so much so that the doe didn't bother looking up.

"You're not very good at that, are you Master Altin?" Pernie said. There was no judgment in her tone. She merely observed.

"No," he replied. "I'm not. I haven't used one of these things since basic training." He didn't want to admit that he was sore and feeling weak.

"I can probably get the baby with my sling," she offered.

"No. I'll get it," he said, not wanting to subject her to such a thing.

He drew the bow back again, grimacing, and fired another shot. This one was worse than the first. Pernie giggled. The doe remained oblivious to the shot, the errant projectile seeming little more than an insect buzzing by; but the child snickering did make the deer look up, forcing the pair of hunters to dive for cover in the grass.

"You sure you don't want me to get the little one before they both run off?" Pernie offered. "At least Taot could have a snack."

"I'm sure," Altin said. "I'll get it this time." He wanted to cast a seeking enchantment on an arrow, but he pushed the thought aside. First off, he didn't have one memorized, and secondly, he was no longer using magic anymore. He'd sworn it off, so he was going to have to shoot this deer just like anyone else would have to do.

"What's that?" Pernie asked as Altin rose up on his hands to peer through the grass and see if he was clear to take another shot.

"What's what?"

"That, around your neck."

He looked down at the fast-cast amulet now dangling a few inches from the ground. "It's an amulet. I made it for bringing my tower close to home. It's just in case something goes wrong."

"What can go wrong?"

"Nothing," he said. "Now be quiet so you don't scare the

deer away."

"It's not very pretty," she observed.

"Yes, well, it only has to work."

"How do you make it go?"

"You don't 'make it go.' You just strike it. Like a match."

"Oh," she said.

He got back up onto one knee and fitted another arrow to the string. Pernie fell silent as Altin drew back the bow, this time trying to remember everything his drill instructor had said. He took careful aim and released another shaft. This one was too low and hit the ground early, sliding through the grass and coming to a stop right between the doe's front feet. She jumped and darted off, perhaps thinking it was a snake, and she didn't stop until she was eighty paces from the tree. The fawn followed along behind her, bounding through the grass as if its feet were made of springs.

"Damn it," Altin cursed, which set Pernie to giggling again. Altin cupped his hand over his mouth. "Sorry," he said. "That's a bad word."

Pernie was still giggling.

Now what was he going to do? Getting food for Taot was going to take forever at this rate. He debated going back and demanding that Nipper slaughter the hog anyway. He did have the authority if it actually came to that. However, he really was not in the mood for another argument. Yesterday had really worn him out.

"Master Altin," Pernie asked innocently, "why don't you just use your magic?"

"I can't," he said.

"Why not?"

"Because I can't."

"Because why?"

"I just can't, that's why."

Pernie watched him for a long while. He could tell she desperately wanted to ask him why again, but was managing to hold her tongue.

"Come on; it's going to get away." He got up and trod through the knee-high grass, stooping as he moved and trying to stay downwind. Pernie waded along merrily behind him, arms out and grinning as the blades of grass tickled the soft skin on the undersides. Once they were in range, they crouched down again. Altin pulled another arrow out. He glanced over at Pernie who returned his look with a happy smile. He sighed, and then took another shot.

He got the doe this time, only he hit her in the hind leg, high and in the middle of the thigh. She let out a screech and took off in full flight, her fawn once more following behind.

"Damn it," Altin cursed again.

Pernie didn't giggle this time; she just stood up, watching the deer run away and waiting for Altin to make another move. When the pair was almost out of sight and Altin still hadn't done anything, she looked up at him with wide, expectant eyes.

"What?" he said, pinned down by those blinking blue irises and feeling somehow very small.

"Aren't you going to chase her down?" she asked. "So she don't die a horrible death, all sick and miserable, oozing pus and dying torture-like?"

He groaned. "Where do you come up with this stuff?"

"Gimmel says you got to chase them down if you make a bad shot like that. He says the goddess gets mad if you make them get sick and die on their own, all hurt and stuff." She paused and then added, "Plus, yer supposed to be a better shot. That's why I practice all the time." She patted the length of rope tied around her waist, which Altin realized was her sling.

"Well we're not going to catch them now," Altin observed as the doe, while limping noticeably, still managed to diminish into the distance at quite a clip. She was headed for the woods.

"Use your magic then," Pernie said as if it were such a simple thing, though with urgency in her voice that spoke to her belief that there was something huge at stake. "You're not supposed to let them die."

"I told you I can't. I'm not using magic anymore."

Incredulity filled her little face. "You mean never?"

"That's right. Never."

She clearly didn't understand. "But what about the deer?"

"Forget the deer. I'll just tell Nipper I need a hog. Let's go." He turned and started back towards the horses on the hill.

Pernie didn't follow; instead she took a few steps closer to the woods. Altin figured she would come if he just pressed on, but when he was half the distance to the horses and she had still not caught back up, he stopped and turned around. She continued watching the deer as they ran towards the trees.

"Pernie," he yelled. "Come on. It's time to go."

She did not come, and he was forced to go back to where she stood. When he got close to her, he realized that she was crying, the sound of it carrying to him on the wind as he approached.

"What?" he asked, frustrated and desperate all at once.

"I don't want the goddess mad at me," she managed to say between sobs of increasing severity. "Gimmel says the Great Huntress will gut you in the night if you treat her creatures mean. I don't want to get gutted, Master Altin. Gimmel says it's a terrible way to die."

He wanted to tell her that Gimmel was a twit and that there was no such thing as a Great Huntress anyway, but it was clear that that particular tactic probably wouldn't work. His mind churned as he sought a way out of his predicament. "Listen, Pernie, the goddess will understand," he said at last. "Maybe she'll even come down and pull the arrow out. The gods do things like that sometimes. The doe will be fine."

He caught himself even as he spoke, realizing that he was doing it again, setting the world to revolve around his needs, centering everything on his beliefs. Forget anyone else. Do anything, say anything, just so long as everything moves his way. And once again he'd managed to make Pernie cry. He was getting good at that. Making girls cry.

The word "menace" flitted hauntingly through his mind, and he felt the rage begin to boil once again, filling him with its heat and its necessity to act. "Fine," he said, snarling, and he then began to chant. A moment later he appeared right between the doe and her fawn just as they had come into the edge of the shelter of the woods. Before they could leap away, he reached out and placed a hand on each of them, calling up the still-familiar lightning spell in his mind and releasing it with a word. In an instant, the deer and her fawn writhed and died as the powerful currents burnt their flesh and turned their blood to steam inside their veins. Finally they fell motionless to the ground, smoking heaps of sundered meat, as Altin ground his teeth with the anger of feeling trapped. And he was trapped too. He knew it now with palpable certainty. His magic was a curse, an inescapable reality. He could feel the truth of it with all his heart and soul, and he realized that he could never be rid of its effects; it would find him even if he didn't want it to. Which meant he had no other choice, he had to be rid of himself instead; he had to go away.

Still angry, he teleported himself and both deer corpses back to where Pernie stood. She clapped giddily and jumped up and down. "I can't wait till I'm old enough to do that," she said, tears forgotten and drying on her cheeks. She stared down at the two charred corpses, smoke still coming off of them with the scent of fresh burnt hair. "Magic is going to be so much fun."

"You can wait," he said. "And it's not fun." With that, he

stooped and slung the doe across his neck, a mighty heave that sent pain like lightning jolting through his already aching back. He groaned, feeling as if mountains could not weigh as much as this damnable doe now did. He wheezed under the weight as he staggered through the grass, headed towards the horses on the knoll.

Pernie followed a few paces behind, dragging the fawn along by its hind leg and humming the tune to "My Cat's Paw" with a contented smile upon her face. She didn't even mind that Altin never spoke another word the whole way home. That was fine. She could be happy enough for two.

Chapter 33

The vaccine made by the *New Guinea's* crew proved efficacious, and just in time too, at least for those who were still alive when it arrived. Captain Asad survived, if barely, as did Orli and Doctor Singh. Of the ship's one thousand twenty crew members, only one hundred and forty-six remained alive. So, while the vaccine was seen as something of a victory by those who survived the disease, for the rest of the fleet, the events aboard the *Aspect* were a terrifying example of a battle horribly lost and one that gave the measure of their enemy as well. And the worst part of it was, the enemy had returned.

Orli had particular familiarity with this latest development as she had been reassigned to the position of first-shift communications officer and was now stationed on the bridge. Unfortunately, the reassignment had less to do with her skill in the area of communications than it did with her being one of the nine remaining officers on the ship. When the calls had gone out to the rest of the fleet for volunteers to re-crew the *Aspect*, few had taken the offer up. Despite the vaccine having proved successful, there just weren't many people willing to take a chance in exposing themselves to an alien disease that had proven itself capable of wiping out nearly an entire crew, particularly one that could shift its own genetics seemingly at will. Most expected it was simply a matter of time before the organism adapted to the new vaccine and came at the crew again, although there weren't many willing to say such a thing out loud just yet. The bottom line, however, was that there had been a few who had agreed to come: a handful of nurses and some engineering folks willing to help out under the condition that they could go about in hazardous material suits at all times and that they were given triple pay, which they were allowed on both accounts. All told, the *Aspect* was now running on roughly a quarter of its crew and everyone was pulling double shifts and, apparently, would be for a long, long time to come. What couldn't be done by those onboard or by remote from another ship simply wasn't done at all.

The captain, in a live address to the assembled crew, and one that completely violated fleet protocol for it was neither recorded nor transmitted to the rest of the fleet, assured everyone that once enough time had passed, the rest of the fleet would see that the disease was in fact gone and would eventually "find their collective balls." Then relief would come. The address helped a little, but the truth was, nobody believed anyone would come aboard the *Aspect* now, not in the bottoms of their hearts anyway, likely not even the captain himself. For most though, there was a strong sense of being "in it" together now, and that was something new; they were in it and in it for the long haul. The survivors shared a bond that was stronger and much deeper than what had existed aboard the *Aspect* prior to the disease. Before, they were simply shipmates—stuck together for over a decade, true, but not so stuck that there hadn't always been, at least lingering in the backs of their minds, some possibility of a getaway. The occasional inter-ship transfer promised the option of a change of scene, or at least a change of faces, if anyone ever really had some pressing reason to find another place to be. Transfers were an option even though they were rarely done. But now it was different. Nobody was going anywhere, and everyone knew it. Including the captain.

Which is not to say, in giving his address—or in his acceptance of the fact that things aboard his ship were no longer going to be as neat and tidy as he'd always kept them in the past—that he was about to give up his strict sense of military discipline. The realization that the human dynamics aboard the ship were different now did not, for Captain Asad, change anything at all where discipline was involved. In fact, for him, discipline was the very thing that was going to make their new circumstances work. However, he was more willing to forgive past transgressions, and it was with very little hostility that he accepted Orli as an officer on his bridge.

In fact, in the first few days of her reassignment, the captain had been very patient in helping her learn, or relearn, various elements of her new post—elements that she had been thoroughly trained on during her time as a student in the Fleet Academy. Unfortunately, no help that he gave, nor any coming from Roberto, could make her stop wishing she hadn't spent the entire semester of her coms class flirting with that damnably gorgeous Cadet Fogart rather than paying attention to what was being taught. Besides the fact that Fogart had turned out to be a total jerk, leaving her broken hearted and feeling like a fool by semester's end, she was now stuck struggling with the results of that distraction, fighting to remember just what the hell it was she was supposed to have learned and what she was supposed to do at this station now that she was here. But the operations were coming back. Slowly. Just not fast enough to make her feel comfortable in the role if the orbs attacked again. If the fight got hot, she did not want to be the one stuck coordinating communication between the five ships currently on the scene. She was still too clumsy for that.

And an attack could come at any time as three new orbs hovered out beyond their ships, clustered together roughly a hundred kilometers away and waiting. Neither Orli nor Roberto was able to determine if one of them was the same one that had run off before, but the captain suspected that the smallest of them was in fact that very one. He said he could "feel" it, and Orli had no reason to doubt that he was right.

"Find out if engineering can muster another missile battery if we use up one that's loaded now." The captain's order came unexpectedly and caught her staring absently at the image of the orbs hovering on the screen.

"Yes, sir," she said, punching at her panel reflexively.

"Maintenance," came the voice on the other end.

"Oh. Crap," she stammered, blushing. "Not you. Sorry. Wrong button." She killed the link with a stab of her index finger and glanced out of the corner of her eye to see if the captain had noticed. Maybe he hadn't.

But Roberto had. He leaned near enough to whisper, "God, you suck," with an evil grin. He straightened himself and went about pretending to study trajectory charts taken from the last encounter with the orbs. Orli knew better than to think he needed those now. She knew full well he'd already analyzed every last movement that the orbs had made and had done so at least a hundred times. He could recite from memory their speed at every moment from beginning to end on every pass, how many milliseconds between surface shifts, the angles—and lack of angles—of each maneuver they made, and the distances maintained from the ship and between one another for every pass. In short, there was nothing he did not know about how they had moved. And yet, even he admitted that "we're screwed if we get more than three orbs to a ship." "I can take two," he'd said. "Three if I have to. Maybe. But four, forget it."

He'd already given seven ship-to-ship conferences to the fleet's bridge crews regarding the strategies he'd figured out. "The bottom line is, you need to have multiple attacks going off in perfect unison," he told them. "You need lasers and nukes in the same place at the same time, so regardless of whether the orb goes soft or hard, you have something nasty to shove right up its ass. And it's still going to need some luck." Roberto's simple sounding plan was much like Doctor Singh's design for the "three-legged vaccine," formulated to hit simultaneously whichever organism the disease tried to manifest, disallowing it the opportunity to avoid one through becoming another. The difficulty of Roberto's strategy, however, was that it could not be computer controlled due to the impossible movements of the orbs, shifting as they did in flight as if not ruled by physical law, and so the gunners were on their own to place their shots. Which was also why Roberto insisted he could only get three.

"Hey, I'm good, but I'm not a magician," he'd said when Orli tried to encourage him that four orbs were still within his realm of expertise. "Three tops. We only have two lasers. If three come at once, well, we're going to get hit by one as it is. We can take one hit, if it's not too hard. And if we can take one orb out right away, then we're down to just a pair. Then I'm golden. But four just gives them too much opportunity."

It seemed that perhaps the orbs knew this too, for they continued to hover in the distance for several days after initially showing up. Apparently they were waiting until two more came, which they did. And a sixth showed up the day after that.

"Now I'm worried," said Roberto as they both watched the recent arrival moving in to join its friends. The Hostiles made no attempt at a formation, and they arranged themselves loosely with nothing to give evidence of structure or hierarchy amongst the group.

"We have four other ships with us," Orli reminded him. "We should be fine."

"Those guys have never done this," he said.

"They'll be fine. Have faith."

"I have faith that those orbs are assholes. Everything else is still up in the air."

"Necessary chatter only," ordered the captain, pointing at the blinking orange light above the main console on the forward wall. "We're at orange, remember?"

"Aye, sir," they said together. Orli could hear Roberto mutter "asshole" again under his breath.

"Get the admiral's ship, tell them we have six now," the captain said. By the time she'd pulled up the channel, he changed the message to "seven."

Pleased that she actually called the right ship this time, she relayed the message as two more orbs were slipping into view.

"Holy shit, man," said Roberto. This time the captain did nothing to rebuke him for the unessential remark. Roberto figured he agreed.

"We're sending Echo squadron," came the reply from the admiral's ship a moment later.

"Tell them to hurry; now we're up to nine," Orli said before realizing she was technically putting words into the captain's mouth. Still, it seemed like they should know.

"That's still two days out," said the captain. "The Hostiles are reinforcing too fast. Faster than we can. Tell the admiral to get Delta moving too. Frankly, tell him I'd advise gathering the fleet."

Orli relayed the message. It was ten minutes and two more orbs later that the reply came across the speaker. "Delta on its way. Bravo too. Rest of fleet holding for now. Keep us posted."

Captain Asad shook his head but nodded grimly. He

wasn't happy with the news. Orli confirmed receipt of the message and terminated contact. The three of them sat in silence staring at the screen. An hour later another orb showed up.

"Damn," muttered Roberto as it came into view. "That's a big one." Orli zoomed the main sensor in on the newest arrival to give them a closer look.

It was indeed huge, at least twice as large as the largest they'd seen before. It almost looked like a small moon. She grimaced as she looked at it and shook her head. Even the captain let out a grunt.

"What the hell am I supposed to do with that?" Roberto asked. "All things being relative, the shaft that comes out of that thing is really going to stick it to us. Seriously. Our lasers aren't going to push that thing's projectiles anywhere. No way."

"You'll have to use missiles to do it too."

"They're too slow. They'll never make it. Not for the push."

"Plan ahead."

Roberto rolled his eyes. "Right," he said. "I'm on that." He made no attempt to mask the sarcasm in his voice.

"Lieutenant Junior Grade Levi, if you don't wish to be an ensign again, I suggest you stow the attitude and focus on your work."

Orli could tell Roberto was about to pop as he tried to hold back some remark regarding the worthlessness of rank when one is dead, but despite bulging eyes and a screwed up left corner of the mouth, he managed to keep it in, if narrowly.

Two more orbs arrived.

Roberto groaned. "Well, let's hope they don't attack until Delta and Bravo show up. Maybe with enough extra lasers we can still coordinate pushing them aside."

"I'm more concerned that these things stop reinforcing

soon," said the captain. "If they bring many more we'll have to tell Delta and Bravo not to bother coming at all."

"Well I hope they don't attack *and* they stop reinforcing," said Orli, agreeing with them both and trying to lighten up the mood. What was the point of being surly and negative in a time like this? It wasn't like they hadn't faced death already just a few days before. This was just another round.

"Good call," said Roberto. "I'll vote that way with you."

"Focus," said the captain a moment later. "Here they come."

Chapter 34

Three more nights went by before Taot finally came awake. Altin was seated on a crenel staring out morosely from the tower wall, his vision blurred into the green cloud of the Great Forest's canopy where his thoughts had turned inward on himself. His perch was a fortunate one, for in mid-daydream Taot began to stir. What started as a grunting sort of noise quickly became a tantrum of terrifying might.

The huge beast woke suddenly with the last memories of orcish arrows, spears and icebolts firing in his mind. He roared and blew a reflexive gust of fire across the battlements by which the small hairs at the back of Altin's neck were singed—a good thing Taot's head was faced the other way. The dragon tried to heave itself up onto its feet, but its legs were weak and stiff, and one had been turned beneath him long enough as he slept for circulation to diminish, reduced to the point of putting the leg itself "to sleep." The numb limb collapsed under Taot unexpectedly and brought forth yet another rumbling cry, this time pain and rage. Pebbles rained down from the cliffs as Taot's confusion rattled amongst the rocks.

Flapping his great wings in what approached a panicked state, Taot again tried to rise, but by this time Altin had begun sending him some telepathic thoughts. He sent images of the ruined village and all the orcs lying dead into Taot's mind. He sent the sense of a hot desert wind and a full stomach along with that as well. He sent the sense of calm.

Taot flopped about a moment longer, reluctant to believe at first, but finally his dragon's brain caught up with his instinctive body and both began working in the present again. Altin quickly filled in the history of what had happened since the dragon's fall, and included as best as possible the nature of his wounds and the many visits by Doctor Leopold, including images of the removal of the spear and the arrows in his wings.

Unfortunately, convalescence was a foreign concept for the dragon, and Altin had to struggle to get the idea across as Taot once more began to try to rise. The dragon's forceful thoughts were clear, he wanted to return to his lair, but Altin insisted that staying here, close to him, close to deer and Doctor Leopold, would be a better choice, at least for another week. Taot could not fly, nor could he even stand for very long, and Altin was unwilling to leave the dragon in his cave subject to daring predators until the mighty beast was truly mighty once again. Ultimately, and only after being bribed with the promise of fresh venison, Taot eventually acceded to Altin's insistence and settled in to rest.

When the dragon was safely sleeping again, Altin stared down at it ruefully, once more moping over what he was going to do. He was feeling a little less guilt now that it seemed Taot was going to mend, but that didn't change much else. In his internal debate over which course to take regarding his magic, the pendulum had swung back to burning out his mythothalamus again. But he was not going to do it just yet. He needed his magic until Taot was nursed fully back to health. Which vexed him. His life, his habits were too caught up in the magic now. He was as dependant on his magic as a skunk was on its stench; awful as it was, take the spray away and all you're left with is a rather clumsy cat. Altin didn't relish the idea of becoming a clumsy cat, but he knew he'd never be able to just stop casting either. He could never simply stop using magic anymore, a fact made perfectly clear by the evidence of the deer in the meadow the other day. He couldn't escape the magic even when he tried, which was why he had to fry the magical organ in his mind. But still, resigned as he was, it was a depressing concept now that he was resolved to get it done. He still had so many questions as to why his life had to come to this. There were so many things that didn't make any sense.

If he was a Six, like everyone said he was, then he was probably going to kill himself eventually anyway. And he was fine with that. He always had been. It's not like he'd been racing to his death on purpose, but he had always been perfectly resigned to having death looming all the time. He honestly didn't mind. Frankly, he'd never given it much thought. He always felt he was a Seven anyway, somehow destined to avert the rule of Six. But none of that mattered anymore. Not now. Not sitting here watching Taot slowly recovering from a narrow escape from death that was entirely Altin's fault. Altin knew there was no other way. It was as clear as water in a mountain lake what he had to do, because he knew, deep down, that he would never change. He could never stop using magic, no matter how hard he tried, and he could never stop posing a threat to everyone that mattered in his life. And that was the heart of it all, the root of his frustration over his life having come to such a pass.

For eight hundred years Tytamon had managed not to kill everyone he met by mistake. Tytamon had control. So what was the difference? Was it just luck? Was it time and experience? Or did the Ancient One have skeletons buried in his vault? Somehow Altin didn't think he did. So it must really be the damnable law of Six. Altin hated that idea, but he began to believe it had to be the case, began to believe that's why they called it the *law* of Six instead of something else.

And Tytamon was an Eight after all. Tytamon had full circularity. He had the perspective of all the schools of magic, each one giving insight into the possibilities of those on either side around the "ring." Even if Altin had proved to be a Seven, it wouldn't change a thing. Altin did not have the "perspicacity of roundedness" as it was called, and so there were things that he was always going to miss, things he did not know, things he could not know, at least not until it was too late. "You do not know what you do not know" was the magician's curse, made worse with the more schools of magic a sorcerer has access too. Unless the sorcerer is an Eight. Then they are fully round.

Altin took out his guild card and studied the marks around the ring. He ran his thumb over the blank spot where his divination rank should have been, emptiness with scores on either side. He should have had a rank in that. All his life he'd felt it in his heart and mind and soul. It really did seem to break the rules, him skipping over it like that. He wondered if maybe he had some mental block. Knowing whether he truly was a Six or not was the one answer he wished he could have before he went and burnt the magic out for good.

Just then, Taot let out a long, slow wheeze as he fell into the deepest slumber, breaking Altin from his reverie. The sun had already dropped out of the sky. Altin hopped off the battlements and gazed down at the dark green form of his resting reptilian friend. Somehow the sight of him there made the young mage decide there was no reason why he shouldn't give divination one last try. Sort of a parting shot, a magical farewell. One last attempt to see if he really was only just a Six. And if he could do it, if he focused this time and truly gave the attempt his full ability, maybe this time, just maybe the gods would answer why, before he let his magic go. Before he blinded the magical eye of his mythothalamus. Besides, if it wasn't divining that he lacked, then it wasn't anything. He'd always known, somehow intuitively, that he had never been meant to heal. He was too selfish for that. He knew it instinctively. The recognition didn't even come with any guilt. Divining had to be the missing link.

He went downstairs to where the *Divining for Beginners* tome was still lying on the floor. He picked it up and took it to his bed, lighting the candle on the nightstand as he sat down. Curling his feet under him, he sat upon the bed and began to chant the words that would bring a sense of Tytamon's location to him, wherever the elder wizard was. The divination wasn't going to work the same as a seeing spell would, nor would it work like a telepathic nudge. According to the book, he would just have an intuitive sense instead. He would have an impression in his mind, an image that he might have to interpret to understand.

As he chanted, allowing the cadence of the child's song "My Cat's Paw" to lead him along, his mind wandered to little Pernie who'd been humming it the other day. He could see her in his mind's eye towing the fawn along. She reminded him of his sister, and Altin suddenly understood why he had never liked the song. Neechy had sung that song. They both had, in the orphanage growing up.

He caught his thoughts drifting and realized he was not focusing on the spell. That or else he just couldn't do it and he really was a Six. But he was not giving up so easily, and he started once again.

It still didn't work, and no images of Tytamon came into his head. He went back to the beginning of the book, the parts that he had gone through too quickly, and read them again, this time forcing himself to patience, to the degree of focus that he'd always had for things that were important to him. He read every word twice, despite their childish tone. And then he started chanting once again.

He sat there, cross-legged amongst a nest of wrinkled blankets, with his eyes closed for quite some time, singing the spell and seeking a simple understanding of where his master was, when finally he got the sense that Tytamon was standing in the room. His brows furrowed as he tried to further focus the image down, to refine the impression that seemed as if he'd finally made a divination work, but then Tytamon cleared his throat.

Altin's eyes snapped open to find that Tytamon was in fact standing at the door. Altin groaned. So much for divining, he thought. He laughed. What a fool. For a moment he'd actually thought the spell had worked.

"Divining, eh?" said his mentor. "I thought you'd given up on that."

"I had. But I'm trying it again. It's the least likely school for me to kill anyone with."

"Oh, you're wrong about that. Divination is the most dangerous of them all. Why do you think they put it at the top of the circle of schools?" He came into the room and walked over to the window, gazing out into the darkness. He stood there for quite some time before he finally spoke again. "I was going to talk to you about the opening in the wall and about the orcs, but I understand Kettle took that upon herself."

"Aye, she did."

A long silence followed as Altin stared absently into his book and Tytamon the night—it seemed Altin had been at it for quite a while.

"So now what?" Tytamon asked. "I divined your mood the other day. You're in an uncomfortable place."

Altin nodded.

"That's why you've got that book?" Tytamon indicated the book in Altin's lap with a nod as he turned back and took a seat at the table in the center of the room.

"Yes."

"What are you looking for?"

"I just wanted to know why things have turned out the way they have. But I suppose it doesn't matter in the end. I'm going to quit casting as soon as Taot's healed." He paused, and looked up for a moment from the book. "I just wanted to see if I really am a Seven rather than a Six, if being a Seven is why I've been nothing but a plague. It's not in the history of Sixes to kill everyone but themselves. I wanted to know if maybe that's the Seven's curse, to kill everyone else instead. At least then I could tell myself I didn't have a choice." He expected Tytamon to protest or to say something wise and introspective like he always did, but the old man acted as if he'd barely heard a word.

"Another school would help," the ancient mage superficially agreed. He reached a gnarled hand out and tore off a bit of Altin's ever-present bread. Altin regarded the loaf with a shake of his head. He didn't deserve the service of those people he'd put through such a horrible ordeal.

Tytamon chewed slowly, gazing into the candle sitting near the bread. "I heard Kettle told you about your family. Rumor has it she was a bit more abrupt than I would have been in choosing how to let you know those things."

"Yes. She let me have it all right." Altin turned a page in the book, though he wasn't looking at the words.

"Well, I'd been putting it off. I'm sorry it had to come out like that."

Altin nodded and turned another page.

"You're not a bad magician, Altin. And 'menace' is too cruel a choice of words."

"She told you that, eh?"

"Yes, she told me the whole thing. She's very upset. She didn't mean to hurt you. She was just afraid. You do know she raised Pernie since the girl was eight months old?"

"Yeah, I know. I don't blame Kettle. I deserved everything that I got. Probably more."

"Well, that's why I came up here. I wanted you to know that you are a good man, Altin. You just get in a rush sometimes."

"A rush that kills people," Altin said. Tytamon had never referred to him as a "man" before. It felt... unfamiliar. He let it go. "I really don't know what I should do. I think burning out my mythothalamus is the safest thing to do."

Tytamon let him talk, taking another chunk of bread.

"I've tried to think if there were maybe some other way. I thought maybe I could become one of those reclusive wizards like you read about in books, stuffed off in some swamp somewhere, isolated from everyone, somewhere where it's safe. I even thought I might just go live in outer space. I could be the Galactic Mage, far away, safely drifting beneath the stars. No danger to anyone but myself. But that feels like it's letting me off the hook. And I could change my mind someday, come back. Blinding myself to magic is the only way."

Tytamon shook his head as Altin spoke, shifting in his chair as if there were something crawling up his leg. But he waited until Altin was through. "Feeling sorry for yourself is not the answer, and you know it as well as I," he said when Altin was finally done.

Altin went back to flipping through the book.

"Altin, you're not the first mage to lose someone that he loves."

Altin groaned silently, sensing that now one of the old man's stories was on the way for sure. He rolled his eyes, still staring at the page. He knew what he had to do. Tytamon could talk until he was blue in the face; it wouldn't change a thing.

Tytamon understood the essence of Altin's resolve and stood up, stepping closer to the bed. "Altin," he said as the younger mage leafed through the divination book. "There's something I want you to see."

The sound of soft fabric collapsing to the floor brought Altin's attention up from the book to Tytamon. The ancient mage had turned his back to Altin and let his robes slip to the ground revealing in his nudity a body so scarred and hideously wrecked that Altin had to look away. Half of the old man's left thigh muscle and buttock were gone; and the flesh up and down his entire left side was wrinkled and twisted far beyond any damage that time could possibly have wrought. He'd been mangled, as if burnt and chewed and soaked in acid all at once, the skin mottled, discolored, and undulant like a meat pie that's been stomped. It took Altin several moments to recover from the shock.

"What in the name of Mercy's tears is that?" he asked as Tytamon pulled his robes back up.

"That is the mark of *my* arrogance, Altin. It's what happens sometimes to mages regardless of how strong or clever they think they are. I was inches from adding Eights to the list of dead magicians normally saved for Sixes." Altin's eyes were wide and staring, rapt, as the old man straightened his garment and returned to the chair and took another pinch of bread. "But that's not the worst of it, Altin. I, like you, would not necessarily have regretted my own death. That is a price we have always been willing to pay. Both of us. That is an acceptable and familiar risk for mages like you and me. It is harm to others that we must suffer and that we must always try to avoid. And, sadly, despite our efforts, it is often inevitable."

Altin had to think about that last part for a while. "So what are you saying? That people are just going to die because of me? That I should get used to it? Carry on? Stiff upper lip and all that rot?" Altin couldn't believe what Tytamon had said. "You can't possibly be serious. I can't live like that. I won't. Not now. Not knowing what I know. If that's the case, then I'm definitely going to burn my mythothalamus out."

"You have to find the balance, Altin. There is always middle ground."

"I'm not interested in middle ground. Not if people are going to die, not everyone that I love. I can't carry that kind of guilt. Not anymore. That's something you just can't understand."

Tytamon pulled another chunk of bread from the loaf and held it near the candle flame for a while, toasting it absently as he considered Altin's words. When it was warm enough, he pushed it into his mouth, his moustache squirming above his parchment lips as he chewed. He swallowed and then leaned forward in his chair.

"Her name was Kelline. She was my wife for thirty-seven years. A powerful Four—two Z's, a W and an H." He laughed a moment, a sad sound. "You think *you* can cast big fireballs?" Altin watched him closely and could tell that the old man was on an inward trip. "Anyway, we were young, and I was smart, too smart; I'd convinced myself I was smarter than anyone else alive. And so we decided to go to Kolat and have a look around."

"Kolat?"

"A tiny island far to the south of Kurr. It's a terrible place. It's where I got the Liquefying Stone."

Altin nodded, his own mind flashing back to that dark spot he'd seen looking down at Prosperion from the moon.

"We heard about it from an old pirate down in Murdoc Bay. He told us stories of a place where the creatures were so horrible and dangerous that the monsters of Kurr seemed soft and cuddly when compared. The pirates call the island

'The Heart of Magic,' but nobody ever listens to pirates and their wild tales. Nobody except for me. And I dragged Kelline along.

"Oh, she was happy enough to go, don't get me wrong. And I've allowed myself to recognize that as the years went by, but she'd never have gone had it not been my idea. But we went. We were young and bored. We just wanted to see if the pirate stories were true.

"They were. It is the heart of magic, Altin, but in an unexpected way. You see, the whole island is made of volcanic rock and of Liquefying Stone. There are huge deposits of the stuff everywhere, and it's almost impossible to cast a spell without being in contact with the stone. Which is why the creatures are so hideous and malformed.

"And they are malformed. You can't imagine how much so. You've never seen such terrible things. Monsters, twisted into forms that are so hideous they are indescribable with words alone." He whispered a chant under his breath and illusions began to dance about in the air above Altin's bed, images of beasts that were little more than twisted wads of mangled limbs with eyes and teeth and wings jutting haphazardly from anywhere but where they should have been. The younger mage recoiled in horror with each successive scene. His mind suddenly returned to the misshapen skull on the shelf in the small basement room of Tytamon's tower. It suddenly made perfect sense.

"Mercy save us," Altin muttered as he watched the illusions that Tytamon spun before him in the air.

The images winked out a moment later, and Tytamon's story went on. "But the beasts were not the trouble, Altin. The trouble came from what at some point must have been a race of men. There were tribes of these things, these men, who roamed about the island with appetites to make a swarm of locusts seem a sated lot. They were voracious and savage and cruel, and they had magic that was beyond anything you have ever seen. Animal magic, but tempered by just enough intelligence to make it unstoppable by any force I know. They'd survived the Liquefying Stone, warped and remade, but somehow they'd survived.

"Think about it. An entire race, capable of magic just like us, and one that has miraculously managed to adapt, to live in the excess of the Liquefying Stone, mutated over time by the endless effects of the stone's presence at almost every cast. They were burnt and warped into something that no longer looked like man, but they were close enough still that Kelline and I could recognize them for what they were, or for what they used to be. And they recognized us as well. And hated us.

"When they attacked us, almost immediately upon our landing on the shore, of course we reflexively began to cast defensive spells. Apparently I was on a patch of sand that had no pieces of the yellow stone in contact with my feet, but my Kelline was not so lucky. The fireball she conjured engulfed us both in flame, but her much more than me. She burnt her mythothalamus out on the spot and never cast another spell.

"I fell to the sand and rolled into the surf, putting out the fire burning through my clothes. Quickly then, I got up and tried to put her out as well. She was screaming, and I knew she couldn't cast a water spell. I rolled her burning body into the waves. By the time the water extinguished her, it was already too late. She died right there on the beach, in agony, and with me watching the entire time."

He paused for a long while, and Altin thought perhaps the elder mage would be unable to go on, but at length he got his voice back. "When it finally occurred to me to look to see if our enemies were gone, I saw that Kelline's fireball had killed them all. She got them. Every last one. She'd saved me as the last act in her amazing life." He paused again, eyes glassy. "If only she could have lived."

They both sat silently for a while, Altin unwilling to say a thing. Finally Tytamon shook himself and resumed where he'd left off. "Anyway, that's when I discovered the Liquefying Stone. I fell to the sand next to her body and screamed and cried for a while, delirious with pain, in my body and in my heart, and then, in that delirium, I tried desperately to bring her back to life.

"As you know, I'm only an F-ranked healer, so I'm lucky to mend a broken toe, but as I was casting uselessly into her decimated body, I began to realize how much mana was pouring in. My leg was lying across a piece of the Liquefying Stone. The amount of mana I was pulling was incredible, and I could stream as much as there was available in the sky. And I did too; I thought the gods were giving me strength.

"But obviously I couldn't bring her back, not even a Z can resurrect the dead, but still I tried. It wasn't until later that I figured out that the incredible mana draw was due to the yellow stone."

Altin nodded, understanding now what price his Liquefying Stone had cost. What it had truly cost. In a way, it made him feel even guiltier than he had before. The price of his progress in human lives was large, and possibly still mounting. The bodies were really piling up, back into time. But he also realized that he was no longer all alone. Tytamon's tale was no different than his own. Only in the details, in the names of who was dead. He wondered how many more lives Tytamon had taken along his path through magic and a span of eight hundred years.

Tytamon blinked his eyes dry as he finished his tale, but he sat silently for a while, staring blankly into the air. Finally he stood. "She was a good woman, Altin. I've never recovered from her death. But she would never have wanted me to quit. And neither would your parents have wanted you to quit. I did not know them, but I am certain I am right. They would not have wanted you to run away." He walked slowly to the door, turning back to add one more thing before going out. "But that is a choice you have to make. At least I've said my piece."

Tytamon left without another word, just a wan smile as he disappeared down the stairs. Altin watched him go and gave a long and weary sigh. Maybe Tytamon was right. Maybe his parents wouldn't have wanted him to quit. He just wished they'd lived long enough to say it to him themselves.

Nonetheless, Tytamon's words opened up the truth that was buried in Altin's heart. He wasn't supposed to burn his magic out. He was a caster, and he was doing what he was supposed to do. What everyone wanted him to do.

He began to think of all the people who encouraged him every time they spoke. He thought of Kettle and Aderbury and Doctor Leopold. All of them loved what he'd been doing all these years; they'd attached a tiny portion of themselves to his dream, their hopes linked with his, tied to him and his seemingly impossible quest to reach the stars. He gave them something to root for in a world where life could be empty and often cruel. Blinding his magic or hiding away in outer space would only be another injury forced upon those who cared about him and the wonderful things he might discover with his gifts. He thought of little Pernie then, Pernie who idolized him, who hung on his every word, what would she think if he quit, if he threw it all away, ran from it like a coward into the night? Quitting would let her down most of all. She wanted to be like him. She would never quit, not with her tiny tiger's heart. He wished he had half the guts she had. But he still had time to make it right.

Balance was the key. He had to find the middle ground. If he was truly meant to do this thing, to keep pressing out into the deepest parts of an eternal night, then he was going to start with what he'd been leaving out all along. He was going to find his divination skill. At least he could be a bit more rounded if he did. He wasn't sure why, but he understood it now, what had been blocking him before. There were too many things he hadn't wanted to know. Too many things he'd been afraid to find out. But the lavamoth was out of its chrysalis now, and he couldn't put it back. There was nothing left but to fly into the fire.

He picked the book up from where it had fallen into his bed. Turning back to the page that began the simple spell, he started once more to sing its song, and by morning he'd actually made it work.

Chapter 35

Altin took his success with the divination spell, elementary as it was, as a sign. It was the approval from—from somewhere—that he was supposed to continue on. And he also knew that Tytamon was right. He'd known all along that he could never quit being a magician, that the people who had loved him long ago would have wanted him to press on, to keep on with his work in space. But he still needed some time to let his new world view soak into his head, so he decided a few days after hearing Tytamon's tale to take the tower back out into space. Where better to have some time alone?

He cast the double domes, intent on never leaving Calico Castle unprotected again, and even included an illusion of the tower and curtain wall as well, making it appear as if everything was still in place. When it was done, he one-hopped himself and his recuperating dragon out into the stars—while largely recovered, Taot was still too weak to be left in his den alone, and Altin was determined to keep him close for at least a few more days.

The dragon was unperturbed by the sudden transition into outer space, and Altin discovered quite by accident that the darkness put the beast to sleep straight away, which was even better than at home, for the dragon badly needed the rest and was growing more anxious with every passing day.

Given the added bonus of Taot's fitful slumber, Altin let himself drift among the stars for quite a while, studying the sky and beginning to contemplate the resumption of his quest to reach the star that he had chosen as the place he was going to get to next. He was staring out at it, dreamily half asleep himself, when he noticed a flash of light far off in the direction of his tiny target shimmering in the night. At first he thought it was just another star, and the pulse of light was gone so fast that he wasn't sure if he'd actually seen a pulse at all.

He scanned the area carefully, this time more awake. He was fairly sure he'd seen a flash, but if he had, there was nothing out there now, only a million tiny lights. Perhaps it had just been a trick of the lamp burning on the table near the stairs, some wayward reflection bouncing off the shield. But no sooner had he written it off as being exactly such a thing, he saw another flash, which was immediately followed by two more.

"What do you think that is?" he said to the dragon sleeping near the wall. He wasted no time starting the seeing spell that would get him a better look.

Though well familiar with blind casting, he still had to guess at the distance between himself and the flashing lights, and his opening cast left him still a bit too far away, but not so far that he couldn't run his vision towards the flashing lights without having to make a second cast. He sped his sight along until at length the flashes brought him to where he could see tiny specs of light floating in the distance like a glowing cloud of gnats. He moved in closer, slowing his vision as he drew near, and he watched in awe as a most amazing scene played out before his eyes.

It seemed he'd come across a great battle between a knot of the coconut monsters and a new form of creature that looked remarkably like some kind of frozen snake. There was a handful of these new monsters: stiff whitish things, long and blocky looking with glowing scales in places along their lengths that illuminated their shiny skins and everything around them like giant lightning bugs. They moved slowly, breathing fire from their arses, and Altin had to wonder how anything so sluggish had any chance against the battering rams of the speedy, aggressive spots.

However, the stiffened snakes did have beams of red light that shot out from underneath their throats, and they spat little pellets trailing blue fire that exploded into the giant flashes of nearly blinding light that Altin had seen from far away. Altin concluded that they were dragons of a sort and perhaps capable of holding their own against the spots after all.

He debated bringing the tower forward so that he might view the spectacle in person rather than through his sight, but as he watched the coconut monsters sweeping in and bashing at the snakes, and as he saw how the pellets were exploding virtually everywhere amongst a net of the searing red lights, he decided that perhaps the seeing spell was a safer bet for now.

The lumbering dragons were outnumbered by at least two-to-one, although the coconuts moved around too quickly for him to count them accurately, but he could see that there were only five of the silvery snakes currently in the fight. The longer Altin watched, the more he realized the snakes were probably going to lose despite their pellets and red lines of light. Still, the scene was a mesmerizing display of movement and brilliant energy.

As he watched the glorious dance of death, he couldn't help wonder how long these battles had been going on out here, how many times these two types of creatures had clashed and fought and died—and with the people of Prosperion ignorant of it the entire time, ignorant of everything beyond their own, tiny little world. The recognition was humbling, and he clutched the parapet unconsciously as he continued to watch the scene unfold from the safety of a sight-wrought bird's-eye view.

Two of the snakes teamed together against one of the coconuts, and Altin found himself letting out a cheer as the ball-beast ruptured into a spray of the orange ichor that served the spots as blood. Watching one of those nasty things blown apart was certainly nice to see. But then, unexpectedly, the furthest snake from him exploded in a flash of light so bright it made him step reflexively away from the granite wall he gripped, the movement breaking his concentration on his spell.

"Damn it," he cursed before recasting the seeing spell.

The frozen snake was completely destroyed by the time Altin's Sight had returned, and large portions of its length were tumbling slowly away, spinning as they drifted apart amongst a cloud of glittering dust and debris. Score one for the coconuts, he thought as he watched. This meant that the odds were now slightly worse for the snakes, given that they had only taken out one of the spots in the overall exchange. A one-for-one trade was not going to work in favor of the snakes.

One of the pieces of the decimated snake was coming slowly towards the location where Altin had his vision parked. The segment had gone completely dark, its glowing scales extinguished when it died, and its torn edges were bent and jagged, looking remarkably like they were made of metal, perhaps of iron or maybe tin. This detail caught his eye, and he pushed his vision to intercept the broken segment before it was beyond the illumination still coming from the snakes that remained alive. He wanted to have a closer look.

His first impression had been correct; the portion of the snake was indeed made of metal, or something like metal, and even its ribs seemed more like beams than bones, but beams made of metal rather than wood. And the snake was hollow. Looking directly into it from its broken end revealed that its guts were not soft and filled with blood, but were compartments built in perfect geometric shapes, like rooms. Altin knew immediately that he was looking at a ship.

He plunged his vision through the darkness and through the nearest wall, heading into the parts invisible from outside. He found himself immersed in absolute blackness as he pushed his vision blindly forward hoping for some signs of life.

He went through another wall and came into a room where a strange bluish fire was burning on an angular thing that reminded him of a writing desk. The pale blue light was enough to illuminate a dismal scene. There were things, manmade things, floating all about. He saw a cup and broken chair floating oddly in the air. There was a boot as well, and something that might have been a belt. And there was a corpse floating up against the roof.

Altin recoiled when he saw it, flinching unconsciously as it slowly turned, drifting like a body bobbing in a stream. The face, a man's face, was bluish and cracked open, frozen solid and looking exactly like the mouse had after Altin had sent it to the moon. Altin gasped, and once again the distraction broke the Seeing spell.

"Good gods," he muttered as goosebumps prickled up and down his back. "Those are men out there." He knew instantly that he was required to go and help, chivalry demanded it, and he wasted no time in getting his tower to the location of the fight.

By the time he arrived, another ship had been destroyed by the coconuts' attack. In fact, Altin's tower nearly emerged in the exact same spot as one of the larger segments of the broken ship, the twisted wreckage blown into the area by the force of impact during the time it had taken him to cast;

he missed merging with it by a matter of only a pace or two.

He shuddered and tried to quickly assess what was going on. Four coconuts were taking up positions that made it clear they were intent on attacking the ship closest to where Altin's tower had appeared, perhaps a few hundred paces to Altin's left. The ship was looking pretty battered, its armor dented in places and venting what looked like steam, and Altin was fairly sure it wouldn't make it through the next attack.

He had to teleport his tower close enough to the ship to make a defensive cast, and upon emerging from the teleport, he immediately began a merging teleport spell directed upon two of the approaching four. Instantly, the two spots became one, the sudden combination rupturing the newly formed mass in a gout of orange as the other two sped on and set their shafts careening at the ship. The ship's red streaks shot out, as did those of a ship several hundred paces beyond it on the farther side, and the two remaining battering rams were deflected harmlessly aside. Altin jumped his tower into the path of the second pair of orbs and cast another merging spell as they came in range. A moment later they were crushed together too, spewing their orange blood and spinning harmlessly away.

There were nine of the coconuts left, and Altin noticed that one of them was absolutely huge. He and his new snake-ship friends still had a lot of work to do.

Apparently the coconuts recognized where the new threat was coming from, and four of them were now streaking at his tower, using the same formation as the four he'd met when he'd first discovered these hostile spots not so long ago. He wondered if those he'd killed had somehow managed to warn the others, telling them how best to fight him off. He grit his teeth and hoped his Combat Hop was still going to do the trick.

It did.

The four stony beams flew harmlessly past as his tower dodged magically to the side, and Altin had to suppress a gloating sing-song that threatened to come upon his tongue. The wrong cadence could undermine the spell he was about to cast, the spell he had prepared for yet another merge. Focused, he finished the chant, and two more coconuts would not be furthering the fight.

Three more spots were coming at him from the left, however, apparently hoping to catch him off-guard while he fended off the other four. Two of them met with the merging fate straight off, and the ship he'd helped a moment before managed to take the third one out as it passed his tower by.

That's when the big one came, moving towards Altin at a speed almost too great for him to see. It streaked in so fast that Altin barely had time to gasp. It was enormous, looming up at him like a rounded mountain as it approached. He grimaced as he waited for its giant battering ram to emerge, figuring the weapon would be as big as the tower was or more. He braced himself and hoped his Combat Hop enchantment would still be able to keep him safe. It should, he thought. He hadn't put any restrictions in the spell regarding how big the coconut missiles could or could not be. Still, he closed his eyes and cringed.

But the giant spot did not throw its enormous spear at all. In fact, it came right up against the Polar's shield and pressed against it tight. Altin swallowed hard, realizing he was about to be introduced to a new element of coconut battle strategy. The spot's rough surface shifted to a softer, almost hotcake brown, and it began wrapping itself around his tower like a great fleshy blanket, oozing around it like melted wax until the tower was nearly halfway consumed, embraced almost entirely within the mass. The whole tower shuddered with the contact, waking Taot, who let out an irritated growl.

Altin immediately feared for the integrity of the shield. There was no way Polar Piton had ever considered anything like this. Panting with the rush of adrenalin, Altin began to cast a spell to teleport outside the creature's grip. But, to his horror, he could not. The mana was being pulled away from him, drawn out of his reach as the giant spot sucked it from the space around the tower with such fervor that Altin couldn't catch a single thread; it was like trying to use a teaspoon to dip water from mighty Kilgore Falls.

Several places around the surface of the shield began to pulse where the coconut's flesh had started probing the magic barrier in selected spots, and there were tendrils coming out of its skin, thick as Altin's arm and hollow at the tip like pieces of dark bamboo. The spot appeared to be trying to push them through the shield, and the whole tower was shaking violently with every thrust the monstrous creature made.

Altin needed the Liquefying Stone to compete with his assailant's mana draw, and realizing it belatedly, he spun to get it just in time to see the wooden bowl tumble over the parapet's edge.

"Damn it," he cried. He immediately made to cast the teleport that would take him to the ivy bed below.

"Damn it," he cried again. The monstrous orb was channeling the mana too fast for Altin to grasp enough to cast even a simple teleport spell. He had to run downstairs instead.

By the time he got outside the tower and around to where the wall was butted into the shield he realized he was really in it now. He had no way to get across the wall. "Gods be damned," he spat, and ran back into the tower. He got a rope from the lowest room and ran out from the second floor onto the curtain wall. The tower was shaking terribly and Taot's irritated growl had grown to something angrier and far more menacing.

Altin hastily tied the rope to a merlon and slid quickly to the ground. He ran to where the wooden bowl had landed in Lady Synthia's writhing ivy bed and, glancing up, saw that the giant spot had already pushed three of its tendril tubes completely through the shield. "Mercy's light," Altin breathed as he searched frantically through the mass of shifting vines. Where was the gods-be-damned stone?

That was when Taot let out a mighty roar the likes of which Altin had never heard from him before, a roar so loud Altin had to clutch his ears. He looked up in time to see the dragon climbing up onto the parapet, stretching the whole of his body and reaching out with both front feet to lean against the shield, extended to his fullest length. His hind legs flexed as he raised himself, his back claws gripping the stone powerfully, crushing the granite edges and raining crumbles of rock down onto Altin's head. The enormous reptile craned his sinuous neck upward towards the top of the dome and began spraying it with iron-melting fire. His head darted up and back, snuffling and snorting along the surface of the shield, sometimes nipping at the spot's protruding tubes, sometimes nipping at the air around him. He roared again and played another jet of dragon's flame all around the shield for what felt to Altin like an eternity. He had no idea the dragon could breathe so long a single breath. The furious dragon sprayed flames everywhere, alternating back and forth between dousing the shield and blasting into the empty air with an endless-seeming spew of volcanic heat. The beast was furious and to Altin his frenzy seemed random, even mad, despite considerable focus on the tubes that were sticking through the shield, which suggested he knew what was happening. And by the gods, the racket he was making was louder than a thousand beating drums.

Altin, even forty feet below, had to cower from the heat as Taot seemed to have utterly lost his mind. The dragon moved around the battlements, shuffling his forelegs along the inner surface of the shield as his head continued snaking up and down, darting everywhere, bobbing and spraying flames at the gods-knew-what. Altin cringed and felt the heat beginning to singe his hair as his dragon apparently went completely mad.

After several minutes of Taot's fire storm, the temperature beneath the Polar's dome became unbearable. Altin was forced to lie down and wriggle beneath Lady Synthia's enchanted vines, hoping that the lingering magic would give him some protection from the heat. He sent the dragon a mental shout, admonishing him to stop, but Taot was completely beyond control.

The dragon went on like that for several long minutes, leaving Altin cowering beneath an insulating blanket of fire-resistant vines that actually began to steam. He wondered if this time he really was going to die. It seemed ironic really, to come this far into space only to be killed by the dragon Tytamon had told him he never should have tamed.

Finally, however, the roaring and the flames came abruptly to a halt. The tower stopped trembling and a molten silence was in the air. Altin lay beneath the vines for several moments before he even dared to move. But eventually, tentatively, he poked his head out from his groping green concealment and had a look around. The air was hard to breathe, so hot it hurt his lungs, and, frankly, felt as if he'd come near to the point of having been cooked alive. But Taot was no longer standing on the wall.

Altin looked up and saw that the giant coconut had detached itself and was flitting back out amongst the other spots, all of which were still attacking what remained of the group of armored ships. Maybe Taot had scared the thing away.

He couldn't watch and ponder long, however, for the grass growing up amongst the ivy— the normal, unenchanted grass—was smoldering around him, and with a yelp of pain he realized that his robe had caught fire somewhere near his knee. He quickly snuffed it out, and as he did, he noticed that the hair on his arms had blackened and that some had gone to ash. Taot had gotten very close to going too far.

He felt around and finally found the Liquefying Stone and replaced it in its cloth within the bowl. Then, with the absence of the monstrous coconut, he teleported himself back up into his rooms. Once there, he climbed the stairs to the battlements cautiously, peering out to see if Taot had regained possession of his wits. He found the dragon curled up against the wall again, panting loudly and sounding like twenty bellows being pumped at once, apparently having exhausted himself with the incendiary episode.

Altin probed him with a thought and retrieved a sense of satisfaction from the dragon's weary mind. Whatever it was, the dragon was convinced that some kind of threat was past, though the sense of what the dragon tried to convey made no sense to Altin's mind at all.

"Well, that was close," Altin said, cautiously stepping out into the open floor. "You almost roasted me alive." As it was, the space inside the Polar's shield was like an oven now. He decided that having a dragon with him in space was probably not a good idea and vowed to take Taot home as soon as this battle could be won.

And win it he and his snake-ship allies would, for there weren't that many of the ball shaped monsters left now that all was nearly said and done. Once Altin merged two more, and the furthest ship took out the smallest one. With those destroyed, the three that remained moved quietly away. Apparently they'd had enough. Altin watched them until they were gone from sight, the giant one the last to disappear. He hoped that they'd given up completely and were headed now for home, but he suspected they were not. Nonetheless, it was with jubilation that he watched them fade into the night. Victory was theirs.

He turned and let out a whoop, jumping up and down and thrusting his fists into the air as he gave a cheer in the direction of the nearest ship. "We did it," he yelled at them. "Look at them run!"

Chapter 36

"All right, someone tell me that I'm actually seeing this," said Roberto staring at the screen. "Tell me I'm seeing some dude in a dress dancing on a castle. Either I'm seeing that or I got battle fatigue or something."

"You're seeing it," said Captain Asad. "We all are." He too seemed reluctant to take what the monitor showed at face value. "Pewter, you getting a reading on that?"

"No, sir, not a thing," she said, not exactly lying. She hadn't had the presence of mind to try. "Let me give it another sweep."

Captain Asad shook his head as he watched the man in the medieval tower jumping up and down and shouting silently in the cold of space. "I'm not buying it," the captain muttered beneath his breath.

"I'm just glad it's not only me," said Roberto. He paused then added, "And just to make sure we're all perfectly clear on this, that is a dragon with him right?"

"Yes," confirmed the captain. "Or something that looks like one."

"Assorted stone, sir," reported Orli after a sensor pass. "Mostly granite with some limestone too. Various others. Organic life. He's real by this thing." She indicated the console with a turn of her hand. "The dragon too. It all reads real."

Roberto snorted. "As if you'd know what a *real* dragon looked like on a scanner grid."

"Says reptile to me," she responded a bit defensively. "And that's as close as I need to get."

"Quiet, both of you," said the captain. "It's obviously a Hostile trick. They've already proven that they are capable of guile, and there's far too much granite going on out here for this to be a coincidence."

"What kind of trick includes blowing up half your own ships, or orbs, or whatever the hell they are?" Roberto asked.

"They may not value life the way we do. They may not even be alive. The deaths could be part of the ruse. This might be a holographic trap."

"Why the man and the tower then?" Roberto did not sound particularly convinced.

"Maybe," suggested Orli, "they're trying to create a setting that they think will make us feel at ease. You know, give us a little slice of home."

Roberto shook his head as he continued staring at the screen. "If that's what they think Earth is like, they need to update their files."

"That may be exactly what we're seeing here," said the captain. "This might be the impression they got from us, taken from some ancient television show beamed out a long time ago."

"Or," put in Roberto, "maybe the feudal age was the last time the orbs flew past the Earth." He was mostly kidding and expected the captain to cut him off with a curt remark.

"That's possible too. In any case, keep an eye on him. If whatever he was doing to the orbs is real, he could just as easily do the same to us."

Orli punched up the zoom on the monitor and stared deeply into the image on the screen, studying the tousle-haired man who was apparently delighted with something as he leapt about. "I don't think so," she said after watching him for a while. "He doesn't look like the type."

A distant quality in her voice caused them both to turn on her and Roberto to crook his head as he squinted into her face. He spent a moment scrutinizing her and then he laughed. "Oh shit," he said at last. "We got a hormone alert. Don't tell me you're into him somehow." He studied her a second longer as she gazed into the monitor on the wall. "Good God. You are." He laughed again. "You realize he's wearing a dress, right?"

Orli blushed, but ignored the thrust of Roberto's remark. "Just look at him. Come on. You're a people guy. Does he really look like the kind of person that's going to... blow us up?"

"Well, I'm not willing to trust your intuition," said the captain, "regardless of how he appears. He may look like some kind of medieval man, but the fact is, he's more likely an aspect of the Hostiles' plan. They didn't wipe out the entire populace of Andalia, a planet as technologically capable as are we ourselves, without being gifted in trickery. Levi, lasers locked on that tower, and hair-trigger, you got that? If he so much as blinks the wrong way, blow him straight to hell."

"Yes, sir," Roberto said and punched the targeting coordinates in. The tower wouldn't stand a chance. Although quietly inside, Roberto hoped that Orli was right. He'd never had to kill a man before, and he didn't want that dude in the tower to be the first, even if he was wearing a stupid looking dress.

"Pewter, what's the status on the orbs?" demanded the captain. "How far have they gone?"

She tapped at her console a few times and brought the orbs up on the left half of the main screen. It took a moment for the distances to come up. "Eight hundred kilometers and holding, sir."

"I didn't figure they were going to run away. What's the status on our remaining ships?"

Orli took a few minutes to gather all the data, but the other two ships were doing well enough, having taken no damage that couldn't be fixed despite the long and heated fight. But the *Vaunted Angel* and the *Beijing* were both destroyed. Only one escape pod had made it out, and that carrying only three. Doctor Singh was seeing to them now. Bravo, Delta and Echo squadrons were still on their way, Bravo and Delta still mostly two days out. But help was on the way. Hopefully, this time their reinforcements would arrive more quickly than the Hostiles' did. Only time would tell.

But for now there was little left to do but watch the man in the tower, who had, after a few moments of celebratory dancing, gone still and now stood studying them; and did so for quite some time. They could see his lips moving as he looked up at them. "Dude's loco en la cabeza," Roberto said, tapping himself on the side of his head. "Check him out talking to himself like that."

"I talk to myself," Orli said.

"Kind of makes my point, doesn't it?"

"Shut up," she said through a smile. "Besides, he could be talking to the dragon."

"I swear to God, if that dragon starts talking back, I'm out of here."

"Now what's he doing?" she asked.

They watched as the man in the robes closed his eyes and began to sway rhythmically, snaking his arms from high to low as if tracing a column of hourglasses stacked one upon the next.

"I think he thinks you're hot," said Roberto. "Check him out." He repeated the man's curvaceous gestures but a great deal more emphatically as if describing the outline of a buxom woman to his buddies at a bar.

"Shut up," she repeated. She looked down at her modest bosom and laughed. "I wish I was built like that."

"Me too," he said.

"Shut up."

"Never."

"Both of you shut up," said the captain, looking up from a damage assessment report.

They each had to hide grins as the tension of battle began to drain from them, leaving giddiness in its place. Besides, seeing that tower out there was the highlight of nearly eleven years—at least for now, before it revealed itself to be some form of insanity or turned out to be a Hostile trick.

The man in the tower continued to speak and sway for a moment more before clapping his hands together once and bringing the dance abruptly to a halt. He stood motionless then, his eyes still closed and his hands reaching absently to the stone wall before him for support. He didn't move for a very long time. Seeing him like that made Orli uncomfortable. She felt vulnerable, and she wasn't sure if it was for him or for her. "What's he doing?" she asked after nearly seven minutes of the odd behavior.

"How should I know," said Roberto. "He's a whack-job in a dress. What do you expect?"

"It's a robe, not a dress, and how do you know he's a whack-job?"

"Have you even been watching this?"

Orli did not respond, and they sat and watched the man for another four minutes, after which he abruptly opened his eyes and stepped away from the wall. He waved. He looked right at them and waved, a sure movement, as if he was certain that they were watching him.

Orli had to stop herself from waving back. "Hi, castle man," she said under her breath.

Roberto laughed. "You're pathetic."

Orli looked innocent. "What?"

"A whole fleet full of men, not one good enough for you, and then some guy in a dress shows up and bam, you're ready for Camelot. And I thought I needed therapy."

"You do. And it's not that. He's just very... interesting."

Roberto snickered. "I bet."

The man on the tower waved again then seemed to hesitate. He bit his lower lip and glanced about as if searching for something nearby. He stopped and looked back up at them, raising a hand, this time indicating the number one.

"One what?" Roberto said, squinting as if somehow that might help him to better understand, unaware that he'd become as immersed in what was happening as his friend beside him was.

The man repeated the "one" gesture and followed it by presenting the palm of his hand as if wanting them to stop.

"He's telling us to wait," said Orli. "He's going somewhere I think."

And he did, for he turned immediately and ran down into the tower, out of view.

"Arm the lasers," the captain ordered. "Arm them now."

"They're armed, sir," Roberto answered, snapping out of the hypnotic trance that watching the medieval man had come to be. He moved his hand towards the key that would set the lasers off.

"Captain," Orli nearly gushed, "he told us to wait. He obviously means no threat."

"That or he needs a moment before he does something I don't want to see." The captain wasn't taking any risks.

"Roberto, if you shoot that laser without honestly knowing we're in danger, I will never speak to you again."

"Pewter, if you countermand an order of mine again, I will shoot you where you sit. Do you understand me?"

The man came running back up the tower stairs, and Orli's eyes flitted back and forth from the screen to Roberto's finger like a bullet caught in a twenty-second ricochet. The man was waving a piece of paper and a feather, and he was sloshing ink across his wrist from a bottle gripped tightly in his fist. He said something again, for they saw his mouth move as he stopped and set the paper down on a disheveled looking table that was sitting near the door.

He flashed a rather boyish grin up at them as he ineffectually wiped at the ink on his arm with the bottom of his robes. His legs were very white, and Orli had to suppress a snicker as she saw that he wasn't wearing any shoes. How could that man possibly be a threat?

He finished wiping off his arm and then, with another slightly less sheepish grin, he began drawing concentric circles on the paper. He drew three rings, in the center of which he drew a circle about the size of Orli's palm, which he then filled completely in with ink, having to dip his feather in the ink pot several times to get it done.

"You realize that he's actually using a feather pen, right?" said Roberto.

"A quill," she corrected him.

"Whatever. You read too many books."

"It appears your friend has just drawn himself a target," said the captain, moving to stand between them both. It was true enough; what the man had just drawn could most easily be described as exactly that. It was just like those projected down in the firing range, only paper and just in black and white—or black and slightly yellow as this particular paper seemed to be.

When he was done, the man held his paper aloft so that they could see it clearly on the screen. "Be ready, Lieutenant, I believe he may be making some kind of threat."

The man took his paper and set it down in the middle of the floor. He looked up at them and curled his hands inward, touching his fingers to his chest and obviously pointing at himself. He then reached outward, pointing up at them.

Then he pointed at himself again. Then back at them. Then he pointed at the paper, at himself, and, oddly, jumped onto the paper. When he was done with his strange ritual, he looked up at them and raised his eyebrows quizzically, as if expecting something now from them.

"What the hell was that?" Roberto asked.

The captain's answer came deliberately as he worked through the possibilities in his mind. "I think we are to be his target, and he wants us to know that he is planning to stomp us?" He hesitated, but concluded, "That's what I make of that."

"Are you kidding me?" Orli said, unable to control her ever-loosening tongue. "He's saying something about landing on that spot. It's about the paper, like he wants us to come down on it somehow."

"Maybe," Captain Asad allowed. "Just stay alert, Lieutenant. I don't want you missing our chance because you get caught up in his guessing game. More likely than not, that's entirely the point of this exercise. And Pewter, keep an eye on those orbs."

"Yeah, Pewter, the Hostile orbs, not his dreamy greens," said Roberto.

"Will you stop?"

"You're the one defending him."

"I'm the one who's actually paying attention to what he's trying to say."

"Oh, is that what you're doing?" He snickered again.

"Just shut it." She was actually annoyed.

"Both of you shut it."

The man in the tower stared up at them patiently for quite some time, and Orli felt like there really was something they were supposed to do. Without thinking, she flashed a pair of forward docking lights to let him know that they were at least still watching what he did.

"What the hell was that, Pewter?" the captain asked,

seeing the movement of her hand.

"Nothing," she said. "Just letting him know we're still here." The captain started to growl, so she added, "You know, so that he knows we're keeping an eye on him."

"Some of us more than others," Roberto goaded, but Orli ignored the remark.

The man turned and took the paper up from the floor and held it out to them, shaking it a couple of times, then placed on the floor again. He took a long step back from it and began beckoning them with exaggerated motions of his arm, every so often pointing invitingly at the paper on the ground.

"See?" said Orli, but they could only watch.

The man seemed to grow impatient after a while and once more took the paper off the ground. He went to the wall and stared up at them again for quite some time. Finally, he nodded as if coming to some conclusion on his own. He held the paper out once more, then, putting it on the wall, he pointed at it, then back at them. He made a spreading gesture with both arms, moving his hands from in to out as if swimming the breast stroke in the air. He moved briefly to a large wooden bucket near the wall, opposite where he stood, and glanced into it for a moment before returning to where he'd set the paper down. Then he closed his eyes and began to say something as his body started to sway. A moment later the paper vanished.

"What the hell was that?" Roberto said for what seemed the hundredth time today.

"Some kind of trick," said the captain. "Part of the hallucination disappeared. Just be ready to melt him if he makes a move."

"Oh, I'm ready."

"'Yes, sir,' is the accepted response to an order."

"Yes, sir," Roberto said, wincing. Despite the captain being somewhat stuck with him and Orli now that the disease had killed most of the officers aboard the ship, things weren't *that* comfortable on the bridge. He'd better watch his mouth. Silently he blamed Orli for her rebellious influence on him. That's when Orli gasped.

"Look," she said. She'd been watching the medieval man's expectant face ever since the paper target had disappeared, and, for whatever silly reason, it had occurred to her to look around the bridge. And there it was, lying on the deck eight feet from the captain's chair. The paper was on their ship.

"Oh, you have to be kidding me," Roberto moaned. "Seriously, someone tell me what the hell is going on."

The captain put his hand on his sidearm and turned back towards the monitor on the wall. "I do believe your peaceful man is actually targeting us."

"No," Orli said. "That can't be it at all."

"Now what's he doing?" Roberto said, nodding up at the monitor where the man had once again begun to speak and sway.

"Let him have it, Lieutenant. Fire, now."

"No!" screamed Orli as Roberto tapped the button with his thumb.

The man vanished as the laser's red beam streaked down to where he'd been standing on the stone. Vaporized instantly, Orli knew, though none of them had ever seen a ship's laser shoot a man before.

Orli screamed again, tears springing to her eyes. "What have you done?"

That's when the sound of someone clearing his throat spun them all around.

Chapter 37

Altin had grown impatient when the people aboard the ship could not grasp what he was trying so desperately to say. He assumed the problem was that they were reluctant to teleport one of their own into a stranger's tower, and he thought perhaps it might be because Taot was giving them a scare. He really couldn't blame them for that, toothy brute that Taot was, and along with the recent fire-breathing episode, so he decided he had to take the initiative instead. He was confident that he'd found the right people, his exploratory seeing spell having ultimately brought him to the metallic vessel's bridge. He had little doubt that the stern-faced man could be anyone other than the captain of the ship, and perhaps royalty as well, which was why he decided that that was where he needed now to go.

He cast the parchment target into their room and then followed the spell with a quick glance into the scrying basin to make sure that none of them had gone to stand on the drawing, perhaps misinterpreting his intent as wanting them to stand on it and be brought back to the tower by a teleport of Altin's doing rather than their own. Surely they knew that he could not do that—no one could—but he wasn't about to take a chance, just in case they didn't know. It was possible they didn't have a teleporter on board to advise them in such things, as good ones could be awfully hard to find.

But they weren't standing on his parchment, so, seeing that it was safe, he teleported himself onto it instead, hoping they did not take his arrival as being unfathomably rude. One certainly never did something like this back at home as it would be considered a colossal breach of maritime etiquette. Such an offense would find you keelhauled or even worse.

He landed right on the target he had drawn, and, seeing them all still facing into their viewing wall, he politely cleared his throat. It was only then that he realized that they had actually taken a shot at him with one of their ship's red lights, and the thought occurred to him that he might have just made a terrible mistake.

His confirmation came a moment later as the stern-faced man spun and, with reflexes like a snake, fired a hand-held version of the red light straight at Altin's chest. The slender blonde woman let out a horrified scream as the red light struck him with brutal force, like a pinpoint blast of Taot's breath, and then everything went dark.

He woke up sometime later in a room with the whitest lights he'd ever seen, bright yet somehow ghostly, glowing from behind panes of misty glass above. There was a low chirping sound, slow and rhythmic, coming from a strange panel filled with blinking lights behind him on the wall, and there was a man with deeply brown skin leaning over him and looking quite pleased as Altin came to. The man smiled and said something Altin couldn't understand, his words coming on a wave of coffee-scented breath that was comforting in a room permeated by otherwise unnatural smells.

It took a moment for Altin's head to clear, and once he realized what had happened, he suddenly checked to see if his hands and feet were bound. They were not. He breathed a little easier.

But why had the stern-faced man shot him? What could he possibly have done? Was his intent really that hard to understand? Altin had done nothing to suggest that he was going to be a threat. Which meant that these people might be the naturally violent sort, like orcs. Perhaps they were space pirates. That idea certainly made sense. Except why would they bother to save him after shooting him like that? Maybe they needed him to get them into his tower, particularly if they had no teleporter of their own. Or maybe it was for torture, and they wanted secrets of the Queen.

The chirping sound on the wall grew more intense as his mind ran through the possible motivations behind the stern-faced man's attack. It occurred to him he might be overreacting just a bit. He was awfully far from home. Just as he had never heard of men like these, they probably had never even heard of his Queen, much less needed any secrets she possessed. He needed to gather his wits; that's what he needed to do.

He tried to raise himself out of bed, but by the gods he was weak. How long had he been unconscious lying there like that? He suddenly clutched the sheet that was covering him and sought the wound he'd taken in the chest with his eyes. Someone, presumably the kind-faced man, had attached odd-feeling white bandages onto the area where Altin had been shot, and they were held in place with some sticky strips of something that felt like parchment pressed quite thin. Onion skin, maybe? The whole place left him feeling out of sorts. Lying here, actually on this ship, was much different than it had been when he'd been seeing his way around. For one, it seemed much brighter, too bright. And there was the most curious of smells. Unnatural, not quite metallic but definitely not perfumed. Something in an alchemist's lab perhaps, but not from any he'd ever frequented on Kurr. It was completely alien.

He looked about tentatively. The room he was in was obviously a hospital ward; although the beds were odd shaped and made with lots of metal rails. Each one looked like it had a hundred moving parts, and he wondered what kind of people needed beds as complicated as all that. There were no other patients in the room; it was just he and the doctor, and that infernal chirping on the wall.

As he took in his surroundings, a rectangular section of the wall slid open, and in came the blonde woman with the very short hair. He remembered hearing her scream just before he'd been shot. He wondered why she cut her hair like that, barely hanging past her ears. She had an exquisite face though, pale as porcelain and nearly as translucent too. Her nose was narrow, like the statues of Mercy always were, and her eyes were large and of the deepest blue. But her clothing was immodest beyond belief, thin cloth, like hosiery, and all one piece, stretched about her fit body, revealing absolutely every gentle curve of the woman's nubile form. He could even see the faintest trace of her ribs when she breathed, not to mention just about every other thing. My gods, he thought, an aggressive corset was one thing, but this? Water-soaked muslin hardly revealed so much. Modesty aside, she was lovely, and she moved just like a cat, with purpose and with grace. He noted that she wore one of those miniature red-light weapons at her hip, hanging from a belt and secured by a strap about her thigh. It was the same type as the surly man had used.

Which brought his mind back to why that man had chosen to shoot him when he'd first arrived. While undeserved, he didn't suppose the reason for the attack was entirely a mystery: the unauthorized boarding of a ship was definitely taboo. But still, the episode was just an accident in the end, one that he hoped he would have a chance to make them understand.

As the woman approached him with a tender smile, he decided that perhaps they might have already figured out that very thing, maybe even divined it while he was unconscious in the bed. She certainly didn't seem as if she were going to attack him with the red light now.

She said something unintelligible to the kind-faced man and then moved up to Altin's bed. She stood a pace away as if expecting him to make a move. He lay back into the pillow and pulled the sheet modestly over his chest, unable to avoid watching hers as it expanded and contracted with every measured breath. She was striking, and her uniform certainly did nothing to impede his view. Women did not dress like this at home.

She noticed where his eyes had gone and a pinch of red came upon her cheeks. Altin was ashamed. What was wrong with him, gawking at her like that? Had he lost all self control? She was clearly no bordello tramp, and that was obviously her peoples' customary garb. He berated himself silently for being so ungallant. "I'm sorry," he said. "I'm not myself right now."

Which was true enough, and she smiled, saying something unintelligible in response. Her voice was sweet, like flute music carried on a breeze, and Altin once again had to check his wayward eyes. She grinned at him this time, and it was his turn to show a blush. She turned to the man that was obviously Altin's doctor and said something else to him. He answered back, and she actually clapped twice before plunging her hands quickly to her side, suppressing a smile and whatever it was she had been about to say. She blushed again, and then, with an embarrassed grin, uttered two short syllables and turned and left the room. Her backside was outlined just as well by the stretchy cloth as was her front, and Altin had to discreetly turn his head. He did not want these people thinking he was as licentious as they must already think him rude for having snuck upon their ship.

The chirping sound behind him was pulsing more quickly again, and the doctor came to him and pushed him back into his pillow with a knowing smile upon his face. Altin hadn't realized that he'd sat back up again.

He wasn't sure how much longer he was in their hospital, because there was absolutely no sense of night or day on board this ship, but he awoke at some point later and felt remarkably improved. He peeked under the stack of white cloth stuck to his wound and saw that the hole made by the red light was large and colored a ruddy brown, still angry looking, but apparently going to heal. The repair work certainly wasn't very neat. He wondered if the injury had been terribly severe or if their doctor just wasn't very good. He had to admit that having access to a Z-class healer like Doctor Leopold could spoil one to lesser healers when the situation came. Still, he was grateful to be alive as he sat up and swung his feet out of the bed.

He realized he was naked with a gasp, suddenly glad that the blonde woman hadn't just come walking through the door. The doctor saw him sit up and came to him, presenting him with his old gray robes, recently laundered and folded into a perfect square. That was very considerate of them, despite the curious odor the laundering left behind, another unnatural smell, artificial if such a thing could be said of scent. The doctor said something that sounded polite, and Altin thanked him as he unfolded his robes and slipped them on. Someone had taken the time to patch the holes with some of the same stretchy cloth that these people seemed so inclined to wear, and Altin pushed a finger into a patch just to see what it was like. It was much thicker than he'd surmised, and seemed very strong despite being elastic like nothing he'd ever felt before. These were definitely a strange people, he thought. Very different than folks on Kurr. He would have to watch his manners. And he needed to figure out their language too.

The doctor was speaking to him again; his voice sounding very pleasant, though Altin couldn't understand a thing, and he nodded politely and smiled back at the man. Yes, he was definitely going to have to do something about the language barrier. He caught himself reflexively wishing, once again, that he had the power to divine, but it occurred to him suddenly that in fact he did. Granted, it was a newfound skill, perhaps only a few days old, but still, it was not like he didn't have the gift now that he'd pushed himself past his mental block. He knew for certain that there were language spells he could try once he got back to the tower and found them in a book.

Thinking of the tower, he was reminded of Taot lying out there all alone. Altin suddenly had a pressing need to know how long he'd been recovering. If it had been more than two or three days, Taot would be raving mad, if not sickened by the lack of food. Or worse. The large creature was hardly in a condition for a fast; he needed every bit of nourishment he could get.

He waited until the doctor turned around before quietly muttering the words for a telepathic check. The dragon was still asleep. That was good, and Altin did not bother to wake him up. Maybe he hadn't been recovering for all that long. Still, thinking of the dragon reminded him of the fiery events of the recent past, and he realized that it was urgent that he take the dragon home; having Taot out here was a danger to them both. If the dragon accidentally killed him, it had no way of getting back. Altin promised himself that they would go soon. He did not bring the dragon out here to die.

The doctor was speaking into a square scrying mirror, an interesting spell that Altin had never seen, and in it was reflected the face of the stern man who had shot Altin with the beam of light. A moment later, the doctor cancelled the spell with a tap upon the mirror's edge and turned to Altin, explaining something in his foreign tongue. Shortly after that, the man who shot Altin was standing in the room. Altin grew immediately tense.

The tall man said something to Altin, his voice icy and sharp, and he spared not a single smile. Altin was intimidated by the man and simply nodded back, anxious for him to go away. He was absolutely sure now that this man was at least the captain of the ship, if not these people's king; he was the embodiment of command. Altin bowed when the man finished talking and seemed about to leave the room, at which the man's stern face became even more so, his thick black brows knitting together in a frown. The man's eyes were deep and severe; they made Altin nervous. The captain studied him a moment longer then looked briefly from Altin to the doctor. The doctor shrugged, at which the captain's face returned to stern neutrality and he stepped out through the sliding portion of the wall without another word. There was something about men like that that made the end of conversations painfully abrupt, no wasted pleasantries or awkward lingering goodbyes. Altin wished sometimes that he could pull off that kind of thing, affect a bearing that put others on their guard. He could face Thadius down with composure like this ship's captain possessed.

A few moments after the captain left, the blonde woman came in again, this time accompanied by a shorter, stocky fellow with dark skin, like the captain's, but not so dark as the doctor's was. This new fellow was the other man that Altin had seen up in the captain's observation room. These were a very tawny people, he thought. Excepting for the blonde.

She was just as intriguing as before, and her companion seemed to like to laugh a lot. They stood very close to one another, and she frequently touched him on the arm. Altin wondered if they were husband and wife, although they didn't seem to say as much with what passed between their eyes. Still, they were very friendly with one another, and Altin found himself struck with an uninvited jealousy. He caught it before it could take root and wondered if he was going out of his mind. Clearly the adventures of the last few days, on top of the emotional week he'd just been through, had put him out of sorts. He forced a smile onto his face and beat the silly feelings down.

They talked at him, and to each other, for a few moments more before she moved up to him and put her hand upon her chest. "Orrrr-leeeeee," she said to him, speaking slowly. She repeated it again, this time rapidly. "Orli." She smiled. Then she turned her slender hand over in a gesture clearly meaning that it was his turn to say his name.

He spoke his as she had, slowly once, and then at normal pace. "Allll-tin," he said. "Altin."

She beamed at this announcement, her smile revealing perfect teeth and setting a spark alight in her deep blue eyes. "Altin," she repeated. Then she slapped the stocky fellow lightly on the shoulder with the back of her hand, turning to face him with a grin. "Roww-bur-tohhh" she said, prodding a finger deeply into his arm at each syllable in a gesture that was clearly meant to be an irritant to the man. "Roberto." She smiled back at Altin again as the stocky fellow gave her a withering glance, seemingly both annoyed and entirely amused.

Altin repeated the man's name carefully just as he had hers. Roberto grinned and nodded, stepping forward and putting out his hand, saying something that once again Altin missed. If it was the same gesture as they had back at home, Altin was meant to take his hand and shake it, so he did. The man had a powerful grip. Roberto grinned again. He said something else that ended with Altin's name. Altin smiled back. A chorus of smiles all around.

Altin decided that Roberto had kind brown eyes, despite

a mischievous something lurking in them too. The stocky fellow turned back to Orli and stabbed her in the arm with a thick finger as a measure of revenge. He said something that from its tone was meant to be intimidating, at which point she laughed. Roberto looked back at Altin with a helpless expression on his face and offered up a shrug. His smile immediately grew warm again.

Altin then learned that the doctor was known as "Sing." When he spoke it back, once again everyone laughed and seemed happy. Maybe only the captain had the personality of a gorgon's mate. Which of course was just Altin's luck.

What followed were several long, agonized moments of failed communication. They simply couldn't get past the names and endless smiles. After many of these well-meant-but-futile attempts to found the beginnings of common speech, Altin grew impatient to give divination a try. The conversation had gotten to a point where he felt like they were wasting time. With the dragon alone out in his tower, he needed to move this meeting along, and he wanted to make at least one attempt with a divining language spell.

However, he'd learned his lesson regarding teleporting in and out of the ship, so he needed to find a more discreet way to get out to his tower and back, and he knew immediately how: the small room with the watery chamber pot he'd had occasion to use a few times during the last few days. His doctor had gleaned Altin's need for such accommodations at one point and Altin had to admit to being entirely amused—albeit a different approach than the simple enchanted teleport for carrying out the waste in chamber pots back home, he thought the rush of blue water was certainly an aesthetic touch; he might even consider introducing the little waterfall idea to Aderbury when he got home as it was just the sort of thing that the pampered bourgeoisie in Crown would gladly pay a few extra silver pieces to have superfluously added to their pots.

He raised a finger, indicating that he wanted them to wait, and then went into the tiny room with its waterfall-enchanted amenities. He closed the door behind him, but he could hear Roberto laughing about something through it as he began to cast. As quietly as he could, he teleported himself back to his room in the tower outside the ship.

He ran down to his library and rummaged through his books. He'd been pretty haphazard about collecting divination works, but he did find one large and musty old tome that had some language spells inside; it was a huge book, nearly half as wide as the table at the center of his room, and he grunted as he pulled it off the shelf. He leafed through its giant pages and eventually found one that seemed like it would work. He didn't have time to study it here, however, for he didn't want them growing suspicious at his already rather longish visit to the tiny private room, so he quickly teleported back and stepped out into their ship's bright unwavering light.

The smile evaporated from Roberto's face as Altin stepped out holding the giant tome clutched against his chest, and even Orli seemed to be taken by surprise. The look in her eyes suggested she felt as if he'd let her down, as if he'd betrayed her in some inexplicable way. His heart emptied like a basin drained. How could he tell her it was only just a book?

"No, no," he rushed to say. "It's not like that at all." He set the book down on the bed, its weight pressing deeply into thin, unnatural feeling sheets. "Just watch and you will see."

He opened the book and had to flip back and forth several times to find the spell again. The three of them were suddenly speaking in agitated voices, and Altin could see Roberto's fingers twitching near his red-light gun.

Realizing this was not working as he had planned, Altin stopped and moved away from the book. He pointed to it, his expression exasperated as he grew weary of so much mistrust. "Go," he said. "Look for yourself. There's nothing there. It's not even an offensive spell. By the gods you people need to relax." He wondered what had happened to them to make them so distrustful all the time. He wondered if all of them were like that. It didn't bode well for the future if they were like this across their entire race. But still he waited; let them check the book themselves.

He knew, of course, that if they could not speak his language, they likely could not read it either, but he hoped his message was clear all the same. He set his hands on his hips and sighed loudly with his desire for a bit of faith. He tapped his toe and crossed his arms, waiting. They just stared at him for a while. Which was fine. They could stare all they wanted, but he would not cast until they checked the book.

Finally Orli made a move as if she was going to have a peek, but from the sound of Doctor Singh's words, he did not think it was a good idea. Before she could get close enough to touch the book, Roberto stepped in front of her and pushed her back with the sweep of a straightened arm. He said something indecipherable, shooting Altin a sideways look. Altin knew exactly what he'd said. He decided he liked the man.

Roberto examined the book for a few moments, flipping through all the pages and turning it around and over several times. Finally, apparently convinced that it was just a book and not some enchanted firetrap, he set the book back on the bed and returned to Orli and Doctor Singh. Altin continued to wait, raising an eyebrow at them as he persisted with the tapping of his foot against the floor. He would wait until they asked him to carry on.

After a brief conversation, finally it came. Roberto swept his hand out towards the book and muttered a pair of words. Altin smiled and with an inclination of his head stepped back up to the magic tome. He had to leaf through it again to find the spell; it was titled "Common Tongue." After a few moments, he found the page and began to read the spell's description aloud:

Common Tongue is cast in an initial area of three by three paces and has a duration of seven days, affected outward in space and time by the caster's divining rank. Common Tongue allows the user to speak and recognize in all its forms the languages of the selected persons within the radius of the spell so long as their intent is to be understood by said caster. Anything said in secrecy or with the intent to deceive will not be understood and requires the use of the Greater Common Tongue spell (see next chapter). The components for this spell are a quill, a sheet of parchment, an ink pot and a lock of hair from each person with which the caster intends to speak, including one of the caster's own. The hair should be taken from the vicinity of the ear and samples should be of roughly corresponding size.

What followed were instructions for casting the spell itself and a diagram for laying the components out. Altin didn't like the secrecy thing, but a quick glance at the spell Greater Common Tongue showed that it was forty-three pages long. He didn't think he had that kind of time or expertise, so he decided to stick with the six-page version for now. He realized that getting cuttings of their hair was likely going to be an interesting trick as well. And he needed his quill pen, parchment and pot of ink, which meant he had to go back to the tower. He wondered how they were going to take his making another trip into the waterfall-pot room so soon, but he had little other choice.

Once more he raised a gesture asking for them to wait, and again he locked himself in the tiny room. Roberto said something again, and Altin heard him laughing, apparently at his own joke. It only took Altin a moment to get the things he needed, and he was back in less time than it took to butter toast.

Orli grinned as Altin stepped out from the cramped little room with a large quill pen, rolled parchment and an ink pot in his hands. She giggled, nodding an I-told-you-so at Roberto as Altin came back up to the bed. Roberto made some comment in reply that made all three shipmates laugh out loud. Altin was perfectly happy to be the butt-end of a joke. He was about to join them in their mirth.

He set the parchment on the floor in the center of the room with the ink pot centered on it. Then he laid the feather quill next to the ink pot, turned precisely as the spell's illustration showed. From there, he went to a metal tray where he'd seen Doctor Singh keep many of his instruments. Searching through the implements there, he took a finely made pair of scissors from the towel upon which many shiny objects lay. He returned to the parchment on the floor, and, making sure that all three of his observers were paying careful heed, he clipped a finger's-breadth pinch of hair from a curl jutting out behind his ear. He set it beside the inkpot, opposite the feather just as the spell directions instructed that he should do. When he was done, he looked up at them and gave an audible sigh. This is where it might get interesting.

He took them all in with a gesture, then, holding up the scissors, he pulled taut another strand of his own hair and made as if to cut. He didn't though, pointing to them instead.

They spoke back and forth as they watched him point them out. Judging by their voices, none of them seemed to be sensing any threat. Encouraged, and with his heart pounding like a trapped rabbit in a box, he took a step towards the beautiful woman and reached half the distance to her almost white-blonde hair. There he paused. "May I?" he said. She studied him for the briefest of moments and then smiled once again. She turned her face slightly and tipped her head away, exposing her ear and a length of exquisite neck as she offered her trust to him and her hair to the scissors in his hand.

He closed the distance and saw that his hand was trembling as he took a snip of hair from just behind her ear. It was soft like down and smooth as a unicorn's mane. From this proximity he could smell her too: she smelled like flowers and moist earth—not perfume, but real, which seemed odd to him considering she lived in such a place as manmade as all of this—and there was something else too, *her* scent, the scent of her skin. She was intoxicating, alien and alive. Frightening even.

Embarrassed, having caught himself in this silent reverie, he hoped that he had not too obviously delayed or been flagrantly uncouth. He took her hair quickly to the parchment and set it atop the little pinch of his, finding the sight of the two mingled together very satisfying to see. He straightened and went to the others, taking clippings from them both, each of them more than willing to oblige. Soon the pile contained a lock of hair from all four people in the room.

Altin replaced the scissors on the tray and then went back to the magic book. He went over the spell carefully, page by page. He could hear the three of them talking in the background while the spell took him nearly twenty minutes to learn. Normally he would have spent another hour making sure he had it down, but he felt that he had the need for haste. They were indulging him, he knew, and growing impatient if his gauge of Roberto's voice was any clue.

Finally ready to cast, he turned to them and smiled, once more giving them the hands-up gesture, asking them to wait just a moment longer. Then he began to cast. He was vaguely aware of them talking as he did, the sound of their voices rising, growing increasingly agitated in time with the rising cadence of his song. At last he reached the end of the incantation and released the magic with a short command. "Mar-du!" he said with hard emphasis on the second syllable. And with that, Common Tongues was cast.

Chapter 38

"... he has rhythm," Roberto was saying as Common Tongue's effects came upon the room. "Not bad for a white boy."

"Stop it," Orli said, realizing as she spoke that Altin had finished his lovely chant.

"Hello," Altin said unexpectedly. "Can you understand me now?"

All three crewmates stepped back in utter awe.

"Holy shit," said Roberto, the first to find his tongue.

"See," said Orli, regaining her composure as well. "I told you." She turned back to Altin. "Yes, I understand you fine. Can you understand me too?"

Altin's face-splitting grin was answer enough.

"What did you do?" She was looking around the air above them as she spoke, as if hearing words for the very first time. "It's fantastic. Like magic."

Altin's face wrinkled a bit, his frown mixing with his smile. "Well," he hesitated, not wanting to make her feel foolish. "It is."

She giggled. "What did you do?"

"Yeah, man," Roberto chimed in. "What did you do? This is insane." He was looking around as Orli had, trying to locate the source of sound, to find the device stuck or floating somewhere that would explain what was going on.

Altin continued to regard them with furrowed brow. These people certainly were odd. Maybe they'd never seen a diviner before. That seemed unlikely.

"Well, the spell is called 'Common Tongue,'" he said. "To be honest, I wasn't sure that it would work; I've never cast this one before." He didn't want to admit that, but it seemed the right thing to do, honesty and all. What he really didn't want to admit was that, at twenty-two, he'd only just recently made divination work. Saying so was like admitting he was seven years old again, so he decided to just leave that last part out. But apparently something he had said left them speechless anyway, and a few moments later Roberto was looking at him through narrowed eyes. Altin suspected Roberto was having a hard time believing a magician could cast such a complicated spell on the very first try, so he added, "I've had a lot of training, and it really wasn't that complicated of a cast. The next one, well, that will be a bit more work I assure you. Forty-some-odd pages long."

That didn't seem to help. But, apparently whatever he'd said didn't bother Orli or Doctor Singh, the latter of whom stepped forward and put a hand on Altin's shoulder in a gesture that was warm. "Magic or no, that's a nifty trick." He clapped Altin on the arm as well. "Very impressive."

"Thank you," Altin replied, grateful for the praise. He finally had a chance to make a good impression on these people after sneaking in and out of their ship so many times.

"So where are you from?" Roberto asked, apparently past whatever had been troubling him, at least for the moment. "We don't get a lot of towers floating around out here."

"Oh, of course," Altin said, "I suppose you don't. I haven't had time to build a nice ship like yours. A very good idea, this. And you're quite right, we've not been properly introduced. I am Altin Meade of Calico Castle, in service to my master, Tytamon the Ancient, in turn in service to the Queen." He saw their frowns and realized how silly that all must sound. "From planet Prosperion," he added to make the matter clear.

Roberto studied him for several breaths then began to laugh, a long, deep laugh, from the belly, so hard he had to bend at the waist and put a hand on his thigh to brace himself.

"Roberto," Orli scolded, "stop it right now. Stop. It's not funny." Doctor Singh echoed her remarks, equaling her tone.

After a moment, Roberto straightened, still struggling with an unruly grin that desperately wanted to play upon his lips. "I'm very sorry," he muttered, barely keeping the smirk at bay. He bowed politely—although too deeply considering Altin had no royal blood—and the whole thing went awry when something of a nasal snort escaped near the bottom of the sweep. Orli kicked Roberto in the shins.

"Forgive him," she said, stepping between Altin and Roberto and putting four soft fingers on Altin's wrist. "Roberto is the ship's idiot; just ignore him like I'm going to do for the rest of his life if he doesn't stop acting like an ass."

The heat of her anger towards her swarthy friend was no match for the fire burning up Altin's arm, joyous energy thrilling through his body from where the gentle touch of her soft hand pressed against his flesh. He had to force himself to stay focused on the diplomacy at hand.

He wasn't sure why she was so upset with Roberto, but he could tell that her wrath struck home, for the chuckling fellow stopped choking down guffaws a moment later and apologized again, this time sounding entirely sincere.

"Sorry, dude," he said, looking Altin squarely in the face. There was no trace of mockery in his dark brown eyes. "That just came out. There's been a lot of pressure around here, you know? And I wasn't kidding about not seeing towers out here. Honestly, it's just, you know. It seems so impossible that I had to laugh. Seriously, no offense?"

"None taken," Altin readily agreed. "I should think, after seeing your powerful ships, that my dilapidated tower would be quite an unexpected sight." Then, to move them all beyond the awkward moment, he added, "Although perhaps not so much a sight as the coconut beasts." He knew as soon as he said it that this was not going to be what they called the monsters they had fought.

And of course they all immediately frowned, clearly trying to figure out what he meant, but Orli came up with it an instant later. "Hostiles. We call them 'Hostiles,' or simply just an orb. But they do kind of look like coconuts, now that you mention it. Except without the husk."

A smile burst upon Altin's face. "Yes, that's what I thought too. No fur, but coconuts just the same. But you call them Hostiles. That does seem a more fitting term. It certainly suits their disposition." There was a moment's pause as he looked into her face. He caught his breath as she turned her eyes up and locked gazes with him, the depth of her stare sending what felt like lightning coursing through his flesh. She stunned the words right out of him. He felt the length of their silence, and it started something of a panic in his chest. He tried to blink out of her paralytic charm as tunnel vision threatened to close him out of thought. There was something diplomatic he should be saying, some words to facilitate an escape. Finally, like a rope dangled to a man that has fallen down a well, a thread of thought somehow wormed its way into his head. He spoke it slowly, trying to find his breath. "So what happened to make them so... hostile?"

Her eyes lingered in his for a moment, and he was almost willing to believe she was having the same kind of trouble that he was. He could only hope such an audacious thing.

But then, that was absurd. He didn't even know her. She was an alien woman, from some far off land, breathtaking, perhaps, but as foreign as any human could possibly be, perhaps more foreign even than an elf. And she was a warrior no less, lithe and sinuous, and with that red-light weapon slung across her hip. What use would a warrior have with a country bumpkin like him? A soft bookworm had no appeal for a woman such as this. He needed to collect himself. Besides, he had a role to play. He was, in a sense, an emissary of the Queen. His behavior would reflect heavily on his entire planet. He forced himself to composure. She seemed to sense his inward shift and took her hand away.

"We have no idea why they attacked," answered Doctor Singh as the roar of confusion and desire finally faded from Altin's ears. "They just appeared one day and the fight was on. They killed everyone on Andalia, or so it seems; but we have no idea what provoked them. It's possible the Andalians did something to bring it on, but they were not forthcoming if they did. And there were hardly any messages to let us know that they were under attack at all. It appears we may never know what started all of this."

"And your people are not from this Andalia, I take it?" Altin said, quickly catching up.

"No, we're from Earth," Roberto put in eagerly, perhaps trying to make up for his behavior from before. "We're almost five light-years from Andalia. We've been out here awhile, but only just discovered the Hostiles a month or so ago."

Altin didn't want to appear ignorant, but he had no idea what most of Roberto's statement meant. He was ecstatic, however, to discover that there were multiple worlds of humanity. This was remarkable and entirely as he'd hoped. "Well," he said, carrying the energy of the revelation into his words, "we shall have to dispatch them quickly and be on with the celebration of our mutual discovery. I'm delighted to find others out among the stars." He paused, then added, "If that's not too bold to say."

"Not at all," Doctor Singh assured him. Altin had hoped Orli would be the one to react to his hospitable remark, but she seemed a little put off for some reason now. The doctor pressed on, "How far away is your planet? Which system are you in?"

A quizzical look consumed Altin's face as he wrestled with the question. Common Tongues was not without its obvious communication gaps. It did nothing to fill in understanding where ignorance came in. "Well," he began, "I'm only a blink of an eye away from home, but it took me several weeks to make it out this far. I'm not sure how I would quantify it though. The whole thing is terribly new to me; I've only just begun."

It was their turn to be confused. "So your planet is only a few weeks from here?" Doctor Singh said after a brief delay.

"No, it took a few weeks to find... 'here,' wherever 'here' is exactly, but now it's only a matter of a moment to get back and forth. Teleporting, you understand."

"That's what you've been doing in the can, right?" said Roberto. "Teleporting? That's what you do?"

"The can?"

"You know. The bathroom, over there." Roberto pointed to the tiny room with the waterfall pot and the flowing basin inside.

"Ah, yes, well, sorry about that. I figured you knew. Your captain—I'm assuming that was the man who shot me—seemed not to appreciate it so much the first time, so, to be safe, I thought it wise to be discreet."

"Ok—and I mean this totally not to be an ass—but you're really saying you're using magic for all this stuff, seriously, is that what I'm getting here?" Roberto was doing little to hide the incredulity in his voice.

Orli sighed, but did not intervene. He hadn't asked anything they weren't all thinking, and his question was at least almost halfway polite.

Doctor Singh looked like he might say something in response to Roberto's question as well, but Altin could tell the older man wanted the answer too. Asking about magic seemed like such a stupid question, though. If he hadn't seen the doctor using the scrying mirror, Altin would have thought the entire ship was crewed by blanks, which was fine with him, if a bit risky given the Hostiles and the danger they could present. Heading out this far with no mage, or only just a few, seemed reckless; although it certainly would explain the poor maneuverability of their ships, not to mention the trouble they had in dealing with the orbs. However, a crew of blanks could not account for the red light beams, nor could it explain the glowing scales on the outside of the ships, the exploding pellets, or any number of other things. But, regardless of their obvious access to at least a few magicians, these three were clearly hoping he would answer the question and put some of their doubts finally to rest. He was happy to oblige.

"Yes, I do magic. I can get my Teleporters Guild card for you if you like. I have it back in my tower. I'm a Seven, though my card says I'm a Six: I have a teleporter home with a Z,R,Q,L, zero, K and, well, I don't know what my divination is just yet...," he blushed, realizing Orli was going to find out he was still a foundling when it came to that particular school. He tried to fudge past that part as vaguely as he could. "I'm sort of just figuring that school out—it's a long story; I was a Six up until three days ago. Oh, and a Y." He shrugged. Nothing to do about it now; the moon was up and the werewolves were about.

Once again the three of them were staring at him with vacant expressions. Roberto was the first to speak, blinking deliberately as if to clear his eyes. "Ok, so let's say I buy it.

What else can you do? Something we can see. So far we can't see any of it. Not that I'm saying I'm not mostly convinced. Just, you know, it's really hard to believe."

"Well, what would you like to see?"

"I don't know," said Roberto, thinking. "Can you, what, maybe... how about turn me into a frog or something?"

"Roberto!" Orli gasped, flashing her tender blue orbs at Altin apologetically again as she punched Roberto in the arm. She turned on her friend. "What is wrong with you?"

"I am not offended," said Altin, coming to Roberto's defense. There was nothing wrong with the question that he had asked, and Altin had resigned himself to these people being at least somehow partly blank. Besides, he was an excellent transmuter, and polymorphing animal forms was easy enough to do, assuming he had the right spell memorized. "And yes, I could do that if you liked. I would have to go back and get a book, however, as the spell isn't fresh in my memory just now."

Roberto rubbed his arm as he flashed Orli a look that spoke of vindication. He turned to Altin with measured patience and said, "I can wait."

He was serious, and Altin grimaced at that. It seemed rather a waste of time, given the newness of their acquaintance after all. And why would he want to be a frog? Why fool around with such silliness? But, he reminded himself that the customs of men from faraway places always seemed strange at first. "Very well," he said. "I shall return in a moment."

He started for the "bathroom" as they called it, but Doctor Singh stopped him before he could go in. "You don't have to do that. We don't mind if you... teleport from here."

"All right," said Altin. "Just don't move, okay. You saw what happened to the cocon... to the Hostiles when they got put together in a teleporting merge. We don't want that to happen to us."

They all nodded politely, watching, waiting, none of them really gathering what Altin had said just yet. Altin began his spell and in a moment he was gone.

They all stood in silent awe as he disappeared with a hiss of rushing air—well, all except Roberto who immediately lost his mind. "Okay. Goddamn it, did you see that shit?" He crossed the room to where Altin was, and waved his hand in the air where the medieval man had disappeared. "Seriously, that's it. What the hell is going on?" He walked around the area where Altin had been standing, looking for something, anything, to explain the inexplicable fact. "Well, it's official. Doc, I need something, man, because it's all coming apart up here." He tapped his temple with a finger, rather brutally.

"That was something of a surprise, wasn't it?" agreed the doctor.

Orli only smiled, half a smile, the other half of her mouth was tight as she contemplated what she'd just observed. She wanted to believe, but magic seemed like such a stretch.

"Jesus," said Roberto, still struggling with a threat to everything he thought he'd ever understood about the universe and things. "That scared the shit out of me, if you want the truth. Like seeing a ghost or something. Look, it gave me chills." He held his goosefleshed forearm up for all of them to see.

Doctor Singh was on to more important things. "Did you hear what he said about the Hostiles? About us not moving. Do you realize what he implied? What power that could be?"

"What are you talking about?" Roberto asked.

"What he said, about not moving, about being merged. It explains the odd bloating of the orbs before they ruptured. If our new friend is saying what I think he's saying, he was using his... teleport... to move them inside of one another, and that is how they died. It would be like me slamming you and Orli together so hard that you both became one mass. One dead, bloody mass." Roberto raised an eyebrow speculatively as he considered that, freezing for a moment as he realized where he stood and suddenly took a long step back to stand once more beside his friends. He stared with horror at the spot where Altin had just been, where he himself was standing only a second ago, and began to shake his head.

Still, his expression suggested that he didn't want to believe; how could he accept what he just saw as magic? There had to be some kind of trick. The captain's theory was looking better all the time. At least the captain's opinion still had some grounding in physics and established principles of the universe. In fact, the more he considered it, the more likely the captain's scenario became the realistic answer, the likely one. Occam's razor to be sure. He announced this to the other two. "No. This is bullshit. The more I think about it, the more I think some sort of hallucination is probably more in line." He laughed nervously. "You know, Doc, you almost had me going there. Both of you. But I'm thinking the orb shot us up with that combo virus crap and now we only think we're cured. They just used that disease to get inside our heads, and now they're using it to generate mass hallucinations or something along those lines. That dude ain't even almost real."

The pitch of Orli's voice rose slightly with each successive word she spoke. "Giant space balls generating mass, synchronized hallucinations through psycho-conductive pathogens? Are you kidding me?" She shook her head with a look on her face that bordered on amazement. "How is that a better hypothesis than Altin's using magic?" She had to inhale and exhale slowly to keep from getting mad. Besides, she liked the way his name felt as it played upon her lips.

Roberto started to answer, but Altin's sudden reappearance startled them all to silence. Once again he was holding a book, although much smaller than the last. "All right," he said as if he hadn't been gone at all, "a frog is a little more complicated than would be a creature closer to your size, so it will take me longer to do than if you could settle for something on the order of a dog or a deer—you understand, something closer to you in mass. But, whichever you like. I'd like to get us past this part and onto more fertile diplomatic ground."

His matter-of-fact tone unnerved Roberto, and the burly Spaniard began to suspect that there was a chance Altin might be serious about what he said. Altin was staring at him patiently without the slightest twinkle of humor in his eyes. Roberto faltered under that gaze, under the expectant looks from his crewmates doing nothing to intervene, unwilling to take the chance. "No," he said. "You know what? I think I'm good. Never mind the frog. Or the dog. I believe you."

Altin looked up from the book. Now there was a twinkle in his eye. "Are you sure? I mean, neither one will take that long. I can do a frog in about fifteen minutes or so. And a dog, well, I can have you licking our feet in less than five."

"Oh, do that one," Orli chimed in at once, flashing a villainous look at the cringing Roberto. Hearing her speak made Altin happy. "We'd love to see that," she said, eyes glinting. "Wouldn't we Doctor Singh?"

"Very much," the doctor said, grinning and nodding emphatically.

Roberto glared at them both, traitors in the flesh, then turned plaintively to Altin. "No. Seriously, it's fine. I'm sorry I brought it up. No dogs. Please."

Both the doctor and Orli were laughing hysterically by the time Roberto finished pleading for his human form. Roberto, at first trying to retain his sour face, eventually had to laugh as well. He looked over at Altin and nodded with respect. "Ok, you got me, man. That was a good one, I admit." He clapped Altin on the shoulder, conceding defeat.

Altin, somewhat at a loss, just smiled and nodded back. He felt as if he'd only caught about half of what was going on.

"Come," said Orli taking Altin by the wrist for the second time that day. Slender yet strong, her hand closed around his arm, gripping him tightly as her touch once more set the lightning coursing through his veins. "We should at least give you a tour," she said, "since we've obviously been so rude." She flicked her eyes at Roberto, shooing him away. "How does that sound to you? Would you like to see our ship?"

"Count me out," Roberto cut in before Altin made his reply. "I have work to do." He winked at Orli, they both knew he was off duty for six more hours.

"A tour sounds wonderful," Altin said as his palms grew slick with sweat. She could lead him into a wyvern's lair and he would gladly go.

Chapter 39

Altin and Orli did not get very far before discovering that once they left the area where the Common Tongues spell had been cast they could no longer understand what one another said. They'd gone perhaps a hundred paces down the long white hallway when Altin finally felt the need to point it out. He hated to spoil the contact with Orli as they walked along, but by the end of the corridor, he realized that he would not be able to just contentedly stroll along to the music of her voice forever; at some point, he was going to have to say something back, for if he waited too much longer, the revelation might be embarrassing to her. Reluctantly, and not until they were nearing another of the ship's sliding doors, he told her about the range of his divining language spell. As soon as he spoke she understood—in that she could not understand a single word he said. They both laughed and then went back to the hospital room.

"I'm going to have to enchant something portable, or we'll never be able to leave this room," he said on their return. "Either that or I'll have to enchant your entire ship, which I suspect would be the task of months if not a year."

"Enchant?" she asked. "What do you mean by that? Like something permanent?"

"Yes, exactly. It might take me a bit of time, because, as I said, I'm rather new to Divining magic. However, I'm not new to enchanting at all, so I should be able to come up with something that will work. We just need it to be portable so that we can communicate as we move around."

"Well, will it interfere with radio waves?" she asked, unclasping a silver button from where it was attached near the collar of her uniform. "If not, we could use this. That's what it's for anyway. Communication I mean." She handed him the small device, not much bigger than the tip of his thumb, and let him take a look. The object would do fine.

"Are you sure you can do without it?" he asked. "It may take me some time to get it done. Again, divining is rather new for me."

"It's fine; I have another one I can use. How long do you think it's going to take?"

"Well, I'm not sure. A few hours at the very least. It might even take a day or two. But, something like that. Plus, I need to send my dragon home; he's been out here far too long." Altin knew as he said it that he no longer had any intention of accompanying the dragon home. Taot was going to get delivered right into his cave. Clearly, given his display the other day, practically burning them both to death, the dragon would be able to keep any nosy predators at bay. He might not fly for another week or two, but Altin no longer feared for his safety in the cave.

Orli gasped as he said the words. "No," she said. "You can't send him away. I was kind of hoping I could say hello."

"To my dragon?" His brows knitted nearly together with concern. He hated to tell her no, but it probably wasn't safe. "Listen, dragons are an unpredictable lot, and he's been sick. Did you see him during the fight, blowing fire all around?"

She nodded.

"Well, that's not normal. He's never done that before."

She looked disappointed, her delicate lips curving to a pout. "It's okay. Maybe some other time."

He groaned inside. "He doesn't like anyone. He's horribly rude that way."

She smiled, barely. "It's okay, really. I understand."

He groaned again, this time not just inside.

She put her electric hand on his arm again, heating his face and flesh. She certainly was an aggressive thing, despite her incongruous sense of tact. "Altin, I really do understand. Animals are like that. I'll meet him some other time, when he's feeling better."

Altin could no longer let discretion hold him back, not with the pounding in his chest. "I'll make him behave. It will be fine." He simply could not let her down. Not even a little bit. And Taot was probably still asleep. He would send a telepathic warning before he brought Orli to the tower.

"No," she said. "Really. I'm not sure I'm ready to be barbequed anyway." She laughed.

He sent a gentle probe to Taot's mind, almost disappointed to find that Taot was awake. Finding him so, he projected a sense of visitors and that there was nothing to pose a threat. The dragon returned an impression of unconcern but accompanied that with a sense that neither Altin nor his guest would be safe if Altin didn't find the dragon something to eat fairly soon. Altin assured the beast that he would supply food the instant he was in the tower.

"Everything will be fine," he told her. "I just checked with him. He's just a bit cranky right now is all. I need to feed him as soon as we get back."

"You mean you can talk to him? Like, with E.S.P.?"

"I'm not sure what that is, but if it's on the order of telepathy, then yes, that's exactly how it works. Dragons are remarkable that way, one of a handful of telepathic beasts. I take it you don't have dragons on your world."

"No," she grinned. "At least not in the last several million years."

He nodded. Prosperion had seen its share of species go extinct as well. "All right then, are you ready to go?"

She stared blankly at him for a moment until it slowly dawned on her what he had just proposed. She felt her hands begin to sweat and found herself more than just a little terrified. "You mean now? With a... teleporting?"

"Yes. Unless you have another way."

She swallowed hard. She wondered how much trouble she was going to be in. She *was* off duty though. What she did with her own time was, technically, up to her. Wasn't it? But unauthorized departure was definitely against the rules. However, she loathed the rules. And though she'd never actually thought about it before, she'd always wanted to meet a dragon. "No," she said at last, as her skin tingled and her heart began to race, "let's go say 'hello.'"

Altin grabbed his books from where they lay upon the bed and began to chant the spell. A moment later they were standing in his room. At which point he blushed to the deepest crimson, realizing what he had done. "Oh my," he said, eyes wide and expecting her to be mortified. "It's really not what you think." He stammered and, tossing his books aside, tried to straighten the blankets on his bed. "Oh my. Oh my. You'll think me a scoundrel." He turned to look at her, clearly horrified by what he'd done, then abruptly darted up the stairs, calling down to her as he went, "I'm terribly sorry. I honestly meant no insult at all. Please don't think me so depraved. I just... I'm unendingly sorry. Please forgive me."

Orli said something that he couldn't understand, and she was fanning herself, obviously surprised at the temperature Taot had created with his fiery tirade. It was also obvious from her tone that she was baffled by his sudden shift in attitude. And, once again, he'd forgotten about the ten-step radius of Common Tongues.

He came back down the stairs, shielding his eyes with a hand so as not to gape at the woman in his boudoir like some predatory lout, and ran down to the first floor of his tower to get some parchment, a quill pen and some ink. He came back up, displaying the objects to Orli while maintaining the properly discreet aversion of his eyes, and then went up to the battlements hoping that she understood. Apparently she recognized the purpose of the objects, for he happened to glimpse her nodding as he shuffled past. She had a grin on her face that suggested that she was mildly amused. He marveled at how forgiving the woman was as he skittered up the stairs.

He set the items down upon the battlement floor, roughly centered, but close enough for the spell area's outer edge to overlap with Taot's resting place. The dragon eyed him expectantly and licked its teeth.

"Oh," Altin said. "One second. I'll be right back."

He ran back down to his rooms where Orli, clearly waiting for permission to approach the area wherein the dragon lay, had gone to his bookshelf and was leafing through a book. Her alabaster skin was beginning to shine as the heat hanging in the air brought a sheen of perspiration to her flesh, luminously wet, reflective and smooth like fine marble under the lights in Mercy's temple or that of some other feminine divinity. He wanted to smile at her, but did not want her to misinterpret his gaze for lust, particularly given that he found himself with more than a seed of it stirring in his loins. Her uniform was unparalleled in inspiring such ungallant thoughts, more so than anything he'd ever seen.

The whole of discomfiture was made worse by the fact that he had to approach her to get to the crate of food, which was not too far from where she stood.

"Excuse me," he said, face turned away from her and still blushing red, "I need to get Taot something to eat."

Apparently she sensed his predicament and stepped to

the other side of the bed. She was still smiling, almost a smirk now, as if she had figured out exactly what was on his mind and yet found it amusing just the same. That didn't help at all.

He hadn't checked the crate before he'd brought his tower back out into the stars, and there wasn't much left inside. There was, however, still an entire ham and three turkey legs, plus a wedge of cheese and some bread. He wasn't sure the dragon would be interested in the latter two, but the rest would suit him fine. The meager portions wouldn't fill the dragon up, but they would keep hunger at bay until Altin could send the great beast home.

With an unintentional glimpse at Orli, now pretending to leaf through the book as she watched him with an unashamed stare, he loaded all the food into his arms and trundled up the stairs. He dumped his haul near Taot's head and watched with satisfaction as the dragon began to eat. The ham was gone in the matter of a blink. Altin sent the dragon a promise that he'd teleport him home in just a moment, but that he was going to bring someone up. He asked that the dragon behave when Orli arrived, but, as usual with dragons, no promises were made. Taot sniffed the air near the stairs and sent back to Altin's mind the sense that he didn't need to eat her just yet. That was as close as Altin was going to get.

Altin ran back down the stairs, growing breathless with all his labor and the stress, motioned for Orli to wait and went down to the bottom floor in search of some scissors with which to cut their hair. Of course he didn't have a pair. However, he still had his service dagger hanging on the belt suspended from a peg on the back of the door. So he pulled that from its scabbard and headed back upstairs, wiping the dust from its pommel as he went.

Orli greeted him with a smile as he reentered his bed chamber and, for whatever reason, this time he did not avert his eyes. She certainly didn't make him as uncomfortable in this circumstance as other women might have done. He would have to thank her for that. Most women would have been outraged. However, as he approached, she saw the dagger in his hand. He realized, as her hand moved down to her red-light weapon, that she was not quite so comfortable as he had assumed.

"Oh," he said, stopping and stepping back. "It's for the hair." He reached for another lock of his hair, and sliced it neatly with the knife. "See." He held his newly pruned spell component out for her to see. "For the spell."

She immediately recognized his intent and her posture became more relaxed. Still, the moment had taken something from the energy that been heating up the air quite aside from anything Taot had done before.

Altin flipped the dagger around in his hand, holding it by the blade, and offered it pommel first to her so that she could cut her hair herself. She smiled, clearly relieved, and took it. He made a quick gesture to his own ear, reminding her to take it from the area specified by the spell. She was rather clumsy with the knife and took a somewhat longish cut, twice the size required by the spell. He wondered if maybe he should have offered to do it after all. Gods, what was it about her that made him so out of sorts?

She returned the dagger to him with the sample of her own hair, which he took, smiling, and then beckoned her to follow him up to the battlements. Once there, he placed the dagger on the table, discreetly halving the sample Orli had cut and slipping the extra portion behind the lamp so that she would not know that she'd made a mistake. Then he went about placing the samples on the parchment and setting up the rest of the ten-pace radius spell that would allow them to communicate. The spell was cast a moment later, and, still out of breath, he could finally apologize for teleporting her into his bed chamber as if he thought her some common tart.

"What?" she stammered as soon as he'd prattled out his long, dissembling explanation of chivalry and proper etiquette. "Is that what that was all about?" She giggled, almost childlike, and blushed a little pink into her cheeks. "I admit, I thought it might be something like that, but chivalry has been dead so long on Earth I really figured it had to be something else." She looked him square in the eye, and a smile came upon her perfect lips. "You really are sweet, Altin. I've never met a man like you."

His cheeks caught fire as if Taot had just breathed directly in his face. He used the dragon as his excuse to divert her attention from his blush. "Thank you," he managed after a moment. "You're very kind to say it." He stepped to the dragon and patted it on the head. "This is Taot, my dragon." He paused. "Well, he's not really mine. He's entirely his own, but we have something of a partnership."

Orli regarded the dragon who was just finishing off the last of the turkey legs, the bones popping and crunching as they were crushed between its powerful jaws. She clapped her hands and laughed aloud. "He's magnificent! And so huge. Whatever made you want to cram an animal this big up here in such a tiny space?" Before Altin could answer she added, "Can I pet him?"

A bit surprised that she was not more cautious, and a bit impressed, he queried Taot to see if he was going to stand for a stranger's touch; the dragon was never amenable to such things, but it was always worth a try. The sensation the dragon returned to Altin's mind was entirely unspeakable, inappropriate beyond all measure, and he could not believe that Taot would assume such base and lustful things about Altin's purely chivalrous motives regarding the woman standing here. Taot was an unremitted and lascivious beast, and clearly expected little more from Altin than he expected from himself. And in addition to assuming Altin had such carnal plans, the dragon apparently approved of Altin's "choice of mates" as well—including an appalling appreciation for her scent. Altin's blush could not have gotten any deeper red, though there was a lurking voice inside him that wished he dared be so bold.

"Good gods," was all he managed to get out.

"Does that mean I can't pet him?" Orli asked, sounding a bit disappointed as she took a step away from the dragon lying on the floor.

"No," Altin said as the pricks of heat slowly faded from his face. "Quite the opposite. He seems to...," he paused, appropriate words not at hand. "It's fine. Go ahead."

Orli moved cautiously to the dragon and reached a hand slowly out towards his snout. As no fire erupted to consume her, she pressed her fingers against the very tip of his nose where it was pointed, almost like a beak. The skin there was scaly, hard like industrial plastic and just as smooth. The dragon made no move to bite her, and so her confidence grew.

"There's some softer skin just behind his ears. He likes when you rub him there, if your hands are strong enough. Don't be afraid to dig right in, or he won't even know you're there."

She followed Altin's instructions and found the spot that he was speaking of. Rubbing the thick skin was rather like trying to knead body armor, but, using both hands, she managed to pull it off. Taot let out a low rumble that rattled the stone beneath her feet. She echoed it with a less stentorian version of her own.

"Oh, Altin, he's amazing," she said after petting the dragon for a while. "So beautiful and strong." She cooed at the dragon and spoke to it as if it were a puppy or soft kitten in her lap.

Altin grinned and watched her with warmth filling his chest like hot water being poured into a bath. She was so innocent, standing there like that, sweet and pure, yet clearly not like any other woman he had seen. She was strong and confident, even assertive, but not like Lena or any of the other girls he knew, and not crude like the women who fought for the Queen with knives and swords; she was not a hardened warrior despite the red-light strapped to her thigh. Orli's was a different kind of strength, an alien one, entirely unique. And she was exquisite to be near.

That was when the button she had given him began to squawk from inside the pocket he had dropped it in. He could not make out the words, as whoever spoke had not been included in the translation spell he'd cast a few moments ago. But whoever it was, they were clearly quite upset.

"Oh shit," she said as the button sounded off. She spun and stared out at her ship. "They can see me standing here."

"Who?" said Altin. "Is that the captain yelling there?"

"Who else?" she replied. "You'd better take me back."

Judging from the captain's tone, Altin could tell that it was true. "All right," he said, his heart breaking at the thought. He handed her the device, but she did not take it. She closed his hand around it with both of hers; he could feel the wetness in her palms as they wrapped around his fist. "Enchant it, like you said." She went to the table then and took the dagger from where he'd placed it coming up. She deftly sliced another sample of her hair from behind her ear and turned to him with a grin. "If we keep this up, we'll both be bald." She laughed and handed him the lock of white-gold hair. "Can you send me back alone? I think you might be safer here." She glanced down at the silver button in his palm and gave a semi-shrug. Altin knew exactly what she meant.

"Yes," he said, his hand going absently to the dark patch upon his chest and the wound that lay beneath. "Perhaps you're right about that."

The silver button nearly exploded with the violence of

the captain's next command.

"I need to go, Altin."

He'd never wanted to kiss anyone so much in his entire life, but he tore his eyes away from her and went to the scrying basin, calling up the hospital room where they'd first met. It was empty. With agony in his heart, he turned, smiled, and sent her back.

Chapter 40

"What in the hell did you think you were doing, Pewter? You just leave the ship with the first swinging dick you meet? Are you out of your fucking mind?" Captain Asad was fuming, his brown eyes wide and his voice booming from deep inside his chest like explosions from some unseen engine catastrophe. "I should have you shot for unspeakable stupidity, not to mention aiding and abetting the enemy, dereliction of duty, unapproved leave and treason. My God, Ensign, what the hell is wrong with you?"

Orli leaned defiantly into the wind of the captain's tirade, too rapturous from her moments in Altin's tower to let the words get beneath her skin. Being there with Altin and his dragon was the most fun she'd had in her entire adult life. Altin was alive, a real man from a real place, not some sterile military robot like everyone in the entire goddamn fleet. Let the captain shoot her. She didn't care. She finally felt alive. For the first time in memory, she lived, as if something had come awake inside. And besides, she'd just scratched a dragon behind the ears. How dangerous could the captain possibly be?

Her silence only made matters worse. "Speak up, Ensign,

what the hell were you doing down there? Tell me your infatuation has not endangered the entire fleet. Did you even have yourself decontaminated before coming back aboard?" He didn't wait for her reply. "Of course you didn't. You're too busy thinking with your cunt to have one thought for the safety of this already decimated crew. Goddamn it, Pewter."

The veins in his forehead were enormous, thick wires trying to swell through his heated flesh. He'd always been a surly man, but she had never in ten long years ever seen him get like this. She actually believed she was in real danger of being shot.

"I'm sorry," she said, her voice trembling now. There were a million emotions coursing through her veins, fear was only one. "It seemed harmless."

"You can't be fucking serious." Flecks of spittle flew from his mouth, luminous particles of irritation launched at her, given light by the glow from the console by which he stood. "Harmless? Boarding an alien vessel without permission. And alone, no less. That doesn't seem stupid beyond the pale?" His eyes bulged with incredulity, the whites tinted blue by the same light that illuminated his apoplectic spit.

"Well," she stammered, "not once you get to know him. If you just took the time to talk to him like we did...," she gestured to where Roberto normally sat, but their shift had still not come back around. There was only Lieutenant Mitur sitting there, and he didn't appear to have any intention of helping her.

"Some of us have duties to the rest of the crew. Some of us think about other people besides ourselves. You have a duty to the goddamn crew, Pewter. To the rest of us. To the fleet."

Orli began to recede into herself; clearly nothing she could say would abate the captain's wrath. And so she stood silently in the storm of his assault, her unfocused gaze absently aware of the panel lights flickering behind him until at last his anger had played itself mostly out. He stood there glaring at her for a moment in silence, a looming presence in the dimness of the bridge. He seemed to swell almost, as if frustration and rage inflated him from within, but at last he relented and his presence normalized. After a very measured breath, he spoke again.

"You're lucky I have no other choice," he said. "Otherwise I'd be sticking you in the brig. And the first second I have an actual crew again, that's exactly what I'm going to do. You have my word on that. You're living on borrowed time, Ensign, trust that. You better hope the rest of the fleet never decides it's safe to board my ship again, because on that day you're through. Now get out of my sight. If I see you in that tower again, I'll fire the lasers myself. Do you hear?"

"Yes, sir," she said. "I'm really sorry. I didn't think it was going to be that big a deal."

"Get out." He looked as if he wanted to spit on her for real, so she turned and immediately went away.

Back in her room she cried into her pillow for nearly an hour and a half. This place was so horrible. God, she just wanted to go away. She wished they'd left her back on Andalia, even if there were Hostile spores hiding in the dirt. Who cared? At least there'd be no one there to make her feel like shit every time she made a move. Goddamn it. This ship was such a fucking nightmare. She hated it. She hated the fleet. She hated them all. Every last one of them in their goddamn matching clothes and matching words and matching every-fucking-thing. Goddamn it. She wished Altin would come and just take her far from here. He said his world was only a few moments away. Maybe that was true. Maybe he could teleport home as easily as he could teleport from his tower to the ship. Maybe it really was that easy.

Or maybe it was just a dream. Maybe the captain and

Roberto were right. Maybe it was some horrible Hostile ruse. Maybe they really could control everyone else's mind. It did seem awfully hard to believe. The magic. The dragon. A man that was more than simple lust. That really was impossible if she thought about it very long.

She raised a trembling, tear-dampened hand to her ear, to where so much of her hair had recently been clipped. The ends were blunted in three distinct places, cut with no concern for aesthetics or for style. If this was all a dream, then the Hostiles didn't miss a trick.

But it couldn't be a trick. How could it possibly be? The way he blushed, the rustle of his robes. My God, the tables were all burnt. So was the carpet on his floor. She had smelled the smoke. And the clutter. The half-eaten bread. The sound of bones crunching in the dragon's mouth. And it had been so terribly hot in there. How could the Hostiles create a hallucination so completely real, so filled with the most random things? And why? Why would they feel the need for so much insignificant detail? It didn't make any sense.

Or at least it didn't make any more sense than did a magic man floating in a tower with a dragon out in space. She sighed and sniffled all at once, the combination giving her the hiccups in its wake. She sighed again and curled up into a ball. Maybe she could go to sleep. A few hours to at least dream that he was real. She had just enough time for that before her shift came back around and she had to return to her post up on the bridge. Where the captain was. She shuddered and rocked herself to sleep, visions of green-eyed sorcerers and rumbling dragons whirling in her mind.

Her alarm woke her in what seemed only an instant after that, an atonal clarion of misery. It was time to go back to work.

"They're regrouping," Roberto informed her when she sat back down in the com-station chair. He pointed at the main monitor with his chin as he started shaking his head. "Look how many now."

Any vestiges of lovesickness that may have been haunting her were immediately whisked away. At least twenty orbs were now visible on the screen, and another appeared even as she watched. "Good God," she said. "How far away is the rest of our help?"

"That's your job, Pewter. I suggest you make some attempt to do it now." That from the captain, of course.

"Yes, sir," she said. "On it." She was never going to have his favor back, but she had to at least make an attempt. The cessation of his contempt had been nice to have in those few days that followed her contribution to the cure; she'd actually been able to relax, almost enjoyed being on the bridge—at least during those moments when they weren't under attack. For a time he'd at least treated her with respect. But deep down she knew that this time the damage was permanent. She sighed and pulled up the data from the fleet. All three squadrons should be arriving at any time, and she made the announcement as soon as the specific distances came up. "Twenty minutes to Echo, forty for Bravo and Delta to arrive. They're almost here, sir."

He made no answer, and the raw fury radiating from him confirmed her sense that the friendly banter on the bridge had come completely to an end. Roberto sensed it too, and, unaware of her brief foray down into Altin's tower, he shot her an inquisitive glance.

She waved him off, indicating with a shrug and the expression on her face that the answer would have to wait. She returned her attention to the com.

"Twenty seven," she announced as she picked up a handful of orbs coming into scanner range but not yet on the screen. "Five incoming."

"Tell the admiral to bring the entire fleet." Then a moment later, he said, "Stow that." Three more orbs had just joined the growing swarm. "Just radio our report."

She did, and after a moment, the admiral's face appeared upon her screen. She punched it up to a quarter of the large monitor on the wall. After a brief exchange between the captain and the admiral, it was decided that the rest of the fleet should assemble a half-day's distance from where the *Aspect* currently was. The three squadrons already on their way were to continue coming to their support, but the rest of the fleet would gather in full at a distance first, and then move in to help if there was anything remaining of the smaller group. Deciding to leave the four squadrons to fate was a hard decision to make, and both men walked away from the conversation looking grim. It was not the kind of decision Orli ever wanted to have to make: deciding who was going to live and who was probably going to die. The callous emotional distance required to make that kind of call reminded her of the first few hours of vaccinations when the crew was dying faster than the doses could be brought. No, she never wanted to be party to that again.

After his exchange with the admiral, Captain Asad sat quietly in his chair watching the screen without comment as Orli occasionally announced the latest tally on the orbs' steadily growing swarm. They were up to nearly a hundred by the time he finally spoke. "Any idea what your friend over there is going to do?" He was looking at the portion of the monitor that still kept Altin's tower securely in its sight. Orli had been glancing at it occasionally too. She wished she were there. If the orbs were going to kill her, she'd rather die with him.

"He said he had to send his dragon home. That's all I really know. I wasn't over there long enough to learn anything else. He had to recast his language spell, so we didn't get much chance to talk."

The captain grimaced at the use of such ridiculous words, but let it pass. "Do you know if he's planning on staying long enough to fight?"

Her first instinct was to say, "Why the hell should he? You shot him, you fucking ungrateful ass?" But instead she managed to say, "I have no idea," though not without a tremendous amount of restraint. Thinking of Altin like that stirred up an emotional force that had her hands trembling against her console by the time she finished speaking on his behalf, her skin moist and slightly sticky where it pressed against the glass. The fact that the captain considered Altin a potential ally after treating the magical man so poorly was both evidence of the captain's recognition of Altin as a potent military force and of the captain's sense of just how dire their circumstances had become. The former had to be more painful for him than the latter was.

She looked up at the monitor and saw that the dragon had just disappeared. She said as much aloud. The captain nodded and gave the briefest hum.

"He must have teleported it home," Roberto said, daring to butt into the captain's ominous mood. He heard the captain grunt again. He hesitated, reluctant to go on, but, given the obvious misery that had settled upon Orli since the last time he'd seen her, he felt that whatever had transpired between her and the captain, he would rather come down on the side of his best friend. "Captain, with all due respect, you are wrong about him. The magic is real. I saw it too. So did Doctor Singh. He does it."

"Lieutenant, I'm too old to believe in fairy tales, and not spiritual enough to believe in miracles and myths. There is no such thing as magic. The hologram of the dragon has simply been shut off."

"Fine, sir, call it what you like. Matter transmission. Dimensional shift. Whatever. But that don't change it. The effects are real. I've seen them. I'm telling you: it's real."

The captain nodded. Clearly he'd considered that option, but he was just not sure how he wanted to proceed from there. The whole idea of magic was ludicrous, but the circumstances were such that any options had to be taken into account, even ridiculous ones. And at this point, it probably didn't matter if Altin turned out to be friend or foe anyway. With a hundred orbs out there, they were all going to die shortly after the orbs decided to attack. What difference did it make if it was by the onslaught of a hundred Hostile shafts or some trick of that enigma out there floating in a tower made of stone? The only difference was that the robed man at least presented the possibility of being an ally, however unlikely that might seem. And, once again, it would make little difference in the end.

Four more orbs flew in and hovered with the rest.

"They're here," Orli announced a little while later. "Echo is finally here." She quartered the view on the monitor again to allow the image of five long Earth ships to appear approaching on their starboard side, slivers of glowing metal hope, white against the darkness out of which they came. "Finally someone else is here." She punched up the location of the other two squadrons and found they too were only a short time away, and in the span of half an hour, their numbers had grown to eighteen.

Unfortunately, the orbs now numbered one hundred and thirty-two.

Roughly an hour later, after the commanders of the other ships and Captain Asad had worked out a tentative plan for their defense, the captain addressed her once again. There was an aspect of reluctance in his voice that she had never heard him use, resignation and something else. Humility? It couldn't be, not after the vehemence of his tirade.

"Pewter, do you think you can get him back, so we can talk to him again?"

At first she thought he was talking about the commander of Echo squadron and started to punch that ship's com officer back up on her screen.

"No, Ensign. The magician. Can you get him to come back to the ship? We need to find out what he's planning to do, if he's going to fight again—assuming he ever was." He couldn't help adding the last.

"Oh," she said, surprised. "Well...," she stammered, thinking on it for a moment. Her bottom lip slipped unconsciously inward and she pinned it gently against her lower teeth with the press of the upper row. How was she supposed to get him back? She had no way to communicate. Although he did still have her com link. She wasn't sure how his enchantment was going to work though, or if he'd even gotten it done. But it was certainly worth a try. "Maybe," she said, letting go her bottom lip. "Let me see."

She deactivated the com link on her shoulder, the replacement that she'd pinned on before she'd come back up to do her shift, and reactivated the original as default on her personnel screen. Then she keyed it up and began to talk. "Altin," she said. "Are you there? Can you hear me?"

For a long time there was nothing, but finally his voice came back over the speaker. She couldn't understand a thing. Apparently he hadn't got his spell to work. Or else it didn't work as she had hoped. Either way, at least she had his attention. It was a start.

"Altin, I need you to come back. Please come back. We need to talk to you." As she spoke she must have let out a bit more emotion than she thought because Roberto turned to look at her with narrowing eyes and one brow raised.

"Wow," he said after studying her and without the usual sarcasm in his voice. "You're serious, aren't you?"

Her eyes misted and she only nodded back. He really had no idea.

Roberto bowed his head, humbled by the raw intensity of her gaze. "He's a lucky man."

"It won't matter either way if he doesn't answer soon. Pewter will be dead with the rest of us if we don't figure out something soon. Get him up here, Ensign. We need to work his... magic... into the plan." Orli could tell that it pained the captain to use the word, but she nodded and tried again.

"Altin, come up here, please," she said again. "The captain needs to speak to you. Can you at least try to understand what I'm saying? Come up, come up, please."

Roberto leaned over to Orli's com and punched the key, "Yeah, dude, seriously. Get up here, man. The shit's about to hit the fan."

Altin appeared a moment later on his tower top, looking up at them. He closed his eyes and started chanting, then stopped a few moments later and went back down into the tower again.

"Where's he going?" Roberto said, but the question was answered a moment later as Altin returned with a sheet of parchment, upon which he drew invisible circles with his finger. He placed it on the parapet and once more began to chant and sway. A moment later the parchment disappeared from where it sat upon the wall. Orli immediately turned and looked to the place on the floor where the first paper target had appeared. Sure enough, the blank parchment was now lying on the deck.

"Stay away from it," she announced. He's going to appear right there. If you stand there when he shows up, you're both dead."

The captain didn't look impressed, but he made no move towards the yellow paper lying there.

"Captain, since I'm already doomed to imprisonment anyway," she went on, "I can promise you that if you shoot him again, I'm going to blow you straight to hell." She had no idea she'd been going to say the words until they were already past her lips. Both she and Roberto recoiled from what she said.

Space was not as cold as the look the captain gave her in exchange for that remark, but Altin's arrival postponed that for another day.

"Don't shoot," were the first words out of his mouth when he appeared, both hands up defensively in the air.

"We were just discussing that," Orli said. "The captain promises to behave." Then she paused. "Hey, I can understand you now."

"Yes," he said. "I figured out the enchantment on your pin. Here, you can have it back."

"But I couldn't understand you just a minute ago."

"Yes, well, Common Tongues has a radius as you'll recall. We have to be within ten paces of this for it to work."

"Gladly." She smiled, willing the emotions in her heart out through her eyes and into his.

"What's he saying?" the captain asked. "And how did you learn his language so fast?"

"I didn't," she said. "He's enchanted my com link so that we can understand one another's language. We have to stay within... ten paces for it to work." She chuckled. She loved the way Altin thought of things. She looked back to him. "Why can't the captain understand?"

"Your button is only enchanted for us, remember. I only had our hair."

"Oh, of course. I forgot about that." She relayed this detail to the captain who seemed resigned to this unending trend of fate, the irritant of Pewter's indispensability.

"Of course it's just the two of you." The captain's words had to slide out from behind a sneer. "That's fine. Listen, just ask him what he intends to do about all those orbs out there. I'm guessing there are too many for whatever it is that he actually does, but ask him anyway. Ask him what's his plan."

Orli nodded and looked back to Altin. "The captain wants to know what you plan on doing about all the Hostiles gathering out there now. He wants to know if you are going to stay and fight."

"What Hostiles?" was Altin's response.

Orli pointed at the screen, directing the sorcerer's gaze. "Those."

"Whoa," said Altin, taking a backwards step. "By the nine gods, that's a lot of coconuts." Orli actually laughed. How could he remain so unperturbed?

"So what are you going to do?"

"Well, I hadn't thought about it up till now. Honestly, I didn't even know that they were there. I was just working on the enchantment for your button and doing a few menial things. I sent Taot home. He's very impressed with you." His cheeks turned slightly pink at this last part, and he quickly moved along. "He ate all my food, so I sent my crate back to be refilled. I even tidied up a bit in case you ever decided to come back again. I'm usually not such a terrible slob."

Orli laughed and highly doubted that. She'd already pegged him for being the cluttered kind, and she'd wondered why almost everything in his tower looked as if it had been burned. The table on the tower top made sense enough, having seen the dragon do its thing, but the one in his room was somewhat blackened too. And the rug was horribly scorched as well. General mayhem seemed to prevail in Altin's medieval home, and tidiness didn't seem to be one of Altin's traits. Which made him unlike anything on the ship.

"Well?" demanded the captain. "What's he saying? What's he going to do?"

"One second," Orli said, cutting the captain off. "He's not done explaining. Try to be polite. Altin's people are very courteous. Unlike ours. You're just going to have to wait."

"What's he saying?" Altin asked.

"He's saying that he's sorry for being such an asshole and that he just can't help himself."

Altin frowned. "That's not what it sounded like."

"Well, it's what he should have said. Actually, he still wants to know what you're planning on doing about all of that." Once more she gestured at the view upon the wall.

He grunted and scratched the stubble on his chin, staring up at the growing Hostile herd. "I don't suppose there's a teleporter or two on one of these other ships is there? That would really help a lot. And maybe a conduit as well?"

She wrinkled her face up at that, shaking her head, and then it finally dawned on her what Altin was missing that she was not. "Altin, we have no spells. There is no magic on our world. Not one tiny bit. To be honest, we don't even believe in it anymore. Or we didn't until meeting you."

Altin matched her frown for frown before nodding that he finally understood. "Okay. It's not exactly what I thought, but I suspected something similar might be at work." He looked back at the growing mass of orbs up on the screen as his nodding slowed to motionless. He looked as if he were about to say one thing and then changed his mind to ask something else instead. "Then how did you get out here?"

Understanding his question came slowly, but finally she smiled. "We call it technology. You know, science and math. We figure stuff out and then we make machines." She motioned around herself with a hand, presenting the ship as evidence. "We're pretty good at it really."

He smiled and nodded again. "Yes, I can see that. Although, I have to say it's not working so well against these... orbs."

"No, it's not," she agreed.

"What's he saying?" the captain demanded again.

"Hush," she said to him. "Stop trying to interrupt. I'm finding out." She asked Altin to carry on.

"What your ships need is a version of my Combat Hop. I think that spell would make a huge difference. Your ships move awfully slow." He looked back out at the cloud of orbs and made a clicking sound in his cheek. "Although, to be honest, I doubt that it will prove to be difference enough now. They came at me in a formation of only four awhile back and managed to get in a lucky shot. If they come in groups of five or ten, I'm thinking that kind of luck will eventually win the day."

"But do you think whatever that is you're talking about could buy us time? We have reinforcements on the way. We just need to stay alive. We have over a hundred ships, if we can just hold the Hostiles off long enough for the fleet to arrive."

"I make no promises," he said. "But I'm certain it would help."

She clapped her hands again and saw Roberto roll his eyes. She shrugged at him. She didn't care how childish she looked. "So what does... Combat–whatever do? The captain will want to know."

"Oh, it's simple really. It's just a short teleport, enchanted in place with many possible directions for it to go. I've actually worked out the specific description for those battering rams that the coconu–Hostiles use, so that part is already done. When they shoot the stone beams at us, the Combat Hop engages and my tower teleports away. I'll have to figure out how to make it work for something as large as one of your ships though; I've only ever cast it on my tower. Modifying the spell will take some time. But I'm sure that I can do it if the Hostiles decide to wait."

"So you're saying it just moves us somewhere else when they shoot?" She wanted to be clear.

"Yes, that's precisely what it does. Although you'll want to spread your ships far enough apart. The spell doesn't care if there is someone else already occupying the space. Generally speaking, it's a last-ditch defense, and it was never intended for use amongst a crowd."

"Well, we don't have a lot of options at the moment as it is."

"I believe you are right about that," he said, looking once more at the scene depicted on the wall.

Orli relayed what he had said to Captain Asad who looked dubious at best. But he was under orders from the admiral to talk to the magic man and report whatever came of the conversation back to fleet command. He did as much while Altin and Orli chatted privately in their mysteriously encoded spell. Their secrecy annoyed him greatly. Roberto actually began to look a bit jealous too, hating to be left out.

In the end it was decided that, as the captain stated before, they had so little chance of survival as it was, anything that might buy them time until the fleet could arrive in force was a chance that they should take, however ridiculous it might sound. But the final decision was left to each individual ship's captain, and they were given their choice regarding admittance for the magician upon their ship, and they were reminded that if there was still contagion aboard the *Aspect*, the robed man might be bringing that along as well.

In the end, only four of the other ships agreed to let Altin come aboard. Most thought that Captain Asad and his crew had lost their minds, a residual of the infection, the general consensus being that Altin was in fact a hallucinogenic Hostile trick. And even amongst those captains who did believe, or at least who were willing to hope that somehow Altin could actually do what he said he could, few were willing to risk infection by the disease that had decimated the *Aspect's* crew now that Altin had been aboard. Which is why there were only four of the eighteen that agreed to receive the Combat Hop.

Orli reported all of this back to Altin who simply shrugged it off. "That is their choice," he said. "And I'm not worried about some disease. There's nothing Doctor Leopold can't cure, no disease beyond the Healers Guild but death. Nobody dies from disease back home. At least very rarely, and usually it's a blank." He blanched as he said it, hoping she didn't take offense at the latter part.

She pointed out the willing ships on the monitor, apparently unbothered by the reference to her magical powerlessness, and he said that he would teleport his tower just above each in turn when he was ready to enchant their ship. He made her promise that she would explain the requirements regarding the parchment targets to each captain so that they all completely understood. She came up with the idea to have them flash their docking lights five times to let him know that they were ready for him to arrive. He agreed that this was a good idea and prepared to teleport back to his tower to begin working out the details of the spell.

"Hurry," she said as he was just about to start his spell. "And..." she paused. What else could she say? He was obviously a man of extreme decorum. She was afraid to scare him off. "And be careful."

He smiled at that, and his face became so bright that it felt to her as if he shined down upon the entire universe, the look of grim determination that had been his countenance a moment before replaced by jubilant innocence revealing that she'd found the perfect thing to say.

"I will," he promised, and a moment later he was gone.

Chapter 41

Working out the details of Combat Hop to the point where the spell could encompass an object as large as Orli's ship was the project of several hours. Technically, just adding more mana to the spell should make it work, but Altin had other things to check as well. He wasn't going to make any mistakes. Not this time. Not after meeting *her*. And more mana was not what was slowing the process down. The problem was that the spell he'd written required that its anchor be embedded within the Polar's shield; it was the immersion in the shield that allowed Combat Hop to be so easily spread around an area as large as the surface of the tower and its foundation rock. At first, that seemed as if it would be easy enough to do; his initial thought being to encapsulate the ships in pairs of Polar's domes butted up to one another like two halves of a split coconut. The thought was ironic. However, it wasn't helpful in the end, because, try as he might, he couldn't find any way around the spell requirement that the Polar's shield be anchored firmly to the ground. The element of "ground" was too critical an aspect of the spell to be bypassed, which meant he had to enchant Combat Hop on the entire ship—steel plate by steel plate—an entirely different thing.

The original spell from which his version had come to pass had the advantage of a person's sense of "self." The Earth ships had no such thing; they had no will or concept of "being," no accepting thought to which the spell could be attached. Worse, the ships' hulls were not even magically wrought; they had no merged metal from some transmuter's spell, the casting of which would have left some residual energy to which Altin might bind Combat Hop, so Altin was reduced to pouring through his sparse assemblage of divination books hoping for anything that looked like it might suggest somewhere else to begin.

Finally, as he sat on his bed, crossed legs buried beneath a mound of tattered old tomes, he found a spell that he thought might give him the insight that he sought. The discovery was fortunate, for he'd gone through every divination book he had. In the last volume, his most advanced, was a spell called "Curiosity" that promised "answers for a caster willing to see." The book was ancient, the edges of its yellowed pages gone brown and crumbling ragged parchment flakes like dried skin that worked their way atop this letter or that, masking commas and quotation marks or even truncating a word. He wiped them away, sending some sliding down into the crease and some tumbling into his lap. He ran his green-eyed gaze along the lines carefully, his lips silently pronouncing words he'd never spoken before, his fingers tracing script penned gods-knew-how-long ago. He worried that the spell might be outside his competence. He was horribly new to divination for a spell like this. But failure meant letting Orli down. And that was not going to happen, not on his watch. In his heart he knew that she was the reason he was here, the reason he had come so far from home. Hers was the voice that had been calling to him all these years, and he wasn't going to let her die.

Behind those thoughts was a sinister one as well, a

skulking sense of craven and selfish need that came lurking into the dark parts of his mind. It was cowardly, this thought, and without any of honor's sense, but Altin found himself thinking that, if this battle was going bad, he would go get her and carry her away. Even if he had to take her against her will. He would not care if their entire fleet hunted him down, chased him forever for having kidnapped one of theirs and taken her to Prosperion. He did not care. She would not die out here in this vast and endless night. Not while he could still draw a breath. Not even if she hated him for it somewhere down the road. She only had to live.

He didn't want it to come to that, however, so he worked furiously to figure out the spell. The instructions were as ambiguous as Neven'Na'haria's ever-changing head, and, unlike the mythical figure, it was unwilling to show him a helpful face. However, after several hours and an excruciating headache, he finally managed to get it down. Or so he hoped.

Straightening his legs that had long gone to sleep, he sat at the edge of his bed and slowly began the chant. The spell required no components and was entirely based in focus and time, so, with eyes closed, he sang the song that, in theory, was going to leave an impression in his mind, an image or sense that would address the question he wove repeatedly back into the spell, an impression of the "thing," whatever it might be, to which he might attach his Combat Hop.

The effectiveness of this assumed, of course, that he could understand what the impression meant. This was the real problem with divining. Given how completely little he knew of anything regarding Orli's "technology," he felt his chances were ultimately pretty grim. The odds were he'd get an impression of something that meant nothing to him anyway, like a knight trying to explain the advantage of shifting his charger's lead to someone who's never ridden a horse. He wished he'd had time to rummage through Tytamon's library; he likely could have found a more certain way if he had, but, given the gathering of the orbs somewhere out beyond his view, he had no opportunity to do such a thing. Besides, what would Orli think if she found out that he had gone? She might think that he had run away, and that would never do.

And so he chanted well into a second hour of the spell, his mind open to receive the product of his inquiry, meticulously held blank, staring into darkness maintained through force of will—and still nothing. He felt himself growing weary. And then, finally, as he was about to return to the beginning of what would be his divination's last chanting loop, he saw an image like a dream. In his mind he dimly saw Orli's ship with a shimmer around its length, not entirely unlike that seen when something touched upon his Polar's shield, a flicker like a ripple of hidden light. He got a sense of lightning and something tugging him to the ground. And then it was gone.

But he knew exactly what it meant. The image did not seem vague to him at all, not as he had feared. He'd seen an aura flickering around the ships when the Hostile rams pounded into them. He'd assumed it was part of the Hostile attack, something that happened on impact, but now he knew that it wasn't that at all. Orli's people had a shield of energy all their own, and according to the feel of the divination, it was a suitable anchor for his Combat Hop.

Tired, and weak with hunger, he hadn't eaten in what had to be over a day, he went back up the battlements and waved a sheet of parchment in the air towards Orli's ship. A moment later he saw several amber lights and two bright white ones flicker on and off five times in a row.

With a quick glimpse into the scrying basin just to be sure, he sent himself back to the *Aspect's* bridge. "I have it," he announced when he arrived. "I'm sorry it took so long. I had no idea you had a protective shield."

She looked puzzled, but her face showed that she was happy he was back. "Yes, we do. I'm sorry. I should have told you that we did."

"You could not have known," he said, not wanting her to feel one instant of regret. "It was I who should have asked." He was invigorated just by seeing her again, his hunger gone completely from his mind. Had she told him to leap off of Mt. Pernolde just then, he would have been grateful for the sound of her voice even as he fell. But there were serious matters at hand. He forced his mind to focus.

"All right, if you're ready, I'm prepared to give the spell a try."

Orli conveyed this to the captain who, looking doubtful, nodded.

"Go for it," she said.

"All right. Here goes." He closed his eyes and began the spell that would enchant the ship with Combat Hop. He plunged his mind into the mana flowing all around them, it seemed so thick out here in space—though he could feel it steadily flowing towards the growing mass of orbs—and he grabbed a stream of it intending to feed it into the ship's protective shield. But when he searched for the shield he found it difficult to see. Its power was manaless and almost indiscernible until he figured out how to look. But eventually he found it. Their shields were nothing like his Polar's shield was, not even remotely, but they were made of energy just the same, and so he tried to slip the mana cord inside.

Suddenly everyone was shouting, loud enough that his concentration broke, and he had to let the mana go. The force of the spell's incompletion threw him to the floor, and he had to grasp his head as the pounding in his skull nearly knocked him out. He threw up, and for a time his vision went completely dark. It came back to him, oddly, in eerie shades of red, and sound returned to him as well.

The captain was yelling at him, and Roberto was yammering on about something urgent too. Only Orli seemed to be concerned about Altin lying on the floor, and she was on her knees beside him, her hands cradling his face.

He blinked up at her, his vision still hazy as he tried to make the red glow that filled his vision go away. It was disconcerting and hardly helped him see. He was only vaguely aware of commotion around him as Orli wiped the bile from his lips gently with her sleeve. "Altin," she called to him through the blur that filled his brain. "Altin, are you okay?" Her face hovered above him, angelic but nearly lost in the bloated darkness that was barely held back by the blood-red light.

He shook his head, but could not clear the ringing from his ears, and several moments passed before he could focus enough to muster a coherent thought. Finally, raising an arm to indicate he was recovered enough to stand, he drug himself to his feet. A bit ambitious—he nearly fell, and Orli had to catch him and hold him up awhile. It was at least another minute before he could see.

When he could, he looked around the bridge and saw that the three of them were watching him closely, scrutinizing him each in their own way: Orli was clearly concerned for his safety as she propped him up; Roberto was uneasy, his trust threatened, but beginning to relax and prepared to call whatever happened an accident; and the captain, by his posture, by his hand gripped around his red-light weapon and ready to draw, clearly saw Altin as a continued threat.

The captain's glaring mistrust annoyed Altin to no end. As his thoughts became increasingly clear, he decided he did not like the man at all. The Iris Leopards of String got their name because, according to the stories anyway, they only attack after they see themselves reflected in a victim's eyes. There had to be something of those leopards in the captain as far as Altin was concerned. Altin had done nothing to earn so little faith.

"Tell them not to yell again," he said. "They can't break my focus when I'm casting a spell as complicated as that. There's no place for the mana to go. They'll burn me out. It was lucky I'd just begun."

He could tell that Orli wasn't sure quite what that meant, but she was quick enough to apprehend the essence of his point.

"I'm sorry. We didn't know. I was yelling too." She could feel him standing on his own, and released him to test his strength. He appeared to be okay. "What happened, though? You scared us when it all went dark. You shut down everything on the ship." His quizzical look prompted her to add, "Or something did. It would be an amazing coincidence if it wasn't you."

He had to wait for his head to clear a little more before he could concentrate enough to figure out what went wrong. He frowned and blinked a few more times; he still wasn't seeing right because the red lighting would not go away. But he forced himself to think the whole cast through, going back through every moment of the cadence bit by bit. As he did, normal light returned. He was glad that the horrible red glow had finally faded from his eyes. It helped him think.

"There we go," Orli said, sounding calm. The captain snarled something too.

"What did he say?" Altin asked.

She grimaced. "Basically, he's glad that the power's back and there was no permanent harm."

Altin was certain that the captain's comments had not been so benign, but he knew it was important to figure out what went wrong. "Give me a moment to try to figure it out," he said. "Let me think."

He closed his eyes and muttered a few words, playing out into the mana stream again, this time only intending to have a look. With a filament of mana so thin as to hardly be a thread, he tapped the shield around the ship as lightly as one might test a pot handle with a finger to see if it was hot. The gentle probe told him exactly what he needed to know, and he let the spell go only moments after he'd begun. He came out of it as Orli screamed at the captain to "put the laser down," and as both Roberto and the captain were shouting as loudly as they could. He saw that the lights were flickering back on as well, darkness dissipating the moment he opened his eyes.

Altin turned to regard the captain and simply shook his head as he saw that the captain's red-light weapon was leveled at his head. That man was incapable of trust. However, Altin was even more surprised when he turned back to Orli to find that her weapon was drawn as well. It was pointed at the captain's chest. Altin blanched and let out a muffled grunt. This was an unexpected turn. He needed to end this standoff quickly before it got out of hand.

"Tell him I know what I did wrong."

She hardly dared to look at him, keeping her eyes on the captain and his raised red-light gun.

"Tell him," Altin repeated. "Tell him it was an accident, but that I have it figured out. I almost broke your shield. I did not know it was so...," he cut himself off, unwilling to call it weak. "I did not know it was so delicate. I won't make that mistake again."

Orli repeated what he had said. The captain was apparently unwilling to believe.

Roberto said something to the captain then, which the captain countered with whatever he said next.

"Oh for God's sake, Captain," Orli nearly spat, "if he wanted to kill us, he would have done it already. How can you possibly be so fucking naïve? Jesus. Just shoot us both and get it over with then."

Altin decided he might have been a bit quick in assuming

Orli had nothing of the hardened warrior in her. It seemed that she was not completely soft and gentle after all.

"Tell him I can do it now," he said, hoping he still had time to save anyone from being shot. "Although your lamps may flicker once again, I will not put them out." He realized that their shield was somehow connected to their lamps, and perhaps much of their other "technology" too, and Altin understood what he had done. He'd simply pushed too hard. Their shield was as brittle as an egg shell and had to be treated as such. But he could do it now. "Tell him," he urged again.

Orli repeated his message, adding a few words of her own. Roberto seemed once more to have to back her up. Eventually the captain gave in.

"Do it," Orli said at length. "But you better do it quick. I'm not sure the captain's up for a whole lot more."

"I will. I promise it will be all right this time."

She smiled her winsome smile, and once more he began to chant. This time he cast the spell slowly, poking the mana into their shield with the care one saves for threading a needle or petting a hatchling chick. And finally it was done.

He came out of the spell and, as expected, saw that the lights were coming on. "Sorry about your lamps," he said. "There's nothing for that I'm afraid."

Orli told her shipmates that Altin's spell was done. He watched as the two of them looked about the room, as if searching for some evidence that the magic was in place. Roberto, after a few moments like that, said something to Orli in a clearly questioning tone.

"He wants to know if we have to do anything to make it work."

"No. There's nothing. It simply will. I can't promise it won't dim your lamps every time. But they should come back on as they have these last two times. You should know that your whole ship is going to have moved to another place. The shift might be disorienting if you're not ready for it, as your ships will be blinking out of the way each time an orb sends one of its battering rams. It's an unsettling spell at first. It took me some time getting used to it when I began using it back at home. But you will grow accustomed to it too. Everyone does."

She smiled up at him, her face so beautiful and pure. He was so glad he'd finally made the spell work. He could not have endured failing her.

She turned in response to a tone coming from her seeing mirror and began chatting with a face that appeared within its shiny surface. Watching her using that device certainly made it seem as if there was magic taking place, a kind of sight merged with telepathy. It was an interesting combination, and the image was remarkably crisp and clear. He wished his scrying basin could be used to summon sound. From the half of the conversation he could make out, it was obvious that the other ship was eager to find out if Altin's spell was going to work.

The captain said something that was little more than a snarl as he stepped over and had a few words with the man on the other side of Orli's looking glass.

Finally Orli turned back to Altin, saying, "The other ships are ready for you to come."

"Tell them about the targets on the floor," he warned. "I don't want any more accidents." He looked sideways at the captain and added, "Or any more red lights in the chest."

She nodded, her face an oasis in the black desert of this eternal night. "I did."

"Tell them again, just to be sure."

She stepped up to him and kissed him on the mouth. He nearly swooned. By all the gods, she was an assertive thing. "I'll tell them," she said, laughing as he blinked his vision back. "Now go."

He smirked, and let the feel of her lips radiate across the

landscape of his body like the warmth of the sun rising over a dew-cooled hill. Though tired, haggard and hungry, he had enough strength now to enchant a thousand ships.

He wanted to say something appropriate back, something a hero from Prosperion's epic myths would say at such a time, but she silenced him with a finger on his mouth. "Just go. And hurry back." He smiled again, glad that she had saved him from appearing inarticulate.

Still a little dizzy from her kiss, he closed his eyes and began to chant. He had a lot of work to do.

Chapter 42

By the time Altin had enchanted the last of the four ships, the strength borrowed from Orli's kiss was almost entirely gone. He left the bridge of the final ship to a host of grateful, if perhaps slightly skeptical, smiles. The captains of the other vessels were far more congenial than Orli's captain was, and all in all, the experience was a pleasant one. Orli's people were a colorful bunch, not only in their many shades of skin, but in their love of laughter too. He found that even though he could not understand any of them, most of the people that he met were fast to smile and quick to laugh. They all seemed ready to want to like him and to clap him on the back, and, in truth, he was happy to meet them as well. However, once he was back in his tower, all of the energy simply drained from him and he collapsed onto his bed.

He needed sleep so desperately that he could hardly think anymore. His head lolled to the side, cradled in the soft embrace of his pillow, and he saw the empty space where his food crate normally sat. His stomach growled as if reminding him that the crate should be sitting there and that he hadn't eaten in what felt like months. He wondered if Kettle had had a chance to refill it yet—assuming she even would, given how mad she was at him. He looked over to the bread sitting on his table and gave a grunt; it was likely as hard as stone. He didn't have the energy to get back up anyway, though perhaps he had enough for one more cast. He could retrieve the crate and set it down right here, right within his reach. He was so hungry.

With enormous effort he swung his legs around and sat up with his feet upon the floor. He struggled with his vision, blurred as it was, and had to blink several times just to bring some liquidity to the dryness that gave his sight a haze. A long rumble traced its way through the maze of innards beneath his ribs. He took a breath and forced himself to clarity.

Fighting for focus, he began the cast that would bring the crate back from Calico Castle with something in it for him to eat. He closed his eyes and carefully sounded the measured cadences that underlay chant, and after slightly more time than it normally took, his crate finally arrived. But it was too late for Altin, the spell sapped the last of his strength and he fell back into the bed, unable to rise again. Breakfast would have to wait until he slept. He just hoped the Hostiles would not attack before he had time to eat. He didn't think he could cast again without fuel.

But there would be no such luck, for when he awoke a few hours later, he found that hunger was the least of his concerns. A thin rain of dust was falling down from the ceiling and most of his books had just crashed noisily to the floor, and those that did not hit the floor, landed on his head.

He shook the fatigue from his mind and mounted the stairs at a run. When he reached the battlements, he saw that his tower was spinning wildly, giving him a nauseating view of the Earth fleet as it wobbled in and out of sight while the tower cartwheeled through the night—he'd been hit, and he hadn't reset the stasis element of his Polar's shield.

He spoke the word that stopped the spin and quickly looked about trying to assess his circumstance. His mouth fell open as he looked out into the sky. Orbs swarmed everywhere, and Altin couldn't even begin to count just how many there were darting about like a cloud of bats dipping insects from the surface of a pond. There had to be at least five hundred, probably more. And they were attacking the ships just as Altin had feared they would, in ordered formations of eight to ten, sending organized waves, patient enough to do their work right this time, and clearly with enough numbers in reserve to keep up the attacks until they finally did. Apparently his Combat Hop was working well enough though, for he could see that the ships he'd enchanted were indeed blinking in and out of sight, a flashing play of light reflecting off the long bright ships as they appeared and reappeared randomly amongst a crisscross of red-light beams and the occasional white flash of an exploding pellet bomb. He was glad of that. But he knew from experience that it only took one lucky shot—or one unlucky Combat Hop—and the light play would become a fireball instead. He needed to help them out. And most of all, he needed to get to Orli's ship.

He realized immediately, however, that he had troubles of his own, and it seemed that the orbs might be aware of who it was that had introduced this magical element into the Earth fleet's options for defense. Or else they knew where their real problems actually lay. Two groups of ten orbs each were hovering on either side of his tower, but not moving yet. Perhaps they had paused, thinking their last shot had done the trick, but the righting of the tower proved them wrong and so they came for yet another pass.

They darted in together at their incredible rate of speed, and in unison twenty giant battering rams were hurtling on their way, staggered in distance so as to arrive not quite all at once. Altin watched them streaking in, thinking that avoiding them would be like dodging hailstones the size of cottages. Gritting his teeth, he braced for a concussive blow, then thought to release the stasis spell again "just in case," hoping it would mitigate the damage if the Hostiles did get another lucky strike.

Combat Hop took him out of range, however, and all twenty missiles hurtled out of sight. Altin rushed to get a teleport-merge started, and a moment later two of the orbs were spinning broken into the night. He managed to get a second pair before all of the orbs had recaptured their weapons and regrouped for another pass. He got a third pair as they came rushing towards him, their spherical masses bursting open just before his tower blinked safely away at the approach of the hurtling granite rams. He managed to finished off two more pairs as the orbs streaked silently across his field of view. And he got another as those that remained turned and tried to get away, teleporting up to them and capturing them in his crushing magical grip before they could get out of range.

"Hah, hah," he laughed. "Run, cowards. A teleporter is here. And I'm not afraid to break the rules!"

His jubilation was brief, however, as one of the Earth ships was suddenly enveloped in a brilliant ball of explosive yellow light. A moment later it broke in two, its halves drifting apart, spurting flames and clouds of debris from many places along its battered hull. Altin could see human bodies amongst the wreckage being jettisoned from openings in the decimated ship, and his heart nearly fell from its place inside his chest.

"Orli!" he cried, leaning so far forward in his attempt to see that he nearly tumbled over the wall. In a panic, he suddenly realized that with all the Combat-Hopping about, he could no longer tell which ship was which. They all looked so infernally the same. He had no idea if that had been Orli's ship.

He threw himself on the floor near his scrying basin and muttered into it, willing Orli's face to come into its view. It did not. At first, all the world went dark as Altin felt himself begin to curl up and die.

But then he realized that Combat Hop had made her ship move. She was no longer where she was supposed to be. Scrying was like teleporting, you had to know precisely where you wanted the spell to appear or it could not do its work. Orli was no longer exactly where he thought.

"Tidalwrath's fits," he cursed, scanning the sky in hopes of some miracle that would reveal which ship was hers.

But he had his new divining spell. He cursed again for having wasted precious seconds having not thought of it before. *Stupid mage, gather your wits.*

With a cherished image of her held in his mind, he began the chant that cast to the tune of "My Cat's Paw." He just wanted to know where she was. He prayed to all nine gods as he began, swearing reverence to them forever if only she were still alive. A moment later he knew that in fact she was.

Not only could he sense that she was still alive and on her ship, he could also feel the depths of her unprecedented fear. He knew in that instant that she was not so much the warrior after all. There was not one drop of battle lust coursing through her veins, not one iota of her was thirsting for a kill. The only thing keeping her focused on the task at hand was her will to live. She fought on with stubbornness alone, stubbornness and the desire to save her friends. And the Hostiles were trying to take that away from her. To take her away from him.

He felt the rage come back to him again; the old rage; the familiar one; the burning, primal hatred that he'd felt down in the canyon where Pernie had been taken by the orcs; and sadly, the same one that had filled him on that day his sister died. He felt it pour into him like the waves of demons summoned upon the isle of Duador, a seething mass of acidic hate that could now be channeled at his foe. It did not blind him this time, not as it had when he was young. At least not quite. The sound of "menace" bounced around inside him, a thin strand of consciousness that could just keep him from losing touch. He would not lose sight of Orli, no matter what he did. His magic would not hurt the ones he loved; he was never doing that again, but he could use his anger to break some rules.

Letting the divination go, he strode over to the wooden bowl behind him and took up the Liquefying Stone. Gripping it in his fist, he swung back to look into the scene raging above. It was time for the coconuts to die.

The combined power of Altin's rage and the Liquefying Stone transformed what had started out as merged pairs of Hostiles into merged dozens, then fifteens, then twenties. Range became less of an issue too. He teleported his tower defensively out in front of the struggling knot of ships. He floated before them all and defied the entire host of orbs to come at him alone. Many of them did.

For every wave of eight they sent at a lumbering ship from Earth, they sent a wave of twenty, and then forty, as they realized that Altin was the most imposing force. But Altin did not care. Huge lumps of merged Hostile orbs were now tumbling away from the battle like disfigured mountains, melted volcanoes murdered and trailing long lines of glowing lava goo. The entire scene seemed a tiger's pelt for all the streaks of orange and black striping across the stars. And still Altin raged. Not even bothering to chant, not needing to. Raw magic, happening with just a thought.

His tower was struck twice in the randomness of Hostile luck, made more likely by the ever-increasing size of the formations the Hostiles were sending at him now. But still he did not care. Better him than her. "Send them all," he screamed as the fury and the lust for killing boiled inside his veins. On a surge of emotion twenty-four Hostiles became a massive broken mass.

Every time an Earth ship blew apart, Altin sung his Cat's Paw song, feeling Orli with his mind and heart, just to know that she was still alive. As long as she was there, he could continue in the fight. He could not allow himself to think of any other fate.

"Send them to me. Send them all," he screamed again as he merged three waves of thirty into one unfathomably large and decimated lump, ninety gone in a single "shot." He had gone to a place beyond bloodlust. He had never felt so alive, so focused on any singular goal in all his life. Save her. Save her at any cost. He was exultant in his love and in his rage. He could feel his mythothalamus nearly glowing with the heat. This was power.

He sent out a telepathic call daring anything that might hear it to come and take him on. There were at least three hundred of the orbs still racing through the night. And it seemed as if they heard him, for suddenly the attacks on the Earth ships came abruptly to a halt.

Altin felt the resonance of his telepathic taunt reverberate in his mind like a well struck drum. He grinned as he saw the remainder of the orbs begin to form into several groups from ten to thirty each. He laughed at them, and spat out into the air over the parapet. "Come on," he shouted on telepathic waves as his teeth ground like a miller's stone.

He clutched the Liquefying Stone so tightly that it broke the skin, slicking the stone with the spill of blood, but he did not feel a thing. He grabbed an ocean's worth of mana into his head and cast it out like a net over the nearest cluster of the orbs, defying with savage disregard the distance "required" by his spell as he drew the net tight around them, squeezing them all into a wad as he collapsed it and ruptured the lot of them with a cosmic pop that sent a measure-long gout of ichor spewing across the darkness like a burst boil. He cackled with maniacal delight and plunged back into the mana to gather up another net to cast.

The orbs sent their formations at him from every side, groups coming from everywhere, and coming wave after wave after wave. His tower blinked in and out of sight, dodging battering rams with instantaneous speed, though from time to time one of them struck it a glancing blow. He'd left the stasis spell off, and he no longer cared if the spinning made it impossible to see. He saw within the mana now, and he was a creature of the Liquefying Stone. He crushed the orbs as they soared past; it was like grasping grapes and making wine in magical fists. They died in an endless spray of orange, spitting their juices into the night time and again, yet still coming, undaunted by the scattered husks of their broken fellows spinning away with each successive pass. They were undeterred, no matter how many Altin merged. On and on they came. And Altin crushed them as fast as he could.

It seemed as if he might actually destroy them all too, so long as his shield held out, but then, just as he was feeling certain that he would, just as the last three waves of them came at him from top and bottom and side, just as they came in what was going to be their final pass, they got their lucky shot—and actually, they got three.

Staggering their attacks just enough to have weapons incoming in perfect increments of space and time, three of the huge battering rams slammed brutally into Altin's Polar shield. Miraculously, the shield itself held up, but Altin's tower could not. The impact shook the ancient stone so hard it knocked loose the tower's entire outer wall. The battlements collapsed, falling outward and crashing to the ground, bringing Altin with them, tumbling down amidst a jumble of giant blocks of stone. He had only the vaguest sense of falling before he hit the ground, and then, with a hazy image of Orli's face and crushing sense of regret, the light that was in them slowly left his eyes.

Chapter 43

Orli screamed. A long, horrified "No!" that leapt from her lips as if it were a living thing forced out of her body by the heat of agony. She sprung from her chair and ran to the portion of the viewing screen where Altin's broken tower could be seen amidst the stars, a cloud of dust still rising from the tumbled heap of stone lying at the tower's base. She placed her hands on the monitor, fingers clutching at either side of the image as if she might somehow hold it together, might, somehow, put it back. "No, no, no," she muttered beneath her breath, a frenzied whisper as she clawed at the image frantically. But she couldn't put it back. The unfathomable magnitude of the loss stunned her, spreading outward from the core of her body like a blast wave of godless cold, freezing her in place. Helpless. Several moments passed before she could scream again, a long and piteous wail rooted in death of hope. The sound carried louder than her thin body would visually admit, and her anguish lingered for a time as it echoed through the bridge and down the elevator shaft causing crewmates on every deck to turn towards it with looks of fright.

"Pewter, get back to your post. We can't help him if you don't do your job. Sit down, damn it," barked the captain.

Vaguely, she felt Roberto's arm slip around her waist, gripping her firmly, but pulling her gently away from the enormous viewing screen. "He's right," Roberto was saying from somewhere far away. "Come on. Sit back down." He half dragged, half carried her back and pushed her down into her seat. "Come on, Orli. He needs you now more than ever. Snap out of it. Focus. We can still save him."

His words came to her dimly, as if he'd whispered them from the opposite end of the ship. But she heard them, reluctantly, and suddenly the horrified lethargy was gone, or at least suspended for a while.

Twenty orbs remained, and of the original eighteen ships, seven still survived—three of them enchanted with Altin's Combat Hop. The Hostiles had apparently figured out early in the fight that some of the Earth ships had been magically enhanced, and they had made a point of going after the unenchanted ships in force, perhaps intent on thinning the fleet's numbers down. But whatever the reasoning, assuming the Hostiles did any reasoning at all, the effects were devastating to those who'd been too intimidated or too skeptical to let the wizard come aboard their ships. Nonetheless, the *Aspect* and six others were still alive. Victory was possible now; it was still a long shot, but at least they had a chance. Altin had given them a chance. But it seemed the Hostiles had decided now was the time to go after the enchanted ships instead.

A wave of eight orbs was coming at them now. "Focus," she heard Roberto say again. "Bring up *Pegasus*."

She tapped up the Echo squadron ship and could see the weapons officer's face in profile as the link came up on her screen. "Here," the man said, a long cut on his cheek marking where his face must have hit the console following one of the Hostile's "lucky" shots.

"*Pegasus*, on my mark, lasers on the top two, left. Stagger missiles at intervals of a hundred feet," Roberto said once the link was made.

"On it," said the man.

"Not too close on the near side. I'm not in the mood for friendly fire."

"No worries, *Aspect*. I got you, mate."

The orbs came in, always with that impossible speed, and, as expected, in came a barrage of giant, pulverizing shafts, eight of them, primitive granite slabs capable of decimating all this modern technology while irony had a laugh. Roberto fired lasers into the sandy spots of the uppermost pair just prior to the release of stony shafts, and he sent a battery of missiles off in a scatter all around the pair, anticipating their infuriating dodge abilities. He barely got them fired before Combat Hop went off, sending the ship into momentary darkness and the navigation computers into temporary disarray.

Used to the sequence of events by now, Orli and her bridge mates waited impatiently as the computers recalculated their position from readings taken from nearby stars and as the other systems came back online. Though it seemed like hours, the systems restored themselves in seconds and finally they could look to see if their counterattack had had any significant effect.

"Fuck yeah," Roberto shouted. "Got them both."

And he was right, for both orbs were bleeding spouts of glowing goo as they moved away from the ship. One was totally ruined, broken open like an oil drum blown up from inside, and the other, while not completely destroyed, didn't appear to have enough glowing guts remaining to carry on with the fight. It retreated, moving back to hover at a distance behind what remained of the Hostile host, trailing a thin line of the luminous ichor as if unraveling a spool of red-hot copper wire.

"Bring it on, bitches," Roberto bellowed at the monitor on the wall. "You brought this shit on yourselves."

Another wave, ten this time, was hurtling at the *Lima* in the group of Bravo squadron ships, and Roberto was instantly retaken by the gravity of the fight. "*Lima*," he barked at Orli before the captain could get the same word out. Orli tapped it up. "Which one you want?" Roberto queried to their weapon's officer. "Lower left," came the woman's voice.

"On it," Roberto said. "You want to call it, or on my go?"

"You're the only one hitting anything out here," the woman said. "On yours."

"Roger," he said. "Lasers on the shafts, spread the missiles wide."

"I know what to do," the woman answered. "It's the goddamn timing I can't get down."

"Who's got another pair?"

"*Pershing's* got the top one on the starboard side," came a voice over general com. "I'll do my best to make it count."

"Just let them have it on my mark, most of them release at the same damn time. We'll leave the laggers to magic and some luck."

"Roger," came the *Pershing's* reply.

"Here they come. Be ready...," Roberto said, his voice somehow calm and charged all at once. "Now." He jammed his fingers into the glowing lights on his console that would fire both lasers and a pair of missiles from the *Aspect's* arsenal to help with the *Lima's* defense.

Again Roberto was right on target, and another of the orbs broke open and sprayed the surface of the *Lima* with its phosphorescent blood. The *Lima's* own weapons did some damage to the second as it whistled past, though it was not a killing blow. Still, from the cheer that came across the channel, she was happy with her shot. "Goddamn," she said. "I finally hit one."

"Nice. Now focus. *California* has incoming too."

Orli had already tapped them up.

And so began a dance of death that went on for nearly half an hour. She and Roberto, driven by their reactions to what had happened to Altin right before their eyes, became a force that was a magic of its own. Together they brought ship-to-ship communication that had been chaotic and laced with fear prior to Altin's downfall into something more like a finely tuned machine. Computers might not be able to anticipate the magic-using orbs, but human instinct could. Roberto had been coordinating a lot before, but now, as Orli's whole body and soul worked only for the battle's end, her focus was supreme. She had the links to the various ships open before Roberto could tell her which one he wanted her to call. Pretty soon, he was barking orders to the weapons officers with no more thought for hierarchy or command. He simply knew what had to be shot, when and by whom. Even the captains realized right away that Roberto was on his game, and soon the airwaves were silent but for his singular voice and the occasional victory cry as one orb after another burst into a gush of glowing orange.

And finally it was done. The last of the orbs, the only two that remained, went crushed and leaking off into the night.

Orli didn't even wait for the sound of cheering to finish in her com speaker before she was down the lift and sprinting through the corridors headed for an emergency pod. Never had there been such an emergency in all her life. She could hear the captain's voice on her com link ordering her back to her post, but there was nothing he could say. He could sooner command the Andalians back from extinction than he could have gotten her to stop.

She stabbed the hatch release at the pod dock at least twenty times, mashing its infernal blinking button over and over with her finger, breaking a nail and violently bending her slender fingertip backwards against the joint. "Open goddamn it," she shouted at the console as the hydraulics slowly pushed the hatch outward from the pod.

Finally a space opened wide enough for her to squeeze through, and she wriggled inside, jamming the pod's hatch button again with her palm. She threw herself into the seat and waited for it to close, breath coming to her in ragged pants. The six seconds it took to release the tiny escape craft from the launch tube was an agony of years, and Orli could hardly see the controls through an impatient mist of tears. "Hurry up," she screamed at it again.

Once out of the ship, she engaged the throttle and quickly closed the distance between her and Altin's tower, which was now drifting slowly away from the fleet. It turned slowly as it moved, tumbling gently, end over end, as if it were falling through a dream. The tower's shield shimmered as it spun, flickering as if it might wink out, and it was no longer invisible as it had been when Altin had first arrived. She stared through Altin's shield, seeking him out with frantic eyes. But there was such a mess. The inside of his enchanted dome looked like some macabre medieval snowglobe robbed of festivity, its snowflakes transformed to misery and the nightmare of Orli's breaking heart. As she drew closer she spotted him lying amidst the debris, and she brought her tiny craft right up to the tower's flickering energy field. It wasn't until the pod's docking hatch window was bumping gently against the shield that she realized how little there was that she could do, how helpless she really was. All she could do was watch. The tower had no docking bay, no way to get inside.

But she could see him there, only a few feet from where she was. She could see him lying in a crumpled pile, wedged horribly amongst a jumble of giant stones and ivy that seemed to stir as if caught in an inexplicable breeze. A flow of crimson issued from him, from a wound she could not see, and painted the flat surface of the granite block over which he lay with red lines that branched as they ran, tiny rivers that carried his life away. The dark blood flowed from him steadily, spreading like a scarlet shadow being cast, and she could tell from the volume of it, as much as from her time in sick bay, that he could not hold out for long.

What was worse, as she stared at him she realized that his back had been broken when he fell. Broken in two. From the way his body was folded over the edge of the granite block, an acute angle like a towel tossed over the back of someone's chair, she knew she had no chance of saving him at all. Even if she could get inside the dome, there would be nothing she could do.

She screamed again and tears began to run as freely as did Altin's blood. She couldn't just sit out here and watch him die. She needed to go to him. To be with him so he didn't have to die alone. Alone out here in this awful empty place.

Frantic, she steeled herself again, forced herself to think. She searched the pod's instrument panel, seeking anything that might get her in. The laser! she thought. I'll cut my way in. She began tapping at the keys. Almost too late, she realized through her frenzied grief that even if the laser did cut through his shield, she would only freeze him where he lay. She stopped only a keystroke from having begun to cut.

The last gasp of hope left her on the sigh that followed. Tears came again, burning from her eyes as she sobbed and pressed her face against the pod's bubbled window glass, fogging it with her breath as she watched, helpless and overwhelmed with grief.

Then a movement coming from around a still upright portion of the tower wall caught her eye. At first she thought it was just the ivy, moving in that incoherent breeze, but as she sought the movement out, she saw the most unexpected thing. A child had arrived.

She watched in a hazy dreamlike state as a little blonde girl came out and picked her way carefully across the rubble of giant broken stones. The going was slow, for the gray blocks were much bigger than the girl, and she had to stop occasionally to shake off tendrils of ivy that kept catching at her feet. But the child was resolute and continued to work her way steadily over and around the heap of decimated stone.

Orli stopped crying, her tears in check as the impossibility of what she saw caught somewhere in her chest. For a time she could no longer breathe.

The girl was a scrawny little thing, no more than six or seven years old. And even through her horror and her grief, part of Orli's mind could not help wondering what the child was doing there. Altin hadn't mentioned anyone else; in fact he'd been quite clear that it was only he and the dragon that had come. She wondered if Altin was married, and if this girl was Altin's child. But the thought quickly went away. He would have had to get an early start to have a child as old as this. Wouldn't he?

She shook herself and realized that she had to get the child out. Concern for the girl broke through the trauma of her inability to prevent Altin's death. They had to do something; they couldn't just leave her out here alone. She found a moment's composure and immediately called back to the ship. "Do you see her?" she asked.

"We see her," came Roberto's voice, doing double duty now and having to cover the communication's com.

The girl, hair frosted grayish in places with dust from the collapse, and with a trickle of blood running down her cheek from where a stone must have grazed her head, picked her way to the place where Altin lay. She stared down at him and appeared to be speaking to him urgently. When he didn't answer, she fumbled around inside the collar of his robes for a moment and then, placing two small hands beneath his neck, she gently lifted up his head. She pulled something from around his neck, slipping it over his head and then, struggling some with the weight of a grown man's skull, momentarily dangled what she'd taken in the air.

It was a small red amulet hanging on a leather cord, and the girl regarded the gemstone only briefly before gripping it firmly between her fingertips. She looked up then, pausing, and stared right out at Orli staring back. She gave a tired little smile, waving once, and then, placing her free hand on Altin's chest, she struck the amulet against the bloody stone upon which she knelt. And then they were gone. All of it was gone. The tower, the girl and the incredible green-eyed mage. Gone. As if it had all just been a dream.

Orli plunged her face into her hands and sobbed violently, her whole body convulsing and tears running down her wrists. All of her that mattered left when that tower went away.

Nearly twenty hours would pass before Roberto could finally coax Orli back aboard the ship. He tried to warn her that the captain was in a fit, that she shouldn't have run out there in the pod without having at least gotten permission first. But Orli no longer cared. All she wanted was to die.

Chapter 44

Orli lay on the hard bunk in her cell in a state nearing catatonia. She had lost weight, down to a scant ninety-seven pounds, and her lean runner's body now hovered on the brink of wasting away. Doctor Singh had been sneaking nutrient powder into her water for the last two months just to keep her alive, but it was difficult to sustain someone who had so completely given up.

At first he'd thought it was just a case of broken heart, for word got round shortly after the fight, and certainly after the trial, that Orli had fallen for the robed man from planet Prosperion. However, the pall that settled on her was more than just a case of lovesick lament. No, what Orli had was the total abandonment of hope. The loss of her newfound love had brought back the deep depression that she had only barely kept at bay, a malignant creeping darkness that seeped like oil from a ruptured tank and spread slowly into everything, smothering any positive emotion that it found. Losing Altin had simply been the final straw the way the doctor saw it, one tragedy too much. Orli was not cut out for living decades in outer space. She never had been; it just wasn't in her genes.

Roberto and Doctor Singh were the only ones who saw

her now, excepting her father, the colonel, who came by occasionally and sat before the Plexiglas cell in his bright yellow contamination suit and tried not to weep as his daughter lay unresponsive and in a state of emotional decay. Sometimes she would sit up and talk to him, but usually not. It was much the same for the doctor and Roberto too. When she did, the conversations were generally the same regardless of who was sitting outside her cell:

"Hey girl. You're finally awake."

"I am."

"How are you feeling?"

"Fine."

"You need to eat more."

"I know."

Usually an uncomfortable silence would follow, and then she would ask, "Is he back?"

The answer was always the same. "No."

Generally at that point she would lie back down. That was it. Frankly, her hopelessness was too depressing for most, which was why there were no regular visitors left but the doctor and her Spanish friend. Only they had the stamina to endure her desolation anymore. Her decline was enough to be almost as contagious as the disease she had helped them all survive.

Doctor Singh was sitting outside her cell on yet another uneventful visit, watching her through the glass, when he got a glimmer of hope that at least today might be one of Orli's days to talk. Even a few words were better than none. But it turned out to be just a twitch, as her arm nearest the wall jerked up towards her ear as if she had an itch. He thought her attention to such stimuli was promising; it could mean a resurgent concern for the condition of her body, but after a while he gave it up as hope. She settled back into motionless, and Doctor Singh settled back into watching her, lost inside his thoughts. But then her arm twitched again, once more shooting up to scratch beside her ear.

She did it again, three more times. He assumed she must be dreaming, reaching up to where Altin had taken cuttings from her hair; she did that often enough, dreamt of Altin. He heard her speak the young man's name from time to time in bouts of restless sleep. He felt so sorry for the girl. They never should have brought her into space. What had the colonel been thinking?

Her arm twitched again and then she sat up, flicking at her shoulder as if she'd woken to find a spider crawling there. Then she lay back down. But the doctor saw that she had knocked something away, and whatever it was came scurrying near the glass.

Doctor Singh bent down towards the floor and squinted at the impossible sight. There was a lizard standing on the deck, no longer than a scalpel and barely twice as thick. This was impossible, however, for there were no animals on the ship. And unless he had completely lost his mind, there was a note tied to this lizard's back as well. He immediately called for the guard to open the door to Orli's cell.

The lizard was apparently unafraid of people, and Doctor Singh had no trouble scooping it up off of the floor. And there was, in fact, a note strapped to its narrow back. He untied the string and unwound the strip of yellowed paper from the creature's torso. He handed the lizard to the waiting guard, both of them beyond curious to see what was written on the note. He opened up the paper, holding the yellowed parchment taut between both hands.

He couldn't read a word.

"Damn," he said.

"What's it say?" asked the guard.

"I don't know," replied Doctor Singh. "But I bet I know who it's from." With an order that the lizard not be lost, Doctor Singh ran back to sick bay holding the note before him as if letting it out of his sight might make it go away. He ran straight back and into the area where Altin had first cast his language magic and had spoken to them all. It was just a hunch, but the doctor was hoping he might be able to read the note while standing there.

He could not.

He stared down at the paper, trying to will it to coherence, but still the markings made no sense to him at all. The disappointment struck like a physical blow, and the walk back down to the brig seemed very long.

"Well," said the guard when Doctor Singh returned, "you figure out what it says?"

"No. It didn't work." He studied the note sadly for a while, but at length allowed a melancholy smile to come upon his lips. At least Altin was alive. Or at least the doctor hoped he was. That discovery might be enough to bring poor Orli back. "Give me the lizard," he said reaching out his hand.

The guard handed it back to him, and Doctor Singh carefully wound the note back around the lizard and secured it once more with the string. Then he went inside the cell.

"Hey, you're not supposed to be in there unless she's sick."

He shot the guard straight through with his dark eyes. "She's sick."

The guard took a step back and raised his hands defensively. "It's cool. Go ahead."

Doctor Singh sat on the edge of Orli's bed and placed the lizard on her chest. He stroked her hair gently and called her name. "Orli," he said. "Orli, wake up, child. Someone's sent you a note."

Orli turned her head away from him, staring blankly at the wall.

"Orli," he persisted. "Wake up, girl. I think Altin's trying to communicate with you."

She turned her head back, looking up at him with eyes

that were sunken and red-rimmed. She spoke the name in a hoarse whisper. "Altin?"

"Yes," he said. "Look." He nodded towards the lizard on her chest.

She raised her head enough to see the tiny creature staring back at her. It rotated its head slightly, almost expectantly.

"Read it," he said. "I think Altin sent a note."

She reached up and took the lizard gently in her hand, sitting up as she did. "What did he say," she said. "Did you read it?"

"I can't. His spell in sick bay is gone. Or else it doesn't work in context with a note."

She fumbled with the string, her fingers unused to doing anything these last few months, but finally got it off and took the note from around the lizard's body.

Dearest Orli,

I'm sorry for the long delay, but it seems I had a bit of trouble there at the end of the fight. I am fine, and Dr. Leopold says that I may be able to cast again in perhaps a month or two. Please write back and tell me that you are alive. If I don't hear from you, my recovery will have been in vain as I have no intention of going on without you. Speak my name and throw the lizard to the floor, it will return to me.

All my love,

Altin

i.a. Taot sends his regards.

When the tears finally stopped, Orli's eyes filled with fire. "A pen. I need a pen." She looked up at Doctor Singh who only shrugged.

"I haven't had a pen in years."

"Get me a goddamn pen!" She was frantic, even furious. She looked at the guard. "There has to be something to write with on this ship. Get it!"

Startled, he took a step back from the ferocity of her

command. These people are all so touchy, he thought. He hadn't had this much activity down here in a while. But, despite her being the prisoner and all, he couldn't help being caught up in what was going on. And besides, nearly everyone in the fleet saw Orli as something of a romantic hero; most had been disappointed upon hearing the verdict of her trial: guilty on all counts. But, in the end, rules were rules, and if discipline fell apart, well—the fleet couldn't run on anarchy. And so she'd been locked away.

But that did nothing to help him find a pen. Such devices were just not in use anymore. He shrugged, splaying his hands out helplessly. There was nothing he could do.

"I have an idea," blurted Doctor Singh. "Wait right here." Then he was gone. Orli had never seen him run like that before. He was like a little boy again. She felt like a little girl too. Her emaciated body was filling up with the possibility of joy. Altin was alive. That was all that mattered. The rest would work itself out in time.

The doctor came trotting back, panting. "I'm too old for this," he said as he flopped down on the bunk at Orli's side. He handed her a small, cylindrical device with a long button mid-way down.

"A laser scalpel?"

"I turned it all the way down. It might be low enough to use. Try it, just be ready to put the paper out if it gets too hot."

She nodded and spread the note out on her bed. She pressed the button and tentatively wrote a word. The scalpel worked perfectly, charring the paper lightly wherever the light beam struck. It was only a matter of moments before Orli had completed her brief reply:

I am alive. Come back to me. I love you.
Orli

She tied the note back onto the lizard and did just as Altin had instructed, speaking his name then tossing the lizard to the floor. In a blink it was gone.

Doctor Singh let out a hearty laugh. "How about that," he said. "What a remarkable thing."

Orli smiled a dreamy, wistful smile and lay back down on the bed. "What a remarkable thing," she repeated. "What a remarkable thing."

Chapter 45

A tightness wound around Altin's guts as more and more moments passed, a dread serpent winding its way amongst his intestines, coiling round and tightening with each moment that Orli did not respond. *She could be writing me back a very long note*, he told himself as he lay breathing meticulously slow and struggling not to panic as seconds were ticking past.

Doctor Leopold came back into Altin's hospital room and waddled up to his bed. "I was right," the doctor said, spreading the eyelids of Altin's left eye wide with a pair of thick fingers and staring deep inside. The doctor had had garlic pheasant for lunch, which now caused Altin to wince, the motion pulling his eyelids free from the doctor's grasp. The doctor frowned slightly at this, but continued speaking as he reclaimed the escaped folds of skin and spread them apart again. "You'll be casting in no time. Within a month or two."

"I know. You just said that half an hour ago," Altin complained as Doctor Leopold switched to the other eye. "And what's taking her so long?"

"Well I should think you'd rather like the news," the doctor answered. "It's certainly good enough to repeat." He stared through Altin's pupil briefly, his seasoned breath heavy and audible, then pulled away, leaving Altin to blink a few times as he added, "And what is taking who so long?"

"Orli. She should have answered by now."

"Answered what?"

"My note. I sent a homing lizard. It should be back by now."

The doctor looked surprised, his voluminous chins piling up at his throat and causing his neck to swell beneath his ears as he recoiled a bit. "I didn't know you'd gotten her imprinted on one of them."

"She imprinted through Taot. Like I did."

"Ah, well, all the better for you both. Perhaps she can get you to stop moping about and speed your recovery along."

"She's not answering." Altin would not say more. He could not say more. To speak the dread aloud was to give the serpent in his guts permission to further tighten around his soul. What if she hadn't made it through the fight? What if the Earth ships had been destroyed? He didn't think he could bear it if that turned out to be the case. Until Aderbury had given him the homing lizard idea an hour ago, he'd allowed himself to hope, even to assume. But Aderbury had sent him the homing lizard now, and he had sent it off in search of her. Now he was forced to face the fear for real.

"Well, you did say it's an awfully long way away," considered the doctor, pushing Altin over onto his side and pulling up his patient's bedclothes unceremoniously. He prodded his pudgy fingers deeply into the muscle on either side of Altin's spine, roughly and right in the center of his back where it had been broken in two. "This hurt?" he asked as he dug into Altin's flesh and caused him to gasp.

"No," Altin grunted, "except that you're pushing too hard."

"Good," said the doctor. Righting Altin's bedclothes with a practiced yank, he let the young mage roll onto his back again. "How do you know the lizard has even gotten there? How long did it take you to travel all that way?"

"An instant," Altin said. "Once I knew where it was. You know how teleportation works even if you don't have the school."

"Well, it might be different for the homing lizards."

"They're Z-class. Just like me. Trust me, it's already there." He paused, unwilling to say it, but thinking, assuming there's any *there* to be. The doctor read it in his face.

"Altin, if those people have machines that can do half of what you said they can, I'm sure the girl is fine. Besides, the lizard wouldn't have gone anywhere if there was no 'her' for it to find. Right?"

Altin hadn't thought of that. That was a promising idea. But still, he was too long immersed in the practice of grief and worry to be over-buoyed easily by hope. "Then why is she taking so infernally long to answer back?"

Doctor Leopold was still formulating an answer when the tiny lizard appeared on Altin's shoulder and began chewing on his ear. Altin felt the nibble and immediately snatched the creature up. His hands trembled, frenzied as he clumsily detached the note. When he was done reading it, he leapt out of his bed and captured the portly doctor in a powerful embrace, or at least as powerful as he could muster given his long stay lying here in bed.

"She's alive, she's alive," he yelled triumphantly into the doctor's face.

"Good gods, boy, let me go," sputtered the doctor, taken totally by surprise. "Get off me, lad, and get back into your bed."

"Don't you see?" Altin said, dodging the already wheezing doctor, who clamored to grasp his patient and stuff him back in bed. "She's alive!"

"I fancy she'll be unhappy to discover you're not after

you undo all these months of healing," the doctor gasped and finally got Altin by the arms. "Lay down or I'll cast a sedative on you."

Altin was not stupid, and he quickly realized what he had done, putting all his recovery at risk. He was strong, and nearly well, but he still needed another week for the Healing to complete itself; his bones were still brittle where the mending had been done. He stopped immediately and let the doctor lay him down, but the ear-to-ear smile was not put to rest at all. "She's alive," he said. "They did it. I just knew they would."

Doctor Leopold was kind enough not to point out Altin's recent melodramatic negativity as he tucked the covers around Altin so tightly as to nearly have him bound. Altin grunted at being swaddle so, to which Doctor Leopold responded by saying, "By the light of Luria, boy, do you have any idea how many healers have spent months of their lives crawling around in you?"

Altin sobered immediately upon seeing the expression on the doctor's face. Doctor Leopold actually looked as if he'd been truly terrified. "I'm sorry," Altin said after a moment to catch his breath. "You're right of course. I lost my head."

"The bones in your back are made of little more than glass. You can't afford to lose your head."

"I know. I promise it won't happen again. Besides, no news will ever be as good as this, as knowing Orli is still alive. What could ever move me so much as that?"

"See that nothing does or you may never move again." Doctor Leopold was clearly unnerved by his recent scare and had to dismiss himself from the room. Altin had put a tremendous collective effort in jeopardy by jumping out of bed, the depths of which he really had no idea. His recovery was already being written up in medical journals across Kurr, touted, and rightly so, as the most advanced feat of spinal healing done to date, a modern marvel and a testimony to the incredible pace of medicine under the auspices of the Queen.

Altin relaxed and allowed his pillow to encompass half his head. He didn't need to leap about for joy. He didn't need anything. He already had what he needed lying there on his chest: a note, written in her own sweet hand. Words to live for. Contented, and with the anxious python in his guts vanquished by the sweep of Orli's pen, Altin could finally get some rest.

What followed was a seven-week correspondence via homing lizard as he continued his recovery. With each exchange the depths of their desire increased, and with it their love and health. Another thing that increased as letters were exchanged was interest, outside interest from, well, almost everyone.

News of their correspondence got to the high places in each of their respective realms, and it turned out that the Queen wanted to meet the admiral with the same enthusiasm that the admiral wanted to meet the Queen. And so it was with some awkwardness for Altin that Queen Karroll conscripted his love letters to Orli as a way to offer an invitation for the fleet to come to Kurr. Her argument for this avenue, while embarrassing for Altin, was logical, as she had no other way to communicate with them: Altin was the only one on Prosperion that was in contact with the alien race.

"Tell them to come immediately," she commanded Altin as he was sitting up in bed one morning, only a few days from being allowed to go home. "I intend to throw a royal ball. The largest in history."

This was her sixth visit to Altin's bedside since she'd discovered his relationship with beings from another world, and he was at least beginning to get used to her company. He found, as Tytamon had said, that despite her commanding air and self-indulgent ways, she was entirely a "good old gal," though Altin would never say as much aloud—she was a good old gal with access to a guillotine after all. And there was the elf that followed everywhere she went. The only elf on Kurr. The royal assassin. A spooky creature to be sure.

No, no point making his opinion known, but she was a light-hearted soul. And the fact that demanding to read Altin's letters was embarrassing for him did not faze her in the least. "I *am* the Queen you know," she told him when first she'd seen him blush. "And I do delight in love despite its tendency for being such a tragic thing. Which is why I refuse to participate. But, that shouldn't stop you from giving it a go."

He'd smiled, still blushing, and it was at that point that the Queen officially declared him Prosperion's liaison to the people from planet Earth, immediately after which she'd said, "Tell them to set the date most convenient for them to arrive, and the rest will take care of itself." She'd waited perhaps four seconds before urging again, "Tell them," and then began cycling her hand through the air at him as if he were already taking far too long.

"I'll tell her," he said. "But I'm not sure what she will be able to do. They've tossed her in the brig as you've already seen." He glanced at the pile of Orli's letters on the table by his bed, all of which the Queen had recently read.

"Child, they're dealing with the Queen. And you said yourself they've never met another living race besides themselves. Of course they'll listen to what your dear Orli has to say. And of course they'll come."

There was a hesitance in his aspect that she noticed right away.

"Don't you worry about that girl. I will insist she's brought along. It will be a condition of diplomacy. You have my word." She patted him on the cheek. "Now lie down and do as the doctor tells you. I need you healthy so that you can take Lord Chamberlain and a few ambassadors up to meet them as soon as you are fit." With that she turned and left, the dark shadow of the elf known only as Shadesbreath vanishing behind her as if he'd never been in the room at all.

A date was set for the ball not long after. The admiral was more than happy to come and meet the Queen but insisted that the fleet would get to Prosperion on its own. Altin had offered to bring teleporters out to the fleet so that they could transport people, or even ships, back to Prosperion right away, an idea that the Queen loved, being as impatient as she was, but that the admiral had adamantly refused. Altin didn't really blame them. They wanted to come on their own terms, equal, not beholden to their hosts to send them home when the ball was done.

And so Altin had to wait. He tried once to sneak aboard Orli's ship and managed to stay long enough for a kiss, but the guard outside her cell had come running after some alarms went off. In truth, the guard had actually let them have a little extra time, giving them a few moments to stare into each other's eyes, but in the end he insisted that Orli make Altin leave. The guard, while sympathetic, had no desire to be in a cell himself. Particularly not now that the captain was in such a mood.

Captain Asad thought the whole business was a reckless course to take. Having seen what one of "them" could do, meaning Altin and his magic, it felt like suicide to him to send the whole fleet "straight into their trap." He maintained that the orbs were just a hoax and had been all along with their shifting skins and transitive three-part disease. While he was reluctant to call it "magic," there was no doubt that these people had abilities that were as mysterious as magic, something that became increasingly clear after the Prosperion ambassadors had arrived. However, his belief in magic-seeming phenomena only proved to him, and not a small number of others amongst the fleet, that the Hostiles had in fact been the ruse that would bring the whole fleet into the skies above Prosperion. The orbs had been the bait.

And then what? If Altin's performance during the Hostile fight was real at all, then the power his people possessed was unimaginably great. Such consideration presented the possibility of danger in that the fleet would be at the mercy of Altin's people should their mysterious powers be turned against the trusting people from planet Earth. And there would not be one thing that the Earth ships could do, not if Altin's power was real. And it was this sense of being inexorably drawn into a Hostile plot that put the captain in a mood.

From the stories Orli got from friends who resumed visiting as she became more bearable to be around, she was almost glad that the captain left her in the brig. Roberto made his shifts on the bridge sound as if he were the target at a firing range. But Orli wouldn't have minded either way, bridge or brig; it made little difference to her. She was going to a royal ball. She was going to dance with Altin and feel his hands in hers, see his eyes gazing into hers, and there was nothing in the universe that could take the joy of anticipating that away. The Queen had even promised her a dress. "Your gown will be as fine as mine," is what the Queen had said via Altin's note. Orli couldn't wait.

And finally the day came. Seven and a half months later, ten ships of the fleet's remaining eighty-nine were orbiting Prosperion, not far from its pink-hued moon. The rest would wait just outside their solar system, in case things went as Captain Asad and a few others feared they would.

In truth, however, the people of Earth's first trip to Prosperion did not go poorly at all. They were met with nothing less than vast and unending courtesy. Queen Karroll had a forty-acre compound cleared for their landing craft two measures out of Crown. She'd had time as the Earth fleet travelled to have the compound walled, gated, and filled with several orderly rows of outbuildings and one central structure to serve as command post for their admiral and his staff. No expense was spared, and even the royal gardeners were employed to plant and grow oaks and elms that were large enough to throw shade amongst the buildings should the springtime sun be too warm for the Earth folks' ship-bound skin, not used to such a thing.

All in all, the compound was spectacular and gracious, and Orli gasped at it as she stepped out of the landing craft and stood mesmerized on the ramp. The wind made a whispering sound as it blew through the grass, and she could smell lilac, heliotrope and mignonette. There were other scents she'd never smelled before, flower varieties she had never seen. She could hardly wait to touch them all and see what colors they would show. She looked up, squinting as the sun shone warmly on her face. There were birds up there, soaring in the sky, and their calls mixed with the trumpets that were being blown by men in fluttering tabards standing atop the walls. A grasshopper landed on her sleeve. She took it gently into her hand, tilting her head and giving it her sweetest smile. What a beautiful creature, she thought as it leapt back into the breeze.

She looked around for Altin even though she knew that he would not be there. This was their space, he had told her that. The Queen insisted that they have a place they could call their own. In fact, the horns were blowing to announce the changing of the guard. The Queen's men had been ordered to depart when the Earth forces were ready to take control of their new fort. Orli was actually surprised to see that the admiral had agreed to do such a silly thing, but she watched from the loading ramp as marines moved to station themselves around the upper wall.

How stupid, she thought. What kind of a message was

that to send? But then, what did she know about diplomacy and military force? Maybe it was expected from them, a sign of strength or some odd form of respect. Apparently a lot had gone on in the lord chamberlain's meetings with the fleet.

But none of that mattered to her. At last she was finally here. She was free of her cell and in the incredible contrast of a real "outdoors." What made the situation even better was that she was here on the orders of a queen. The Queen. A royal pardon of sorts. Too bad it hadn't worked for her on the ship these last few months. But that no longer mattered, not now, not here.

She stepped down onto the grass and moved amongst the straggle of officers and those few lucky crew members who'd been allowed to come. "At least a few hundred," insisted the Queen in one of Altin's letters. "What good's throwing a ball if there's no one there to dance?"

Orli went through the receiving line and was assigned a room in one of the buildings near the outer wall. Once inside, she tossed her small travel bag onto a bed that was little more than a wooden bunk. A mattress lay upon the crude frame that looked as if it might be filled with straw. It was. She had to laugh at that. What a wonderful thing. How quaint. She lay on it. It was softer than anything she'd ever lain upon before. She turned and pressed into it with her hand, marveling at how straw could be as supple as this mattress was, and then she noticed the tag sewn into the mattress seam. "Enchanted by Murphy. Do not remove." She laughed again. She knew immediately that she loved being here more than any place she'd ever been. Even more than Earth. Earth was a gauzy memory, lost to distance and space, a place of origins and loss. Here, this was beauty and reprieve.

Something nibbled on her ear.

Used to them by now, she took the homing lizard from

her shoulder and untied the message on its back. "It's me," was written on the parchment scrap, followed by, "Where are you? What number is on the door?"

She glanced up, but the number was outside. She put the lizard on the bed and quickly went out to look. Seventeen. She went back to the bed to reply, but realized she didn't have a laser scalpel at hand. She ran her eyes around the room. There was a quill pen in an inkpot sitting on a tiny desk near the wall. She smiled yet again, her cheeks beginning to hurt from being so happy for so long and all at once.

She wrote her room number on the note and retied it to the lizard's back. Speaking Altin's name, she tossed the lizard to the floor, where it vanished as the creatures do.

She didn't hear anything from him again for quite some time, so she decided to go out and have a look around. There were manicured gardens all around the little village the Queen had built for them, and there was even a small fountain in the middle of what might be construed as a town square. The buildings were all made of wood, and from appearances looked for all the world as if their roofs were made of thatch. She laughed again, joyous through and through, and had to reach up to rub her aching jaw. It didn't seem possible that there could be so many things to make a person smile.

As she turned down an unpaved lane that separated a row of buildings, she could see their landing ships parked in the grassy field a few hundred yards beyond the little town. Such an odd sight, those metal boxes sitting there in contrast to everything else around. Such an ugly sight. She turned her back on them so that they were no longer in her view.

She studied the wall for a moment. It wasn't very high, fifteen feet at most, made entirely of stone, large hewn blocks that measured three or four feet at every edge. This must have been a colossal project to get done in time for the

Earth ships to arrive. She absently wondered what it was that the wall was supposed to keep away, or was it as the captain said, meant to keep them all locked in?

She turned to the huge iron-bound gates as the thoughts were going through her mind, and immediately she knew. The gates were thrown wide, chained back and open, inviting anyone to leave. The walls were meant to make them feel secure, perhaps free from a thousand gawking eyes, but no more sinister than that. And there were some gawking eyes too, for she could see that out beyond the gates quite a crowd had begun to grow. People from the city were filing into the meadow beyond, obviously hoping for a peep at the people coming down from outer space. Orli realized that it must be very exciting for the denizens of Kurr to see such an unprecedented sight. And she wanted to meet them too.

As she walked up to the gates, two marines stationed on either side stopped her, the larger of the two barking an authoritative, "Halt."

She looked at them, their laser rifles clutched firmly in their hands, and she could only shake her head. They bore the insignia of the *Pershing* on their sleeves, and she'd never met either of them before. "I'm going to say 'hello.'"

"We have orders to keep people from going outside," said the big man, standing squarely in her path.

The shorter one's face wrinkled up a bit as he stared at her. "Hey, you're Pewter, aren't you? From the *Aspect*?"

"Yes," she said. "I am." Then she turned to the serious fellow and added as she pushed past him without a backwards glance. "Shoot me if you have to. But, I'm going to say 'hello.'" Orli was done with orders.

Her enchanted com link did nothing to help her understand what the Prosperions had to say as she approached, but the slow murmur of "Orli" told her that the young marine was not the only one that had figured out who she was. She smiled, warmed by the sunshine of their joy, their happiness at seeing her and touching her with their reaching hands when she drew near. She felt like a celebrity, and their acceptance was such a contrast to the derision that she got on Captain Asad's cold and lifeless ship.

She spent nearly twenty minutes mingling with the people and learning many of their names before she heard her own name come barking across the breeze. "Pewter," yelled the captain, "you were not authorized to leave."

She smiled at the little boy she was talking to—his name was Peety—and gave him back his toad. "Thank you," she said. "He's a wonderful little pet." She took her time in turning back to face the captain. She was enough of a diplomat to know this was not the place to face him down. "Coming," she said.

As she strode through the tall grass, headed back towards the gate, the sound of horses' hooves and wagon wheels turned her gaze towards the west. A coach was rumbling down the road, little more than two tracks worn in the grass by the passing of construction carts, and it was headed towards the gate, drawn by four black stallions upon whose coats the sunlight glinted in a mesmerizing way.

The gilded coach stopped before the gates as Orli came around it from behind. She stood near Captain Asad as the coachman leapt down from the driver's seat and opened up the carriage door. A tall, lanky man with a beaked nose and a conspicuous mole beneath his left eye gazed at the captain and gave the slightest bow. He was exquisitely dressed, and he had a leather case tucked beneath his arm. "Are you a person of authority?" he inquired of Captain Asad.

"I am," said the captain.

"I am Perfuvius Needlesprig the Third," he announced with an imperious air. "And I come with a summons from the Queen." He handed the leather case to Captain Asad who opened it and stared at the parchment letter inside with a frown.

"I can't read this," the captain admitted as it occurred to Orli that she'd just understood everything that this man had said.

It was Perfuvius' turn to frown. "Damned enchanters can't get anything right," he mumbled to the coachman. He snatched the letter back. "I will read it for you. It says, 'It is the will and desire of Her Royal Majesty Queen Karroll, Overlord of Kurr and Defender of Right, Purveyor of Justice and Keeper of the Realm, that the Lady Orli Pewter of the forces of Earth and serving upon the great warship *Aspect* be delivered in person to the auspices of the Royal Dressmaker, Perfuvius Needlesprig the Third,'" he paused, adding unnecessarily, "That is me," before continuing on, "'...that Lady Pewter might be properly attired for the royal ball that is being thrown largely on her behalf.' It is signed by the Queen herself." He turned the document back so that they both might see the large, flowing signature on its lower half, accompanied by what could only be the royal seal.

"I'm Orli Pewter," she said before the captain could open up his mouth.

"Pewter...," the captain started to say, but she smiled and cut him off.

"It's a royal order, Captain. You know as well as I do that it's bad manners if we don't do whatever the Queen demands."

"Indeed," agreed Perfuvius Needlesprig the Third as his footman made a gesture that invited Orli to step up and into the gilded coach.

"We'll have to run it by the admiral first," said the captain, fighting for control. "There are security issues to be discussed."

Orli was already climbing into the coach.

"Let me know how that goes," she said as she settled comfortably into the carriage's cushioned seat. The interior smelled like leather and perhaps too much of Master Needlesprig's cologne. All in all, delightful. She waved to the people still gawking at her through the window on the opposite side of the coach. Peety hoisted up his toad. She flew a smile at him and another for his pet, and a few moments later, they were bouncing along their way, Perfuvius Needlesprig the Third eyeing her up and down and muttering about fabrics, colors and just what to do with her too-short but gorgeous platinum-blonde hair.

Chapter 46

The ball, formally titled "The Royal Earth Ball," took place one week after the ships from Earth had settled on the ground. Altin had been waiting restlessly for seven long months for that day to finally come. He and Orli had gotten quite a bit of time to see one another in the days that came before the dance, but never enough to suit his insatiable desire to be with the woman that he loved. Master Needlesprig hogged her most of the time, and when she wasn't being royally attired, either Queen Karroll or Kettle were monopolizing her time. Even Pernie had taken to following her around like a little puppy hoping for someone to throw a stick, and Orli was incapable of resisting the child's charm.

Orli told Altin at one point that Captain Asad was going to have a stroke if she got any more attention than she already was.

"Don't worry," Altin had said to that, "he's in no danger then. You can't get any more attention than you do." They both laughed because it was true.

Kettle had taken to pinching Orli's cheeks by the time she was on her third visit to Calico Castle's now quite busy kitchen, and Roberto gained six pounds from his week of visits and humorously declared his eternal love for Kettle in his most romantic Spanish tones. This, of course, made the much older woman blush to her ears, though it did nothing to discourage her from cooking her finest and most decadent recipes whenever the Spaniard came around.

Finally, the day of the ball arrived, and Altin found himself standing on the palace steps waiting for Orli's carriage to arrive. Aderbury was standing next to him, both men dressed in the formal uniforms of the Queen's Reserve.

"You'll be fine," Aderbury was saying. "Stop worrying already. You've already seen her ten times since they landed. Relax."

"I know. I just want everything to go well. There are so many people now. So many coming together all at once. And her captain hates me. And I can't dance a step without stepping on someone's toes."

"Stop it," Aderbury said. "You're going to work yourself into a fit. Go get a cup of wine."

"She might come while I'm inside."

"Gods. You're pathetic."

A carriage rumbled up and deposited its occupants onto the crimson carpet that ran up the stairs from the curb to the titanic palace doors. It was Thadius Thoroughgood and his parents, the baron and the baroness.

Courtesies were exchanged as the couple and their dapper son came up the steps. "Nice work, Master Meade," said the baron as he shook Altin's hand in an enthusiastic grip. "Nice work indeed. A real honor. We're proud of you, my boy." The baron's familiarity was a bit out of sorts, for, in truth, Altin had only met the baron twice before, but it was nice to receive his praise.

"Thank you," Altin said.

"Yeah, nice work, old boy," said Thadius, though his tone seemed to mock the words. "Even a blind pig sniffs a truffle every now and then, eh?" He laughed as if he'd meant it as a joke. Altin smiled politely back, but only for the baroness' sake. She seemed to recognize his kindness, and then tugged her husband up the stairs. Thadius delayed for just a moment more. "I hear the Earth girls are exotic," he said once his parents were safely up the steps. He leaned down and gave Altin a conspiratorial wink. "I bet they just love to dance." Altin winced as the butterflies had seizures in his gut. "Maybe I'll have a go with yours."

Aderbury grabbed Altin's arms, hugging him from behind as he prepared to pounce and rendering him incapable of doing anything foolish that might ruin the entire night. "That's what he wants," Aderbury hissed.

Altin ground his teeth and forced himself to breathe.

"Easy there, old man," jibed Thadius. "Don't want to start something you're unable to carry off." His hand was resting lightly on the pommel of his sword. It was true; Altin could not beat him if it actually came down to a conventional duel. But a nice fireball to the face would have melted Thadius' smugness straight away. Aderbury squeezed him and demanded that he "let it go." Reluctantly, he did.

Thadius grinned and gave a derisive snort. "Of course not," he said, and bounded up the stairs to catch his parents before they had time to reach the castle's enormous bronze-cast doors.

"By the gods I hate that man," said Altin when Thadius was gone.

"Most people do," said Aderbury.

"Women don't."

"True. But only the silly ones."

"I hope so," said Altin, and let out a long and lingering breath.

Aderbury was about to tell him to quit worrying again when Orli's carriage finally came rumbling into view. Once more she was in the charge of the royal dressmaker, and her arrival did not come without a considerable amount of pomp. The Queen had gone overboard to make Altin's beloved feel every part the princess on her visit to their world.

Her entourage consisted of both front and rear guard, six knights apiece, in full armor burnished to a mirror's shine, and included a herald in the Queen's own livery to announce Orli's exit from the coach. The coach itself had two footmen, plus the coachman and a seated guard. Altin's thoughts upon seeing who that particular guard was were captured perfectly by Aderbury's remark. "Good Guano and the Bats of Gore," he muttered. "She gave your girl the royal assassin as a guard?"

"So she did," Altin agreed incredulously as he eyed the unnerving elf sitting silently by the driver's side. He smiled as he shook his head in disbelief. Queen Karroll had been better than her word.

The shadowy elf slipped from the carriage seat and disappeared into the crowd that had gathered to watch the guests arriving to the ball, all of whom began to murmur and lean, curious to see who it was that had just arrived with such an entourage. A footman ran round and opened up the carriage door as the other blew a few blasts on a long brass horn. The herald waited until the footman had finished with the horn, then, pounding his staff upon the stone, announced the royal dressmaker by title and by name.

Perfuvius Needlesprig the Third stepped out, doffed his hat, and gave a florid bow. The crowd clapped politely as he moved up to the first step to wait for the rest of his party to be announced.

The herald pounded his staff once more on the stone beneath his feet, this time announcing in his great bass voice, "Lieutenant Roberto Levi. Weapons officer of the great warship *Aspect* and hero of the Hostile War."

Altin waved and called out as Roberto stepped down and stood beside the carriage step, again to a smattering of applause from the growing ranks of the curious crowd. He gave Altin a grin and a nod, then turned and reached a hand back up inside the coach.

"The lady Orli Pewter," began the herald as Orli finally could be seen. A hush fell across the crowd as she stepped lightly down onto the carpet covering the steps. "First Ambassador from Earth and Advisor to the Queen," the herald went on, "communications officer of the warship *Aspect*, creator of the cure and heroine of the Hostile War." A ripple of awe moved across the crowd as Orli straightened herself and flashed perfect white teeth up to where Altin stood. The crowd was nearly as mesmerized as Altin was himself.

The healers must have spent the entire week casting growth spells on her hair—and the illusionists doing much the same in hiding the growth so that no one would know it was being done and spoil the effect. The luxurious display of molten gold was piled upon her head was a miracle to behold. Coils of it, curling ropes that wound like captured waves, were bound up and held together by enchantments and a few jewel-encrusted combs whose gems sparkled almost as beautifully as did the radiant flaxen mound, glimmering in the dual lights of a setting sun and a rising, reddish moon. A few strands of hair, as if on accident, tumbled down and curled about her neck, teasing upon her pale white cleavage and delectable collarbones. A single diamond, round and cut to sparkle like the blue irises of her eyes, was bound securely at her throat, held in place by a narrow strip of shimmering black silk, the perfect contrast to her snowy skin.

Her gown was made of Sunshine Silk, a fabric so lustrously yellow it made daffodils envious to the point of withering away, and it shimmered nearly as much as did her hair. Her slender waist was put to excellent use, and the royal dressmaker had made her modest bosom rise to its best effect. Strings of pearls were sewn into her bodice and her skirts, and the whole affair was held together and augmented at every pleat and fold by golden thread and enchanted lace that sparkled as much by magic as by reflected light. Orli was literally aglow.

Altin gaped as he watched her start to climb the stairs, her movements graceful, her willowy arms slender and toned, ivory fleshed and vanishing into white gloves, elbow length and tailored to her delicate hands. She was simply astonishing. To look upon her was almost painful, like a giant clutching him around the chest making it difficult to breathe, and he was unaware that he'd begun to lean towards her, tipping down the stairs as if gravity had a twin that now emanated just from her. Aderbury had to grab him by the back of his coat when it seemed he might run down the stairs and take her into his arms. "She's supposed to come to you," Aderbury said softly in his ear. "Don't ruin it for her. Let her have her moment."

Aderbury was right of course, and Altin stopped before he'd descended another step. But she was so beautiful. No one had ever been so beautiful before.

Orli, however, was not as inclined to formalities as Altin was, or at least as Aderbury was, and, despite the gasp of hopeless resignation that came from Perfuvius Needlesprig the Third when she suddenly bounded up the stairs—he'd worked so hard to get her trained for just this moment too— she rushed up and into Altin's arms.

"Oh, Altin," she said, kissing him and making Aderbury blush to match the darkest wine, "it's like a fairy tale. Just like one. I've never been so happy in all my life. I've found heaven. And you are the angel that brought me here." She kissed him again as Roberto and the royal dressmaker came up to stand behind her on the stairs.

"Ahem," said the royal dressmaker, clearing his throat and fearing that their kiss was beginning to grow scandalously long. "I'm sure my lady should like to keep her tongue behind her teeth," he admonished quietly, then cleared his throat a second time. "It won't do to make a scene." He was whispering, but all of them could hear.

She pulled her face away from Altin's, although she kept their bodies close, and turned to face the man who'd been her patient tutor throughout the week. "You're right," she said. "I'm sorry. I'll try harder to restrain myself once we get inside." She winked at him and gave Altin another kiss.

"Woman, you better hope they don't have some kind of decency laws here," Roberto said with a grin, "or you're going to get us all put away."

Altin let Orli go long enough to introduce Aderbury to Roberto, his newfound friend from Earth.

"Well met," said Aderbury.

"Great to meet you too," said Roberto. "Looks like you and me get free reign on the rest of the girls inside, eh?" He gave a hearty guffaw, for which Orli punched him in the arm, quite out of keeping with the elegant gloves encasing her slender hands.

"You being a pig is what will get us in trouble if anything does. Try to behave. Just this one time in your entire life."

Aderbury only laughed, placing a hand on Roberto's epaulette. "No my friend, I'm afraid all the single ladies are yours to court. I've got a bride somewhere inside lost amongst the crowd, no doubt telling scandalous personal secrets about me, for which I will suffer the sounds of snickers throughout the night." He used that as his segue to urge them all inside. "Speaking of whom, we should go up before she gets completely out of hand."

"I can't wait to meet her," Orli said, taking Altin's proffered arm. "And those stories sound very interesting. I'm looking forward to hearing them all." Aderbury pretended to be frightened, and the group climbed up the carpet and entered the vacuous royal hall.

Once again the Queen had spared no expense, and all the

best illusionists had been brought in to animate the walls. The east wall depicted a scene from the Battle of Andeon Hill, a famous battle of the Unification Wars that was renowned for the awesome collection of siege weapons and conjurers gathered there. The scene repeatedly played out the opening salvo of the royal army's initial attack, a rain of fireballs, boulders and burning pitch that fell upon the great orc stronghold for approaching an hour and a half. The illusion reset itself when the fortress finally fell, and anyone paying attention could watch it all happen once again. The west wall showed Margorian Falls, a magnificent waterfall in the depths of the Great Forest that fell for over a thousand feet. And on the south wall, through which they entered, was a giant manticore curled up as if asleep, but every time anyone came or went, the ferocious animal suddenly woke up, opened its mouth and then chomped down ferociously, its teeth coming together like a portcullis gnashing through the doorway. Most of the guests were quite amused by this, and they enjoyed the fun of watching one another being "eaten alive"—or being thrown up as Roberto pointed out sometime later in the night. The north wall alone was unenchanted, sufficing instead with its ancient tapestries and the dais upon which the royal throne now sat, and in which rested the Queen. This was the seat of power, and there would be no enchantments here.

The little group was separated from the Queen by the milling crowd. Here and there pockets of people gathered in clusters, chatting noisily beneath elegant chandeliers, each one a swarm of glimmering diamonds and bright candles dangling from silver chains attached to the enchanted ceiling above. Forty paces up, the ceiling had become a bright blue sky, filled with clouds upon which sat round-faced cherubs who smiled down at them and, on occasion, threatened mischief as if they might drop some fruit or pour a cup of wine upon the heads of the people down below.

Most of the guests were beyond being amused by such things, at least were the folks from Kurr, but more than a few members of the fleet could be caught snickering as they looked up from time to time and caught some clever enchanter's little private joke.

As the five of them stared across the room, waiting for their eyes to adjust to the dim light, the disparate styles of dress became immediately apparent to them all. The assemblage was an odd shuffling of dissimilar cultures and opposite styles of dress. The contingent from Earth all looked very much the same, their uniforms nearly identical excepting for ribbons and other demarcations of rank and acts of valor. But the denizens of Kurr were an entirely different lot. Their baroque style and opulent elegance seemed a luxury stolen from another time, at least it did for Orli, and the visual feast of all this color and pageantry was rapture in her eyes.

As she came in, she spotted her father standing with the admiral and Altin's mentor, Tytamon, whom she'd met the day after the Earth ships had come down. The trio of wizened men all stopped to wave at her and her entourage across the sea of heads, the colonel giving her an adoring wink just before the herald's announcement that "Altin Meade has arrived" got the attention of everyone in the hall. The crowd fell silent, eager to turn and pay respect to the man who had "discovered" outer space, but that silence was broken by a wave of murmured awe. The crowd gawked as they turned as one and froze, amazed in the discovery of Orli standing at his side. Her cheeks reddened as she heard the intake of at least a thousand breaths and felt the heat of twice as many eyes. She was humbled and exhilarated all at once.

A second herald began the long-winded announcement of titles and honors again, during which time Orli glimpsed Doctor Singh in conversation with the immensely large man Altin had introduced as his own doctor, Doctor Leopold.

Doctor Singh gave a subtle wave and smiled at her as the enormous fellow raised his goblet high in lieu of being so discreet. He grinned broadly at her before taking a long draught of the Queen's expensive wine.

When the herald had finally introduced them all, the Queen summoned them to the throne, staying the resumption of noisy socializing amongst her guests for just a moment more with a gesture of her hand. The crowd parted before their small company, making way as they approached. Even the musicians playing in the corner let their tune fall temporarily away.

After the appropriate genuflections, the Queen came forward on the dais and began to speak. "At last," she said. "The guests of honor have finally seen fit to arrive, trusting to the patience of the monarchy." She winked at Orli, having personally arranged the timing of her arrival for maximum impact. "I won't bore you all with a long and ceremonious speech, as I know most of you are eager to get back to drinking all my wine." There was a round of collective laughter. "Fortunately for you all, the more humdrum aspects of the early diplomacy between our two worlds have already taken place safely behind closed doors, sparing you all the trials of my stubborn attitudes." She turned her gaze to the portion of the room where the admiral and his chief advisors stood. "Except for you, you poor man," she said looking directly into the admiral's eyes. "I do appreciate your patience with my blunt questions and ignorance of your world." He bowed deeply to show his mutual respect.

"Which means there is really only one other matter to attend to before we can all find the bottom of a glass." She turned to the small group standing before her on the steps. "Altin Meade, come forward."

Ugh, he thought, swallowing hard as he mounted the singular step between himself and the Queen. He was already being watched more closely than he liked.

"Kneel," she ordered as he approached. She turned and drew her sword from the scabbard hanging on the back of her throne. As she laid the shimmering blade upon his shoulder, he felt his stomach fall out through the bottom of his boots. "I dub you Sir Altin Meade," she said, picking up the blade as she spoke and moving it to his other shoulder. This can't be happening, he thought. "Knight of the Realm," she concluded as she took the sword away. "Rise and be recognized." It *was* happening. He had to hide his trembling hands behind his back as he complied with her command.

She took him by the upper arms and turned him towards the assembly. "I give you, Sir Altin Meade," she said. "Kurr's first galactic mage." The entire chamber exploded in thunderous applause. Altin smiled, embarrassed and thrilled together, then looked down at Orli whose face shone brighter than a universe of suns. Her eyes were wet, glistening with tears of pride that she could not stop from running down her cheeks. He wanted to kiss the watery gems from her soft skin, to taste the salt upon his lips. Imagining it gave him some respite from the discomfort of a cheering crowd.

But he would have to wait; both of them would, until they'd done their service to the meeting of two distant worlds. And they did their duty too, all of it: Orli had to dance at least three dozen dances, and were it not for her runner's heart and the months she'd had to recuperate from her malaise, she'd never have made it through. Altin was not so lucky, and after dancing with what felt like every woman in the realm, not to mention no small number from the fleet, he found himself nearly gasping for air as he collapsed into a chair at the table ostensibly reserved for him and Orli and their retinue—a table that had seen little use since the dancing began. The truth of the matter was, he'd only spoken to Orli twice since the music had resumed, and he'd only gotten to dance the first dance in her arms, from there diplomacy had taken the upper hand.

Grateful for at least a moment's rest, he sat and gulped down a cup of wine, willing his heart to stop pounding and vowing to get more exercise when he got the time. He saw a flash of yellow in the churning mass of dancers and began to smile as he recognized Orli by her dress. But then he saw who was holding her and found himself rising from his seat. Thadius.

"Easy now, Sir Altin," came the Queen's voice unexpectedly from behind. Her hand on his shoulder prevented him from getting up.

He turned and tried to rise again. She stayed him with a look. "If she can be taken from you so easily as that, she never was yours to begin."

"Anyone but him." Anger began to burn within him as if some wicked alchemist had poured acid into his heart and now stirred it with a stick.

"Oh, I know him well enough," Queen Karroll said. "I'm the Queen. It's my job to pay attention to such things."

Altin grunted and glared into the dancing throng. The Queen sat down next to him in a casual, familiar way.

"Believe in her, Altin. Relax and enjoy the night."

Fear of losing her was not what gnawed at Altin's heart. Loathing did. The very idea that that man's hands could violate even a strand of Orli's silken hair infuriated him; that his vermin fingers might press against her flesh was too much to bear. He felt the rage starting to build inside and he had to fight desperately to keep it from rising up, but the Queen was looking straight into his soul. She gave him a look that only a queen can give. He growled silently as he pushed the emotions down. He should say something to his monarch, but he couldn't think of anything appropriate, so he sat quietly and ground his teeth instead.

Queen Karroll smiled, genuinely amused. "Youth," she seemed to lament. "Firm bodies but soft heads." She laughed. "Cheer up, the song is over now. Put on a knight's face, here she comes."

Altin shook himself and forced a smile.

Thadius accompanied Orli back to the table, but the smug look he'd been about to drop in Altin's lap melted away as he saw the Queen reclining comfortably beside Altin and grinning back at him as he approached. "Master Thoroughgood, you dance divinely," said the Queen. Altin was amazed at how her words could say the one thing while her tone so clearly stated something else, seeming instead to say, "You are an embarrassment to your family, and I hope some day you might grow up." Altin didn't have to say a word as Thadius bowed deeply and made excuses, retreating back into the crowd.

"He is an amazing dancer," Orli agreed after a draught of wine. "He simply glides across the floor."

Altin did not allow himself to grimace, or at least he tried to hide it behind a swallow of his own wine. He could not be angry with her, she was only pointing out the truth. And though he didn't want to dance anymore, he did want her next dance to be with him if she decided to go again. Hating to have to follow up the skill of Thadius' nimble feet, but unwilling to risk Orli to yet another of the endless dance requests, he asked her anyway, making a preemptive strike. "Would you like to dance again?" he said. "I can't dance as well as Thadius, but I do love staring into your eyes."

Orli beamed, and the Queen nodded approvingly, smiling as if her job was done. "I'll leave you two a moment's peace," she said. "Having the Queen hanging around has to be worse than having one of your parents sitting here." She paused long enough to cup a hand on Orli's cheek. "You look beautiful, my dear. The jewel of Earth. Your people must be proud." She didn't wait for Orli's reply, turning instead and barking at the Earl of Vorvington who had just gone staggering by. "Don't you run from me, Vorvington. Where's my six thousand crowns?"

Apparently the earl had not expected the Queen to be loitering amongst the crowd. Before the Queen moved to chase the indebted earl down, she paused long enough to add, "Altin, make sure you and Aderbury come see me in the next day or two. You boys have a lot of work to do." And with that she was gone.

At last they were alone.

"Well, do you want to dance again?" he asked.

"Do you?" Something in her eyes suggested that she already knew the truth.

"I would walk across the Lava Seas of String if that's what you wanted me to do."

"Well, I hope my dancing's not that bad."

"No, no," he stammered. "That's not what I meant at all."

She laughed. "I know, silly. I'm teasing you." Her expression softened. "I'm sorry. I shouldn't do that to you. Your people are so different than mine. Your people seem to say what they really mean."

He shrugged. "Some of us do. Not all. I expect our two peoples are very much alike, even where we're different."

She nodded and took another sip of wine. "Ohh," she gasped suddenly. "Who is that Roberto is dancing with? Wow. She's gorgeous."

Altin followed the direction of Orli's eyes out onto the floor where he saw Roberto whirling about gracefully with the buxom Lena in his grasp. Both dancers seemed rapturous, laughing as they spun, twirling and weaving amongst the other couples like a pair of feathers bobbing on a breeze. Altin grimaced but followed it with a laugh. "Oh dear," he said. "That's Lena Foxglove. Roberto's got his hands full with that one."

Orli laughed back. "I'm sure that's exactly what he has in mind."

The twinkle in her eyes made Altin reach once more for the concealment of his wine. Perhaps Lena and Roberto were perfectly suited for one another after all. As a means of escape to more comfortable conversational ground, he observed, "Roberto's been here for barely a week and he already dances better than half the people in Crown."

Orli smiled, seeing that it was true. "Yes, he's got great rhythm. Ask him and he'll tell you that dancing is the gift of his Spanish heritage."

"While I do not know precisely what that is, I can see no reason to dispute the claim. He is amazing."

She laughed and let her eyes follow Roberto and the lovely Lena as they whirled through the center of the room. Altin just watched Orli. There was nothing else to see.

He could tell as he regarded her that she was tired, her breathing still quick from the exercise of a long night on the floor, and perspiration glistened on her bosom as her chest heaved intoxicatingly with every indrawn breath. The delicate bones and soft curves of pale flesh were highlighted by the glow of the chandeliers above, stirring his desire.

His palms grew moist and his heart began to thump against his chest as a daring plan came into his mind. He sent a thought to Taot, wanting to find out exactly where the dragon was. He learned that the dragon was just finishing off a fat and juicy elk.

Altin grinned inwardly, and placed his hand on Orli's warm, damp arm. "Have you ever ridden a dragon?" he asked.

She stared blankly at him for a moment, and then her eyes widened as she grasped what his question implied. She blinked at him, hope and disbelief mixing with raw emotion to set her perfect face aglow. He gazed back, his pulse racing as he sensed something opening in the depths of those limpid blue gems, something deep beneath, allowing him inside as if the last tissue of restraint was torn away. A purely sensual expression came upon her face. "I'd love to."

They snuck out together, hand and hand, giggling and

darting from column to column like giddy thieves skulking through the night until they found a shadow safe enough to allow Altin time to cast. A few moments later found them in the moonlit meadows not far outside of Calico Castle's ancient walls. Taot was still crunching on a bone.

Ignoring the shockingly lewd assumptions Taot's thoughts imparted as Altin communicated his desire for the dragon to take him and Orli for a ride, he arranged for conveyance with little trouble at all. Well fed, the dragon was happy to oblige.

Soon they were soaring along the treetops of the Great Forest's endless canopy, just barely above, and so close that the tip of Taot's tail dipped occasionally into the uppermost branches, slapping noisily at the broad leaves as they glided by. Orli screamed with delight at first, her face thrust into the wind until tears ran from the corners of her eyes into her slowly unraveling coiffure. At no point in her life had she ever been so rapturous as this.

Altin was euphoric too. Orli's slender body was pressed against him with her arms clutched tightly about his waist and her breasts pressed firmly into his back. She felt so real to him finally. So alive. Not just a person in his dreams. He could feel her breath upon his neck, warm as she snuggled into him, wriggling close to him for protection from the chill that came with the dragon's speed. He felt her sigh with contentment against his skin. "I love you," she whispered.

His smile nearly touched his ears. "I love you too."

With the slightest pressure of his knee, he urged Taot into a graceful, gliding arc that turned them directly into the light of the luminous crimson moon. Luria in her quarter phase, the red phase known as the Lovers' Kiss.

The End

Made in the USA
Lexington, KY
22 September 2012